10.⁰⁰

AN AFFAIR TO REMEMBER

KAREN HAWKINS

AN AFFAIR TO REMEMBER

An Avon Romantic Treasure

AVON BOOKS

An Imprint of HarperCollinsPublishers

This is a work of fiction. Names, characters, places, and incidents are products of the author's imagination or are used fictitiously and are not to be construed as real. Any resemblance to actual events, locales, organizations, or persons, living or dead, is entirely coincidental.

AVON BOOKS
An Imprint of HarperCollins*Publishers*
10 East 53rd Street
New York, New York 10022-5299

Copyright © 2002 by Karen Hawkins
ISBN: 0-7394-2786-5

Printed in the U.S.A.

The men of the St. John family are outrageously handsome and possess far too much wealth. It is enough to make one ill.

Viscountess Hunterston to Miss Sophia Canterley,
while sipping lemonade at the
Woodhouse Charity Masque

Prologue

It's true that the St. John men are far superior to all other men. I wish just one of them would find me superior to all other women.

Miss Sophia Canterley to her mother, Lady Fetchwythe, while driving in Hyde Park

Kiltern House, England
May 1, 1816

"And last, to my cousin Anthony Elliot, the estimable Earl of Greyley, I leave the sole care of all five of my beloved children."

A complete, stunned silence met the solicitor's words. The silence stretched and grew, punctuated only by the rustle of stiff black bombazine as people turned toward the back of the room where the Earl of Greyley lounged in a chair, legs stretched before him, hands shoved into his pockets. But although the assemblage waited, the earl gave no reaction.

The solicitor was disappointed. Mr. Hebershem had expected *something*. A startled blink. A quick frown. Anything other than bland acceptance. After all, the earl was a noted bachelor and one of the most successful, wealthy men in England. As such, he could hardly be pleased to learn that he had just inherited five notoriously unruly children from a cousin he'd openly abhorred.

Fortunately for the solicitor, the earl's half brother was not so reticent. "Bloody hell, Greyley," Lord Brandon St. John said, amusement gleaming in his blue eyes. "You've just inherited an armful of babes."

"Babes?" the earl drawled in that lazy, deep voice that was peculiar to the head of the Elliot family. "If they're anything like cousin James, they're devil's spawn."

Lady Putney leaped from her seat in the front row, her black mourning dress a compliment to her falsely colored hair. "How dare you impugn my son's name!"

Greyley turned a bored gaze to the woman. "It's the truth. James Elliot was a nip farthing, a scoundrel, a cheat, and a liar."

"I'm afraid he's right," Lord Brandon agreed thoughtfully. "Didn't know how to dress, either. Never saw a man more given to wearing stripes with dots."

"*Oh!*" Lady Putney turned to Mr. Hebershem. "My son would have never left his beloved children to that"—she cast a look of virulent dislike at the earl—"*man.*"

"Careful, Greyley," Lord Brandon warned his brother. "She has thrown down the gauntlet and calls you a *man.* Such rudeness."

The earl ignored him. "Lady Putney, if you have issue with the will, then take it up with your son. *He* wrote it."

Her face reddened. "My son is dead."

"So he is," the earl said with a sardonic glint. "I must assume, then, that you know what he wished. I daresay he spoke to you about it frequently?"

A nervous titter arose. Everyone knew Lady Putney and her son hadn't traded a word for over ten years. "My relationship with my son is no concern of yours," she said stiffly.

"My concern is for my grandchildren." She turned to Mr. Hebershem. "Isn't there *something* you can do?"

Mr. Hebershem was not used to members of nobility asking for ways to disinherit an earl. Especially not when the earl in question was sitting a mere fifteen feet away. "I, ah, my lady, you can't mean to—please, madam. Lord Greyley has the care of his cousin's children unless he voluntarily assigns their care to someone else."

Lady Putney turned to face Greyley, but he held up a negligent hand. "Don't."

"But you don't even want them!"

"No, I don't. But I have never shirked my duty, and I'm not about to begin now."

A faint stirring of appreciation warmed Mr. Hebershem. Few knew the extents to which the Earl of Greyley had gone to salvage his family name. Since he had assumed his responsibilities at the age of seventeen, he had pulled the Elliots from the dregs of their own waste and ruin. He had paid their debts, bettered their lands and profits, smoothed over scandals, and brought the entire, unruly family to heel.

In a normal man, the wear and tear of such an endeavor would have had some sort of effect—left him ill or wan or perhaps just bitter. But Lord Greyley's broad shoulders seemed to handle the heavy burden with ease. Oh, it was true that Mr. Hebershem could detect a slight hint of arrogance that had not been present before. But that was, after all, only natural.

Lady Putney's numerous chins quivered. "Greyley, if you think for one moment I'm going to accept this, you are sadly mistaken. Those children cannot—"

"*Mother.*" Rupert Elliot, Lady Putney's last remaining son, stood and crossed the room to his mother's side. Tall and lanky, his dark hair falling over his pale brow, he stood out among his Elliot relatives, his fashionable attire nearly as well wrought as Lord Brandon's.

Rupert frowned down at his mother. "You have said more than enough."

"But I—"

"*No*," he said again, more firmly this time. "You will not make a scene. Not here. Not now."

The two glared at each other, the room fraught with tension. Just as Mr. Hebershem thought Greyley would have to intervene, Lady Putney flushed an ugly red.

"Oh very well," she snapped. "But I will not be silenced forever." She freed her arm from her son's grasp and plopped back into her chair.

That was the end of the theatrics, and Mr. Hebershem reluctantly finished reading the last few paragraphs of the will. The second he reached the final word, Anthony Elliot rose in an unhurried manner from the small, spindly chair and glanced down at his half brother. "Thank God that is over."

"Over?" Brand stood and picked an invisible piece of lint from his perfectly pressed coat. "You have a nursery to open, a governess to hire, ponies to buy—"

"My man of business can take care of such nonsense. Dalmapple will find the task invigorating."

"Anthony, I don't think you understand. Five children? That is a very heavy responsibility."

"I've been taking care of the entire Elliot family since I was seventeen. How much trouble could a few children be?" Anthony lifted a brow. "I suppose you will be sending news of my misfortune to Marcus?"

"As the oldest, he will want to know." Brand hesitated, then placed a hand on Anthony's shoulder, his expression serious. "Anthony, I know you don't—if you need any help, we are here for you. The St. Johns always support their own."

"I am not a St. John."

Brand frowned and squeezed Anthony's shoulder. "You were raised a St. John, and a St. John you are."

Anthony wasn't sure he believed that. His true father had died when Anthony was quite young and he'd been raised by his stepfather, James St. John. Anthony's mother and her new husband had been deeply in love and had rapidly produced five more children, four boys and a girl. Anthony hadn't minded—he'd enjoyed his little half brothers and sister. But he'd always been aware that he was not one of them. "Brand, thank you for coming to this debacle. I suppose I owe you something in exchange?"

A sudden flash of humor lit Brand's blue eyes. "Now that you mention it . . ." He reached into his waistcoat and withdrew a thick silver ring, heavily decorated with circular carvings.

"Good God. Mother's ring," Anthony said. Their mother had believed that whoever possessed the talisman ring would meet his life's mate. Her sons, however, thought of the ring differently. They had early on dubbed the ring "the family curse" and then spent a considerable amount of time attempting to fob it off on one another. "I thought Chase had that blasted thing."

"He did. I discovered it in one of my riding boots after he visited last week."

"So hide it in his boot the next time you visit him."

"Yes, well, I was hoping you'd do the honors. He'll be expecting it from me."

Anthony sighed. Normally he stayed out of this little game since the ring wouldn't affect an Elliot. Still, it was the least he could do after Brand's show of support. Anthony held out his hand.

Brand dropped the ring into it and grinned. "I'll owe you for this."

"Yes, you will." Anthony deposited the ring in his own pocket. It seemed like a fairly easy request considering he'd just agreed to take on five unruly hellions.

He almost grimaced at the thought. Despite his outwardly calm reaction, inwardly he was seething. Cousin James must have laughed uproariously as he'd written that damnable phrase in his will. Anthony was quite certain the cretin had done it with no other thought in mind than to make his life miserable.

And who could blame him? Anthony had single-handedly forced the Elliot family to become . . . better, he supposed it was, for want of a more accurate word. At least more respectable and certainly more financially mature. In return he'd earned their deep and undying hatred for imposing his will on the lot of them. He tightened his jaw. It was a good thing he was used to such. It had been his life for almost eighteen years now.

He glanced about the room now, noting that not one of his erstwhile family dared meet his gaze. None except Rupert Elliot, who offered a deprecating shrug and a half smile as he escorted his nearly hysterical mother from the room. Anthony returned the smile with a brief nod. Rupert was the only Elliot who showed any promise of overcoming his upbringing.

Anthony rubbed his neck wearily. Perhaps he was being unfair. Perhaps James's children held the same promise. After all, he'd never seen them; and they were young, after all. For several minutes he mulled over this fact, an idea hovering. There must be some reason fate had given him these charges—perhaps *here* was his chance to prove that the Elliot family was not ramshackle by blood, but by the circumstances of their upbringing.

The thought took hold. It grew and expanded as Anthony considered the myriad of possibilities that lay before him. By

God, he'd raise the children to be models of propriety. That would show the doubters who believed that once an Elliot, always an Elliot.

His boredom banished, Anthony took his leave of Brand. He had to prepare Greyley House for the imminent arrival of five soon-to-be-perfectly-behaved children. The time had come to put to rest the last, unfortunate ghosts of his Elliot ancestry.

Chapter 1

The Earl of Greyley's sins have finally caught up with him. It couldn't have happened to a more deserving man.

Lady Fetchwythe to the Dowager Duchess of Roth,
while taking a breath of fresh air
on the terrace at the Hotchkiss soirée

Greyley House, outside London
June 15, 1816

"**Y**our brother will not be happy to see us."

"Nonsense." Sara Montrose, the Countess of Bridgeton, regarded her husband from across the rumbling carriage. "Anthony will be delighted we came to visit."

"Not if you engage in your usual heavy-handed match-making attempts," Nick said, a warning threaded through his silky voice.

"Me?" Sara slipped off her shoe and rested her foot on the edge of the seat opposite hers, very near her lord's muscled thigh. "Heavy-handed?"

He lifted a brow, his blue eyes fixed on her with unwavering regard.

"Truly, Nick, I only wish to see if he is well."

"Hm."

He said no more, and after a moment, Sara frowned, a niggling worry settling between her shoulders. Her husband suffered from horrendous headaches, though it had been almost six months since he'd succumbed to an attack. "You seem out of sorts. Is your head—"

"No." Nick's gaze softened. "I'm fine. And so is Anthony. Leave him be, Sara. He's over thirty and well able to live his own life."

Sara wiggled her toes once more. "I just want to visit my brother. Surely there's nothing wrong with that."

Nick snorted inelegantly, responding to her not-very-subtle demands by capturing her foot. His warm hands cupped her ankle as he kneaded the pad of her foot. Sara closed her eyes, almost purring as his hands made their way up her calf.

But before he could proceed further, the carriage rumbled to a halt. "Damn." Nick sighed and released his hold.

Sara hurriedly pushed her skirts back down and thrust her feet into her shoes just as the footman opened the door.

Moments later, they were climbing the stairs to Greyley House. Surrounded by a wooded park, the house sat on a small knoll and cast a forbidding shadow across the front lawn. Large and square cut, the manor conveyed all the welcome of a mausoleum.

"It makes me yearn for Hibberton Hall," Nick murmured.

"We won't be long." She was just as impatient to return home as he. She hated leaving their daughter for more than a day or two at most. The thought of little Delphi made Sara sigh. She would say what she came to say to her brother and then leave, not that Anthony would pay any attention. He rarely did. Still, it was her duty as his sister to keep a watchful eye on him and to offer advice. Whether he wanted it or not.

She and Nick had just reached the top step when the door opened and a horse-faced woman dressed in a sturdy traveling pelisse stomped onto the portico. A bandaged dog was tucked under her arm, a flowered bandbox dangling from her fingers.

Her clothing proclaimed her a step above a practical servant, but the state of her coiffure made Sara pause. The woman's long, dull blond hair tangled to one side, a mass of feathers seeming to grow from the lump.

Jenkins, Greyley's most proper butler, followed hard on the woman's heels. "Miss Turner, pray reconsider. They were only teasing—"

Miss Turner whirled to face the butler. "Teasing? Were they teasing when they rubbed poor Fanny with catnip and then locked him in the loft? That orange tabby in the barn frightened him so badly he nearly had a seizure."

"It was never proven that the children—"

"Are you suggesting that my sweet little dog opened the window in my room, climbed down a trellis from two stories up, and locked himself inside the barn loft?"

Sara's glance slid to the nearly bald dog. He was as fat as a stuffed hen, his legs splayed in a most unattractive way. He truly was an ugly specimen. As if aware of her thoughts, the dog turned his bulging eyes toward her and lifted a lip to display crooked, yellowed teeth.

"Miss Turner," Jenkins entreated. "If you'll just listen! I'm certain your beloved Fanny is an excellent dog. But His Lordship was most insistent you stay for the contracted length of time."

"Not for a hundred pounds!" Miss Turner descended the stairs at high speed, her chin so high, she didn't see either Nick or Sara standing to one side.

"*Two* hundred pounds?" Jenkins said swiftly.

But it was a lost cause; Miss Turner never stopped. As she reached the drive, a lone carriage rattled from the stables and pulled to a halt. Miss Turner sent one last, virulent glare at Greyley House, hugged her ugly dog, then clambered into the carriage.

Jenkins had by this time noticed his master's sister and her husband. His face colored and he quickly stepped forward. "My lady! My lord! I didn't see you! Please accept my apologies. We're in a bit of an uproar today and—"

"I'm sorry we didn't let you know we were coming," Sara said quickly, trying to soothe the ruffled servant. It was a sign of how badly things were faring at Greyley House to see the usually stoic Jenkins so overset.

"The earl is expected any moment." The butler opened the door and escorted them inside. "A fire has been laid in the sitting room in anticipation of his return. I will light it now and bring some refreshments while you wait."

Sara smiled pleasantly, but her attention was already diverted to the foyer. Someone had added two sets of imposing armor at the bottom of the stairs, and a new tapestry adorned one wall.

Anthony loved old things. As the years passed, his house looked more like a museum display than a home. It was yet another sign that he needed a wife. Before Sara could point out such an incontrovertible truth, Nick's hand closed over her elbow and he firmly guided her toward the sitting room.

They crossed the foyer and Sara noted other changes; one of the bottom spindles on the stair railing was missing, and the mirror in front of the entryway displayed a large crack.

Jenkins caught her inquiring gaze. "Master Desford's cricket ball." He opened the door to the sitting room and bowed low. Just as Sara and Nick passed inside, a sound came from upstairs. It began as a low rumble, then increased in volume to a roar, passing directly overhead, then moving away.

"Large mice, perhaps?" Nick murmured, his gaze on the ceiling, a wry twist to his lips. "Or a pack of demons. Must be one or the other."

Jenkins politely did not answer and Sara wished Mrs. Stibbons was about. The talkative housekeeper would have given her all the information any one could want. As it was, Sara barely waited for the door to click shut behind the stoic butler before she whirled on her husband. "Anthony has gotten in over his head." As if to validate her words, a huge crash sounded, followed by a deadly silence.

Nick's blue eyes lit with mischief. "You know, my dear, this visit may actually afford us some amusement."

The sound of booted footsteps approaching the door stopped any reply Sara might have made. The door flung open and Anthony entered the room. Tall and broad-shouldered, he made the generous chamber seem small.

Unlike her other brothers who were all made on more elegant lines, Anthony was roughly masculine, his hands large and powerful, his face seemingly hewn from rock. The Elliot blood showed in the straightness of his brows and the sardonic curve of his lips, making him appear cold and impersonal to those who didn't know him.

"Sara!" he said, a frown resting on his brow. "To what do I owe the pleasure?"

"Nick and I were passing through on our way home and thought to see how you fared."

To Sara's chagrin, her brother didn't appear the least gratified to see her. "How long are you staying?"

Sara frowned. "Only for an hour. But if we're not welcome, we can leave—"

"Don't be ridiculous. I'm always glad to have you visit," Anthony said briskly. Normally, that would have been true. But now . . .

Six weeks ago, his life had been perfectly ordered, his goals to reestablish the Elliot name firmly in place. Anthony rubbed the back of his neck and tried to ease some of the tension that tightened his shoulders. Perhaps he should purchase an estate in America; he *could* send the children there. If that didn't work, there was always India. Anthony suddenly realized Sara was talking.

"—she just stomped off. I cannot believe a governess would behave—"

"Wait." A sinking feeling weighted his stomach. "Not Miss Turner?"

"Weren't you listening?" At his blank gaze, Sara made a disgusted sound and came to stand in front of him, tilting her head back to stare directly in his eyes. "We ran into your governess as she was *leaving*."

"Bloody hell!" He'd paid a fortune for her and for almost three days, he'd experienced some semblance of peace.

Unaware of his turmoil, or perhaps in spite of it, Sara continued, "Miss Turner is gone. It appeared as if her hair and her fat dog had experienced some sort of accident involving feathers and catnip."

Damn it to hell! He turned to the door and yanked it open. "*Desford!*"

Sara's eyes lit with curiosity. "Who is Desford?"

"The eldest of my troublesome wards," Anthony said grimly. "He thinks to force me into letting him and the rest of the children live with their grandmother, but he is mistaken. I'll be damned if I let an eleven-year-old dictate to me inside my own home."

Rushed footsteps sounded in the hallway and Jenkins appeared. "My lord?"

"Find Master Desford and bring him here," Anthony ordered.

"Yes, my lord."

Anthony watched the butler climb the stairs before slamming the door closed. He caught sight of his brother-in-law's amused gaze. "Don't say a word."

"Leave Nick alone." Sara crossed toward the settee. "Perhaps if you showed a bit more patience, the children would not—" She looked down at her foot. A piece of paper had somehow glued itself to the bottom of her shoe. Frowning, she lifted her foot and yanked the paper free, resting her hand on a small escritoire as she did so.

Anthony started to call out a warning, but it was too late. Her slender hand already rested on the edge.

Releasing the desk, she turned back toward the settee, absently smoothing her gown as she went. "Those poor children are probably frightened to death—"

"Sara," Nick interrupted, his gaze fastened on her skirt. "Perhaps the children have been more difficult than you realize."

"You have no idea," Anthony muttered, watching with dark amusement as Sara stared in horror at the inkstains marring her silk gown.

"How did—" She looked at her hand, black streaked from where she'd held onto the escritoire. "Those little devils! Nick just bought this gown for me in London."

Anthony smiled grimly. "It is their favorite trick. They coated the edge of my dresser the first day they were here and I lost two good cravats before I realized what had happened. They've also smeared butter on the seats of chairs and the stems of the wineglasses, not to mention the step railing. Yesterday, for a change, one of them poured honey into my best boots."

Blinking dazedly, Sara sank onto the settee. "That's unthinkable!"

Bridgeton chuckled. " 'Tis war."

"So it seems," Anthony agreed. "The children's mother was a believer in the freethinking line of child rearing. They have had no rules and little discipline. And now Lady Putney encourages them to excess."

Sara turned a questioning gaze on her brother. "Lady Putney? Not James's mother? How could she . . . Is she *here*?"

Anthony's jaw tightened. That was yet another problem. "She demanded to stay until the children had settled. I had thought it would help, since she is a familiar face." And at first, it had seemed that she'd done just that. But lately it had become more and more clear that she was actively urging the children to new heights of impropriety.

Only the thought of the children's reaction if he evicted their doting grandmother made Anthony tolerate her presence. Thank God she'd gone to London for the afternoon. At least he was spared that much misery today.

"She's a horrible, horrible woman," Sara said.

"To me. However, the children seem fond of her." Anthony settled into a chair across from Sara's, but only after he carefully checked the surface and then tilted it over to peer at the fastenings. "Meanwhile, they hate me."

"But you've been so good to them."

Anthony shrugged. He was used to that reaction from the Elliot family, though it was somehow more difficult to stomach when coming from a four-year-old with soft brown ringlets and wide blue eyes. "The children want far more than I'm willing to give. Sweets for dinner, no bedtime, fewer baths, and the right to live with their grandmother. I told them I would die before I'd allow such nonsense, and I think they took me at my word."

Nick glanced at the ink-smeared escritoire. "Who is winning?"

"I will," Anthony said coldly. "One way or another."

"Hm," Sara said, though she didn't look as impressed with Anthony's pronouncement as her husband. "Anthony, perhaps this has happened for a reason. It is time you married. This problem with the children is simply proof of that fact."

Anthony shot her a hard glance. "I cannot, in all good conscience, bring a new bride into this household until I have managed to restore at least a *little* of its former tranquility."

Sara's mouth dropped open for a full moment before she managed to ask, "You sound as if you were already planning . . . To whom?"

"Charlotte Melton."

"Melton. I believe I've heard the name, but I cannot place her."

"That's because she hasn't been presented yet."

Nick's smothered laugh irritated Anthony almost as much as Sara's incredulous expression. "Trust me, she's very mature for her age," Anthony said in a stiff voice.

Anthony had known since the day he first met Charlotte that she was exactly the type of wife he needed to reestablish the Elliot name. She was well bred, quiet, and demure—the exact opposite of the Elliots. With a little training, he was certain he could mold her into an outstanding countess and a charming companion.

"Good God, Anthony," Sara said faintly. "Just how old *is* this girl?"

His jaw began to ache. "Eighteen. She was not able to take her season in London due to the death of her grandmother. I had thought to have the wedding this spring, but I cannot ask her to come here without settling my affairs."

"No," Sara agreed, her mouth pinched with disapproval. "You couldn't launch your problems on a chit right out of the schoolroom. Had you chosen a woman, one capable of dealing with life's little foibles—"

"I would hardly call five misbehaved children 'foibles.' "

"Devils?" murmured Bridgeton. "Imps? Fiends?"

Anthony had used all those names and more, but he refused to admit it.

A knock on the door heralded the entrance of Jenkins. He opened the door wide and stood to one side. "Master Desford and Miss Selena."

A boy walked into the room. Thin and pale, with brown hair that proclaimed his Elliot ancestry, he was tall for his eleven years. A pugnacious tilt lined his jaw.

Anthony looked from Desford to the little girl who stood at his side. Selena was the youngest of the hellions. Only four, she was deeply under the influence of her brothers and sisters. She stood, dressed in a pink gown, sucking on one of her fingers, her face framed by soft brown ringlets, her blue eyes wide and unblinking. No angel could have appeared more innocent.

Anthony frowned at Desford. "Why did you bring her?"

"She wanted to come."

Sensing a trap, but unable to fathom what it could be, Anthony nodded shortly and gestured to Sara and Nick. "Allow me to present my sister and her husband, the Earl and Countess of Bridgeton."

Desford bowed just enough to show his indifference. Selena stared with wide eyes, but said nothing.

Anthony stifled a sigh and turned to Sara. "This is Desford and Selena. Or, as I like to call them, The Bane and The Baby."

Nick grinned while Sara smiled gently at the children. "How do you do?"

Desford looked past Sara to the window beyond, too unimpressed to pretend interest.

Anthony's jaw tightened. "Enough pleasantries. Desford, I wish to speak with you about the ink on the escritoire."

"Oh? Is that why you were yelling like a common drayman?" A flash sharpened Desford's brown eyes.

"Don't act surprised; you knew of it."

"Of course I knew of it." A slow curve touched Desford's mouth. "Selena put the ink on there this morning."

Anthony looked at the little girl. She stared back with wide eyes, still sucking on her finger. "You must be joking."

The boy gave his sister a look. "Tell them, Selena. Tell them it was you."

She removed her finger from her mouth and lisped dutifully, "It was me." She beamed at everyone while Anthony glared at Desford.

The boy's expression shimmered with triumph. "Do you want anything else? We were getting ready to play cricket."

Anthony stood staring down at the boy and the tiny girl, his hands curling and uncurling. He couldn't very well visit punishment on a four-year-old child who looked uncomfortably like a cherub, and Desford knew it. This new strategy was brilliant, and Anthony wondered wearily how many more confessions he was to hear from Selena over the course of the next few months.

Frustrated, he snapped at Desford, "You and I both know that Selena did not think of this little trick by herself."

"Yes, I did," Selena said, suddenly indignant. "All by myself."

Anthony grit his teeth, aware of Sara's interested gaze. "We will discuss this later. Return to the nursery."

Desford shrugged, then bent and picked up his sister, who

glared at Anthony over her brother's shoulder. Jenkins quietly followed the two and closed the door.

Sara turned to Anthony, her eyes dark with understanding. "Oh dear!"

Anthony rubbed his eyes wearily. It was always like this. The children would do something wrong and he would be forced to become a yelling boor in an effort to control them. At first it had worked and they had capitulated before the force of his anger, but they had swiftly banded together until he was outnumbered. Now they not only didn't care when he was angry, they worked hard to keep him in that state.

Anthony was not used to feeling like a tyrant, especially in his own house. He rubbed a hand over his face. Bloody hell, but what had happened to his well-ordered plans?

"There is only one answer," Sara said into the silence.

Anthony didn't open his eyes. He already knew what she was going to say.

She said it anyway. "Anna Thraxton."

"*No.*"

"But Anthony, she is the only one who could—"

"You are exaggerating. She's only been a governess for a year or so. Surely there are better trained—"

"Anna only takes the most difficult positions; I daresay because she can charge higher fees. And she is *always* successful. She even tamed Lord Radcliffe's twins and you remember what horrors they were."

That gave Anthony pause. He'd once had the misfortune of being trapped in a conversation with Radcliffe while the man was taking his sons for a walk. Though Anthony had excused himself with all possible speed, the meeting had confirmed his beliefs that children were best left in the nursery until they were of a more advanced age . . . like twenty. "She transformed *both* of Radcliffe's brats into better-behaved children?"

"In four months. She never takes a position for much longer as she trains her successor while she reorganizes the nursery. Everyone wants to secure her services."

Everyone but Anthony. "I don't care how good she is. Anna Thraxton is the last woman I would allow in my house. She's stubborn, interfering, and impossibly bossy. I'd rather live in my own cellar than have her under my roof."

"Such fervor," Nick said, his smile wicked, "but I suppose I can understand. She's an unforgettable woman. That rich auburn hair implies a very passionate nature."

"Bridgeton, if you have nothing of value to contribute, then pray leave."

"Oh, for heaven's sake!" Sara stood, stopping only when her skirt stuck to the edge of the settee. Making a disgusted sound, she pulled the material free, then stared down at a dark splotch on the back of her skirt. "Glue."

"Glue," Anthony answered dully. His whole house was a series of traps and countertraps, all arranged by a set of impossible brats wanting to live elsewhere. He was tempted to let them. But the hope that he could, somehow and some way, save these few children and prove that the Elliot curse was nothing more than an illusion, kept him bound to his course. He would save them just as he himself had been saved. And by God, they'd be thankful, the whole lot of them, or he'd have something to say about it.

"Anthony," Sara said, "Anna is the only one who can turn this mess about, and you know it."

That was the most damnable part of it—he *did* know it. But he also knew what Anna Thraxton would do if she were allowed under his roof. Before she'd become a governess, forced by necessity to seek employment, she had been Sara's best friend since boarding school. Anna had taken advantage of that relationship to tell Anthony what she thought about everything—including him. It was not an experience he desired to repeat.

Peace was all he craved, now more than ever, and Anna Thraxton was the equivalent of a twenty-four-hour display of fireworks—colorful but exhausting. Why, he wondered, did London's finest governess have to also be London's most irritating female? It was a damned shame.

Sara went to the door, Bridgeton following. "There is nothing I can do for you if you won't listen to reason," she said over her shoulder.

"Well, I won't listen to crackbrained ideas like that. But thank you for coming, anyway."

That put her nose out of joint. And it was with a very haughty air that Sara finally took her leave, her husband trailing in her wake, his eyes glowing with suppressed mirth.

Anthony stood at the window and watched the carriage rumble down the drive. Sara was his favorite sibling—he'd been attached to her since his stepfather had first laid the tiny bundle of baby in his arms. But her marriage to Bridgeton had changed her—happy with her wedded state, Sara was now determined to see as many of her brothers leg shackled as possible. Anthony snorted. If she thought Anna Thraxton was the answer to *that* problem, she was sadly mistaken.

Unbidden, an image of Thraxton came to mind—tall, auburn-haired, and elegant with a Roman nose and the audacious attitude of a born princess. The last time he'd seen her, they had argued over Bridgeton's courtship of Sara, and Anna had used the opportunity to inform Anthony that she thought him a complete idiot.

The words rankled still. No one treated him that way. It

was insufferable and a perfect example of the discord that would cloud the pristine airs of Greyley House if he allowed her into his life. The last thing he needed was an argumentative woman. That decided, he closed the curtain. He would prevail on his own terms, by God.

Overhead came the rushed footsteps of scattering children. From the sound of it, they were headed down the hallway toward the back stairs, their favorite route of escape.

Anthony held his breath, waiting. Seconds later a scream arose, followed by the hysterical gibbering of the housekeeper. He tilted his head to one side, trying to distinguish sensible words from the loud screeching. Something about a mouse . . . and a bedpan.

Shaking his head, he crossed the room, remembering that he was supposed to visit the tenant cottages today. Well, he didn't have time now—he had other fish to fry. Five annoying little minnows, to be exact.

This time he'd hire *two* governesses. Surely with two of them, the children would finally be under some sort of control. And if that didn't work . . . there was always Thraxton. The idea made him wince. Thank God he wasn't that desperate. Not yet, anyway. More determined to succeed than ever before, Anthony went to discover what new havoc his charges had wrought.

Chapter 2

It is a pity about the Thraxtons. Not even the prince can do anything for them now.

The Dowager Duchess of Roth to Sir Alfred Locksley,
at a private party at Vauxhall Gardens

Dandridge House, London
August 3, 1816

Her silk dress rustling delicately, Anna Thraxton pulled off her left glove and tossed the entire contents of her glass of orgeat directly into Viscount Northland's leering face.

To her immense satisfaction, the pudgy lord reeled back, tripped over his own feet, and landed against a tall potted plant—the very one he'd cornered her behind. Leafy plant and damp viscount went sprawling onto the edge of the dance floor, dirt sliding across the polished floor as the music in the ballroom came to an abrupt halt.

Anna set her empty glass back on the table and replaced her glove. "Oh, dear!" she said loudly. "Poor Lord Northland has tangled his feet and fallen!"

A loud snicker met this statement, for everyone knew Northland was a bumbling fool. A few even knew he was also an insistent letch who believed the word "no" meant "make me yours, my lusty lord."

Within moments, His Lordship's anxious mother had rushed to her son's side, a servant had righted the upset plant and brushed away the loose dirt, and the music had resumed. Once again, dancers swirled across the floor, and no one was the wiser that Anna Thraxton had efficiently dealt with one of London's most irritating toadstools.

"Bloody fool," Anna muttered behind her false smile, picking up her skirts and stepping over the dazed lord as his fretful mother patted his wet face with her handkerchief. That was the problem with being an unprotected female— and a poor one, at that. She was a walking target for every dandy with the desire to embark on a senseless flirtation, and she was getting deuced tired of it.

She shouldn't have come, and she knew it. But she had been unable to turn away from what had promised to be a truly magical event as the Dandridges' soirée. Lucinda Dandridge was a particular friend of hers, and Anna had allowed herself to be swayed by protestations of friendship into forgetting one, unavoidable fact—the Thraxtons were no longer sworn members of the *ton*.

Her throat tightened, though she managed to keep her smile rigidly in place. She had once belonged in gatherings such as this; her name and position secured, her bloodlines as pure as anyone else's. But all that had changed last year when Anna had been forced to accept employment as a governess.

Two circumstances had smoothed the way for Anna in her quest to support herself. First, though she had never been the sort of woman given to cooing over babies or collecting stray dogs and cats, she discovered, to her surprise, that she actually *liked* working with children, especially the older ones. They understood her, and she understood them.

Secondly, since Anna had very little experience in being a governess, the only positions she could find were for the more troublesome charges. But most of the children that had been labeled thusly were nothing compared to Grandpapa and his scheming ways.

Anna knew that her burgeoning reputation was based on only a very few successes—five, to be exact. It would take only one failure and the very members of the *ton* who had spread the word that she was a governess beyond compare would just as quickly condemn her. The thought made her chest tighten.

She impulsively smoothed her silk gown, her heartache easing somewhat at the feel of the rich silk beneath her fingertips. It was a pity she possessed the family weakness. Despite enjoying the most pragmatic of characters, she was sadly addicted to fashion, and heaven knew, she did not have the money to support her addiction. In fact, the blue gown was far more dear than she could afford. French by design and cut of fabulous watered silk, it looked wonderful on her tall frame, and she knew it. Still, that did not excuse her for spending money that should have gone for a new chair for the morning room. A chair that did not have a ripped cover or a sagging seat like all the others.

But somehow, as Lucinda Dandridge's pleas for her friend's presence at the soirée increased, the need for a new gown became imminently pressing. Anna had finally succumbed, reasoning that she could buy a new chair with the income from her next position—a hazy bit of logic that she was sure she would find faulty once she examined it in the glaring light of day and away from the mesmerizing effects of blue watered silk.

She looked down at the new satin slippers she'd bought to go with the gown and sighed. No wonder their family was nigh destitute. Of course, she wasn't totally at fault. A good deal of the problem lay in Grandpapa's tendency to disburse their funds on every "guaranteed" investment that came along. Between Grandfather's spendthrift investments and Anna's inability to stay within budget, they had found themselves in dire straits.

Anna had been forced to make a decision—debtors' prison or employment. The decision hadn't been difficult, but it *had* hurt, especially the realization that the second she became a governess, her old way of life was lost forever.

Of course Grandpapa didn't see it that way. He firmly believed that their bloodlines protected them from all harm, though Anna knew better. She straightened her shoulders, aware that people had begun to stare covertly. Damn Northland for drawing attention to her; she'd been careful not to put herself forward, but now . . .

She lifted her chin. Perhaps it was time to leave. She'd make her apologies to Lucinda and—a commotion stirred to life at the door. The crowd parted to reveal Anthony Elliot, the Earl of Greyley, looking devastatingly handsome in his formal black attire.

An older woman dressed in the most atrocious pink flounce tittered excitedly, then said to no one in particular, "Oh, look! 'Tis the Earl of Greyley. I didn't expect to see *him* here."

Neither had Anna. The earl was on her list of "people one should avoid at all costs." He was the half brother of Anna's best friend, Sara, but there'd been an instant antipathy between Anna and the earl—the kind that made her neck tingle as if she were standing in a violent storm, in immediate danger of being struck by lightning. They'd had more run-ins than she could count, and none had left them on speaking terms.

She watched him stop to greet their host. Tall and broad-shouldered, he looked like a giant among ants, his tawny hair the color of a lion's mane—amber shot with streaks of gold. His eyes were the deepest chocolate brown, fringed by such thick lashes that he appeared half asleep.

But Anna knew that air of sleepy watchfulness was a thin guise. Beneath that lazy façade was a mind strong as steel and as sharp as an arrow's tip. Her gaze flickered past Greyley's mouth to his firm jaw, and then slid down to where his powerful thighs showed to advantage beneath the snug black fabric of his trousers. It was a good thing she disliked him so much, she thought with a faint stir of approval. She was very susceptible to men with strong thighs.

"Wealthy, titled, and handsome." The matron in pink flounce leaned toward the younger dab of a female who stood at her side. "Straighten up, Mary! He might look this way. He's a good catch, even with all those children."

"Children?" Mary said, unconsciously echoing Anna's own thoughts. "What children? Mama, I thought the earl was still a bachelor."

"Lud, child, where have you been? Greyley inherited an entire brood of children. And now that he's awash with responsibility, speculation is rife that he will wish to marry. I've heard it said that he's worth twenty thousand a year, too."

Anna barely refrained from snorting aloud. Greyley might be worth twenty thousand a year, but he was also the most arrogant, most insufferable, and most obstinate man to walk the earth.

Mary gasped. "Look, Mama! He's coming this way."

Anna followed the girl's gaze, and sure enough, Greyley was bearing down on them, but his dark eyes were not fastened on the woman in pink flounce, but on Anna. A trill of uncertainty touched her, and her shoulders lifted of their own accord.

Why on earth would Anthony Elliot wish to see *her*? Perhaps he wanted to speak about Sara. Or maybe—

Dear God, *the children*. Anna whirled on her heel and slipped through the crowd, weaving through a crush of people by inserting an elbow here, a polite smile there. She circumvented the earl altogether and reached the foyer as if pursued by the devil himself. Despite the fact that Greyley was a commanding presence, Anna knew it would be some time before he extricated himself from that crowd of milling mamas and their dangling daughters.

She reached the safety of the foyer in what must have been record time, glancing over her shoulder and sighing in relief when she saw no sign of the earl. She called for her carriage, waiting impatiently until it rumbled up.

Anna was just lifting her foot to climb inside when a warm hand closed over her elbow. A hot jolt of sensation trembled up her arm and made her jerk away. Off balance, she reeled backward, her shoe falling from the foot she held aloft and landing with a clack on the cobblestone.

Still wobbling, she was caught in a firm embrace and unceremoniously righted. "Running away?" said a deep, masculine voice. "I would never have thought it of you."

The warm, smoky timbre of Greyley's voice made Anna stiffen and she was immediately released. She placed an unsteady hand on the side of the coach and turned to face her accuser. It was very difficult to be dignified when one had to hold one's stocking-clad foot above the muddy cobblestones, but she thought she managed quite well.

Or she thought she had until she found herself staring into Anthony Elliot's darkly lashed eyes. Pools of melted chocolate, they made her heart race, her skin heat. Fascinated, she found she could not look away. "I am not running anywhere."

He gave the carriage a pointed stare.

"I was just, ah, going home. But slowly. I really wasn't running."

Amusement softened the hard line of his mouth. He waved the waiting footman away before turning the full force of his heated gaze back on Anna. "Leaving without your shoe, Miss Thraxton?"

Anna followed his gaze to where her shoe lay on its side, looking forlorn and alone on the curb. "I suppose I will need that."

He picked it up, then turned to her, his eyes almost black in the faint light. "Get into the carriage. If you attempt to put your shoe on here, you'll drag your hem in the muck."

The street *was* dirty. And they *were* blocking the entry, not that anyone else was leaving the ball this early. Plus it was her new gown, and it would be a long time before she could afford another. Anna allowed Greyley to help her into the low slung coach, his long fingers resting lightly on her arm. Agonizingly aware of his presence, she found herself savoring his warm, masculine scent. She settled on the seat and deliberately leaned away. "Thank you, Greyley. If you'll just hand me my shoe, I'll—"

A warm hand encircled her ankle. Anna was too shocked to do more than stare. Compared to the size of his huge hand, her stocking-clad foot actually looked . . . small. Even dainty. It was a heady experience for a woman used to hiding her large feet beneath the edge of her skirts.

Greyley slipped the satin slipper over her toes and pushed her heel into place. It really was a pretty foot, Anthony noted with something akin to surprise. Long and delicately made, it said volumes about the fact that this was not an ordinary governess, but a lady of quality. And that was what Anna Thraxton was—a lady of quality reduced by her circumstances to take on employment.

But that apparently hadn't prevented her from mingling with her peers. It was something of a shock to see her after so long, looking coolly elegant in pale blue silk that made her eyes seem an even lighter silver than usual, her vivid hair attracting his gaze as surely as a lit flame.

Beneath Anthony's fingers, the warmth of her skin seeped through her silk stockings. Entranced, he slowly slid his thumb across the slope of her foot, relishing the contact. A slow, low heat began to build, brushing over him and leaving a trail of delicate fire.

"I believe my shoe is on." Anna pulled her foot free, arranging her skirts so that they hid her feet. "Lord Greyley, thank you very much for your assistance, but—"

"I must speak with you," he said, struggling to regain his senses. Good God, but the children had indeed driven him to distraction. He was dizzy with relief at finally finding a capable governess. "It's urgent." He rammed his hands into his pockets, ignoring the call from the driver of another carriage that had pulled up behind them. "We can't discuss this here. I will call on you tomorrow and we will talk then."

Her creamy skin touched with pink. "Lord Greyley, I'm afraid I cannot—"

"I wish to hire you and I will pay well."

To his chagrin, he thought he caught a hint of something like hurt in her eyes as she said, "I'm afraid I've already accepted another position with Lord Allencott. I'm leaving this week."

"Thraxton, just hear me out. That's all I ask." He saw her hesitate, and he added softly, "If not for me, then for Sara. I need your help."

Her generous mouth turned down at the edges. "It is very unscrupulous of you to use my friendship with your sister."

It was true; he was shamelessly trading on his sister's

friendship just to get an interview with London's best governess. In the month since Sara's visit, things had spiraled even more out of control. His life had well and truly become a hell, and here before him, her chin tilted at a mutinous angle, her luxurious red hair curling over one white shoulder, sat his salvation. "Miss Thraxton . . ." He grit his teeth. "Please."

Her eyes widened. "What did you say?"

"You heard me."

"So I did." A mischievous twinkle lit her gray eyes. "Would you mind repeating it? I don't believe I've ever heard you use that word before."

Anthony scowled. "You're determined to make this difficult, aren't you?"

"Greyley, I cannot accept your offer, so there's no more to be said." She tilted her head to one side, a thick curl of her hair swinging forward to rest on the curve of her breast. "Still . . . I may know of someone who could help. After all, it had to be quite galling for you to seek me out at all. And the fact that you said please—things must be dire indeed."

A shout arose from the coachman behind them, and Anna nodded as if she'd just made up her mind. "Come and see me tomorrow. Number four, Roberts Street."

"At ten," he said quickly. Anna Thraxton might think she was controlling the moves in this game, but she was wrong. "Until tomorrow." Anthony closed the door and stepped back. The carriage started with an abrupt jar as it hobbled over the cobblestone drive and rolled out into the street. Anthony watched until it disappeared from sight, his fingers still tingling with warmth where he'd cupped Thraxton's amazingly delicate ankle.

He shouldn't have touched her in such an intimate fashion, but the opportunity to rattle her was too tempting. He looked down at his hands and thought of her calf as it rested against his palm, curved and firm. The gesture had been innocent, yet erotic at the same time.

Anthony closed his hands into fists and shoved them into his pockets, his fingers catching a round object. He pulled it out and glanced at it. His mother's talisman ring. He'd forgotten about it. Where in the hell was Chase, anyway?

The thick silver seemed warm in his hand, the strange silver runes gleaming as if just polished. A bittersweet warmth in his chest, he closed his fingers over the circlet. His mother had believed in the power of the ring, but then she'd also believed in fairy sprites that made dew circles in the grass. Shaking his head at such unaccountable whimsy, Anthony tucked the ring away. He missed his mother even now, after all these years.

He'd find Chase another night. Tonight was for celebrating. By this time tomorrow, Anthony would have London's best governess in his possession, and woe betide Desmond and the hordes. If Anna Thraxton was even half as good as rumor reported, Anthony was going to win the war. And winning had become imperative. There was no such thing as bad blood—only bad behavior. And Anna Thraxton was going to help Anthony prove it, once and for all.

Whistling to himself, Anthony turned and made his way back into the Dandridges' house. Things were finally going his way.

Chapter 3

Phineas Thraxton is a taxing companion. The last time
I saw him, he taxed me to the amount of 150 guineas.

Sir Alfred Locksley to Lord Brevenham,
over a glass of port at White's

Sir Phineas Thraxton leaned on his cane and stared out
the window of the tiny, cramped room that passed as the
morning room. He glanced once at the closed door, then
leaned over the windowsill and blew a cloud of smoke into
the chilled morning air. As he stood, he bumped the edge of
the shutter where it hung drunkenly on its hinges. He winced
at the resulting groan of rotted wood and rusty fasteners, a
sad testament to the state of the entire establishment.

He hated this house. Hated every creaking, leaking inch
of it. Narrow and drafty, it was in a part of town he openly
considered deplorable. He took another pull of the cigarillo,
savoring the pungent aroma even as he tried to wave it out the
window.

It was his only vice, and it was a demmed shame his
granddaughter had taken it into such dislike. He deserved a
few pleasures, at least. Especially now that fortune had
turned her back on the Thraxton family. Gingerly holding the

rapidly shrinking cigarillo, Sir Phineas blew a perfect circle of smoke into the air. A noise in the hallway made him freeze, and he relaxed only when he heard Mrs. Duckrow's raw voice raised in outcry at the clumsiness of a maid. The housekeeper might be a termagant, but she didn't interfere with his pleasures. No, that privilege was reserved to his granddaughter, Anna.

Anna was Sir Phineas's ultimate joy. Free spirited, intelligent, attractive, and opinionated—she possessed all the best Thraxton qualities. Phineas had no doubt that, had he not been so foolish as to tie up the family fortune in a series of unfortunate investments, Anna would have found a nice, handsome young man and settled into a life more suitable to her station.

He bit the end of his cigarillo and stared morosely out the window for a long moment, mulling over the unsatisfying aspects of his life and wondering what he could do to fix things. After a moment, he shook himself out of his brown reverie. By God, he was a Thraxton; something would occur to right things. He was certain of it.

Anna's quick tread sounded in the hallway. Sir Phineas took two final puffs, then tossed the cigarillo out the window, closed it, and then hurriedly limped to a chair by the cold fireplace and dropped into it. He'd barely managed to pull a nearby lap rug across his knees before the door opened and Anna walked in.

Tall, auburn-haired, and elegant, with a nose as bold as her spirit, she was a true Thraxton. Every blessed inch of her.

"There you are," she said, her smile warming the whole room. "I was wondering where you'd disappeared to."

"I'm sitting here, dying of thirst."

"More likely you were smoking one of your nasty cigarillos."

He almost returned her smile, but caught himself in time. Thank God his granddaughter wasn't a prude. He wouldn't live with anyone who spouted mealymouthed morality. If he had any complaints, it was that Anna had inherited his own outspoken tenacity along with her grandmother's overly generous heart. As a result, once his granddaughter took it into her head to help someone, neither heaven nor high water would turn her from her mark.

Sir Phineas wished she'd find someone more worthy than he for the focus of her astounding efforts. It would help if it were someone well established. Perhaps even wealthy.

He folded his mouth in what he hoped was a hurt expression. "How can you accuse me of smoking? Didn't I promise I would quit last Christmas?"

"So you did, although you were quite careful not to tell me exactly *when* you were going to quit. I've caught you doing it a total of seventeen times since."

"Unfeeling, disrespectful girl."

"Rude, bamboozling grandpapa," she said, taking the seat opposite his with a grin.

"Don't try to cozen me," he said, though he was more than a little pleased that she was in such good spirits. "I might look old, but I'm as sharp as a quill."

"So you keep telling me." She eyed him from head to toe. "I vow, but you look fresh this morning. Did you sleep well?"

"Like a rock. Didn't even hear you return. Tell me, how was the soirée last night? You didn't stop by to see me when you returned, as you usually do."

Her gaze shuttered immediately. "It was lovely."

Was it, indeed? Sir Phineas leaned back in his chair. "Any interesting gossip to be heard at the refreshment table?"

She shrugged, but volunteered no more information.

Sir Phineas waited patiently. When his granddaughter did nothing more than stare down at the tips of her slippers, he said, "Come, child. I want the latest gossip, descriptions of which women wore the most diaphanous gowns, and which men made asses of themselves. It's the least you can do since I was unable to attend myself."

Anna stood and went to wind the clock that graced the mantel, her face carefully averted. "There was one thing . . ."

"Yes?"

"Lord Northland. He tripped and spilled my orgeat."

Sir Phineas looked at Anna's hand, which was bunched about the clock key so tightly that her knuckles shone white. Damn it all, he should have been with his granddaughter and not tucked into bed like an invalid. "I hope you drew his cork."

The air of tension eased a bit, and she turned to smile at him over her shoulder, a look of great satisfaction softening her face. "Nothing so dire as that. Just a little orgeat up his nose. I think I made my point rather nicely."

It was a pity he hadn't been present to defend his granddaughter. "Wish I could have done the honors for you," he said sourly.

"I handled him quite well myself." She set the clock key back on the mantel, a quiver of some emotion lurking in her gray eyes. "It was a lesson to me. I should never have gone to the Dandridges'. I stepped out of my station by doing so, and Lord Northland's behavior reminded me of that fact."

Sir Phineas had to grind his teeth to keep a scowl from his face. In over seven hundred years, no Thraxton had done more than dally in trade, and it was a demmed shame to see it start now. Not that he was averse to hard work; he understood the benefits of using one's own hands to assist those in need.

But the Thraxtons were *not* common laborers. In fact, there was nothing common about any of them. And seeing his granddaughter slaving for a few pence like a mill worker was heartbreaking.

Anna's gaze suddenly flickered past his shoulder. "Grandpapa, you *were* smoking, weren't you?"

"Heavens, no. Wouldn't think of it. Nasty habit, smoking. Often thought they should ban cigarillos and—"

"*Someone* was smoking. And they caught the shrubbery on fire."

Phineas turned to see a thick column of smoke rising in front of the window. "Damnation, I thought I had extinguished that blasted—" He caught his granddaughter's amused gaze and added hastily, "Don't just stand there, yammering away! Tell Hawkes to put it out before the whole house goes up in smoke. As ramshackle as this place is, it would spark like a tinderbox."

Her gaze narrowed on him a moment, but she obediently left, and Sir Phineas could hear her talking to the butler. A few moments later the smoke gulped, then turned to steam. Cursing the ill fates that hounded him, Phineas pulled himself from his chair and crossed to the window, where he watched Hawkes pour more water on the blackened bush at the bottom of the stairs.

It was almost too much to bear, he thought sulkily. And now he was going to be subjected to yet another lecture on the hazards of smoking. Sir Phineas muttered noisily, hurrying to resume his seat before Anna returned.

She entered the room while he was trying to think of a safer topic than his beloved cigarillos. He cleared his throat. "I say, m'dear, is that a new gown?"

Sir Phineas wasn't conversant with his granddaughter's wardrobe, other than to note that she seemed to have a lot of it. But his innocent remark caused an astonishing reaction; a slow blush crept across Anna's face. Sir Phineas sat up straighter. His granddaughter *never* blushed.

She gave an uncertain laugh. "This old gown? I've had it for months. I am expecting a visitor this morning, and I thought I should . . . I ought to perhaps . . ." She sank into her chair, her cheeks still pink. "I don't want anyone to think I cannot afford to dress."

Well! This was something, indeed. "Is this visitor anyone I know?"

Anna fixed him with a hard stare. "Grandpapa, you are not to have anything to do with him."

Oh ho! So it was a "him"? Phineas assumed a wounded expression. "As if I would meddle in your affairs."

Anna stared at him without blinking.

Phineas tried to wait it out, but her gaze reminded him a tad too much of his dearly departed wife. "Oh, very well," he finally said in a testy tone. "I suppose you're old enough to take care of your own business."

"Exactly." She smoothed her skirts, her coloring returning to normal. "For your information, the Earl of Greyley is coming to see me this morning."

An earl, eh? Phineas squinted at the ceiling, trying to recall everything he knew about the earl. He was a man of fortune, if the gossips were to be believed. And an honorable man, too. And there had been some nattering about estates in Derbyshire and farther north. Hm. This could be just the thing.

Still, it wouldn't do to appear too excited. Anna was a contrary woman, much like her grandmother. So instead of grinning, Sir Phineas snorted. "Greyley's a bastard."

Anna blinked. "You don't even know him!"

"Don't need to. Heard all about him from Lady Pedalshem. She says he's a ne'er-do-well."

"Lord Greyley is many things, but I'd never call him a ne'er-do-well."

"If he's not a ne'er-do-well, then what is he?"

"He's arrogant, pompous, overly concerned with being right at all costs, and—" Anna clamped her mouth closed.

Sir Phineas waited, but Anna showed no sign of continuing. He moved restlessly. "At least admit you think he's a bastard."

She turned her fine gray eyes his way. "I will agree to nothing of the kind. I will, however, admit that he is a difficult person. And unscrupulous. And I daresay he has never had a care in his life. Still, I cannot allow you to malign him for no reason other than hearing a bit of unfavorable gossip."

The rumbling of a carriage sounded outside. Anna stood so suddenly that it appeared she'd been propelled out of her chair by a forceful boot. Her gaze locked on the open window, her lips parted as if her breath struggled for release. The carriage lumbered to the front of the house and then passed by, the sound fading as quickly as it had arisen.

Anna sank back into her chair, her face pink as she self-consciously rearranged her skirts. "He's late, you know. But then he would be."

Demme, but something was going on. Anna wasn't a nervy kind of chit, full of palpitations and silly airs, but she acted like a fluffhead waiting on a beau. This was getting better and better.

Sir Phineas put his hand into his pocket and carefully smoothed his last remaining cigarillos. While he wasn't one to hold with the concept of nobility, he had to admit that Greyley's wealth almost made up for the unfortunate fact that he possessed a title.

Sir Phineas didn't believe in titles, not even his own, although he was quick enough to use it when it served him. Besides, it couldn't hurt to have an earl in one's pocket. "I'm glad Greyley is stopping by. I'd like to discuss a few things with him, and—"

"You are *not* going to meet him."

"Why not? I make it a point to meet any man who comes calling—"

"This isn't a social visit. He wants to employ my services as governess."

Sir Phineas would bet his last shilling that Greyley's library was stocked with the finest of everything from port to cigars. For a marvelous instant, he pictured himself in that luxuriously imagined library, feet on a wide mahogany desk, a glass of prime port in one hand, a freshly rolled cigarillo in the other.

Perhaps even a few great-grandchildren scampering about the room.

The picture warmed him as he cocked a brow at his recalcitrant granddaughter. "Will you accept Greyley's offer of employment?"

"No," she said, her jaw set.

"Won't pay a decent wage, eh?" Sir Phineas shook his head, though he kept his gaze on Anna. "A bastard *and* a nip farthing."

"It has nothing to do with money," she replied hotly. "It's just that I refuse to contribute to Lord Greyley's avoidance of his responsibilities."

"What are you talking about?"

"I daresay you aren't aware of it, but Lord Greyley inherited some children from his cousin."

"Five of 'em, last I heard."

Anna's mouth thinned. "You *knew* about that?"

Since his retirement from society, Phineas had cultivated a network of elderly ladies whom he met during his stroll in the park each and every morning. Due to their unceasing efforts, no word of gossip, true or otherwise, ever escaped his willing ears. "Everyone knows about Greyley and those children."

"I didn't."

"I'd have told you if I'd realized you had a fancy for the man."

That lit the fires. She blazed at him with such a ferocious look that he had to bite his lip to keep from grinning.

"I do *not* have a 'fancy' for Greyley. Or any man, for that matter."

Sir Phineas didn't at all care for the way she was speaking through her clenched teeth. "I daresay that's for the best. I'm not sure I approve of this fellow." Phineas stood and limped to the window and peered down into the street. "I believe Hawkes has managed to put out the fire."

"Until you throw another cigarillo out the window."

"I wasn't smoking, I tell you." As he stood watching the butler, a large, well-sprung travel coach lumbered down the road. Wide and luxuriously appointed with leather curtains and brass trim, it slowed to a stop at the steps. A footman climbed down from the perch and went to open the carriage door.

Anna was once again standing. "Has he come?"

"Lud, no. It's a coal cart, nothing more." The sumptuous travel coach seemed very out of place among the shabby-genteel buildings that surrounded it. But even more out of place was the large and elegantly turned Earl of Greyley, just now descending the steps. Dressed in the height of fashion, but with a quiet style that immediately won Sir Phineas's approval, the earl stood on the front walk and murmured instructions to his footman. Phineas supposed that the earl was a handsome enough man, one who might appeal to Anna's overly fastidious tastes.

"If it's just a coal cart, then why are you staring?"

"What? Oh, the man looks familiar, that's all. I think he's

the same scoundrel who tried to sell Hawkes painted rocks for coal just last month." Phineas dropped the curtain and rubbed his eyes. "Anna, could you fetch my eyeglasses? I believe I left them on the stand beside my bed."

Suspicion darkened her gaze, but she went to the door. "Try not to catch the house on fire while I'm gone."

Sir Phineas waited for her footsteps to fade up the stairs before he hobbled to the door. "Hawkes!"

Dressed in a black coat that had seen better days, Hawkes was the only manservant left in the Thraxton household. As such, he was called on to serve as footman, coachman, valet, and butler, all of which he did with so much enthusiasm that Sir Phineas thought him rather simpleminded.

"My lord?" he asked now, looking annoyingly eager to be of service.

"Someone is about to knock on the door. Please open it before they do so."

Hawkes was gone in an instant and Sir Thraxton hobbled back to his chair.

Moments later, Hawkes stood in the doorway and said in an irritatingly grand manner, "The Earl of Greyley, my lord. He has come to see Miss Thraxton."

Sir Phineas waved the earl to his side. "My granddaughter just left to fetch something. She should be back in a moment. Come and have a seat, Greyley, while we wait for her."

Once Hawkes quit the room, Sir Phineas confirmed his first opinions of the earl as he crossed the room toward him. The earl moved with a grace that belied his large size, and Sir Phineas shrewdly guessed there was solid muscle beneath the neatly fitted coat. The man carried himself with real presence and a sense of contained power that bode well. Very well, indeed. It took a strong man to master a Thraxton female. It always did.

"Hope you don't mind if I remain sitting—bad knees, you know." Sir Phineas motioned for the earl to take the chair opposite his. He watched as the earl examined the chair with the faintest lift of his brows. The red velvet chair was hardly the chair for a man of Greyley's size; it was tiny and delicate looking. Worse, two springs were broken and the worn seat sagged pitifully.

After surveying it for a moment, the earl perched on the edge, relaxing some when it didn't so much as creak beneath his weight.

Phineas decided that a full frontal attack was the only way to cut through the confining civilities before Anna returned. He harrumphed noisily. "So you've come for my granddaughter. An excellent choice, if I say so myself. You won't find a better wife anywhere in London."

Greyley gave a lazy lift of an eyebrow. "I'm afraid you've misunderstood. I am here to offer Miss Thraxton employment, not marriage."

"Employment?" Sir Phineas affected a scowl. "Not asking her to be your lightskirt, are you?"

That should have shook the man, but instead of looking angry or upset, the earl said coolly, "I've come to ask your granddaughter to be governess to my wards, the largest parcel of brats ever to grace the earth."

Sir Phineas gave a grudging smile. "Elliots, I take it."

"Every blasted one of them. They are about to run me out of my own house."

"Not surprised. Don't mean to speak ill of your relatives, but they are bad ones, the whole lot."

"Unfortunately, I agree," the earl said. "However, the children might be spared if they are exposed to the influence of a common set of rules and some discipline now, while they are still impressionable."

"Could be," Sir Phineas said, regarding Greyley shrewdly. "I should warn you—my Anna's a pricey parcel. She's not a woman to be gained without struggle."

"I'm willing to pay whatever it takes. Peace must be restored to Greyley House, regardless the cost."

Sir Phineas's blue eyes shone with approval. "Demme, but you've a direct way about you. I think you'll do very well, Greyley. Very well, indeed."

Anthony glanced toward the door. The man was obviously addlepated. Where the hell was Anna?

The old man chuckled, his thin face bright with humor. He was a tall man, but slender, his skin parchment pale, his white hair neatly brushed back from his temples. From the strength of his prominent nose to his glittering blue eyes, Anthony could tell that here was a man who had lived and not regretted a single moment. A pang of envy hit Anthony.

He frowned. Damn it, why on earth would he envy a man like Phineas Thraxton, a man who had squandered his life on lost causes and, through gross mismanagement of his fortune, had sent his family to the poorhouse? It was ridiculous.

Anthony decided that today had started out dismally and appeared to be getting worse by the minute. He'd risen far later than he'd meant to, mainly because some fool had closed all the curtains in his bedchamber and it was as dark as a tomb. Then, while he was attempting to find a decent waistcoat among the horrid display of florid atrocities his valet had packed, he'd received a missive from Dalmapple, his man of business who resided at Greyley House, who had written in great detail of the exploits of the children in the week since Anthony had left.

Apparently Desford had taken his absence to heart and was leading the others into even worse behavior than usual. It was imperative that Anthony conclude his business in London, mainly that of securing Anna Thraxton as governess, and return home as soon as possible.

Blithely unaware of Anthony's dour thoughts, Sir Phineas leaned back in his chair, lacing his hands over his stomach. "I've been busy this month. Want to know what I've been doing?"

"The last I heard, you were distributing pamphlets on the importance of curtailing the breeding habits of the lower classes."

Sir Phineas waved a blue-veined hand in the air. "I've found a better answer to societal woes."

"Oh?"

The old man flashed a mischievous grin, opened a box on a side table, and withdrew a small, slender yellow bag tied on one end with a pink ribbon. "Here is the answer to every problem the earth faces—famine, disease, pestilence, and sloth."

Anthony looked at the bag. After a moment, he muttered, "Good God."

"Do you know what it is?"

"A French sheath, used to prevent pregnancy."

"I have almost two hundred," Sir Phineas said proudly.

"How . . . delightful. I hope you don't mind, but just, ah, what do you propose to do with them?"

"Convince the crown to distribute them freely to the population. I delivered one to the Prince Regent myself. Seeing as he's fathered an unusual number of brats off that married woman, Mrs. Fitzgerald, I thought perhaps he didn't know what one was."

"I'm sure Prinny was impressed with your thoughtfulness."

Sir Phineas made a sound of disgust as he replaced the French sheath in the drawer. "Prinny's a fool. The old king, now there was a man. He would have taken action. Pity he's gone mad."

"Indeed," Anthony said politely, wondering if Anna was ever going to arrive. His irritation was increasing by the moment.

Sir Phineas leaned forward, his gaze bright. "What I really need is someone to back my plan. Someone who could invest a certain sum in providing more French sheaths for the population."

Bloody hell, the man could not be serious.

Sir Phineas nodded sagely. "I can see you're struck by the thought of being able to do so much good. It's a heady responsibility, but I think you're up to it."

"I'm afraid you misunderstand—"

"Want to know what benefits you'll get? Fame, my dear sir. Fame and the satisfying knowledge that you have altered the course of history."

"How generous of you to offer such an opportunity," Anthony said dryly.

"Oh, don't thank me! I'm perfectly comfortable to stand in the background and let you take all the credit. I've no wish to be a hero."

Anthony was trying to think of an acceptable answer when the door opened and Miss Thraxton entered. Dressed in a pale blue morning dress edged with pink rosettes, her hair artfully curled on top of her head, her white skin gleaming delicately, she looked like no governess Anthony had ever seen. She was the epitome of fashion, an undoubted lady of quality, the warm smile on her lips brightening the entire room. Had it not been for her remarkable nose, she would have been astonishingly beautiful.

She stopped when she saw him, her smile dying an immediate death. "Greyley. When did you arrive?"

"Just now." He stood. "I have been having the most delightful conversation with your grandfather."

Her gaze flickered to Sir Phineas, and Anthony thought he detected a hint of irritation in her gray eyes. "Grandpapa, why didn't you send for me when Lord Greyley arrived?"

"I knew you were on your way. Besides, the earl and I had a lot to talk about. But now I'm tired." He stood, yawning as he did so. "If you two will excuse me, I think I'll take a nap."

"I thought you needed these," Anna said stiffly, holding out a pair of silver-rimmed spectacles.

"So I do." Sir Phineas took the glasses and tucked them in his pocket. "I might want to read a bit before I go to sleep." He sent a piercing glance at Anthony. "I look forward to speaking to you more later, young man."

Anthony bowed politely. "I look forward to it."

Miss Thraxton moved to one side to let her grandfather pass. The light from the window touched her skirts with gold and briefly illuminated the fascinating shape of her legs. Good God, they were endless. Endless and shapely and—

Anthony caught Sir Phineas's amused glance. Damn it, what was he thinking? He was here to offer the chit a position as governess in his household and nothing else. "Sir Phineas, please feel free to stay. Miss Thraxton and I just have some business to conclude and—"

Sir Phineas waved a hand. "You don't need me. Anna's no pink and white miss. She can handle herself." A sly smile touched the old man's lips as he opened the door. "If you don't believe me, ask Lord Northland."

With this cryptic statement, Sir Phineas left, closing the door behind him. Anthony listened to the sounds of the cane steadily thumping along the corridor. After a moment, he glanced at Miss Thraxton, who stood planted in the center of the room, her back so straight he wondered if she wore a brace. To ease the moment, he asked, "Who is Lord Northland and why do I feel that I should pity him?"

"Lord Northland is of no consequence." She crossed her arms under her chest, the gesture pressing her breasts upward. "So, Greyley, you need a governess."

Anthony had to force himself to look elsewhere. Anna Thraxton was far too attractive to be a governess. Or would be, if one liked women who possessed far too many opinions of their own. "Miss Thraxton, let us come to the point. *You* are a governess; I would like to hire you." There. Now all he needed to do was find out her salary requirements and—

"I'm afraid I cannot. As I told you last night, I am already employed. However, I would be glad to recommend another—"

"Miss Thraxton, I need you at Greyley House, not some milksop female unable to deal with the slightest upset."

She jutted her chin mutinously, her eyes sparking with anger. "You may be king of the roost at your house, but here you are nothing more than another person looking for a governess. One of *many*, I might add."

He had no doubt that the desperate parents and guardians of London were flocking to Miss Thraxton's door; he himself was testament to that. But no one needed the best governess in London as much as he for no one had as much to prove. Anthony stifled his impatience. "It doesn't matter who I am—I need you, Miss Thraxton. And I'm willing to pay."

"You don't have enough money to employ me."

"Everyone has a price. Even you."

She made a disgusted sound. "You are the most insufferable, pompous, irritating man I've ever met."

"And you, Miss Thraxton, are the most infuriating, maddening, annoying woman in all of England. But I'm willing to overlook that unfortunate fact because you're also supposedly the best governess to be had. And make no mistake," he growled, stalking closer until he stood not a foot in front of her, "I intend to have you. Now cease this foolishness and tell me your requirements." Good Lord, was he going to have to battle her every step of the way?

Her chin lifted to an even more mutinous angle, her mouth thin with anger. "I was willing to assist you in locating a suitable replacement, but if you cannot at least *pretend* to be pleasant, then I have nothing more to say."

Anthony's temper flared. By God, he hadn't come to London for his health. "You haven't heard me out."

"I've heard more than I wanted to," she said. "Please leave before I call the butler."

Anthony closed the narrow space between them, his body all but touching hers. "Then call him."

"You wouldn't dare," she said, hissing the words through her teeth.

Her chin lifted and, before Anthony could comprehend what she was about, she opened her mouth and called loudly, "*Hawk—*"

Anthony grabbed her. His only thought was to keep her from making such a racket that she brought the entire household into the sitting room. But the frustrating events of the morning and the sudden, enthralling feel of her full breasts pressed against his chest cracked the veneer of Anthony's calm logic and released a torrent of pent-up emotions, emotions that flared to life all too quickly around the fiery-headed woman he now held in his arms.

Thus it was that Anthony Elliot, the always proper ninth Earl of Greyley, did something he never did. He lost control of his carefully contained anger and kissed the woman he wanted to hire as a governess.

Chapter 4

I will never again play cards with Lord Greyley. There is no lower feeling than dealing to a man who never loses.

Lord Brevenham to Miss Devonshire,
over an ice at the Waltham musicale

Of all the stolen kisses Anna had been made to suffer since becoming a governess, Greyley's was different. It wasn't apologetic or furtive, but forthright and passionate. It stormed the frigid barriers she'd erected about herself and shattered her illusion of control, burning a way past her shocked defenses before she could do more than gasp.

Anna responded immediately, though not in the way she should have. Instead of doubling her hands into fists, she found herself clutching Greyley's lapels, pulling him closer. As he deepened the kiss, his mouth searing across hers, she moaned softly, the sound delicious and wanton, urging her on.

And why not? the heated part of her wondered. Why not taste just this one, tiny bit of pleasure? She deserved it. The part of her that lusted after the feel of raw silk, that reveled in the glitter of a diamond pin, that unabashedly desired finery and pleasure and fun—it wound its way through her, heightening her senses, and completely silencing the other, more

logical part that mumbled a warning of some sort, the incoherent thought lost as Greyley's tongue slid across Anna's
lower lip. The erotic gesture sent a shudder of delight straight
to her toes.

One of the brass buttons that adorned his waistcoat
brushed the bared skin at her throat. The cold metal chilled
her reactions, and Anna broke the embrace. Here she was,
kissing a man as if she—and it was Greyley, which made it all
the worse. "Heavens!" she heard herself say. The room was
awhirl with color and silence, her mouth and cheeks tingled
as if they'd both been assaulted by the earl's talented lips.

"Heaven, indeed," Greyley murmured. His gaze was fastened on her mouth, a disturbing glint in his dark gaze.
"Congratulations, Thraxton. You are indeed as fiery as you
look."

Anna thought she could hear a dismissal in his tone and
she stiffened, her heart lurching. By God, she wouldn't be
made a fool of—not this time. "Fiery? I only wish I could say
the same of you," she managed to puff out. "I've been better
kissed by the footman."

The statement shocked her as much as it did Greyley. His
brows snapped down. "Been kissing the footman, have you?
I suppose I shouldn't be surprised."

Anna didn't know about that—*she* was certainly surprised at the information, especially as they didn't even have
a footman. She ran her fingers over her bottom lip and tried
to clear her mind. When had Greyley learned to kiss in such
an expert manner?

She burned to realize what he must think of her wanton
response. She'd never allowed anyone such liberties before.
It must be because he was Sara's brother. Anna had known
Greyley for years, and though their discourse had never been
easy, they had always managed to ignore the heated discord

that echoed between them. Until now. "I don't know why that happened—"

"I do," he said. "I know exactly why it happened."

To Anna's unease, a touch of humor lit his gaze. "What?"

"You provoked me."

"I did no such thing!" she sputtered, anger burning away the last remaining vestige of desire. "How like a man to say such a thing."

"And then you provoked me once more when you compared my embrace to that of your footman's." A faint hint of a grin touched his mouth. "I'm tempted to kiss you again just to prove you wrong."

If Greyley was attractive even when he was ordering her about, he was devastating when he teased. She took an instinctive step back. "Don't you dare."

"I would indeed dare if I didn't think your grandfather would burst into the room and demand I marry you."

Good God, not content to insult her by calling her a governess in that superior tone of voice, now he dared suggest that she might try and trick him into marriage. It was almost more than Anna could stand. "Don't worry about my grandfather. He is much more freethinking than that. Furthermore, I have no wish to marry you. Not now. Not ever. Perhaps this happened just to show us why we shouldn't be under the same roof. I can never work for—"

"You have no choice."

"What do you mean I have no choice? Of course I have a choice!"

"Thraxton, calm down and hear me out. I came here to conduct a business arrangement. Nothing more. I have no designs on your virtue."

"Good," she said, telling herself that the sinking feeling in the pit of her stomach was not disappointment, but rather relief. Despite her irritation, she had to marvel at his air of assurance. Anna suspected that part of Greyley's arrogance came from getting everything he wanted. He was one of those people who forced circumstances and people to his path. It was high time he realized that real life was much harsher than the charmed existence he'd led so far.

She plastered a polite expression on her face, folded her hands neatly in front of her, and said, "Lord Greyley, there is no need to continue this conversation. Lord Allencott is expecting me to—"

"I know, you told me yesterday. I am willing to pay twice what he has offered."

The arrogant ass didn't even bother to ask how much Allencott had agreed to pay. Fortunately, Anna had worked with enough spoiled children that she found dealing with a pompous earl less than a challenge. "Lord Allencott was going to pay me two hundred pounds for three months' service."

"Then four hundred pounds it is. I will send a carriage for you in the morning. It is imperative that the children—"

"You cannot be serious," Anna said, struggling for breath. "You would pay four hundred pounds for only three months' service? Just like that?"

"Ah. I see your point."

He should. She'd lied about Allencott's wages; he'd agreed to pay her only a hundred pounds, and at the time she'd thought it a fortune. "Lord Greyley, I'm certain you'll find another governess who will—"

"Three months will not be nearly enough. I'll need you for at least a year."

She slowly counted to ten. "Greyley, you don't understand. I cannot—"

"It is *you* who do not comprehend the situation. These

children are not your normal terrors. No governess, no matter how talented, could change the comportment of these unruly whelps in such a short time."

Anna gave him a wintry smile. "Lord Greyley, I have *never* failed to improve the behavior of my charges."

"You drive a hard bargain, Miss Thraxton. But then I knew you would. Five hundred pounds, but no more."

Five . . . hundred . . . pounds. Anna swallowed. "For three months?"

"Of course," he said impatiently. "That is far more than I've paid any governess. I'm certain it's more than you've ever earned."

Sweet heavens, it was a fortune. If she could last under Greyley's roof for just two quarters, she'd have enough money to see Grandpapa established in the style in which he was accustomed, at least for a while. Several years, in fact. The thought was so tantalizing that she forgot to voice whatever protests she might have.

In typical Greyley fashion, he took her silence for agreement and turned toward the door. "I'll see you in the morning, Miss Thraxton. The carriage will be here at nine."

Anna blinked. "Wait! As much as I wish it otherwise, I am honor-bound to fulfill my duties to Lord Allencott."

"Stop fretting. I've already taken care of the matter."

Foreboding filled her. "I beg your pardon?"

His self-satisfied expression was dangerously near being a smirk. "I ran into Allencott yesterday and I told him you would not be accepting his offer."

"You . . . you didn't." Anna closed her eyes and pressed her fingers over them. "Please tell me you are teasing."

"Of course I'm not teasing. I went looking for him after the Dandridges' soirée. I told him you would be taking employment at Greyley House."

"You—you—" Anna's temples throbbed wildly and she was assailed with an almost uncontrollable urge to hurl a vase at Greyley's thick head.

"Allencott was most understanding. After all, my situation is much more urgent than his. He has two children, I have five." He looked blessedly pleased with himself, full of masculine logic and stubborn pride.

"Lord Greyley, if you run roughshod over your charges the way you have been attempting to run over me, then it is no wonder they are in an uproar."

"Roughshod?" Greyley's brows lowered. "I was assisting you. It was a damnable nuisance having to track down Allencott. Then I had to sit and talk to him for almost half an hour, and the man is an unbearable bore. I can think of at least twenty other things I would have rather been doing." Greyley's dark gaze ran over her once again. "Make that twenty-one."

"Oh, just stop it," Anna snapped, though her body heated in instant response. She supposed she didn't have any choice—thanks to the purchase of that silly gown, she was horribly short on funds, and by now Allencott would have found another governess. Anna closed her lips over the irate comment she would like to make and silently conjugated four Latin verbs, a trick she'd learned when dealing with especially recalcitrant children. She was in the middle of conjugating *amo* when her breathing returned to normal and she was able to say with some equanimity, "Greyley, let us understand one another. If I accept this position, there are certain rules that must be followed."

"Such as?"

"*Never* again will you speak for me. I should have been the one to contact Lord Allencott, not you. I have a professional reputation to maintain."

"It's not as if he was upset. Besides, he knows he cannot compete with me."

"Neither can the sun, yet still does it shine."

The earl's face darkened. "It isn't a matter of vanity; it is a matter of necessity. As much as I hate to admit it, Miss Thraxton, I am a desperate man. You are the best governess in London. I want you and no one else."

He stood, tall and broad-shouldered, filling the tiny parlor until it looked like a closet. And Anna had to admit that it was mollifying to hear the words "the best" coming from such discriminating lips.

Actually, now that Anna looked, the earl possessed a *very* attractive mouth—it was firm and masculine. And she already knew how those lips felt against hers. The memory sent a hot tingle through her.

Greyley sighed. "Look, Thraxton, I didn't mean to set your back up in my dealings with Allencott. If you're worried that he might noise it about that you are untrustworthy because you're reneging on your agreement, don't bother. As compensation for his loss, I invited him to hunt at Greyley this fall. He's always wanted to come, but frankly, I've never been able to stand his company. He very happily agreed to the exchange."

Anna stiffened. "You *traded* me for a week of hunting?"

"I wouldn't say it like that."

"How *would* you say it?"

He shifted, the floor beneath his feet creaking. "It doesn't matter how I'd say it—I was attempting to protect your interests and—"

"I don't need your protection. Not now, not ever."

Anthony almost winced at the frigid tones that fell from Thraxton's lips. Crystalline clear, each word clinked onto his ears like icicles. Perhaps he *had* overstepped his bounds a bit, though it hadn't seemed like it at the time.

Indeed, Thraxton should have been thanking him, not regarding him as if he were some sort of aberration to humanity. But then she'd always had a tendency to see the worst in everything he did, he decided. It was just like her to make a huge fuss over nothing. He'd conveniently forgotten that part of her personality in his zeal to obtain her services. "You are the most stubborn woman I've ever met."

A proper woman would have taken offense, but not Thraxton. She curtsied. "Thank you, kind sir."

"That wasn't a compliment," he answered bluntly. She was unlike any woman he knew, full of health and vigor. From her height to her incredible coloring, there was nothing ladylike about her. Take her gown, for instance. Even though the cut of the garment was modest—almost severe in detail— on Anna Thraxton it became a siren's gown. The thin material draped over her perfect figure, molding to the contours of her full, round breasts, and clinging in a most disconcerting way to her slender waist and hips. Even the color, a soft innocuous blue, did nothing to blend her into her surroundings. Instead, the color contrasted with the creamy hues of her skin and enhanced the rich auburn of her hair. Anthony found himself comparing her coloring to Charlotte's gentle prettiness and decided that surely such vivid looks might tire a man. Still . . . it was hard to find fault with Thraxton's looks. If it weren't for her nose, she would be stunningly beautiful.

Anthony tried to focus on that proud nose, but his gaze kept drifting down to her mouth where her lovely lips parted in a cool smile, revealing even white teeth.

"Lord Greyley, you may be able to waltz into half the households in London and get your way with such high-handed tactics, but this isn't one of them. You have reminded me what a fool I would be to even attempt to work for you. I have changed my mind—you will have to find someone else to serve as governess to your wards." She turned and walked to the door.

Just as her hand closed over the knob, he heard himself say, "One thousand pounds."

She froze, then turned and looked at him with raised brows. "Each quarter?"

"Yes, damn it," he growled. "And that's my final offer."

Heaven help him, but he'd lost his mind. It was a fortune. No, it was more than a fortune. But he would be damned if he would lose her now. He needed her. No, he silently corrected himself—the *children* needed her.

Her fingers loosened on the doorknob and Anthony could see that she was tempted. He added softly, "A thousand pounds each quarter for a year. Think of what you could do with such a sum."

She didn't say anything for a long time. Finally, she took her hand from the door. "I could buy a nice, snug house in the country and keep it warm day and night for Grandpapa." Her fingers brushed her skirts in a distracted way and she said softly, as if musing aloud, "I could purchase some new gowns, too."

"More than a few," he answered, a little surprised she even cared about such fripperies. Still, he would use whatever appealed to her. "Shall I send a carriage in the morning?"

After a long moment, she nodded. "Very well."

Anthony's shoulders relaxed, and he suddenly realized that he'd been holding his breath. "Excellent. I'll—"

"I have other requirements. With so many children, I will need an assistant."

"That seems reasonable."

"A well-lit nursery and plenty of funds for the purchase of whatever materials I think necessary."

"Anything else?"

"I assume the children already have ponies of their own?"

"Of course," he replied, offended. They were in his care, after all. She should have known he would see to the necessities, if not more.

"Then that should do." She gestured toward the door. "If you don't mind, I have a lot of preparations to see to before tomorrow."

He nodded, but made no move to leave. Instead he watched her, his gaze appraising her from head to toe.

Thraxton crossed her arms over her breasts. "What?"

"It just dawned on me that my sister is likely to hear that I've hired you to serve as governess."

"Not from me. I do not often correspond with Sara." Of all the losses Anna had suffered on giving up her station, the loss of Sara had been the most bitter. Oh, Sara refused to admit that anything had changed, which was why Anna was so determined not to become a burden. She still wrote, but much less frequently, and she made it a point not to be available whenever Sara was in town.

Greyley shrugged. "Be that as it may, it would be improper of me to forget what is due your station."

Her silver eyes hardened. "I'm well aware of my station, Lord Greyley."

"So am I. You are my sister's friend and a Thraxton. Therefore, you might want to bring a few gowns with you." He waved his hand vaguely. "For dinner and such."

Anna's chest tightened. It was the one thing she did not want to happen. She had learned the hard way what happened when she forgot the responsibilities due to someone in her position. "Lord Greyley, while I appreciate your kindness, I am not arriving at your house as a guest. I am coming as a paid employee, and I will thank you to remember that."

His gaze glinted darkly. "Afraid I'll attempt to kiss you again?"

"Of course not," she said, her cheeks heating. "You wouldn't dare."

"You don't know what I would dare. And where you are concerned, it appears that I don't either." He turned to the door. "I will leave you to make your arrangements. The carriage will be here in the morning."

Moments later, the earl's carriage could be heard rumbling down the street. Anna reached blindly for the arm of the nearest chair and sank into the lumpy seat.

Sweet heavens, what had she agreed to? For the next three or four months or longer, she would be in close proximity to the one man in all England who had the ability to make her forget herself and her station. It was madness. Especially after . . . She stood, pushing the unwanted memories away. There was no use in reliving the past. It could not be undone.

Whatever she did, she would be damned if she'd let her unruly feelings get in the way of plain, ordinary common sense. Propriety must be addressed on all occasions, which left no room for any other emotion, not even simple friendship. Even that, she knew, could be fatal.

Meanwhile, she had plenty to keep her occupied. If she was successful in this venture, she stood to make a nice profit, one that she and Grandpapa desperately needed, and her reputation as a governess would indeed be set. All she had to do was calm the children and bring some order to Greyley's nursery. Yet simple as that sounded, Anna knew she'd just accepted the most difficult challenge of her life. Sighing, she went in search of Grandpapa.

Chapter 5

Anna Thraxton has the nose and the air of a Roman Caesar. Both have kept her from making an eligible match.

Miss Devonshire to Miss Prudhomme,
while shopping on Bond Street

Sleep was impossible. First there had been bags to pack and then there were arrangements to be made for Grandpapa. To Anna's surprise, he took the news of her new position at Greyley House without comment. He even allowed her to dash off a missive to their cousin, Lady Dandry, asking if she could come for a visit while Anna was gone. Grandpapa usually complained loudly about having to spend time with cousin Elmira, but this time he merely shrugged.

It was late when Anna finally went to bed. But not to rest. The quiet worked against her, and the memory of Greyley's kiss again intruded on her thoughts. Once there, her mind stopped and lingered, dwelling on the moment in far more detail than necessary.

She was certain the kiss had been exceptional. Warm and firm, with a hint of determined command, the embrace had left her breathless. Breathless and wanting more.

Not that she would pursue such a silly desire. She had

merely been intrigued. Yes, intrigued and . . . and infuriated. That's what had caused her to feel slightly dizzy, all flushed and uncomfortable, as if a slow fever were consuming her. She kicked off her blankets at the remembrance and wished it was light enough to rise. Inactivity was conducive to restless thoughts. She'd have been much happier if she'd been up doing something. Anything other than thinking of the feel of Greyley's mouth on hers.

The bounder had proven his rakehell tendencies by that damnable kiss. He was a man used to getting his own way, a man who had dallied far too long in the immoral arts. Certainly it had been far too well-practiced, far too . . . too . . . She sighed. The kiss had been all together too enjoyable and she knew it.

Fortunately she wasn't a slave to her physical impulses like *some* people she could name. No, she was in control of herself and her surroundings at all time. Besides, there had always been a heated tension between them. It soothed her vanity to know that it wasn't onesided.

Still, she would have to take care that it never happened again; Greyley was a dangerously attractive man. And the entire episode confirmed that he was also desperately in need of some guidance. For that reason alone, Anna was willing to overcome her natural hesitancy in accepting this position. She owed her friend Sara that much, if not more. Anna would set the nursery to rights, and in the process, she'd also do what she could to straighten out Sara's misguided brother.

Of course, the proposition was not without risk. Greyley was arrogant and self-serving, and like other men of his set, he had to have other unattractive qualities. Perhaps he was addicted to drink and gaming; his kiss had proven that he was a practiced rakehell bent on seducing whoever was available. To a man with such a lack of moral rectitude, an impoverished governess would be fair game.

The thought made Anna tingle all over. Excitement at the challenge of proving him wrong, no doubt. How she relished the thought. She would avoid his attempts at seduction, focus her attentions on the children, and win the day.

Best yet, when she left, she'd demand a letter of recommendation written in his own hand, which she would frame and hang over the fireplace in her new abode, a reminder of what could be accomplished if one only persevered. All she had to do was keep her objectives firmly in sight and maintain a safe distance from Greyley.

She sighed in the darkness and rolled onto her side, curling around an extra pillow. In her first position as governess, she had worked for the Harbuckles, a pleasant enough family on the fringe of society. Well-moneyed due to Lord Harbuckle's involvement in the textile industry, and vaguely connected to the Duke of York through a distant cousin by marriage, Lady Harbuckle had seen Anna as a way to further her own social standing. After all, the Thraxtons were related to almost everyone, from the prince on down and Anna had freely mingled with the best of society until only recently.

Thus Lady Harbuckle had treated Anna as a guest, insisting that she eat dinner with the family several times during the week, asking her opinion on fashion, driving with her in the park. At first Anna had been thankful, for she hadn't relished her loss of standing, and Lady Harbuckle had made it plain that she considered Anna something more than a servant. Naively, Anna had welcomed Lady Harbuckle's overtures of friendship.

All had gone well until Lady Harbuckle's younger brother, a glib wastrel by the name of Lord Talbert, arrived for a visit. Handsome in a blurry, undefined sort of way, he had immediately attached himself to Anna's side, despite her determined efforts to keep him at bay. Lady Harbuckle seemed to be amused at her brother's florid compliments and she would not hear Anna's attempts to hint that she was being made uncomfortable.

Anna decided that perhaps she was overreacting to Lord Talbert's wholesome compliments. After all, it was obvious that Talbert was a practiced flirt. Unfortunately, he was also a pompous ass who believed his money and purchased title gave him the right to access the beds of every female in the household. Anna's attempt to ignore the young lord merely urged him to new heights of impropriety.

Things got more and more uncomfortable until one fateful night Talbert, drunk as a fox, forced his way into Anna's chamber. Had it not been for the nearness of her bedpan, which she used on His Lordship's rather hard head to dissuade him from his nefarious intentions, Anna was certain she'd have been ravished.

The ruckus caused by Lord Talbert's cry of pain on being crowned with the bedpan caused the entire household to come running. To Anna's shock, Lady Harbuckle listened to her explanation in cold, disbelieving silence. As soon as Anna finished speaking, Lady Harbuckle had called Anna a liar and worse, suggesting that the entire incident was Anna's fault for "tempting the poor boy."

Anna would listen to no more. She had gathered her things and left. She'd been forced to walk almost seven blocks lugging her overstuffed portmanteau, before she found a hackney to take her the rest of the way.

She arrived home furious and heartbroken, ready to renounce her chosen profession. She'd naively believed that Lady Harbuckle had regarded her as something more than a governess. But now Anna knew the truth—she was a governess and she would never again be friends with a member of her own set. It was a bitter lesson to learn.

A good night's sleep and a week of calm reflection had made Anna all the more determined to succeed. She was a governess, and by God, she'd be the best one in all of England. Furthermore, she'd be damned if she'd let a slug like Talbert thwart her.

True to form, Lady Harbuckle lost no time in informing the world that her new governess had attempted to lure her brother into sin, claiming that Anna had wished to secure the drunken sot as a husband. Had it not been for the Harbuckles' limited social standing and Grandpapa's successful manipulation of his cronies, most of whom were society's most established gossipmongers, it would have been the end of Anna's career.

From that day on, she set rigid rules for her own behavior. Rules that protected her from importuning younger brothers and philandering male cousins who came to visit when their pockets were to let. Never again would she allow protestations of friendship to draw her above stairs. Anna had been successful until Lucinda Dandridge had convinced her to attend her soirée. Anna sighed heavily. Even that small foray into the *ton* had been an error.

Now, apparently not content to err only once, she'd compounded her error by kissing her future employer. There was no excuse for it. And it would not happen again. Anna sat up and tossed the sheets aside. The first pale glow of dawn approached, breaking through the cracks in the curtains and casting long fingers of pale light across the rug.

That was all Anna needed. She hurriedly rose and pulled on a gown. The rest of the morning was taken up in a flurry of preparations that did not leave time for useless wonderings about Greyley's kiss or her own heated reaction.

At exactly ten, Anna sat in a stiff-backed chair by the fireplace in the front room, waiting. The carriage arrived only a few moments later, just as Anthony promised. Anna held her breath as the door creaked open, and Hawkes beamed as he announced the earl. Taking a deep calming breath, Anna stood and faced the earl.

Dressed for riding in buff breeches, black boots, a blue coat stretched across his broad shoulders, he looked devastatingly handsome. He came to an abrupt halt on seeing her. "Good God, what are you wearing?"

Anna's hands went to the stiff skirts. It was an old gown, one she'd consigned to the attic long ago, brought out only for the annual spring cleaning she insisted occur each and every year, much to Mrs. Duckrow's chagrin. Anna suspected the dress, made of stiff gray bombazine, had once been a mourning gown, for it relentlessly covered her from neck to foot. But it was plain and functional, and would serve to remind both her and Greyley of her position in his household.

He lifted his eyeglass from where it hung from his waistcoat and regarded her from head to foot. "Did you make it yourself?"

"No, I did not," Anna replied. "Though you should be glad I didn't for I could have taken offense at your tone."

"You have too much sense to be such a ninny." He dropped the eyeglass and let it swing back and forth on its ribbon. "You look like a nun. What's that gown made of? Sackcloth?"

"No. It's very good bombazine."

"The blue gown you had on yesterday had more . . ." He gestured vaguely. ". . . drapery or something. I liked it better."

"How intriguing," she replied flatly.

"I daresay you don't care what I think of your clothing. Still, I demand an explanation. Women never dress without thought."

"This gown is proper attire for a governess. And *that*, my lord, is exactly what I am."

"Ah. I see what this is. It's about that kiss."

Conceited ass. "It's about our relationship. What happened yesterday can never happen again. It was . . . inexcusable."

He frowned. "I thought it was pretty damned good, myself."

A conceited, *arrogant* ass. Anna smiled through her teeth. "I daresay you did. However, for purposes of our ability to work together in a professional, courteous atmosphere, we must remember our roles. I am the governess, and you, Lord Greyley, are my employer. Kisses are not permitted."

Anthony had passed the entire carriage ride on the way there practicing a curtly worded, but beautifully adept speech voicing that exact same opinion. So he should have welcomed Anna's attempt to draw the lines he'd so carelessly crossed. But strangely enough, he didn't. Instead, her attempts to put him off made him want to get closer, if for no other reason than to prove that he could.

He rubbed a finger along his bottom lip, savoring the memory of that one, brief kiss. "We're to share no kisses at all?"

"None."

Some imp of madness urged him on. "Not even at Christmas? Under the mistletoe?"

Her back stiffened with annoyance and she said with great finality, "Not even then. Not that it matters, for I don't plan on being at Greyley House during Christmas. If all goes well, I will be done by November, at the latest."

He almost felt sorry for the children, facing such a determined governess as Miss Thraxton. She was an intriguing combination of certainty and challenge. Had he any manners at all, he would have let her be. But there was something about the way she stood, all prim and proper, as if she were a good deal better than he, that irked him to death.

She probably *was* a good deal better than he, he conceded fairly. He doubted Anna Thraxton had done anything more reprehensible in her short life than utter an occasional curse, and he'd been the cause of most of those. The truth was that the mere thought of that damnable kiss had been irritating him since yesterday.

The entire incident had caught him unawares. But there was no denying his reaction, one so strong that it lingered with him even as he went to bed last night and caused him all sorts of heated, erotic dreams, all of which featured the prim Miss Thraxton doing a number of not-so-prim activities on, and under, his naked person.

Anthony wasn't a man used to dealing with the impossible. He also wasn't a man given to impulses. His whole life had been dedicated to dealing with the undisciplined actions of his Elliot relatives, and in return his life and actions were focused on precision and discipline. But somehow Anna Thraxton tantalized him. Just the way she looked at him through her thickly lashed gray eyes made him want to beat her at her own game. And right now that game was seeing if she could keep him at arm's length.

Still, it wouldn't do to scare her off. He needed her at Greyley House. "You have my word as a gentleman that I will not attempt to kiss you . . . unless, of course, you *ask* me to."

"That will never happen."

Wouldn't it? It would be interesting to see what exactly *would* happen. "Are you ready to leave?"

"Yes. My portmanteau is in the hallway, as is a trunk."

Anthony went to the door and opened it wide. "After you, Miss Thraxton."

She swept forward, head held at a regal angle, her stiff skirts rustling noisily as she went. Anthony leaned forward as she walked past. She was so tall, the top of her head was at a level with his eyes. It was unusual that he had such access to a woman and he couldn't help but inhale her scent as it wafted by. She smelled of lemon and rose, a tempting combination that made him want to linger near.

He watched as she pulled on her pelisse and briskly ordered her servant to place her things on the carriage. Then, without so much as glancing behind her to see if Anthony was following, she marched outside. He grinned and took his time meandering after her. Perhaps this was indeed the woman to tame the hellions who had invaded his house.

Despite her misgivings about her employer, Anna couldn't help but appreciate the luxurious coach. Large and well-sprung, it boasted all the comforts available. No creaking, lumbering conveyance for the Earl of Greyley. This handsome vehicle would never rattle through a tollgate or cause the occupants' legs to lose their feelings from lack of springs. And even more attractive was the lively black gelding that was tied to the back of the carriage.

Anna felt Greyley's approach and she wondered why she let him infuriate her so. He was being deliberately irksome and she detested the way he lagged behind, watching her with that amused, sleepy glint in his eyes that made her yearn to box his ears. But she was a Thraxton and the Thraxtons had never met an enemy they couldn't subdue.

"Anna." Grandpapa's voice came from directly behind her. "Are we departing already?"

Anna turned. Grandpapa stood at the bottom step, elegantly clad in black traveling breeches and a frock coat of blue superfine, clutching his gold-knobbed cane in one hand. At his feet sat a portmanteau.

Anna looked at the portmanteau. "*We?*"

"I'm coming with you," he said, beaming amiably. "After much thought, I've decided that a few months in the country would do me a world of good."

Good God, no! He had to be teasing . . . but one look at

his face made Anna's heart sink. "You want to come with me? But . . . you've never asked before."

"It's too cold in this drafty house."

"Yes, but . . . it's August."

"The nights still bring a chill." He smiled brightly. "Perhaps I might be of assistance in the nursery. I'm very good with children, you know."

"You'd be bored to tears. None of your friends will be able to visit and—"

"Oh, I can correspond with them. I daresay Greyley would even frank my post, wouldn't you?"

Greyley regarded the older man for a long moment. "Would you refrain from handing out French sheaths to my servants?"

"I'll try to resist," Grandpapa returned, his blue eyes twinkling.

There seemed to be an understanding between the two that set Anna's teeth on edge. "Grandpapa, I've already made arrangements—"

"Cancel 'em." He used his cane to shove his portmanteau at the waiting footman, who obligingly picked it up and went to strap it to the back of the coach. "I've no wish to see cousin Elmira. Boring woman who likes nothing better than to talk about all the dead people she knows." Grandpapa limped to the side of the carriage and the morning sun touched his pale cheeks. His *very* pale cheeks.

Anna frowned. Now that she looked at him, Grandpapa appeared to be limping worse than usual, as well. Was he taking ill?

The earl's lazy drawl sounded at her shoulder. "Let him come, Miss Thraxton. Greyley House has more than enough room."

"But the governess quarters cannot be—"

"You won't be staying in the governess quarters, but in one of the guest suites."

She gazed at him with a suspicious stare, but he just shrugged. "The governess quarters suffered a slight accident involving a large amount of very sticky honey and a pillow full of feathers. Therefore, until it is back to normal, you will be in the guest suite. There is an adjoining room that will suit your grandfather well."

"There," Sir Phineas said, hobbling toward the open carriage door. "All settled then. Greyley, will you be joining us in the coach?"

"I'll be riding," the earl said, glancing at the footman who was even now untying the gelding from the back of the coach.

"If you get cold, feel free to join us," Sir Phineas said airily, as if he'd just conferred a great honor. "I've much to discuss with you regarding the current state of the linen workers in your part of the country. I daresay you hear a great bit about that."

To give the earl credit, only the faintest hint of surprise showed on his face. "I shall look forward to it." He bowed, then mounted his horse with an amazing amount of grace for someone so large. His gaze settled on Anna and he touched the brim of his hat. "I will see you at Greyley House." He turned the horse down the street and urged it on.

Anna watched until he was well out of sight, and then turned to find Grandpapa's smiling gaze on her. "What?"

"Nothing," he said, his smile widening.

But it was something, she could tell. She always knew when Grandpapa had some devilry in mind. And Anna was bound and determined to discover what it was.

Chapter 6

*The Earl of Greyley tells the Elliots when to eat, when
to sleep, and when to breathe. It's a pity he doesn't
also tell them when to leave.*

Miss Prudhomme to Lady Bristol after being rudely ignored by
Rupert Elliot while taking air in Hyde Park

Grandpapa lifted the curtain and peered out the carriage
window. "It will be nice to be in the country. The earl's
lands are supposedly some of the most carefully kept."

Anna's gaze caught something white on Grandpapa's
collar. She reached over and touched a finger to the smudge.
"Rice powder."

Grandpapa appeared mildly surprised. "Wonder how that
got there?"

"You know how that got there! You wanted me to think
you were ill." She pulled her handkerchief from her front
pocket and placed it in his hand. "Wipe your face. You should
be ashamed of yourself."

"No, *you* should be ashamed that I had to go to such
lengths." He wiped the last of rice powder from his cheeks
and said sadly, "It's as if you don't like having me about."

"Nonsense. Grandpapa, I've enough on my plate with
Greyley's charges."

"Oh, you won't have to worry about me," he said quickly. "I plan to help you every step of the way."

"That's what I'm afraid of," she muttered. She eyed her badly behaved Grandpapa for some moments. "Will you promise me one thing?"

"Anything, my dear. Just name it."

"Promise you will not attempt to embroil Lord Greyley in any of your projects."

"I wouldn't dare." He tucked her handkerchief into his front pocket, leaving a broad white smear on the dark cloth. "Besides, I already asked and he said no."

She suddenly remembered the earl's comment about the French sheaths. Anna fell back against the squabs and groaned. "You didn't."

"Just once. He wasn't interested." Grandpapa smiled as if at some inner, tranquil image. "Or at least, he didn't *think* he was interested. But I think he will change his mind."

Anna silently conjugated the Latin word for "cease."

He reached over and patted her knee. "There, there. I vow I will not say another word to him. Greyley will become an ardent supporter of Thraxton interests without any persuasion from me."

"You are mistaken; the Earl of Greyley isn't a charitable sort of man."

Grandpapa pursed his lips. "I wouldn't say that. He *is* the head of the Elliot family."

"I've never heard anything good about the Elliots."

"Ah, but I've never heard anything bad about Greyley." Grandpapa nodded wisely, as if he were a sage. "It must be difficult to remain basically good when one is surrounded by a whole family determined to be bad. And so successful at it that they consider it a birthright. It is all the more amazing when you realize how young Greyley was when he took over the family reins. Not even eighteen from what I heard."

It always amazed Anna how much Grandpapa knew. If only the Home Office had such connections. "I daresay the Elliots were happy to see Greyley arrive." Her fingers brushed over the plush velvet carriage seats.

"They were ecstatic at first. He was young, and they thought him a pigeon ripe for plucking."

"I cannot envision the earl being anything as tame as a pigeon."

"Ah, but then you know him better than the Elliots. You see, Greyley was raised by his stepfather, St. John, who kept the Elliots at bay until the earl reached his majority. Threatened some of them with bodily harm if they so much as talked to the boy."

"Sara has mentioned that her father was very protective."

"Which was a pity in a way. It must have been something of a shock to Greyley to realize just how depraved and deplorable his real family was." Grandpapa absently pulled a rather crushed cigarillo from his pocket and rolled it between his fingers, the breeze from the open window wafting the pungent scent through the carriage. "Born an Elliot but raised a St. John. An interesting juxtaposition—knavery and honor. I wonder which he fights the most."

Anna couldn't picture Greyley wrestling with such weighty thoughts. If there was one thing she knew about the earl from witnessing his actions during his sister's impetuous marriage, it was that Anthony Elliot's besetting sin was pride. Anna supposed it was possible that she'd missed some of his finer traits, though time would tell. She'd have ample opportunity to study him in the ensuing months. The thought lightened her mood, and it was with a sense of anticipation that she waited for the appearance of Greyley House.

After several hours, the carriage rumbled through a wide iron gate, the road falling away to the smoother surface of a well-kept drive. "It can't be much farther," Anna said, leaning forward to look out the window. "We've made excellent time."

"Indeed." Grandpapa put the cigarillo to his nose and took a deep breath. After a moment, he gave a blissful sigh and, with obvious reluctance, put the cigarillo back in his pocket.

Anna pretended not to notice. She wondered what the children would be like. They couldn't be as bad as Greyley made them sound. Still, whatever unpleasant surprises life had in store, Anna could handle them all. She was no stranger to adversity.

She looked out the window just as the carriage cleared the trees and Greyley House came into view. The vista surrounding the house was idyllic. At the bottom of the hill, a stream happily babbled into a blue pond. From the pond, a smooth green lawn rose in gradual slope that was crowned with glorious oaks. All told, it was the perfect setting for a jewel of a house.

But instead of a romantic villa or a typical English manor, high on the hillside stood a square-built house with thick, unrelenting gray walls. Stark, with narrow windows and a façade devoid of frills or ornamentation, Greyley House gloomily surveyed the surrounding countryside. Whoever had placed the house had set it so that the afternoon sun dropped behind it, making the manor appear darker and more sinister in the fading light.

"Good God," Anna said.

"Makes me think of a prison." Grandpapa tilted his head to one side. "But I like it."

"I don't," Anna said in all honesty. She frowned, rapidly

formulating ways to alleviate the problem. "Perhaps the earl could widen the front steps. Or add a portico to hide that ugly door."

"That would liven it up," Grandpapa agreed. He squinted thoughtfully. "Some ivy would help."

"And a flower bed or two. Along the lower wall there." A cacophony of flowers along the pathway leading to the front door would add warmth and color—just the thing to brighten the austere lines of the house. Anna rubbed her hands together, imagining how a small fountain might look to one side of the entryway. Either that or some Grecian statuary.

Grandpapa patted her knee. "It's a good thing you've come, my dear. It appears you are sorely needed."

A wave of certainty flooded through her as she thought of the challenge that lay before her. Greyley House and its inhabitants might be difficult, but she would prevail. There was little that common sense and hard work couldn't accomplish.

The carriage rattled to a halt and a footman sprang forward to open the door. Anna dismounted as soon as the man let down the steps, looking around her with amazement. Now that she was closer, she decided that though the outside of the house was grim, it also possessed a rather stately grace.

She had just walked to one side of the crushed gravel drive to get a better look at it when the earl cantered up on the black gelding. Dust covered Greyley's boots and coat, and somewhere along the way he'd loosened his neckcloth, revealing a strong tanned throat, as if he often rode that way. He looked disheveled and devastatingly handsome.

The earl dismounted and tossed the reins to a waiting groom as an elderly retainer hurried down the steps. "My lord!"

The earl gave the horse one last pat, then turned to his retainer. "Jenkins. How are you? The hellions chase off any more of the staff?"

"Only one downstairs maid, my lord. It has been a very good week."

"Excellent. I rode by the tenant houses on my way. The new thatching looks sturdy."

"Yes, my lord. Mr. Dalmapple was speaking of that only this morning."

Anna eyed the earl speculatively. So Greyley paid personal attention to his tenants, did he? That was interesting information. As interesting as Greyley House.

Greyley turned and met Anna's gaze. Her excitement bubbled over and she grinned. His brows lifted, and for the barest instant, one corner of his mouth curved as if in answer, his entire face softening. Anna's heart thumped a welcoming beat and she took an impulsive step forward.

But then Jenkins made a comment she couldn't hear, and Greyley turned away. Anna managed to swallow her disappointment, though it was difficult. It was strange, but though she'd seen Greyley plenty of times when she'd stayed with his sister in Bath, he was usually dressed in town clothes. Seeing him here, at his stately manor house, dressed in dusty riding clothes and looking more masculine than any male had a right to . . . It was different somehow. More . . . intimate, in a way.

She forced herself to turn away. She was just a mass of nerves. Traveling always made her famished, and neither she nor Grandpapa had eaten more than a few pieces of toast and jam this morning. As soon as they were settled, she'd ask for some luncheon and—

An ear-splitting shriek rent the air. The huge oak doors of the house flew open and a plump woman came running out, her skirts flapping madly. Her mobcap and the heavy set of keys that jangled at her waist proclaimed her to be the housekeeper as she jounced down the steps and came to a halt in front of Greyley. "Thank God you've returned!" she puffed, pressing a hand to her impressive bosom. "We've a plague!"

Greyley's face darkened. "Are the children ill?"

"Lord love you, not *that* kind of plague," the housekeeper said. "I'm talkin' about a *biblical* plague."

"Biblical, eh?" Grandpapa murmured from where he was standing beside Anna. "It appears as if we've come just in time to see the entire household eaten by locusts."

The housekeeper waved a hand in front of her heated face. "Frogs," she intoned. "Large, warty ones."

Anna almost laughed at the astonishment on the earl's face.

"How many are there?" he bit out.

"Dozens! And all in *your* bedchamber. They startled poor Lily nigh to death, they did, when she went into your room to dust."

"The children," Greyley said grimly.

The housekeeper clasped her hands together. "My lord, I'm sure they didn't mean to—"

"Where's Ledbetter?"

"That fribblin' valet went screamin' like a banshee, he did. Says he cannot abide such slimy creatures, jumping here and there and nestin' in your private linens—"

A loud yell sounded from inside the house, followed by a solid thud and a crash. The housekeeper gave a faint shriek. "I do hope that wasn't your new vase! The one you sent from London with instructions to keep it from the children."

"Damn it! That was a Roman urn." Greyley turned and strode up the steps. "Mrs. Stibbons, send a footman to my room with a bucket."

The housekeeper struggled to keep pace with him. "Yes, my lord. I'll keep an eye out for the children, too. Ledbetter saw them peeking 'round the door and he chased them through the house. Almost caught the wee one, he did. Haven't heard a peep out of them since."

Anna gathered her skirts and dashed up the stairs. Here was her chance to establish herself with her new charges. "Lord Greyley! We should speak before you talk to the children about this latest occurrence. In my experience, the best way to handle a situation such as this—"

He came to a sudden halt on the top step. Anna almost careened into his back, tottering for a brief moment on the step below him. When she regained her balance, she found him staring down at her, a determined expression on his face. "Miss Thraxton," he said in that low, threatening drawl, "as much as I appreciate your offer of assistance, my relationship with my wards is my concern and not yours. Your sole responsibility is the nursery and what goes on inside those four walls."

"I thought you wished me to bring the children to a more orderly manner of behavior overall and not just inside the nursery."

"If the children were competently dealt with in the nursery, their behavior would improve in other areas."

"Nonsense."

He stiffened, his voice turning deadly quiet. "I am not going to debate this with you. I have far more important things to see to." He turned on his heel and took the remaining steps two at a time.

Anna started after him. "Lord Greyley, wait! If you will stop being so obsti—"

Something caught her arm just as she was lifting her skirts to sprint up the remaining stairs. Anna turned to find Grandpapa at her side.

He let go of her arm with an apologetic smile and then leaned forward to whisper, "I'm not one to interfere, but you should remember that a man like Greyley is all pride. He will not respond well to anyone making suggestions about his behavior in front of his servants."

Anna looked over Grandpapa's shoulder and saw how the butler and housekeeper were both leaning forward at unnatural angles in an attempt to hear what Grandpapa was saying.

Her face heated. She straightened and said loudly, "Yes, I'm a bit tired as well."

Mrs. Stibbons bustled forward. "Poor thing! Come along, miss. If I know His Lordship, you're not only tired, but starving as well. Didn't think to order a luncheon on the road for you, did he?" The housekeeper sailed past them and on into the foyer, chattering over her shoulder as she led the way.

Surprisingly, the inside of Greyley House was as pleasant as the exterior was forbidding. The entryway lacked a certain warmth and light, but the walls were covered with lovely paneling, and the marble floors were stunning.

The only jarring note were the ornament choices, some of which Anna wouldn't have hesitated to call daunting. Ornaments such as the two ancient sets of armor that seemed to scowl fiercely from each side of the huge, somber mahogany staircase. She placed a hand on one of the monstrosities and sent a telling glance at Mrs. Stibbons. "Greyley?"

"Lord, yes. He dotes on those things, he does, though I've told him time and again that the front foyer is no place for such." The housekeeper turned to the butler. "His Lordship wished us to show Sir Phineas and his granddaughter to their rooms."

Jenkins bowed. "Miss Thraxton will wish to see the nursery, as well."

Mrs. Stibbons plumped her hands onto her hips. "Why would Miss Thraxton wish to see the nursery?"

"Because she is, I believe, the new governess."

Mrs. Stibbons turned to stare, her wide gaze taking in Anna's stiff bombazine gown for the first time. "Lord help you, miss. Are you certain you don't wish to lie down just awhile?"

A look of pain crossed Jenkins's face at the housekeeper's forthright manner, but Anna just smiled. As a governess, she'd come to value servants who included her—they were often able to provide insights that the owners of the house could not. "Thank you, but I'm in no need of a rest. In fact, I believe I'd like to wait here so that I can speak with His Lordship."

The butler bowed. "Yes, miss. The blue sitting room is this way." He turned and trod to one of the many doors that populated the huge entryway and opened it. "I will have some tea brought."

"And some of Cook's scones," Mrs. Stibbons said. She looked shrewdly at Grandpapa. "You, my lord, look a mite knackered, if you don't mind my sayin' so. Perhaps you'd like to rest afore dinner? I'll have a tray brought to your room."

"That would be lovely." He shot a glance Anna's way. "Go easy on poor Greyley. It must be unnerving to return home to find yourself beset with a biblical plague." He smiled and then limped away, following Mrs. Stibbons who talked unceasingly all the way up the imposing staircase.

Anna, meanwhile, followed Jenkins into the sitting room and smiled at him when he withdrew, quietly closing the door behind him. The chamber was large and well lit by a series of narrow windows. Heavy mahogany wainscoting edged the room and echoed the rich red tones of an Aubusson rug, while a large marble fireplace stood at one end of the room. Still, as attractive as the room was, it had a certain unfinished feel to it.

Perhaps it was the furnishings. Placed here and there about the room was an assortment of chairs and benches of varying ages, most of them appearing very, very old, though none of them truly matched.

Anna trailed her fingers along the edge of a small table inlaid with ivory and made a face at herself in the reflection. "Admit it; you're too excited for your own good." Her reflection beamed back at her and she gave a soft laugh.

It was always this way when she took a new position. The opportunity to prove herself was exhilarating. And Anna found children far more pleasant than most adults she knew. Children had faults she could understand: they were painfully honest, given to blurting out whatever wayward thought they had in their heads regardless of where they were or who they were with; they possessed vivid imaginations and a yearning for adventure, which made it very difficult for them to concentrate on the more mundane considerations of their schoolwork; and they had an innate frustration whenever things didn't immediately go their way. All told, Anna understood children very well indeed.

Furthermore, since she was usually asked to attend to the less settled children, Anna had become adept at discovering the sources of their unease. It wasn't all that difficult since she spent a great deal more time with her charges than most governesses. If there was one thing her experience had taught her, it was that most problems came from the family itself, and not just the recalcitrant child.

She wondered what Greyley's charges were like and why they had been acting so inappropriately. Trying to ease her tumultuous thoughts, she walked to a high-backed chair that sat before the fireplace and ran a hand over one of the arms. The seat was covered in ancient purple velvet, the wooden back and arms decorated with delicate ivy leaf carvings. She traced one leaf with the tip of her finger and wondered what she should say to Greyley. If she were to help the children, she would have to win his support. She sighed and wished she could speak to Sara. Of all the St. Johns, Sara was the closest to Anthony. Perhaps she would have some insight.

Things were already looking up. Or they were, if only Greyley would cooperate. Anna was determined to succeed in bringing the children to order. She'd do it if she had to employ witchery of some sort. Grinning a little at her absurdity, she trailed her fingers over the worn red velvet seat of the chair nearest to her, marveling at its smoothness. Almost as smooth as Greyley's voice when he was pleased about something. The untoward thought sent a shiver down her spine.

"Miss Thraxton," the low voice she had been imagining drawled from behind her. "Jenkins said you wished to speak to me."

Anna steeled her nerves and pasted a pleasant smile on her lips as she turned to face her employer, the irascible, aggravating Earl of Greyley.

Chapter 7

They say the Earl of Greyley never invests without first making a list of all possible outcomes, for better or worse. No wonder the man's never married.

Lady Bristol to Viscount Evanstock,
while dancing a country dance at Almack's

Greyley stood leaning against the doorframe, his arms crossed over his massive chest, his heavy-lidded eyes watching her intently. "Do you like the chair? I bought it at a private auction just last month."

The chair? Anna realized her hand was still on the velvet seat. "It's lovely."

"It was King Henry the Eighth's favorite, one he inherited from his own father. Try it. It's very comfortable."

She pulled her hand away and tucked it behind her, amazed at the thought that her fingers had just touched the same place a king's bottom had once rested. Imagine that. And Greyley wanted her to sit there.

Anna wasn't a small woman and she would be damned if the first thing she did while in Greyley's house was break his favorite chair. "No, thank you. I am quite fine standing—"

"Sit." Greyley shoved himself from the door facing and walked toward her, every movement lethal in some way. "It will hold you. It was built in a time when function was first, and style last."

The chair *did* look rather sturdy. Sturdier, in fact, than much of the furniture that graced the salons and drawing rooms in London. Still . . . she met his gaze and then admitted, "I don't wish to break it."

"How much to do you weigh?"

"It doesn't matter how much I weigh. Greyley, we should discuss the children. It has dawned on me that perhaps you don't understand—"

"I understand all too well." His dark gaze swept over her. "I'd guess you were about eight stone?"

Anna stiffened. "We should discuss something else. Something more pleasant." Like having a tooth extracted. Or perhaps the fact that horses always smelled the worst when pulling a romantic-looking carriage.

He lifted a brow. "Nine stone then, just to be on the safe side. Not that it matters. I weigh far more than you and the chair holds me fine." He walked past her to sit in the chair. Once there, he crossed his arms and then looked up at her with a superior expression. "See? It didn't even creak."

Anna's heart gave a strange lurch. He looked so appealing, sitting so close—almost at eye level, a twinkle lurking deep in his brown eyes. She was amazed to discover that he had the same long lashes that belonged to his sister, Sara. Thick and dark, they hooded his gaze, sweeping low and tangling at the corners.

Good God, I must be more tired than I realized. She didn't care how long Greyley's lashes were. Or how incredibly well shaped his mouth was. What she needed was a warm bath and a good meal, and she'd forget what particular shade of brown his eyes could deepen to. She'd pay no attention to the way his hair, the color of ripe honey, contrasted so vividly with his tanned skin. She'd be completely oblivious to the shape of his powerful thighs where they stretched against—

He stood and gestured toward the chair. "You try it."

At least he was no longer at eye level. Of course now his strong neck was right where she could examine it, even touch it if she so desired. She imagined what he would do if she reached out and traced her fingers down his jaw, to the strong cords of his throat. Her stomach quaked at her disgraceful thoughts and she sank into the chair just to put some space between them.

To her surprise, the seat was astonishingly comfortable. The back supported her well, the legs didn't so much as tremble, and the red cushion was even plumper than she realized. "It's delightful."

He sent her a ghost of a smile, then turned toward the window and opened the drapery a bit wider. The sunlight caught his hair and made it appear even more golden. "I've been attempting to transform Greyley House into a proper home since the day I moved in, almost seventeen years ago."

"It's very striking." She looked around the room, admiring the crown moldings. "The outside is a bit austere but in here . . . it's lovely."

He looked at her as if measuring her for more than her weight. "Yes, it is. Not every person can see that." He leaned his arm against the green marble mantelpiece and shoved his other hand deep in his pocket, his gaze never leaving her. "When I was a child, I used to come here every Christmas. It was the only time I saw my Elliot relatives."

"I daresay the house looked vastly different then."

"It looked just like the Elliots—ramshackle and falling apart. I've fixed all the structural damage, of course. Now it's a matter of aesthetics. There is little I can do to remedy the outside, not without losing some of the heritage. But in here . . ." He looked around at the intricate molding that graced the walls and the complex wood trim that decorated the window frames. "One day it will look the way it should."

He gazed at the room, his expression serious, his hair golden against the wainscoting. There was something almost endearing about him, as he stood there, contemplating the changes he'd wrought in his house. She sensed the quiet confidence of ownership in his gaze, and something more. Pride, perhaps.

Suddenly aware that she was staring at him like an awestruck housemaid, she stood and cleared her throat. "I hope you've captured all the frogs in your bedchamber. Have you dealt with the children yet?"

He shrugged, his expression closing. "Mrs. Stibbons's plague turned out to be only eleven frogs in number, and most of them very small and very glad to return to the pond."

"How fortunate." Anna smoothed her dress. "Lord Greyley, we should take this opportunity to establish a few things. If you wish to see a long-term change in the children's behavior, then we must work together. Perhaps we should—"

He held up a hand. "I expected this."

"Expected what?"

"Thraxton, let us understand one another. I do not need a governess to tell me how to deal with my own wards. Any more than you need me to tell you how to teach Latin. You do your job and I will do mine. The problem with the children is that they have had too little discipline in the schoolroom."

A flash of pure irritation stabbed Anna. She managed a very frosty smile. "Lord Greyley, it is painfully obviously that the children are out of control. If they were not, you would never have begged me to take this position."

The earl gave a quick frown. "I did not beg. I asked."

"Need I remind you that you traded me away from Lord Allencott, a man you openly call a bore, in exchange for a week of hunting? I would hardly call that the efforts of a sane, logical man. You were desperate. Admit it."

"I admit nothing except that you are here and you will confine your efforts to the children and leave me be."

Anna swallowed a sharp retort. Anthony Elliot was the most obstinate, self-opinionated jackass of her acquaintance. And sadly, having been a governess, she'd had the misfortune to meet far more jackasses than the average woman. "Perhaps it *is* a good thing we're getting all this out in the open now. Exactly what *do* you see as my responsibilities, Lord Greyley? Beyond Latin, that is."

He gave an easy shrug. "You are to instruct the children to the best of your ability."

"And?"

"You will also give them a basic understanding of comportment."

"But only in the nursery."

"Whatever you teach them in the nursery will carry over. Or it will if it's done properly."

Anna opened her mouth to respond, but Greyley continued. "Furthermore, you will see to it that they are busily employed, follow their schedule, and—"

"Schedule?"

"Yes. I developed it after the third governess left. It is the only thing that keeps the children in check."

Anna managed a frigid smile. "I see. And where on this schedule did it read 'put frogs in master chamber'?"

His eyes narrowed dangerously. "Do you always use sarcasm when talking to your employers?"

"Only when they will not listen to reason. Greyley, I'm known as the best governess in London because I know how to deal with children, and not because I smile and nod every time my employer says a word."

To her surprise, his lips twitched. "I can't imagine you doing anything so tame."

"And I cannot imagine you being so foolish as to think child rearing can be confined to a nursery. Perhaps that has been the problem all along. It will take both of our best efforts if we are to improve the children's behavior."

He regarded her for a long minute, his brow lowered. "You think we need to work together?"

"If they hear the same thing from their governess as they do from their guardian, it will mean more. I will reinforce you and you will reinforce me; like generals in a war. It's simple logic, Greyley."

"Governesses do not tell their employers what to do."

"And you've known so many good ones."

A glint of humor lit his brown eyes. "I'm rapidly beginning to believe there are no good governesses. Just bossy ones."

"Perhaps it is the same thing. We are agreed then?" She held her breath and waited.

Finally, he nodded. "We will meet daily to discuss the children. And I will, of course, reinforce you whenever possible. But I will expect the same from you."

Relief flooded through her. "Thank you." Well, that hadn't been so difficult after all. Perhaps this position would be smoother than she'd—

"Thraxton." He pushed himself from the mantel and walked toward the door. "Come with me."

What was he doing now? Anna followed him out of the room and down the hallway, passing an impressive Flemish tapestry depicting an ancient war scene. They crossed the hall and went through two huge doors.

Anna stopped in the doorway. It was the most gorgeous

room she'd ever beheld. A long row of glass-paned doors that opened onto a perfectly groomed garden let in a swath of light, and sent a warm glow across the gleaming wood paneling and lines and lines of oak shelving. An intricate wrought-iron railing followed a set of steps to a second level walk that circled the room and held even more shelves.

But it was the ceiling that made Anna's jaw drop. A delicate mural had been painted on the plaster, depicting Truth and Virtue at war with Sloth and Ignorance. Soft blue and deep purple mingled with a sunshine yellow and a delicate orchid. The colors alone were worth seeing, but the fineness of the painting held her enthralled.

Anna lowered her gaze to the earl where he stood watching her. "It's lovely," she said honestly.

The hard lines of his face softened briefly. "This is the only room that's been completed so far. One day, I hope the rest of the house will be as inspiring."

Anna let her gaze drift across the rest of the room. A heavy golden and red rug warmed the center of the chamber. The earl's large mahogany desk took precedence in one corner while a hodgepodge of antique chairs was grouped about the fireplace. No two were the same, yet the combination was perfect.

Best yet, the entire room brimmed with books—there wasn't a single empty spot on any of the shelves. Anna walked slowly along the wall, her fingers lightly running over the leather bindings. After a moment, she stopped. "Byron?"

The earl shrugged. "He is all the rage."

"You cannot like him," Anna said, unable to picture the earl reading anything so romantic as Lord Byron.

He glinted her a look, then said softly, " '*She walks in beauty, like the night Of cloudless climes and starry skies,*

And all that's best of dark and bright. Meets in her aspect and her eyes . . . ' "

The words rested in the silence, cupped by the warmth of the room, glowing in their simplicity. A slow tingle filled her heart and expanded, warming her chest, her shoulders, her arms. She found herself nodding. "Byron is one of my favorites as well."

The moment seemed unexpectedly intimate, as if they'd known each other for a very long time and had shared numerous confidences. It was an illusion, she knew. She and Greyley exchanged verbal barbs and not friendship.

To break the hold of the silence, she turned back to the shelves. "Have you read every book here?"

The earl leaned against the desk, his broad shoulders blocking the light from one of the windows. "Not yet. I'm a very deliberate reader, and I savor that which I enjoy most." There was something about the earl's voice that compelled one to listen. Low and melodious, he spoke each word as if he'd considered it, tasted it, and then found it fit to be used.

Anna slanted him a glance and found that he was watching her. "I love to read. It's one of the things I emphasize with my charges."

"If you can get them to do anything, then you will have done more most of the other governesses I've hired."

"How many have there been?"

He made a disgusted sound. "More than I can count." He leaned across the wide desk and picked up a sheet of paper and then held it out.

Anna reluctantly left the books and crossed the room to take the paper. She looked at it then wrinkled her nose. "Ah, the schedule."

"Divided into half-hour increments. I believe you will find everything accounted for—history, Latin, Greek, exercise—"

"Thank you, but I don't think I'll need this." She put it back in his hand. "I don't use schedules."

His good humor melted. "Then how did you keep the children on task?"

"I set very broad weekly goals. Nothing inflexible, of course. Then we establish our routine each morning and work from there."

The earl's brow lowered. "Miss Thraxton, we agreed to work together. The schedule is very important."

"Yes, but expecting children to conform to a strict schedule is not very realistic."

"Why not? I set a schedule for my servants and I have found it very beneficial. They wash the floors on Tuesdays, the linens on Thursdays, and so on. It has made them much more productive."

"Yes, but these are *children*, Greyley. Not servants. Don't you remember being a child?"

Anna looked into Greyley's face and saw her answer. He didn't. He didn't remember being a child. It was as if he'd never been allowed the luxury of playing, of experiencing the unfettered freedom of being young and not having a care in the world.

But how could that be? Sara had told Anna of her own childhood, of escapades and pranks, of swimming in the pond and stealing one of her brother's pocket knives to carve a rabbit out of an old oak stick. How could one of Sara's own brothers not have had the same experiences? Perhaps it was time Anna wrote Sara another letter.

In the meantime, she had to find a way to convince Greyley to let *her* establish the routine for the nursery. She was just grappling with this thorny problem when a soft knock heralded the entrance of the butler.

Jenkins bowed. "My lord, Miss Thraxton's room is ready."

Anna smiled brightly. "Wonderful! I would dearly love to rest before dinner." She bustled to the door. "Thank you for your time, Lord Greyley. I truly enjoyed seeing your library."

The earl lifted a brow, no humor in his gaze. "Running away, Thraxton?"

Anna managed a prim sniff. "I never run. I do, however, walk away from a conversation that promises to spark my temper."

Anthony almost grinned at her frank admission. He couldn't help it—she was honest, which was as delightful as it was surprising. In all his dealing with the Elliots, not a one of them had tried that particular tactic. "Then walk away, Miss Thraxton. We will discuss the schedule sooner or later. There is no escaping it."

Her eyes silvered, humor lurking in the curve of her lush mouth. "We can discuss it after I've had something to eat."

Anthony glanced at Jenkins. "I believe Miss Thraxton is tired and hungry. Please see her to her room and have Mrs. Stibbons bring her a tray."

"I believe Mrs. Stibbons is already seeing to it." Jenkins held the door open and bowed. "After you, miss."

Thraxton gave Anthony a very saucy curtsy and then she left, her skirts bristling as she went. She strode rather than walked, every step vibrating with energy. It was difficult not to picture her trim legs or to ignore the way her gently curved hips swung to and fro beneath her skirts.

The door closed and the latch clicked into place. Anthony shoved his hands into his pockets and shook his head. God help him, but there were unforeseen difficulties in letting Thraxton into his house. She was even more stubborn than he'd thought and too damned attractive for her own good.

Not that that was a completely negative thing. He was a man who appreciated feminine beauty. He just wished the woman wasn't so argumentative. Anthony supposed he couldn't complain; he'd won her willingness to serve as governess to his wards, though that had cost him plenty. Now all he had to do was clearly demark the lines between Thraxton the governess and Thraxton the busybody.

To his chagrin, he remembered the twinkle in her eyes and a feeling lifted in his chest. It took him a moment to realize it was a chuckle . . . She was a handful, that one. And it had been a long time since anyone had been able to make him laugh.

Chapter 8

*I miss Sir Phineas, the old curmudgeon. It's a pity he
had to go and get poor all of the sudden. Wonder if
he'll ever find a way to come about again?*

Viscount Evanstock to the Countess of Chesterfield,
while sitting in the Chesterfield box at the theater

"**L**ooks like it belongs in a harem," Grandpapa said,
staring at the huge blue silk-draped bed in the center of the room. "But I like it."

Anna swallowed. This couldn't be her room. Expensive
blue wallpaper adorned the walls and thick rugs covered very
inch of the polished floor, a perfect setting for the rich
furnishings—a massive wardrobe stood to one side, beside it
was an ornate dressing table, complete with a velvet covered
seat. An assortment of crystal bottles and flagons decorated
the marble top, catching the afternoon rays. But it was the
bed that held one's attention. Heavy blue draperies hung
about the bed, tied back with extravagant red tassels. It was
large enough, Anna was sure, for four or five people. Maybe
six. "This must be a mistake."

"No, it isn't," Grandpapa said with a gleam of satisfaction. "Greyley knows you are a Thraxton."

"I am the *governess*."

"Today, perhaps. But tomorrow . . ." He shrugged, a secret smile touching his lips. "You never know."

"Tomorrow I'll *still* be the governess."

"Hm." His smile faded a bit as he considered her. "I don't mean to say anything ill, but ah, are you going to wear that gown often?"

"Perhaps. It is perfectly appropriate for my position."

"Yes," he said gently. But not for your birth. It wouldn't be wise to appear . . . common."

"Common? Grandpapa, I am a governess. I should dress as such."

"You are also a Thraxton. And you should remember it."

Anna frowned. What was he up to? "Grandpapa, are you—"

"Do you hear that?" He limped toward the door. "I hear the clink of silver. Daresay they are bringing you a tray for lunch, just as they did me."

A knock sounded and Grandpapa swept open the door. Mrs. Stibbons bustled in followed by a thin, slight maid carrying a tray.

The housekeeper frowned at Grandpapa. "Sir Phineas, what are you doing here? You should be resting."

"Yes, but I—"

"You can't rest wanderin' about the house." She took his arm and led him to the adjoining door. "Your room's right through here. You've no business makin' yourself ill. A nice nap'll do wonders, it will."

A faint pout touched the corners of Grandpapa's mouth. He shot a humorous look at Anna. "I am being forced to take a nap. Do you need me for anything, my dear?"

"No. Go and rest. I'm going to eat my luncheon."

With a faint grin, he allowed the housekeeper to bustle him into his bed. Anna listened to his faint protestations and could tell he was enjoying the attention, just as she was sure he was enjoying their well-appointed accommodations.

She glanced around the room, admitting that she loved blue silk almost as much as she loved a well-stuffed mattress. It would be selfish to demand to be placed in a less ostentatious room, as wherever she went, Grandpapa would follow, and he deserved a room like this.

Anna glanced again at the huge bed and noted the mounds of pillows and the satiny smooth sheets, and her skin tingled at the thought of sleeping in such luxury. What was she thinking? *She* deserved a room like this. She smiled and patted a plump pillow back into place.

Besides, Greyley had mentioned that there was some problem with the governess quarters, so it would be ill-bred to complain. And the Thraxtons were never rude. Well, not more than circumstances warranted.

Mrs. Stibbons returned. "Lily, put the tray on that table by the window. I'm certain Miss Thraxton would like to see the gardens while she's eating. We've some lovely roses this year."

The maid did as she was told, her hands trembling as she arranged the silver.

"Now there's no need to rattle everything," Mrs. Stibbons scolded, though her words were softened with an encouraging smile. She glanced at Anna. "Lily's new. Only been here a week now."

Anna smiled at the girl. "Lily is such a pretty name. I always wanted a flower name, though with my height, I daresay I would have been more appropriately named after a bean of some sort."

Lily giggled, her nervousness lessening.

"Well done, Lily," Mrs. Stibbons said, looking at the table. "Pour Miss Thraxton some tea and then be on your way."

Lily did as she was told, sending Anna a thankful smile. The maid quietly finished her duties then left, shutting the door behind her. As soon as they were alone, Mrs. Stibbons turned to Anna. "Thank you, miss. She's a good child, but easily frightened."

"She seems very sweet natured."

"That's her. And you've won her over already, I could see it. Not like that Lady Putney," the housekeeper added darkly.

"The children's grandmother?"

"Yes, and a meaner, more narrow person, I've yet to meet. She came to Greyley only to stir up trouble amongst the children, and so I've told His Lordship time and again."

"If she's been such trouble, I'm surprised Greyley hasn't sent her packing."

"He doesn't dare; the children would be in an uproar. Even worse than they are now, which would suit Lady Putney just fine. She wants those children and she's bound and determined to get them."

It seemed as if Mrs. Stibbons knew all there was to know about Greyley House and its occupants. "I wonder why the children are so badly behaved," Anna mused aloud.

"They're not anywhere near as bad as they wish to be." Mrs. Stibbons smoothed the coverlet on the huge bed and whisked away an imaginary dust mote. "They're just a mite confused, the poor souls."

Anna smiled. "Did you get all of the frogs out of the master bedchamber?"

"Indeed we did. They were very attracted to his neckcloths, they were. Must be the starch His Lordship's valet uses." Mrs. Stibbons made a disapproving face. "Don't know why Ledbetter bothers with such. I've told him time and again that His Lordship doesn't like his neckcloths so stiff, but he won't listen to me."

"Form before fashion," Anna murmured.

"What?"

Anna managed a rueful grin. "I'm sorry. I have a bad tendency to mumble. Tell me, what do the children hope to gain by playing such pranks? They must know they are only making Lord Greyley angry."

"They hope to so disgust His Lordship that he will send them off to live with Lady Putney."

Anna frowned. "Does Lady Putney encourage such behavior?"

Mrs. Stibbons smoothed the edge of a curtain to a more sedate angle. "In my opinion, she's the source behind most of their pranks. She has sway over them, she does. Brings them sweets every time she sees them. And toys, too. Anything to win them over."

"Bribery."

"Exactly. It's what they're used to. I heard tell that their parents were very busy socially and left the children to be raised by a parcel of servants. They've used their knowledge of such to get rid of most of the governesses His Lordship has hired."

So the children were experts on governesses, were they? That was interesting information, indeed. "I daresay His Lordship's gruff manners play very much against him."

"As much as I respect His Lordship, he can be a mite terse. Children don't understand those things, miss. You know how it is."

Anna nodded thoughtfully. "Tell me, Mrs. Stibbons. What is it that the children like to do most?"

"Riding. They love their ponies, they do. And they'd be gone all day if His Lordship would allow it. But he only lets them ride on Tuesday and Thursday mornings. He's quite particular about schedules."

"So I've heard," Anna said dryly. "His Lordship and I disagree on that item. I dislike being held to a set of rules for no reason other than to create the impression of order, whether it exists or not."

Mrs. Stibbons looked doubtful. "That sounds very reasonable, miss. Just don't expect His Lordship to like it."

"I don't expect His Lordship to like it one bit. Fortunately he's not in the nursery. The children are."

"He's there more than you might think," Mrs. Stibbons said.

"In the nursery?"

"His Lordship is very particular when it comes to his responsibilities. He visits the nursery quite frequently to see how the children are and how the new governess is getting on." She pursed her lips. "Seems we've always got a new governess. I'll be glad to see one stay longer than two weeks."

"Oh, I intend on being here for three months, at least," Anna said smoothly. "Whether the children like it or not."

"I wish you luck," Mrs. Stibbons said with a doubtful look. "You'll be needin' it if you are planning on ignoring His Lordship's schedule."

Anna thought she'd need more than luck. She'd need every ounce of her persuasive abilities. Greyley was not a man who welcomed change and he was about to face quite a bit more than he realized.

Mrs. Stibbons stirred the fire, then replaced the poker in the brass stand. "I suppose I should get to work. Do you need anything else, miss?"

"No, thank you. You've been very helpful."

The housekeeper beamed pleasantly, then left.

Anna waited until the woman's footsteps had faded before she tossed her napkin onto the table and leaned over to push open a window. It was a beautiful summer day, the sky blue without a cloud in sight. Below, the garden swayed sleepily in the sunlight, a cacophony of pink, purple, blue and green. The house sat quietly, as if at rest. But somewhere inside the house were five very determined children who were probably even now scheming to oust their new governess, sight unseen.

Fortunately for those five determined children, Anna was not going anywhere. She needed Greyley's funds if she was going to establish a real home for herself and Grandpapa.

Anna knew the general lot of the children of the ton, and Greyley's wards seemed to fit the pattern. Confined to the care of unfeeling servants, and allowed out of the nursery only to be shown to company, many children went weeks without seeing their own parents. Anna's approach as governess was slightly different from most—she tried to improve not only the children's behavior, but that of their parents as well. Most parents did not maliciously neglect their children; they were merely continuing a pattern they themselves had experienced.

Most governesses wouldn't have had the opportunity for frank speech, but Anna's unique position as both a former member of the *ton* and as the most sought-after governess in London had given her access to the lords and ladies she worked for. Like her grandpapa, she never turned from the opportunity to fix some aspect of another person's life.

Schedules, indeed. Anna sniffed. One of the first things she needed to change was Greyley.

For too many years the earl had had his own way in life— she could see it in the way he expected complete and immediate obedience to even the simplest requests. With unlimited funding, a respected and ancient title solidly behind him, and an impressive physique that left him towering over most men, Greyley believed that he knew what was best for everyone.

It was a very dangerous habit for a man to possess, and Anna decided it was one that needed amending as soon as possible.

But how? She was mulling over this particularly thorny problem when a knock sounded at the door.

A liveried footman appeared holding a silver salver. "A note, miss. From Lord Greyley. He said there was no need to wait for an answer."

Anna took the note from the salver, and the footman bowed and left.

The vellum was crisp in her fingers, the handwriting bold and strong, each letter marked with a sweeping flourish. Even if she hadn't seen it before, she would have known Greyley's handwriting.

Thraxton, the note read.

The children will be assembled in the library at two to meet you. Do not be late.

Greyley

Anna crumpled the note into a ball. It would have been polite to have at least asked if the time was convenient. For an instant, Anna toyed with the idea of sending the earl a note telling him that she would be resting at two, that four would suit her much better. But she was ready to meet her new charges.

Anna resumed her seat at the table and buttered her bread with an efficient swipe of her knife. If she was to win the children over, she'd have to start from their first meeting. What she had to do was surprise them, keep them off balance long enough for her to get under their defenses.

She looked down at her stiff bombazine gown. If the children were expecting an average governess, then she was dressed in the perfect manner. Her gaze drifted to the wardrobe that now contained her few clothes. Reworked gowns in a princess's closet . . . but she had one or two items that were not reworked. Her new riding habit, for instance . . . A thought took hold and she smiled. Perhaps Grandpapa was right after all. It wouldn't do to appear like a common, ordinary governess. Especially not before the Elliot children.

They might have been under the care of a wide assortment of governesses, but they'd never met Anna Thraxton before. Fortunately for everyone concerned, that was about to change.

Chapter 9

*Women provide the only true link to civilization. Men
simply are not ruthless enough to survive on their own.*

The Countess of Chesterfield to her friend,
Mrs. Oglethorpe-White, while taking tea at Lady Bedford's

Anna reached the library at exactly two. Greyley
glanced at her as she entered, then looked again, a
frown between his brows.

She didn't acknowledge him at all, but sailed past to the
line of sprites that faced the desk. They stood from tallest to
shortest as if placed in line for a military inspection, poor
things.

Anna ignored the children's expressions, which ranged
from anger to sullen hostility to simple curiosity, and smiled
as brightly as she could. She waited for Greyley to begin the
introductions.

He, however, apparently had other things on his mind. He
lifted his quizzing glass from where it hung on a ribbon at his
waist and looked up and down her form, as if inspecting a
horse. "What in bloody hell do you have on?"

Anna glanced down at her riding habit of sapphire blue,
the large white feather that adorned the hat brushing her

shoulder. The entire ensemble had cost her dearly, and she'd decried her lack of resistance for weeks after she'd purchased it. Still . . . she trailed a hand along the trimly fitted coat. It had been well worth the money, no matter what Greyley thought. "Don't you like it?"

"It fits you," he said, still peering at her through that damnable quizzing glass. "Very well indeed." There was a hint of warmth to his voice that sent a shiver down Anna's spine. Really, she had to regain some control over her traitorous responses. "Lord Greyley, as heartwarming as it is to know that my riding habit has won your approval, I've more important things on my mind. Perhaps you should introduce the children."

He dropped the glass, and his brown eyes seemed darker than usual. "Of course. Children, this is Miss Thraxton, your new governess."

"She doesn't look like a governess," the tallest child muttered, sending her a sullen scowl. He appeared to be eleven or so years of age, with a pale, thin countenance and a reed-slender body. His hair was the Elliot brown, somewhere between a true chestnut and a dull brown, the thick locks standing on end here and there, as if unwilling to bend to a brush.

His dark gaze flickered over her with suspicion. "Why are you wearing your habit?"

"Because I plan to go for a lovely jaunt around the park." She glanced at Greyley, who stood watching her with a faint smile. "I will need a mount."

"I already had one in mind—a bay with an even gait. I think you'll enjoy her."

"So long as she has some spirit, I'm sure she'll do nicely."

"Governesses don't go for rides," the boy said with a superior smirk. "Grooms go for rides."

"I'm not your ordinary governess."

That did not appear to please the boy at all. He scowled. "How are *you* any different?"

"For one thing, I plan on spending time with you. A lot." she said briskly.

His frown deepened. "Doing what?"

"Reading, playing, eating . . . almost everything."

"Everything? All day?"

"Oh yes," she said cheerfully. "From the time you awaken, to the time you fall asleep, I will be there." Most governesses jealously guarded their free time, but Anna had learned to use every moment. After all, the more immersed she was in the lives of her charges, the more influence she had. Once things were better established, she would have no compunction in turning them over to other servants or a groom. But for now, they were her primary concern. "I daresay you are going to get quite tired of me before the day's out."

The boy's jaw tightened. "Bloody hell."

"*Desford*," Greyley growled.

"Master Desford, is it?" Anna said. "How nice to meet you."

He stared back, resentment in his gaze, making no move to take the hand she held out.

That's the way he wishes to play this, eh? She dropped her hand back to her side. "I can see that one of the things we will have to work on are your manners."

He smirked. "I have manners. I just don't find them necessary in my cousin's house."

Greyley's brow lowered. "Desford, I'm going to—"

"My lord," Anna said, "please don't protest on my account. I find challenges stimulating." She met Desford's gaze with a direct one of her own. "In fact, the more challenging the position, the better I like it. It is the other positions, where the children are perfectly behaved, that I deplore."

"Why's that?" Desford asked, clearly unhappy with what he was hearing.

"Boredom," she said airily. "I left one job three months early because I was bored to tears. I simply couldn't stand such perfect children."

He tried to hide it, but Anna could see that she had nonplussed him. It wouldn't last, of course, but she'd given him something to think about which was quite enough for the first meeting. She came to the next child in line. "Who might you be?"

The girl began to dip a curtsy, then caught Desford's gaze and stopped, flushing.

Greyley sighed. "This is Miss Elizabeth Elliot."

Anna examined Elizabeth. Though shorter than Desford, Elizabeth outweighed her brother by a good stone. Plump and red cheeked, she had the air of a country maid. But Anna noted that the child's hair was brushed and braided, a bright red ribbon threaded through the whole in an inexpert manner. "How lovely," Anna murmured, touching the ribbon. "I do so like to curl hair."

As Anna had expected, Elizabeth's eyes lit. "Do you?"

"Oh yes. I have my own irons, too. We can curl it this evening, if you'd like."

"Liza," growled Desford.

Elizabeth bit her lip and Anna could almost feel the child backing away from her. Refusing to bow to such heavy-handed tactics, Anna merely said, "I have some extra ribbons, as well. Some lovely blue ones." Then she stepped on to the next child. "Who have we here?"

The little boy was an exact replica of Desford, but his narrow face was shadowed, his eyes haunted. Anna held out her hand. "How do you do?"

He didn't move, just stood staring up at her. She could feel Greyley at her side. "Richard doesn't speak," he said quietly.

Anna knelt in front of the boy and smiled. "I daresay you will speak when you have something to say, won't you?" She reached out to smooth a strand of hair from his brow. The moment her fingers brushed his forehead, he jerked back, his mouth thinning into a mutinous line.

Anna chuckled. "At least you are still able to think for yourself. I will remember that you don't like anyone touching your hair." Though the child didn't move, she thought she detected a gleam of faint approval in his glance.

She stood and brushed her knees, then went to the next child, a girl of about six with a head of curly hair that longed for a brush, her stout body dressed in a torn and grass-stained gown. "How do you do?"

The girl wiped her nose on a rather grimy sleeve. "I'm Maid Marian."

"Miss Marian Elliot," Greyley said in a tone of long suffering.

Anna had to swallow a chuckle. "How do you do, Maid Marian. I loved the stories of Robin Hood when I was young, too."

Maid Marian glanced at her brothers and sisters, who were all glaring at her. The sight seemed to give her courage, for she straightened her shoulders and then said in a defiant tone, "Desford made a bow and some arrows for me."

"How kind of him! I didn't have a brother to help me and I was forced to make a bow and arrow out of the broom handle and a bit of string and just pretend to shoot. I daresay you are quite good."

"I beat Desford," Marian said in a proud tone.

"Did not," the young boy said hotly. "Liza jostled my arm or I'd have hit the bull."

Marian plopped a hand on her hip. "Liza didn't touch you and you know it! I hit closer to the center than you. Therefore I won."

Anna had to give the child credit—she wasn't about to let Desford bully her. Which was a good thing, because it was painfully obvious that he was their unspoken leader. Perhaps that was the weak link in the chain—none of them was as angry as Desford.

Anna moved on to the last child in line. She was tiny, with silky brown ringlets falling over her brow and shoulders, and thickly lashed blue eyes that focused on Anna with unwavering regard. The child held on to a ragged doll that was missing an arm and one eye. The little girl didn't seem to mind, for she hugged it tightly while sucking on one of her fingers.

"This is my troublemaker," Greyley said. Though the words could have been harsh, they were more a rough caress and the little girl knew it, for she grinned up at him, unabashed. He ruffled her hair, his expression softening slightly. "She looks like a baby, but she's devil spawn from her topmost ringlet to her chubby toes."

"I did it all," she replied proudly, sticking her thumb in the middle of her own chest. "By myself, too."

"So I've been told," he said with mock gravity. He met Anna's gaze. "According to Desford and the others, Miss Selena is the cause of all the unrest here at Greyley House."

Anna looked at Selena. "Even the frogs?"

"I catched them all," she said in a well-rehearsed voice. "With my fingers."

"My, how brave! I dislike frogs myself." She leaned forward. "It's a good thing they don't bite."

Selena's gaze widened and she looked at Desford.

"Frogs *don't* bite," he said, his brows so low they almost met at the center.

Selena appeared relieved and Anna hid a smile as she straightened. "I am so looking forward to being with all of you. Perhaps we should begin with a ride." She turned to face Greyley. "What do you think?"

"The children have rides Tuesday and Thursday mornings. Perhaps you would like to ride with the children then."

"Oh no. I would *much* rather ride with the children today."

It appeared Greyley had suddenly remembered something very sour, for his mouth pulled in at the corners. "Miss Thraxton—"

"It's my first day and I believe it would benefit the children if we could spend a little time together."

The earl took a slow breath, as if to release some sort of inner pressure. "Thraxton, you and I have to—"

"Who," said a shrill voice from the doorway, "is this? Greyley, please tell me you didn't hire yet another governess without asking my advice."

Anna turned to see a woman walking toward them, her hair dyed an unnatural black, her face highly painted, black silk draperies fluttering about her stout form. Her small blue eyes took in Anna from head to foot, noting the expert cut of her habit with a frown. "Who is she? And why is she dressed in such a way?"

At her militant tone, the earl regarded his visitor with a pointed expression.

The woman's mouth thinned, but the earl did not reply. Finally the woman said in a testy voice, "I daresay it is the new governess, though why she has on a riding habit is beyond me."

Greyley's gaze narrowed. "Lady Putney, allow me to introduce Miss Thraxton."

"Thraxton? I've heard that name before."

"I'm sure you have," the earl said smoothly. "The Thraxtons are an important family in Bath. Miss Thraxton is reputed to be the best governess in all of England."

Anna thought she detected the slightest flicker of something in Lady Putney's face, but all the woman said was, "I hope she lasts longer than the others." She turned her back on Anna and began talking to the children. "There you are, my sweets. Grandmama just returned from town with some candies. Come to my room and I'll give them to you."

"Evaline," Greyley said sternly. "You are not to stuff the children with candy before dinner. We have already discussed this."

"Yes, but the children—"

"—do not need to have their dinner spoiled every time you visit the village."

Lady Putney clasped her hands together. "You don't care about the children, do you? You just want them under your control, just as you wish to control everything around you!" She placed a hand on Elizabeth's shoulder and pulled the plump child against her. "Do not fear, my darlings. Grandmama is here to help you."

Anna felt as if she'd stumbled into a very poorly written play. Apparently Greyley thought the same, for he said in a heavy tone, "That's quite enough, Evaline."

"I just want the children to have some candy," Lady Putney said softly, her bottom lip quivering. "Would you forbid them even this one small pleasure?"

The children turned questioning eyes on the earl.

"I said no," he snapped.

His voice seemed harsh after Lady Putney's sugared tones, and Anna grimaced. Heavens, but she had her work cut out for her. The children fixed sullen gazes on the earl while Lady Putney just looked pathetic.

Anna cleared her throat. "Lord Greyley, as I was saying prior to meeting Lady Putney, perhaps the children could go for a ride with me this afternoon. Would you mind?"

Greyley's gaze swung Anna's way. "The children—"

"I'd like to ride," Elizabeth said, breaking from Lady Putney's side. The child's face brightened. "More than anything."

"Me, too," Marian said, stepping forward.

Greyley's brow lowered. Anna placed her hand on his arm and leaned forward to say quietly, "It will do them good to get out of the house."

"But the schedule," he said stiffly.

Heavens, when had the man become so stern and unyielding? She remembered some of the tales Sara had told her about Greyley's youth, and Anna had to fight a sudden giggle. "My lord, I'm surprised you are so attached to the concept of a schedule. There was a time when you were more impulsive."

"Me?" he asked, apparently insulted by the thought.

"When you were thirteen . . . maybe fourteen."

"You didn't know me when I was thirteen or fourteen."

"No, but your sister did, and she told some very interesting stories."

"Stories?" Selena's blue eyes brightened. "I like stories."

"So do I," Elizabeth said.

Maid Marian wiped her nose on her sleeve, her brown eyes hopeful. "Are they funny stories?"

"Some of them are *most* amusing," Anna said in a sun-drenched voice, noting how the earl's eyes had darkened to black.

"I wager they're boring," Desford said, wrinkling his nose.

"No one wants to hear any stories about me," Greyley stated in an implacable tone.

"Not even about . . . oh, what was her name?" Anna tapped her chin, frowning. "What was—ah! Matilda."

His face darkened, a slow touch of red climbing his cheeks. "Sara did not tell you about Matilda."

"Oh, but she did," Anna said gently. "She even brought some of the sonnets you wrote. We even memorized some of the more humorous passages."

"Who was Matilda?" Elizabeth asked eagerly.

"A milkmaid that Lord Greyley once knew. A lovely, red-cheeked milkmaid."

"That sounds romantic," Elizabeth said with a satisfied air. "I want to hear the story."

"Matilda was *not* a milkmaid," the earl growled.

Anna tapped her chin. "How did that sonnet go? I seem to remember . . . oh yes! *'Eyes as bright as coal—'*"

"Thraxton," Greyley said in an ominous voice.

"Yes, my lord?" she said, trying hard not to grin and failing miserably. They were wretched sonnets and she could tell he remembered them all too well.

His gaze glinted. "You are incorrigible."

"Only if forced."

Lady Putney's plump face pinched into a frown. "Greyley, who is this Matilda and why don't you wish the children to know about her?"

"There was no Matilda. Miss Thraxton is merely offering to make up a story," he returned shortly. He glinted at Anna. "I shouldn't let you go, but . . ." His gaze drifted to Lady Putney. "I suppose I shall."

"Excellent."

He didn't seem at all pleased. "You are the most annoying woman I've ever met."

"It's a gift, my lord."

"It's more a curse." He looked at her for a long moment, then waved an impatient hand. "Oh, very well. Since this is your first day, you may take the children riding. But as soon as you return, I wish to discuss that damned schedule."

"Of course." It would be a very short discussion, indeed. There would be no schedule, not while she was the governess. She smiled at Elizabeth, who watched with an anxious expression. "How long will it take you to get ready?"

Elizabeth clasped her hands together. "No time at all!"

Lady Putney stepped forward. "But dearest, I have candy—"

"No, thank you," Elizabeth said politely. "I want to ride with Miss Thraxton."

Marian nodded. "Me, too!" She tugged on Anna's sleeve. "My pony's name is Friar Tuck. He's a piebald and he's very fat."

To Anthony's surprise, the comment seemed to open the door, for soon all of the children except Desford were clamoring to speak about their mounts.

Lady Putney watched it all with a fulminating expression. Stiff with disapproval, she finally drew herself up and left, announcing once more that she'd be in her room with the candy.

The children did not pay her the slightest heed. Anthony's feeling of satisfaction wiped away his irritation. It had been a masterful stroke to secure Anna Thraxton's service— although he would have to discover exactly how much she knew about the almost forgotten Matilda. Damn Sara for spreading tales.

He'd been nothing but a green one, still wet behind the ears and head over heels in love with the downstairs maid, who'd had the good sense not to return his declared affections. He'd done what any other young male of his station had done at one time or another—moped about the house until his parents were driven to distraction, lost his appetite for almost two entire days, and written an excessive amount of very bad poetry. What a fool he'd been. He hadn't thought of the curvaceous Matilda in years.

Miss Thraxton pulled her gloves from a pocket and tugged them on. "I so love to ride," she told the children. "I named my first horse Sweetums, but I had to change it when I found out she was a he."

Elizabeth giggled. "Didn't you know how to tell?"

"Not then. I was only five."

Selena's smooth brow puckered. "How *can* you tell if a horse is a boy horse or a girl horse?"

"What a good question," Anna said, sending Anthony a look so filled with mischief that an alarm sounded deep in his head. "Why don't you ask Lord Greyley? He knows all about horses."

Selena obediently turned her wide, innocent blue gaze toward him, effectively freezing his voice. *Good God, what do I say now?*

Selena tugged on his coat. "Lord Greyley, how *do* you tell a boy horse from—"

"There isn't time," he choked out. He reached to one side and yanked the bellpull. Jenkins appeared immediately.

"Have the head groom ready the children's horses and the new mare for Miss Thraxton."

"Yes, my lord. Is there anything else?"

"See the children to the nursery, will you? They have to change." He was careful to avoid Selena's inquiring gaze. "I assume all of you are going?"

They nodded except Desford.

"Well?" Anthony asked.

The boy shrugged, his hands deep in his pockets, his shoulders rounded. "I suppose I'll go. There's nothing else to do."

"Excellent," Anna said. "You are in charge, Desford. Once everyone has changed, gather them together and meet me in the stables. I'll wait for you there."

To Anthony's surprise, Desford gave a sullen nod. Jenkins held the door open and the children filed out.

Anthony barely waited for the door to close before he sent a glare at Thraxton. "You don't play fair. How the hell was I supposed to answer a question like that?"

She pursed her lips. "Perhaps you could make a sketch."

"A sketch? You expect me to draw—" He broke off at her grin. "Damn you, Thraxton. This isn't funny."

"Nonsense. You need to get used to such questions; they are *your* children now."

"More's the pity."

"Don't tell me that. You care for them; I can tell."

"Of course I care for them," he said stiffly. "They are my flesh and blood."

"That doesn't mean anything. I have tons of relatives and there are several I quite often wish to perdition."

"I was raised differently. I was raised to believe that my family is my responsibility. I do not take my responsibilities lightly."

She looked at him thoughtfully. "I've noticed that. If we're going to discuss responsibilities, there is one thing . . ."

"What?"

She hesitated, then said, "It isn't my place to make suggestions, but—"

"No, it isn't."

"—you really must watch your temper. How can you expect Desford to refrain from cursing when you do it all of the time?" She shook her head. "You are setting a poor example."

Anthony was astounded. No one had told him how to act for years. No one. And yet here was a governess—a *governess*, for the love of God. It was not to be borne.

Worse was the realization that she was right. He did need to be more careful how he spoke in front of the children. The admission was galling, and he glared down at her. She met his gaze with a frank one of her own, uncowed by his scowls, her figure outlined in that damnable riding habit, a faint dimple resting beside her delectable mouth, one strand of lush red hair curling over her ear. She appeared calm and proud and damnably impudent, and he was assailed with the desire to shake her from her certainty.

But he knew where that would lead—to another kiss, just as hot and passionate as before. He'd be damned if he made that mistake again. He turned and strode to the safety of his desk. "I don't need any advice from you, Thraxton. You are here to see to the children and nothing else."

"That's too bad, for I daresay I could do you a great deal of good."

What the hell did she mean by that? But before he could ask, she was sailing toward the door, her hips swaying gently beneath her skirts.

He watched, mesmerized by the thoughts of the long legs that the skirts hinted at. For the fortieth time that day, he remembered the feel of her long, firm body against his when he'd kissed her. He'd wager his best stallion her legs were nearly as long as his. The thought settled into his groin and heated him thoroughly.

Unaware of the torments he was facing, Thraxton reached

the door and turned to toss a gay wave in his direction. "I'm off to the stables to see this horse you have for me. I do hope she has some spirit, Greyley, or I will have to make them saddle another." With an impudent wiggle of her fingers, she disappeared out the door.

Chapter 10

A man in possession of five unruly children must be in want of a good wife. Either that or a very fast horse.

Mrs. Oglethorpe-White to Lord Bristol during the second intermission of the new play

Anthony stared at the door and then slowly sank back in his chair. Good God, what force had he unleashed on Greyley House? It was true Thraxton had temporarily vanquished Lady Putney, and far more quickly than he'd hoped, but that she would dare assume she could correct *him*?

Worse was the realization that she had no intention of adhering to the schedule. And that simply could not be borne. He mulled over all the things he should and could say to her, yet none of them seemed forceful enough. Perhaps she'd follow written instructions better. Yes, that was a possibility. He pulled out a sheet of starched vellum and started to write a pithy note outlining Miss Thraxton's duties, when he realized he was wasting his time.

Miss Thraxton was a woman who would appreciate only direct, face-to-face confrontation. He doubted she'd comprehend anything so subtle as a list of her duties, no matter how plainly written out.

A pounding on the steps told him that the children were now tramping down the stairs on their way to the stables. As their excited voices faded, he was assailed with the unmistakable sounds of peace and quiet.

Perhaps . . . perhaps she was right and there were benefits to allowing the children to ride more often. For one thing, it would keep them out of the house and away from Lady Putney's odious presence. And perhaps, if Anthony was willing to concede this point, he could win some concessions in some other areas. He might even allow Thraxton to set her own schedule for her charges . . .

After a moment, he realized he was staring blankly into the air, his mind not mulling over his recalcitrant governess, but rather that damnable dimple that appeared in her cheek when she was trying not to grin.

"I'm wasting my time," he muttered, picking up an imposing stack of correspondence. He flipped through it for some moments, though his mind kept returning to the image of Lady Putney's face when the children chose to ride with their new governess rather than eat her candy and listen to her spew her poison.

He had to admit that Thraxton was already making a difference. Perhaps he *had* done the right thing in securing her services. Now all he had to do was keep her firmly under control and everything would work for the best. The children's behavior would indeed improve and the world would know that being an Elliot did not necessarily mean one possessed the morals of an ill bred barn cat.

Of course, that was easier said than done. Anthony had spent most of his life since he'd turned seventeen managing the Elliots. He'd turned his back on the usual enjoyments favored by a young man of fashion, refusing the invitations from his school chums to prizefights and other delightfully vulgar amusements. He'd walked away from them all in order to bring the rancid ranks of Elliots to heel. And he'd succeeded, for the most part. But the cost had been high. He hadn't had the time to pursue the usual entertainments.

Not that he'd been a monk, by any means. Over the years he'd warmed his bed with a number of liaisons, each carefully conducted with an eye toward society's rather ridiculous rules. Anthony had been careful to end any affair where it appeared the woman in question was getting more attached than necessary, which happened far too often for his peace of mind. He'd followed the dictates of society and had escaped even a breath of scandal.

All in all, he'd been gifted with an exemplary life. Oh, he occasionally wondered what it would have been like if his youth had been spent on something more frivolous, and there were times when he looked at the charmed lives his half brothers lived and envied their carefree attitudes. But Anthony had more to prove than they. They had been born St. Johns, while he had only the borrowed mantle, one he was determined to earn. He would show the Elliots the error of their lives and prove to all the world that though he'd not been born a St. John, he'd learned the St. John lessons well.

Anthony pushed the stack of letters away and leaned back in his chair, staring at the ceiling. If he had one regret, it was that his stepfather hadn't lived to see his successes. The Elliot fortune was reestablished and the family was no longer the social pariahs they had been. All Anthony needed to do now was to set his own household more firmly in the realms of respectability. And he was about to do that with his marriage.

For some reason, instead of Charlotte's gentle mien, Anthony saw Anna Thraxton's saucy smile. What was it about Thraxton that irritated him so? He didn't know if she was the best governess in London, but she was certainly the most disrespectful. She had no concern for her conduct, other than to win her own stubborn way in every argument. It was maddening, to say the least. But Anthony was not about to let a slip of a governess disrupt his carefully ordered household.

Suddenly too restless to sit still, he rang for Jenkins and ordered a fresh mount brought up from the stables. He'd go and visit his intended. He hadn't seen Charlotte or her parents since last week, when they'd left for a brief visit to London. That would take his mind off the intractable Miss Thraxton.

Within ten minutes, Anthony was riding down the lane. He told himself he was glad that he didn't see his incorrigible governess or the children, though he caught himself looking for them even after he turned onto the main road where they would not have gone.

Twenty minutes passed before he reached his destination— a pleasant stone manor house that sat behind a line of trees. He dismounted and handed his reins to a waiting footman, then approached the front door. The air was just cooling with the approach of evening, and he admired the tasteful arrangement of the flowers that lined the front step. The door was opened by a round-faced butler, who immediately bowed him into a sitting room and left to announce his arrival.

He didn't have to wait long. Moments later, he was joined by a slender, older woman dressed in the height of fashion in an elegant gray dress. Though her brown hair was shot through with silver, her smooth face seemed to belie this one sign of age. She smiled pleasantly at Anthony and held out her hand. "Lord Greyley. What a pleasant surprise."

He took her hand and bowed. "Lady Melton. How do you do?"

"I'm a bit tired from our journey to London. We just returned last night. I'm afraid you just missed Sir Melton. He's gone to visit the colonel."

"I'm sorry I missed him. I hope you don't mind my coming unannounced, but I was impatient to see how you progressed."

She gave a quizzical lift of her brows. "More correctly, you were impatient to see Charlotte."

He bowed again and she laughed. "I never thought to see you so impetuous. Charlotte will be down shortly. Will you have a seat?"

He took the chair she indicated, and a servant brought in a tea tray. For several moments they engaged in desultory small talk, though Greyley listened with only half an ear. His mind was far too occupied with thinking of ways to contain the overly inquisitive Miss Thraxton.

He'd lost ground today, allowing her to sweep the children off for a ride. Had Lady Putney not been present and so obviously wanting the children to herself, he would never have agreed. As soon as he had the opportunity, he would make certain that Miss Thraxton knew he, and not she, was the ultimate authority over the children and everything else at Greyley. He was certain she would disagree, but he was more than ready to deal with her this very moment and would, in fact, welcome the opportunity. A faint sense of surprise made him pause; he was looking forward to the upcoming confrontation.

Anthony wasn't a man who normally welcomed disputes. He liked things and people to know their places and to stay within those confines. It had always been thus with him; everything in its place, and a place for everything. Since the day he'd stepped foot in Greyley House, he'd determined exactly how he'd wanted it to look. And he'd meticulously worked to make it all it should be. Yet still, the house lacked something. Something . . . intrinsic. He stared blankly into his cup of tea and wondered what it could be.

Lady Melton set down her cup. "Lord Greyley, I cannot help but feel that there is some other reason you've come."

"There is," he said. "Perhaps we should move up the wedding date."

A moment of silence greeted this statement and he was uncertain who was more surprised, Lady Melton or him. *What the hell am I thinking?* As if in answer, a picture of Anna Thraxton flew to the fore, sending him that mischievous smile when she'd told Selena to ask him her impertinent question.

He frowned at the memory. Perhaps it *was* time for him to marry, especially if Thraxton was able to restore the nursery to some sort of calm. "Greyley House is in need of a mistress and Charlotte will soon be out of mourning. Perhaps we can marry then."

"It would have to be a quiet ceremony," Lady Melton said in her usual calm voice. "We'll still be in half mourning for six more months."

He shrugged. He really didn't care how big of a wedding it was, as long as he wasn't bothered with any of the details. And he could think of numerous reasons why it would benefit him to get the entire ordeal behind him.

The door opened and Charlotte entered. Anthony stood, eyeing her closely. She was as small as Thraxton was tall, soft and gently rounded. She had wide blue eyes and a wealth of blond curls that tumbled carefully over her tiny ears in the most refined way, quite the opposite of the wild auburn tresses that had shone in the soft light in the library just that afternoon.

Charlotte blushed on meeting his gaze and dipped a perfect curtsy. "Lord Greyley. How nice of you to visit."

Anthony had met Charlotte when he'd assisted Sir Melton home after he'd fallen off his mount while hunting at Greyley. The two men had known each other for some time, but Anthony had never accepted any of Melton's numerous invitations to visit his house until that day.

It had been the end of a particularly trying week, and he had been tired and worn from dealing with the Elliots. Charlotte had appeared like a beacon of light, her shy, perfectly mannered presence a welcome change after dealing with the brash, ill-mannered members of his family.

With the proper training, Anthony was certain she would make an outstanding countess. He took her hand and smiled down at her, noting how her head didn't even reach his shoulder. "How was your visit to London?"

"Lovely," she said in a soft, breathy voice. "I could have stayed forever."

"But Charlotte was very glad to return home, weren't you, dear?" her mother said.

"Oh, yes," Charlotte said, blanching as if she'd committed a major solecism, her lip trembling.

Seeing how tense she was, Anthony asked her if she'd managed to go to Anstley's Amphitheatre to see the animals. That did the trick, for she talked nonstop for several moments, practically glowing when she relayed her fright of the lions. Anthony smiled indulgently, though he scarcely paid attention. Anna Thraxton was wrong—his manners were impeccable. He knew exactly how to behave in company.

Charlotte continued to talk of the dazzling array of amusements in London until Lady Melton gently suggested that Charlotte should return to her room to rest.

She immediately stood and made her adieu, softly closing the door behind her.

Lady Melton took a sip of her tea. "I hope you will forgive Charlotte for chattering on so. The journey was quite fatiguing."

"I hope she doesn't develop too much fondness for London. I am rarely there, except to see to the affairs of my family."

"Charlotte enjoys the sights, but her true love is the country," Lady Melton said firmly.

Anthony nodded, the restlessness returning in full force. He felt . . . dissatisfied for some reason. Before, he'd always thought Charlotte's innocence engaging. Now a slight nagging feeling persisted, as if he hadn't considered some important fact. "Lady Melton, perhaps you could suggest some reading for Charlotte—something to broaden her mind."

Lady Melton set down her cup, a flicker of a frown in her brown eyes. "Of course. Perhaps some Shakespeare?"

"Perhaps." That wasn't exactly what he'd meant, but it was a start. He spoke with Lady Melton some moments longer, then took his leave. Usually when he rode away from the Melton residence, he felt at peace, certain in his future and his destiny. Today, however, all he could think of was Charlotte's excitement about the lions at the amphitheater and Anna Thraxton's deep chuckle when she'd tried to embarrass him in front of his wards.

At home, he was changing out of his riding coat when the sound of voices drifted up to his window. He pulled aside the curtain and looked down to see his wards and their new governess dismounting from their horses. Apparently the spirited mare had met with Miss Thraxton's approval. After dismounting, she lingered by its side and patted it with obvious fondness, saying something to Elizabeth that caused the child to nod and try to stroke the horse's velvet nose.

The horse lifted its head playfully, pulling away from the child, then just as quickly dipping her head to beg for another pat. Elizabeth laughed, a loud, childish laugh that made Anthony pause.

The children had been with him for several months now, yet how often had he heard them laugh? Rarely, if ever. And never while under the care of one of their governesses.

Anthony wondered if he was, in some way, to blame for this. He wasn't a jovial, falsely laughing sort of man. He had responsibilities and little time for frivolous pursuits. Still . . . He watched as Selena giggled at something Thraxton had just said and suddenly a thought hit him. Perhaps in his zeal to correct the children's behavior, he had overlooked certain things. Like the need for warmth, laughter, friendship . . . all the things that had made his relationship with his brothers and sister so worthwhile.

The thought sat heavily on his shoulders for several minutes. He would just have to do better, damn it. Perhaps now that Miss Thraxton was here, things would change all around. For the better or the worse, he wasn't sure. But whatever the outcome, he was reasonably certain he would not be bored. Not in the least.

Chapter 11

What men want more than anything is peace and quiet.
Well, that and a glass of good port.

Lord Bristol to his mistress, Lady Clives-Brandley,
at his rented house just outside Mayfair

For Anna, the ride proved to be a great success. Once away from the stern and forbidding manor house, the children became more talkative. Anna even won a laugh from each of the girls. If only the boys had been as cooperative—Desford remained openly hostile, while Richard ignored her every word. Except once, at the end, when he'd warmed up just for a second . . .

She sighed. It hadn't lasted more than a moment, but perhaps it was a beginning. Anna walked up the front steps of Greyley House behind the children, who scampered quickly out of sight once inside. Anna could hear Mrs. Stibbons scolding about the dusty boots marring her clean floors.

Anna smiled at Jenkins as she walked inside the cool foyer. It seemed abysmally dark after being in the sunshine.

"Did you have a pleasant ride, Miss?"

She dragged her hat from her hair and ran a hand over her tangled curls. "Glorious! The weather is perfect."

He took her hat and handed it to a waiting footman, who immediately turned to take it to her room. "When you have more time, you should try the path by the river. There are some lovely spots and even a waterfall, if I remember correctly."

"Perhaps tomorrow," Anna said, deciding instantly to take the children exploring. If they came to enjoy Greyley's lands, they wouldn't feel so discontented with their lot in life. "Thank you, Jenkins."

The butler bowed. "Shall I have warm water sent to your room?"

"Actually, I could use a hot bath after sitting in the carriage all morning." She grimaced. "I thought the ride would work out all of my bruises, but I fear I only made more."

A faint smile hovered over his mouth. "I shall see to it at once." He bowed once more, then left.

Anna rubbed her shoulder where a stubborn ache persisted, her gaze falling on the suit of armor that stood guard at the foot of the stairs. Greyley had well-developed taste, she decided reluctantly. She might have placed the armor in a less prominent position, which would shift attention to the colorful tapestry that covered the west wall, but other than that, everything was as it should be. Everything except . . . no, something was missing.

She turned around, slowly staring at each object. It was a beautiful area, spacious and filled with an intriguing assortment of items. If only it wasn't quite so . . . dark.

She wondered if Greyley would consider adding a mural on the high ceiling. It would brighten the entire area and make the entryway more inviting. Maybe a sky vista, with a few scattered clouds. Or a group of cherubs, floating on a sea of feathered clouds. "Something brighter."

"Brighter than what?" came a deep voice behind her.

Anna whirled to see Greyley standing in the doorway to

the library, his arms crossed over his broad chest, his dark gaze fixed on her. She pressed a hand to her thudding heart. She wished someone would tie a bell about that man's neck. It would save her heart countless thuds. "I was just thinking that the foyer is too dark."

He raised his brows.

"Not that it's any business of mine," she said hastily, "though I do think you should move the armor to a less prominent position."

"You do, do you?" He regarded her with that lazy, heavy-lidded gaze, just like a large cat trying to decide which end of the mouse to devour first.

Anna decided to take his lack of verbal response as encouragement. "Have you ever thought of having a mural placed on the ceiling?"

"No."

"It's the first place one sees on entering the house," she said, warming to the topic. "It would make a wonderful impression and—"

"Miss Thraxton," he broke in, frustration and amusement warring for a place in his tone. "You cannot stop interfering, can you?"

"I wasn't interfering; I was making suggestions. Friendly, simple suggestions."

"Call it what you will. I'm glad I caught you before you went upstairs. We have unfinished business, you and I."

For some reason, thoughts of their forbidden kiss flashed through her mind. But she could tell by the way he was looking at her that it wasn't anything that pleasant. What could he want? Surely she hadn't—oh yes. *Matilda*. "Ah, yes. Of course. Perhaps after I've had a chance to change—"

"It would be best to discuss this now, while the children are not about."

She supposed he was right; it would be better to discuss this while they had some privacy. Anna glanced cautiously at him from under her lashes, trying to gauge the level of his irritation. He didn't *appear* too upset. He pushed the door wider, and the light from the library brushed the muscled lines of his hip and legs and outlined his powerful arms.

Anna found that she couldn't swallow. Nor could she move. She could just stand. And stare. Goodness, but the man was well built. She wondered how often he rode, for only steady exercise could—

"Miss Thraxton? Do we discuss this now?"

"Oh. Yes. Of course. Right now."

For some absurd reason, she was suddenly aware of how she must look, hot and mussed, her hair falling from the pins. She ran a damp hand over the skirt of her habit, wondering if she was also splattered in mud. "I hope I don't get mud on your rug."

He didn't answer, but stepped back from the doorway, obviously expecting her to follow. A bath was out of the question until Lord High and Mighty had his say. It was just like Greyley to ignore the niceties of life. The thought prickled at her and gave her a new sense of irritation, which she held closely. It was much more comfortable than the heated flickers she fought when looking at his finely muscled thighs.

A hot shiver shook her at the thought and she crossed her arms beneath her breasts as she followed Greyley into the library. Once there, she asked in an ungracious voice, "Well?"

Greyley stood leaning against the mantel, an arrogant pose that suited him well. "I wanted to speak with you about two matters."

"Fine, but first—"

"Have a seat, Miss Thraxton."

There was definite menace in his tone. Now was not the

time to explain how his manner tended to push the children into disobedience. The stern cast of his jaw seemed to tighten, and she swallowed the thought before she could explore it.

Moving slowly enough to let him know what she thought of his ill-mannered tactics, she found a chair, carefully smoothed her skirts, and then perched on the edge of the seat.

"Miss Thraxton," he said, completely unmoved by her silent communications, "I will not be blackmailed. Not by you, or anyone else. From now on, any personal information given to you by my sister will remain in confidence."

Anthony tried to keep his voice even, but firm. He was not an unfair man. But he had to stifle Miss Thraxton's attempts to run more than the nursery. "Do I make myself clear?"

To his immense irritation, she didn't argue or even appear shocked. Instead, she folded her hands in her lap and said meekly, "Yes, my lord."

The gesture was so patently fake that he snorted.

She abandoned the pose immediately, leaning back in her chair and regarding him with a tired, but humorous smile. Her hair had fallen on one side, the thick curls hugging her neck, in vivid contrast to her white skin. "In my own defense, I did not repeat anything that was improper for a child to hear."

"How could you?" he retorted immediately. "I didn't do anything improper. The relationship was as short-lived as it was chaste."

"That one, perhaps. But what about Margaret, or Jane, or that woman from the inn in town—I don't believe any of those flirtations were quite so chaste."

A roar filled Anthony's ears and sought to throttle his thoughts. It was a full moment before he could speak. "The next time I see my sister, I am going to kill her."

"Don't blame her. I'm sure she never thought I might use such information against you." Miss Thraxton's gaze fell on her hands, still neatly clasped in her lap. "But you are right— I do owe you an apology. I'm sorry, Greyley. It will not happen again."

She looked sincere. So sincere that Anthony wasn't sure how to respond. He narrowed his gaze. "Don't bam me, Thraxton."

"I would never apologize insincerely. I'd think you'd know that about me."

Strangely, he did know that. She was irritating and a practiced scamp, but she hadn't a malicious bone in her body. His gaze immediately flickered over that body and he noticed how tightly the coat fit over her breasts, curving around them in a most fascinating manner as if—

He caught himself before his thoughts could progress any further. Damn it, this wasn't how he'd planned this conversation. He raked a hand through his hair. "Miss Thraxton, I believe we should begin again. We've gotten off to an unpleasant start—"

"Nonsense. I had a very good ride with the children. And you were right about the mare; she's a sweet goer." Enthusiasm warmed her voice until it was throaty, as sensual as her glorious hair. "Such a graceful animal."

Anthony found himself looking at the slight sheen of perspiration that touched her neck where it rose above her collar. He remembered cupping his hands about that slender column, of feeling the hot beat of her pulse, of the taste of her on his lips.

His body tightened in response. God, but she was a delectable piece, even with that proud nose.

"It really was lovely," Anna continued, her voice filtering through his jangled thoughts. "Smooth and long. Quite enjoyable."

The words echoed dizzily in Anthony's head. *Smooth and long. Quite enjoyable. Bloody hell, what was she talking about?* "Smooth?"

"The horse's gait." She frowned. "Are you well? You look ill."

He was. He was burning with a fever to taste her again. He grabbed his wayward thoughts by the tail and tried to rein them in. "I'm fine. There was one other thing we needed to discuss. The children's schedule—"

Thraxton stood. Or, more correctly, she popped out of her chair so quickly that Anthony was tempted to take a step back.

"I'm glad you brought that up," she said, her chin level, a warm light silvering her gray eyes. "I'll be certain to set up a schedule that will benefit the children."

"They already have a schedule—"

"Does it include mathematics?"

What was she doing? "Naturally it includes mathematics. And reading and—"

"Watercolors?"

"For the girls."

"French?"

Anthony shook his head, bewildered as to where this line of conversation was heading.

"Ah ha!" she said triumphantly. "No French. I thought as much." She offered him a dazzling smile. "I'll have to adjust their schedule to make room for it. I will begin work on that immediately." She turned and crossed to the door, talking as she went. "It should only take me a week or so to finish it, but I'll put forth the best effort to get it done in a proper fashion."

A week? To finish a schedule? "Thraxton, I don't think you understand the importance of keeping the children on task. They have suffered from a lack of constraint and it is important to provide them with structure."

She stopped at the door. "Greyley, there's no need to be so oppressive."

He blinked, unable to believe he'd just heard aright. "Oppressive?"

"Inflexible. Stodgy. Stiff. Stuffy." She said the last word as if it tasted bad.

That hurt. "I'm sorry you find my company so objectionable," he bit out. "But that does not change your duties. I will have that schedule on my desk by tomorrow, if you please."

"A week."

"Three days."

"Done." She regarded him with a pleased smile. "Was there anything else you needed to say? I really must change."

Anthony didn't like the way she eyed him, as if he were a bull and she a red flag. "Miss Thraxton, you may think this a facetious matter, but—"

"It is obviously important to you," she said, still with that firm smile on her lips. "You'll get your schedule, Greyley. In the meantime, you can work on governing your temper *and* your language." She didn't wait for an answer, but with a swish of that damnably seductive habit, she was gone.

It took Anthony a full moment to realize that he'd been dismissed. Dismissed, discounted, and disrespected. He closed his eyes and slowly, slowly counted to twenty, but still he was a jangled mass of frustration and something else. Something heady and hot. Something that increased his frustration to the boiling point. Something that felt suspiciously like disappointed desire.

He opened his eyes to discover that his hands were balled into fists. It was true—he desired Thraxton, wanted to feel her beneath him, wanted to taste her skin, wanted to dive beneath the trim line of her skirts and feel her moistness. His manhood quivered and stiffened as his vision filled with tight red curls and long, long white legs, of full rounded calves and delicately arched feet.

He shook his head, but the vision refused to leave. Instead it taunted him more. The legs curved, then parted—he moaned and dropped his head into his hands. God help him, but he hadn't lusted this strongly over a woman since . . . well, since the untouchable Matilda, if truth be known.

Women had always been available to Anthony. Coming into his title at an early age, his fortune beyond respectable, he'd been pursued by hordes of matchmaking mothers and their avaricious daughters, all of whom managed to bore Anthony to tears.

Still, it had been no secret that one day he would have to provide an heir. It was his duty, after all. On reaching his thirty-fifth birthday, he'd decided the time was now and he'd gone about the business of selecting a bride just as he went about everything else—carefully and methodically, making lists and checking out financial situations. It was amazing how many of England's great families were insolvent.

He's almost given up hope when he'd met Charlotte. She was everything the Elliots were not—quiet, well-mannered, and gentle. Her parents had trained her well, and she would never embarrass him or cause him alarm.

Charlotte's goals in life would be to see to his happiness and the happiness of their children and to the smooth running of Greyley House. He, in turn, would give her the benefit of his maturity and wisdom, and a handsome amount of pocket money. In return, she would provide him with an heir and make no ridiculous demands of his time.

Unlike Anna Thraxton, who would, he was certain, meddle in the affairs of any man she became entangled with.

The word "entangled" fired his imagination once more, and he was assailed with the image of his new governess, naked and impertinent, her firm round bottom just out of reach, that saucy smile aimed not at him, but at some other man who looked disgustingly besotted.

Anthony slammed a hand onto the surface of the desk, the loud noise dispelling the pictures in his mind. Good God, what was he doing? A liaison with Thraxton would be a mistake of the first order. It was unthinkable.

Or was it? She *was* staying under his roof, which made her convenient if nothing else. And it was certainly no sin in society's jaded eyes to have a mistress. Some men felt compelled to do so, as a measure of their standing.

Anthony rubbed his chin and stared with unseeing eyes at the mural over his head. Anna's exposure to the harshness of life had removed any sort of troublesome innocence she might have once had, not that he thought her experienced in sexual matters. He was fairly certain that for all her bravado, she was untouched in that one area.

The thought tantalized him further, even as he acknowledged it put an end to the possibility of having her as a mistress. She was a handful, was Thraxton, he decided with a deep sense of regret. She met him glare for glare and never so much as flinched. And she was no self-appointed martyr who would cry at the slightest imagined insult. She was also far more attractive than any governess had a right to be. So much so that he'd been in imminent danger of yanking her to him and tasting her impudent mouth no fewer than three times just today.

Perhaps it was her passionate nature that intrigued him so. Whatever Thraxton did, she did with all her heart. It was, he suspected, yet another quality that made her such a good governess, as well as such a damnable nuisance. There would be no light flirtation with a woman like her, and he knew it. As soon as he took her to bed, she'd order new curtains for the entire house. Then she'd set about organizing the furniture, perhaps even ordering that damned mural for the entryway.

Once she'd organized Greyley House to her liking, it wouldn't be long before she cast her improving glance his way and started making suggestions to remake him. There was no way he'd even let any woman interfere with his life in such a way. No, his relationship with Thraxton would be no more than employer and employee.

That decided, Anthony sent for Dalmapple and spent several worthy hours engrossed in the business of running his estate.

Chapter 12

One should never ask a man questions about his personal life. He just might answer and then you, my dear, would have to listen.

Lady Clives-Brandley to her friend, Mrs. Fairfax,
while walking the maze at Hamilton House

After a hot bath and a short rest, Anna went to the nursery, where she found the children huddled together, whispering.

"Hello, children," she said brightly. "Planning something fun?"

Elizabeth started up from the table, her face pink. "Miss Thraxton! We were . . . we were . . ." She cast a wild glance at Desford.

He scowled and said sullenly, "We were planning on making a fort."

Elizabeth nodded, coloring even more deeply. "Th-that's right. A fort. We were going to make a fort."

"Hm," Anna said. She walked to the table and pulled out a chair. With the exception of two chairs beside the fireplace, the furnishings in the nursery were made to the children's size. She settled into the small seat, her knees well over the edge of the table, so she clasped her arms about them. "Perhaps I can help. I used to make all sorts of forts when I was a child."

Desford leaned back in his chair and crossed his arms. "If you've come to teach us, you are wasting your time."

Selena copied Desford's gesture perfectly, her bottom lip thrust forward. "Wasting your time," she repeated.

Anna hid a smile. "I haven't come to teach. That's for tomorrow. For today, I thought we might just have our dinner together."

"Dinner?" Elizabeth looked around. "You're going to eat in here? With us?"

"Of course. It will be much more fun in here with you than in the dining room."

Marian nodded sagely. "We ate in there once. The table came to here." She held her hand at a level with her chin.

"It was horrible," Elizabeth said as if suddenly remembering. "And they made us eat duck." She shuddered.

"With orange sauce," Marian added. "It made Richard sick."

The children all regarded Richard with respect. He sat back in his chair with a sudden smile, showing a gap where he'd lost one of his front teeth.

At that moment Mrs. Stibbons bustled in, followed by two footmen and the faithful Lily, all carrying trays of food. Anna noticed that the meal was simply prepared and that the children ate heartily. Even Desford, who let her know he resented her presence with his sullen glances even while he ate with the gusto of a starved horse.

Lily stayed with the children after Mrs. Stibbons left. The maid quietly sat in one corner and did some mending, watching the children as they finished their meal.

Anna talked to Elizabeth. They chatted about dolls and hair and anything else that Anna thought Desford might not want to hear. Soon enough, he pushed his plate away and got up from the table. He called Richard and Marian with him and they resumed their whispered discussion. Anna watched him through narrowed eyes. "Tell me, Elizabeth, why isn't Desford at Eton? Most boys his age would be there."

"The earl wanted him to go, but Desford refused."

"Greyley gave him the choice?"

Elizabeth nodded. "He was disappointed Desford didn't wish to go. He didn't say so, but you could tell."

"Why didn't Desford wish to go?"

"'Cause the earl is just trying to separate us. Like Grandmama said he would."

Ah. So that was the way of things. "Perhaps the earl just wished Desford to have the same opportunities that he himself did. I believe the earl went to Eton when he was a child. He most likely believes the experience will help Desford."

Elizabeth frowned. "Do you think so?"

"Oh yes. After all, had he really wished to separate you, he would have done so already. He doesn't need an excuse."

"Grandmama says he doesn't want us together."

"Perhaps she is wrong. Adults frequently are, you know."

Elizabeth thought about this for a moment. Finally she turned to Anna, her blue gaze serious. "Are *you* ever wrong?"

"Elizabeth, no one is perfect. All we can do is our best and hope that it is enough."

The girl bit her lip, her brow folded as she considered this.

"There you are, Elizabeth." It was Desford. He stood just behind Anna. "Marian wants you to come and play fort with us."

The little girl cast a quick glance at Anna, who smiled encouragingly. "Go and play."

Elizabeth gave her a grateful smile and hopped up from her chair. Desford turned to follow her, but Anna placed her hand on his arm.

"Desford, Elizabeth was telling me about Eton. I'm surprised you didn't wish to go."

A shadow crossed his face, quickly replaced by his usual sullen expression. "I don't want to go anywhere. Not without my brother and sisters." He pulled his arm free and went to join his siblings.

Anna stayed where she was for another half hour, watching the children play. She quickly learned that while Desford was the undisputable leader, his brother and sisters were by no means submissive followers. Marian especially seemed disinclined to listen to her eldest brother, while Elizabeth questioned his every suggestion. Richard, too, managed to indicate his displeasure by shaking his head in an emphatic "no." Still, Desford managed to win most arguments.

It began to dawn on Anna that for an eleven-year-old, Desford showed an uncommon amount of leadership to bring such a fractious group to point. She was just wondering how to deal with Desford when a shadow fell across her and she looked up to see Greyley.

Dressed in formal evening attire, he looked devastatingly handsome, a snowy white cravat knotted about his throat, his black coat stretched across his broad shoulders. "Miss Thraxton, I wish to speak with you."

"Of course. As soon as the children are in bed, I will—"

"Now." His gaze flickered to the children, who watched with interest. "Please," he added grimly.

Anna sighed and stood, then followed him out into the hallway. Once there, he crossed his arms over his chest and looked down at her with a frown. "Miss Thraxton, dinner is served at seven in the dining room. Lady Putney and I have been waiting."

"I'm a governess here, not a guest. It would be highly improper for me to eat dinner with your family."

"You'll eat with us," he said, implacable as ever.

He really was impossible. But he was also her employer, and Anna was not about to cross that bridge. "Lord Greyley, I cannot—"

"Anna?" Grandpapa stood in the hallway, dressed in his best black coat. He peered at her, a question in his blue eyes. "Ah, Greyley found you. The footman came to tell us it was time to go down to dinner, but you were nowhere to be found."

"I have already eaten."

"Then eat again," Grandpapa said. "Come along, my dear. Everyone is waiting."

Anna tucked a stray tendril of her hair behind one ear. She was tempted. She really was. It would be nice to join Greyley and Grandpapa every evening. She could almost picture herself sitting with them, laughing about some absurd tidbit from the children, feeling like a part of the family. Unfortunately, she knew where such imaginings got one; she'd learned about that from her first position. The memory of that horrid time blurred her imaginations to dust. "Grandpapa, I cannot eat with my employer. It would be improper."

Greyley made a disgusted noise but she shushed him with a single look. "You should know that. Furthermore, I wish to eat with the children. It's important that I spend as much time with my charges as possible, especially in the beginning."

Grandpapa shook his head. "As stubborn as your grandmother. Come on, Greyley. She's made up her mind. I can see it in her eyes."

The earl regarded Anna for a moment before he cut a glance toward Grandpapa. "Sir Phineas, I'm glad you, at least, will be joining us. I daresay you know many interesting tidbits from Miss Thraxton's childhood. She has the advantage of being conversant with mine through her acquaintance with my sister."

Good Lord, the blasted man was going to trick Grandpapa into telling him all sorts of horrid stories about her. Anna opened her mouth to protest, but Grandpapa was ahead of her.

"Oh the stories I could tell," he said gaily. "Did you know that Anna is allergic to blueberries? Swells up like a balloon. One time, when she was six, she—"

"Grandpapa, I don't think the earl is interested in hearing about me."

"Aren't I?" Greyley asked.

Grandpapa waved a hand. "Never think it, my dear. The earl is interested in all his guests. Now, if you'll excuse me, we left Lady Putney alone. Think I'll join her until you two are finished here." He limped away, leaving Anna and the earl in the hallway.

As Grandpapa's footsteps faded, the earl leaned closer. "Come to dinner."

Anna raised her eyes to his, then wished she hadn't. He was so close she could see the gold flecks in his eyes and the firm line of his chin. "I can't."

"You, Miss Thraxton, are my sister's best friend. It is only right that you eat with us in the dining hall."

"That doesn't matter."

"It does to me. It will also matter to Sara."

"I will write to her and explain the situation."

He stayed where he was, his chest not an inch from hers, his face dangerously close. The air about them hummed with vitality and Anna caught herself unconsciously tracing her bottom lip with the edge of her tongue, remembering the feel of his lips on hers.

Greyley's gaze locked on her mouth. "Thraxton," he said, his voice low.

A slow shiver traced down her spine, sending a delicate

feathering of sensation across her skin. She felt drawn to him, as if some force was propelling her into his arms. The moment grew and stretched, neither of them moving. Just as she thought she couldn't fight the impulse any longer, he let out his breath. "If you aren't going to eat with us, what will you do?"

"I plan on resting in my room. I have things to do before the children begin their lessons."

He took her arm, his fingers warm. "Then come. I will escort you there."

Oh no, he wouldn't. Anna wasn't about to go anywhere near her room and that huge bed. Not with Greyley. Not while her mouth still tingled in memory of a day-old kiss. She dug her heels into the hall runner and refused to budge. "I know the way to my own room, thank you."

His brows lowered. Anna wished he weren't quite so tall. She wasn't used to looking up, even a few inches. It was disconcerting and for some unknown reason, it made her want to giggle like a silly girl, which was not something she wanted to be. Ever.

But especially not now. She gave a prim sniff. "Unhand me, sir."

"Unhand . . . you sound as if you think I would ravish you."

"Men pursue women for only two reasons. The first is marriage, which is out of the question—so it must be to form an alliance."

He stood so still he appeared to be a statue. "An alliance?"

"An *unsavory* alliance." Her cheeks heated. It was damnably awkward, but it needed to be said. "I think there has been a mistake. I am not the kind of woman to engage in such activities."

"I wasn't going to do anything 'unsavory.' I was merely offering to escort you to your room. I am being polite."

She eyed him warily. "And that's all?"

"Miss Thraxton, I believe I once promised you that I would kiss you again only if you asked."

Each word he made curved and moved his mouth. Anna couldn't look away. His lips were innately beautiful, as carved and strong as the man himself. There was something about a man who knew what he wanted. Oh, it was an irritating trait, she had to admit that small fact. But it was also damnably attractive. And every time she faced Greyley and his infuriating certainty, the pull of attraction grew stronger. So strong that all she could think about was the feel of his mouth on hers, of his broad chest pressing against her breasts, of his hands . . . "Oh yes," she murmured.

"Yes what?" His gaze flickered across her face, lingering on her lips, her throat. "Thraxton, do you—"

She kissed him. She moved forward a few inches and placed her lips on his, a chaste sort of kiss, but a kiss nonetheless. As sad as it was her calm good sense was rudely ousted by a pair of firm, masculine lips.

Greyley didn't hesitate. He lifted her to him, deepening the touch, his mouth hotly possessive. The heat that simmered between them exploded into an instant conflagration, and her skin flushed from the tips of her toes to the delicate skin on the back of her neck. She couldn't think, couldn't do anything but revel in the feelings that swept over her.

His mouth slid from hers and his breath blew hot on her cheek, tickling her ear and sending shivers of delight spiraling through her. "God, Thraxton," he murmured against her temple. "You taste so good."

So did he. Anna trailed her lips across his mouth, to his chin, and down the strong column of his throat. His cheek rubbed over her hair, the faint stubble catching the long strands. "Your room," he murmured into her ear, his hand sliding across her shoulder to cup her breast.

Thousands of sensations exploded through her as he teased her nipple through her clothing. It was heaven. Anna sank against the wall, held up only by his roving, questing hands and her trembling knees. She closed her eyes and let the incredible feeling wash through her, over and over again.

"Your room," he whispered, more urgently this time. "It's just down the hall. Let me—"

"M-Miss Thraxton?"

Anna's eyes flew open and she turned. There, standing outside the nursery, stood Elizabeth. She looked from Anna to Greyley with wide, shocked eyes. Greyley immediately stepped away, and Anna was left swaying in place.

She cleared her throat. "Elizabeth, Lord Greyley was just . . . whispering a secret."

"Yes," he immediately added. "A very important secret."

He didn't even sound out of breath, damn him.

"What secret?" Elizabeth asked, diverted.

The earl crossed his arms and rocked back on his heels, looking annoyingly smug. "About something Miss Thraxton is *very* fond of doing."

"What are you fond of doing?" Elizabeth asked, looking at Anna with eager eyes. Greyley stood watching, amusement lurking in his gaze.

Amusement, but not a speck of the passion that had so shaken Anna. That jolted her back to life. She smoothed her skirts with trembling hands and pasted a smile on her mouth. "Lord Greyley said that we might ride every day if you and the others wish."

Elizabeth gave a jump of joy. "Every day!" She turned and dashed back into the nursery, shouting her good news.

There was a moment of silence. "Strange," he said, "but I don't recall saying anything about riding every day."

"Well, you did. Right between the 'you taste so good' and the 'let's go to your room.'" Anna straightened her dress, which had somehow gotten twisted. "It was very kind of you to allow us to ride so often. I'm sure the children and I will enjoy it very much." She smoothed her skirts, somehow afraid to meet his gaze. "Lady Putney and Grandpapa will wonder where you are. You had better go."

"Anna, I . . ."

"No. We've said enough."

To her disappointment, he only nodded. "We can discuss this later."

Anna curtsied, then turned and made her way back to her room. Once there, she shut the door and leaned against it, her breath uneven. Good Lord, what had come over her? Whatever it was, it would never happen again. Never.

She'd taken this position intent on bringing order to Greyley House, not to disrupt her own life. And that is what would happen if she allowed the physical bond that fired between the earl and her every time they were alone.

Perhaps that was the answer—she would never be alone with him again. In a large household, populated by a virtual army of servants, that shouldn't be too difficult. Anna prepared for bed, yet she continued to mull over that impetuous kiss. It had proven one thing—Greyley was not as immune to her as he pretended. It wasn't much of a sop to her tattered pride, but it was something. Something indeed.

Anna managed to avoid being alone with the earl for two entire days. Not that it was difficult, as being with the children took all her time. But they proved to be challenging enough. Desford was alternately sullen, resentful, caustic, and rude. The other children tended to follow his lead, though less often as the hours passed.

But it still took its toll, and by the end of the second day, she was so weary all she wanted to do was fall into her bed. Grandpapa took one look at her and ordered her dinner to be sent to her room. Also, he didn't once press her about joining the family for dinner, but had talked quietly, then dropped a kiss on her cheek before leaving her in peace.

Too tired to think, she changed into her gown then climbed into the huge bed. The pillows and luxurious bed coverings enveloped her tired body. She fell into a dreamless sleep and remained that way until something brushed against her leg.

Anna was wide awake in the blink of an eye. She waited, breath held . . . but nothing stirred. She had just convinced herself that she'd imagined it when it happened again. And this time there was no mistaking the feel of dry, slithery scales against her bare ankle. With a loud screech, Anna bolted from the bed, scrambling madly to free herself from the heavy tangle of sheets and comforter.

Grandpapa burst into the room, resplendent in a purple robe. "What's wrong?"

Anna kicked at the counterpane and a small black head stuck out from beneath the lace edge.

"Oh dear," Grandpapa said, his lips twitching slightly. "A lizard."

"I-it was in my b-bed." To her horror, tears welled in her eyes. "It t-touched me."

Grandpapa was beside her in an instant, patting her shoulder. "There, there. No harm done. It's a harmless little lizard, and not even a big one at that."

She shuddered. "Do they bite?"

"Not enough to hurt you." Grandpapa stared at the lizard thoughtfully. "I wonder how he got in here? It's strange it was attracted to the linens. They usually hide in the woodwork."

Anna didn't answer. She had no question about how the lizard had gotten inside the house and into her bed. "Desford. The children have been whispering for the last two days. I knew something was afoot."

Grandpapa pursed his lips. "Seems your instincts were correct."

"Unfortunately." Anna looked at the fallen counterpane, spilled across the blue and gold carpet. The lizard darted from beneath a fold of lace and made his way to the top of the mound, where it sat, lolling its tongue as if it were king of the castle. "I think it's time Mr. Desford and I began to play in earnest."

Thus it was that Desford, who was lying awake at that very moment, congratulating himself on making his new governess scream, was somewhat shocked when the door opened and Miss Thraxton entered. She was dressed in a white night rail, her hair braided, and a large bundle of white clutched at arm's length.

She walked past Richard, who tossed back his covers and sat up, watching with wide eyes as she marched straight to Desford.

"I believe you left something of yours in my room," she said and then shook her counterpane over his head.

Something small and black and somewhat slithery fell into Desford's bed. Or rather, onto his legs, where it immediately burrowed beneath his nightgown and disappeared.

The feel of those tiny suctioned feet on his bared skin made Desford yelp and grab at his night rail. The lizard scrambled to get away and burrowed deeper, finding a hiding spot in Desford's lap. Desford gasped loudly, his face paling as he dug for the small animal. Finally he recovered it, but not until it had traversed his body three entire times.

"Very good," Miss Thraxton said, as if she hadn't watched the entire proceedings with a wide grin on her face. "Take it to the window and let it go."

Desford was tempted to toss the lizard on her, but she pinned him with such a steely gaze that he realized it wouldn't be a good idea. Not now, anyway. Careful not to look at Richard, who appeared to be suffering from a spate of giggles, Desford climbed from his bed and did as he was told, silently planning how he would thrash his brother as soon as Miss Thraxton was gone.

As soon as the lizard scampered from sight, Miss Thraxton reached past him and shut the window. "The next time you put something in my bed, I shall put two of them in yours. Now go to sleep, Desford. We have a very busy day tomorrow." With that she leaned over, kissed him on the top of his head, and left.

Desford stared at the closed door for a long time. She'd *kissed* him. He rubbed his head where her lips had been. Of all the governesses they'd had, not a one of them had dared confront him so directly. And none of them had kissed him.

It wasn't to be borne. He leaped onto his bed and plunked his hands onto his narrow hips and yelled at the closed door. "You think that has solved anything? We have not yet begun to fight!"

Richard's only answer was a choked laugh. Desford threw a pillow at him and then climbed beneath his sheets, where he spent a restless night planning new strategies.

Chapter 13

Lud, you don't have to tell me about the foibles of mankind. I daresay I've slept with every one of them.

Mrs. Fairfax to her niece Viscountess Rundall,
while watching the fireworks at Vauxhall Gardens

Mr. Dalmapple stifled a sigh. For the past half hour, he'd attempted to engage the earl in a meaningful conversation on the possibility of building some new tenants' cottages. Normally the earl would have joined in with enthusiasm; he was a man who took his responsibilities to heart. But this time, he was so distracted that all he did was give faint, monosyllabic answers and stare out the window.

Dalmapple supposed he understood; the earl's wards were enough to drive any man to distraction. Or drink, for that matter. Dalmapple gave a tiny shudder, glad he was both unmarried and childless. He doubted Lord Greyley was aware of the antics that had been going on between the earl's wards and the new governess, though the entire staff was abuzz. Abuzz and delighted—they had all been made to suffer for the children's high spirits, and it was somewhat satisfying seeing them get a little of their own.

He wondered if he should say something to the earl, but

then decided against it. Let Miss Thraxton continue her war without bothering the poor earl. She seemed more than capable of handling Greyley's hellions.

A knock on the door preceded the footman. He crossed to the desk and held out a silver salver. "A note, my lord. From Miss Thraxton in the nursery."

The earl swooped up the note, and Dalmapple watched his expression. The poor man was obviously tied in knots over the whole affair.

"Damn." Greyley tossed the note onto his desk. He cast a dark glance at the footman. "Did you tell her that I wished to speak with her *today*?"

"Yes, my lord."

"And what did she say?"

The footman colored slightly. "I don't believe I heard—"

"*What did she say?*" the earl repeated.

"She said she had better things to do than make up a schedule and that if you wanted one so badly—" The footman swallowed.

The earl was clearly stunned. After a brief moment he said, "I see. That will be all."

The footman bowed, then left, his footsteps muffled by the heavy rug. Dalmapple waited until the door had closed before he delicately cleared his throat. "Is there anything I can do, my lord?"

The earl shook his head. "No. I will handle this matter myself." He stood and smoothed his coat in an uncharacteristic manner.

Dalmapple frowned, noticing for the first time that the earl was wearing an intricately tied cravat. It was quite unlike Lord Greyley to bother with such, especially when here in the country. "Do you wish me to complete the estimates for the new cottages?"

"What? Oh, the estimates. Of course."

The man was clearly distraught. "My lord, I hope you will forgive me, but ah, are the children well?"

"Yes, of course they're well."

"And the new governess? Is she turning out as you expected?"

This time Dalmapple had the earl's entire attention. "No," Greyley said with a thoughtful frown. "She's nothing like I expected at all."

The poor, poor earl. Dalmapple gave a quick prayer of thanks for his canary, two dogs, and three cats. None of them talked back. And only one had what one could call a mischievous disposition. He gathered his papers and stood. "Shall we meet at a later time?"

The earl nodded, his mind obviously already a thousand miles away. Sighing sadly, Dalmapple tucked his papers into his satchel and left.

"What is it today?" Grandpapa asked, peering around Anna's bedchamber. "More rocks beneath your mattress? Or did they spread cookie crumbles in your sheets in hopes of drawing ants?"

It had been three days since Anna had found the lizard, and Desford hadn't budged an inch. If anything, every day he seemed a little more fractious. But that was to be expected. He couldn't like someone besting him at his own game.

She tightened the tie on her wrapper and gave the room a perplexed frown. "I haven't been able to find anything."

"Perhaps you've worn them down." Grandpapa chuckled. "I wish you'd seen Master Desford's face when he bit into his morning toast and found that you'd salted it."

"I daresay it wasn't near as humorous as his expression when he went to put his hand into his saddlebag to get his lunch on our ride yesterday and instead pulled out a neatly wrapped block of wood slathered with molasses. None of the other children would let him have their food and so he came home hungry."

"And angry, I'd wager."

"Yes. I had hoped that would have done the trick, for he's bound to get tired of this foolishness some time or another."

Grandpapa sighed. "Well, I'll leave you to dress. I'm going for a walk. The gardens are lovely in the morning." He crossed to the door, then halted. "Shall I look under your bed for you?"

"I've already looked. Perhaps you're right and Desford is finished." She smiled. "It won't last, but it should put us on an even playing ground, and that is what is most important."

Grandpapa grinned. "If you find yourself stuck to the bedpost or some such thing, just yell out the window and I'll return to assist you."

"Thank you," she said dryly. "You're too kind."

He winked and then left, closing the door behind him. Anna took one last look around, checking under table edges and peering into the wardrobe. Finally, satisfied that everything was as it should be she began to dress. She was just thrusting her foot into her pantaloons when she realized what trick had been played. Someone had sewn the legs of the garment completely shut.

There she was, balancing on one leg, her foot halfway in, but unable to go any further. She tried to pull her foot out, but the garment tangled about her ankle and she lost her balance. She hopped wildly, trying to regain her footing, but it was impossible. Within moments, she tumbled to the ground, right onto her rump, her left elbow catching the edge of the dresser.

Afterward she lay staring at the ceiling, her pantaloons wrapped about one foot, waiting for the ache in her behind to subside. That was it. Today was the end of this little war. Anna peeled the pantaloons off her foot and climbed to her feet. She'd best hurry if she wanted to get to the nursery before the children.

Anna was sitting in the chair by the fireplace when Lily brought the children in. They peeked at her, giggling as they did so. Desford had apparently shared his little trick, for they were all grinning from ear to ear.

Anna refused to admit that anything was wrong. She greeted them gaily, asked about their breakfast, and settled them down to work. They kept exchanging glances and she could see that they were wondering what had gone awry.

She kept them busy for the next hour working on a variety of things when she turned around to find Greyley standing in the doorway. Her heart gave a strange leap. "Lord Greyley. What a pleasant surprise." *Why* did he have to appear now, of all times?

"Miss Thraxton," he returned, his jaw tight. "I sent a note this morning asking to meet with you."

"So you did. But I'm very busy right now," she said, glancing at the children. "Perhaps another time."

Anthony noticed that she seemed uncharacteristically restless. He frowned. "It has been three days. You, Miss Thraxton, owe me a schedule."

"Of course. You'll get one as soon as I have it ready." She walked toward the door as if anxious to get him to leave. "Thank you for coming, but the children and I are very busy today."

Anthony pulled to a halt. She was far too anxious to get him to leave. "I think I will stay for a while. Just to see how things are progressing." He found the largest chair the nursery offered and seated himself. He then crossed his arms and leaned back with the air of a man settled for the duration.

Thraxton did not look pleased to have him there. For several minutes she looked as if she might say something, but finally she shrugged and turned away. Moments passed, during which Anthony noticed that the children seemed uneasy. They glanced at one another and watched Miss Thraxton warily.

Anna finally broke the silence. "Desford, would you bring Richard a new sheet of paper?"

Desford went to rise, but fell back in his chair. He sat, stunned, then scowled and tried to rise again. Once more he fell back into his chair.

Elizabeth blinked. "What is it?"

"Can't you get up?" Anthony asked. He glanced at Anna and surprised a ghost of a smile on her lips, but it was gone before he could be sure.

Desford tried to stand again. This time he made it, but his chair went with him. "It's stuck to my pants!" he said in a voice of blank wonder. He pushed at the chair, and it slowly released and dropped to the floor with a thunk.

The seat was covered with a thick grayish paste. "Glue," Desford said blankly. "Someone put glue in my chair."

Serena placed a hand over her open mouth, her eyes on the seat of her brother's pants. "Desford, your pants are wet. You look like you've p—"

"I know what it looks like," he snapped, cheeks pink. He glared at Elizabeth. "Did you—"

"Of course not!" she said indignantly, tossing her brown curls. "How could I? I was with you all morning."

Desford whipped his glare to Richard.

Richard shook his head, his brown hair flopping into his eyes.

"It had to be someone," Desford said menacingly. "It had to be—" Suddenly he swung his gaze to Thraxton. "It was *you*."

Anthony waited for her to deny it, but instead she smiled serenely. Desford's face reddened.

"I believe I won that trick," she said calmly.

Elizabeth, who had been staring curiously at Desford, suddenly giggled. Which set off Marian and then Selena. Even Richard had a ghost of a smile on his face.

Anthony wasn't sure he liked any of this. "Did you really put glue on his seat?"

"Desford and I have been trading jokes, haven't we, Desford?"

The boy's mouth continued to open and close, his face an alarming shade of red. "You—you—"

"Easy there." Anna lifted her brows. "It's a joke, Desford. Rather like stitching someone's pantaloons closed. Ever heard of anyone doing such a thing?"

Desford shrugged, some of his anger melting away. "Once or twice."

"Yes, well, although that seems like a very funny thing, it is quite possible someone could get hurt."

Elizabeth's giggles ceased. "How could someone get hurt from that?"

Anna pushed up her sleeve. A huge blue and black bruise appeared on her elbow.

"Oh no," Elizabeth said, looking stricken.

"Good God, Thraxton," Anthony said. "Did Desford—"

"Heavens, no." She smoothed her sleeve back in place. "It was an accident. Nothing more."

A flicker of surprise lit Desford's gaze, but he didn't say anything. Anna locked gazes with the boy. "However, I'm certain it's the last bruise I will get."

The boy's shoulders sagged and he looked away. "May I change my breeches?"

"Certainly. We will wait for you here."

The boy ducked his head in a quick nod, then left while the other children went back to their work.

Anthony stood. "Miss Thraxton, may I speak with you outside?"

She sighed but went with him, admonishing the children to finish their work. Once in the hallway she looked up at him with a challenging set to her jaw. "Yes?"

"How many tricks have they played on you?"

"Not so many that I felt the need to run to you."

Anthony frowned. Always before, he heard about each and every infraction committed by the children. "When *were* you going to inform me of this situation?"

"Never. It's my job to deal with the children, not yours. It's what you paid me to do."

He caught her wrist and pushed the cuff up to reveal the bruise once more. "*This* is not part of your job."

She tugged her arm free and smoothed her sleeve back in place. "No, that was an accident. Greyley, when I reach a point where I feel incapable of dealing with the children, you will hear from me."

He looked down at her, at the sparkle of humor that lit her eyes, at the genuine warmth that curved her mouth into a smile, and a sudden well of anger made him curse. "I'm going to put a stop to this right now."

"Nonsense. Let them play their tricks. It will give me the opportunity to play a few of my own. They really are harmless, you know. They've done nothing truly malicious."

"That's not what my last governess believed."

"Then she must have been prone to overreaction. Mrs.

Stibbons has told me every trick the children have played and none of them warranted the attention they've gotten."

She was amazing. There she stood, having been subjected to God knew how much ink and glue and honey, yet she was able to grin without the least bitterness. The morning light glinted on her auburn hair, setting her creamy skin aglow. "Made of steel, are you, Thraxton?"

She gave him a cheeky grin. "I have my weaknesses. We all do." She glanced through the doorway at the children. "They are basically good children. And very bright to have executed some of their more elaborate plans. Desford is a natural leader."

Anthony had no doubt that Desford could lead armies on siege—he'd had the dubious felicity of seeing him in action. "Miss Thraxton, I'm curious. Just what do you hope to gain by operating at the children's level?"

"Respect and perhaps trust. After that it is simply a matter of establishing a few boundaries and we will all deal famously."

"You make it sound easy."

"No, but I enjoy it anyway. I like helping people." She looked at him and tilted her head to one side, her curls swinging across her shoulder. "You, on the other hand, don't like helping people."

Anthony stiffened. "What do you mean by that? I help people all the time."

"No, you take responsibility for them. You make their decisions, rescue them from their faults, pave the way for them to become even more dependent on you. It's no wonder you're always in a bad mood."

Damn it, why did Thraxton have to always see the worst in him, but the best in everyone else? It seemed grossly unfair. "I'm *not* in a bad mood," he snapped.

She eyed him. "Oh?"

His jaw tightened. "Only with you. With everyone else, I'm very pleasant. Ask anyone."

"The children think you the most horrid-tempered man."

"They do not."

"Shall we ask them?"

Anthony glanced inside the door to where the children sat doing their work. Try as he might, he hadn't been able to get close to them. Or anyone, in fact. It was strange, but when he'd come to the Elliots, he'd lost something. Some facet of his personality. A pleasantness, perhaps.

The thought did not sit well, and he glowered. Elizabeth glanced up and caught his gaze. She flushed a bright red and hurriedly lowered her gaze back to her desk. Anthony frowned. Good God, did they actually *fear* him?

"Did you wish to ask the children or not?"

"I'm certain they believe me an ogre. They haven't given me much chance to show them anything else."

"True. But then *they* are children. *You* are not."

"I am the head of my family, Thraxton. I do what I must."

"Yes, you do. And from what I hear, you meet your responsibilities head on. I was just commenting on the fact that you could do it without growling quite so much. Look around you, Greyley. They are not pieces of bad pottery, but people." She offered him a friendly smile as if she hadn't just mortally offended him. "Now, if you will excuse me, I have work to do." With a pleasant nod, she turned back to the room and took her place beside Richard and began helping the boy with his math.

Anthony stood where he was, flexing and unflexing his hands. She expected him to do something, he just knew it. Anna Thraxton was like that, meddling in other people's affairs and trying to change things. But by God, he would have none of it. His life had been perfect before the children had arrived. They would conform to his expectations and so would Thraxton, no matter how saucy she'd become.

He turned on his heel and left, heading for his library and the waiting bottle of port. As he went, he caught sight of the new maid hired to replace the one the children had chased off. She was trotting down the hallway carrying a bucket, humming off-key. She skid to a halt on seeing Anthony, then glanced around her like a wild animal looking for somewhere to hide. Before he could say a word, she saw an open door and scuttled through it as if afraid for her life, the bucket sloshing against her leg as she went.

Anthony's footsteps slowed to a stop. Good God, could Thraxton be right? Had he become so immersed in his own concerns that he was no longer aware of others? Had he become so grim and unapproachable that he was . . . an ogre?

The thought was as unpalatable as it was unwelcome. Still, Anthony prided himself on being fair. If he had begun to display a severe demeanor, he was certain he'd been provoked. First by the Elliots and now by his charges. Damn them all.

For some reason, knowing he was justified did not help one iota. And it was with a very heavy sigh that he went into his library and closed the door.

Chapter 14

It's not that I don't love Mother. It's just that after an hour in her presence, I feel a very real need to float in a vat of bourbon and not swim to shore for at least a week.

Viscountess Rundall to her brother Lord Jessup
on leaving their mother's London town house

"This will not do at all," Sir Phineas told the smirk-faced Elliot ancestors who looked down from their painted prisons on the east wing gallery wall. Greyley's interest in Anna was not progressing at all as it should. Oh, it had begun strongly enough and there was enough tension in the air whenever they were together that it was quite possible the house might erupt into flames. But for the last week, things had changed.

The problem was Anna. She was simply not cooperating and had forced the earl to avoid her like the plague.

"Give the gal the chance of a lifetime and what does she do with it?" Sir Phineas asked the portraits. "Nothing. Not a blasted thing."

He walked a little farther down the corridor, then glanced over his shoulder. Seeing no one about, he pulled his last, lone cigarillo from his pocket. He reverently sniffed it, the fragrant scent sending a shiver of anticipation down his spine. After a long, silent moment, he put the cigarillo back in his pocket with a regretful sigh, and continued on his way.

As awkward as it was, he was going to have to take a hand in the matter. The longer he stayed at Greyley, the more certain he was that this was where his granddaughter should be. It wasn't just the imposing manor house or the wealth of servants. Rather it was the sense of stern formality that permeated every corner of the house, leaving it as musty and molded as a sepulcher. Someone needed to throw open the curtains and stir the dust into a shower of golden motes. And Anna was very good at stirring things up.

The thunk of his cane on the marble flooring echoed loudly down the hall and made him grimace. This wing was as welcoming as a tomb. And even worse was Greyley himself. He wasn't much more lively than the frozen pictures that hung overhead. Except when embroiled in an argument. He livened up very nicely then.

For the most part, the earl spent each day holed up in the library with Dalmapple, his man of business, where they tended to the matters of the estate. Afterwards Greyley would take an hour or two to survey the planting of the fields, the construction of the new stables, or some other item. Then he would return to the library and bury himself once more.

Sir Phineas shook his head sadly. The library was the very room he had imagined himself ensconced in, feet on the desk, a box of fresh cigarillos at his elbow and a glass of port in hand. Someway, somehow, he had to get the Earl of Greyley *out* of the library and closer to Anna. But how?

The earl was expending his time on items better left to his minions. Delegation was the answer. That was how Sir Phineas had run his estate, after all.

To be fair, he'd lost that estate, though that had been due more to poor investments than to mismanagement. But he'd learned quite a lot about investing and once he was back on his feet financially . . . He smiled, leaning on his cane as he left the east wing.

He soon reached the library. The door opened and Dalmapple appeared. Neatly dressed, with a pinched mouth and a pasty complexion beneath a shock of thick, black hair, the earl's man of business reminded Sir Phineas of a sickly cat.

Dalmapple paused on seeing Phineas, managing a faint, condescending smile. "Good afternoon, Sir Phineas. Were you waiting to see His Lordship?"

"Just on my way in," Phineas said.

"I'm afraid he's engaged. Perhaps you could return at a later time—"

"Oh, I won't keep him a moment." Phineas hurriedly limped toward the door. He closed it on Dalmapple's protests and then leaned against the panel in case the imbecile had the poor manners to chase him. After a moment's silence, Phineas heard the gratifying sound of Dalmapple's receding footsteps.

Greyley looked up from where he sat at Sir Phineas's future desk. "May I assist you?"

"Oh no. Just looking for a book to read to while away the afternoon." He limped to the shelf nearest the desk and pretended to mull over some titles. "Hope I'm not intruding."

The earl offered a brief smile. "Not at all." He returned to the papers before him.

Sir Phineas pulled first one, then another book from the shelf. "I daresay you haven't read *Tales of Woe* by Lord Stanwich, have you?"

"Yes, I have. It's about an exploration journey to India in 1767."

Sir Phineas put the book back on the shelf. "What about *Lavinia* by Emma Jenkins?"

"I don't believe I've read that one. It's a novel of some sort."

"A novel, eh?" Sir Phineas tucked the book under his arm, and cast an oh-so-casual glance at the desk. "What are you working on, Greyley?"

The earl sent him a glance from beneath his brows, then sighed and replaced his pen in the well. "I hope you have found your stay at Greyley House pleasant."

"Oh yes. Very pleasant." Sir Phineas pursed his lips thoughtfully. "But I must say that I am worried about my granddaughter."

Anna Thraxton was the last thing Anthony wanted to talk about. Not only had she flouted him on their last meeting, but she hadn't delivered the children's schedule as he had requested. And now, after their last conversation, he felt awkward even asking for it, as if he were being unreasonable or demanding. It wasn't a feeling he relished. In fact, the whole affair was making him very irritable indeed. He made a point of sending Dalmapple to visit the nursery every day, and he was pleasantly surprised to hear how well the children were taking to her instruction. Even Mrs. Stibbons had remarked several times that Miss Thraxton was an outstanding governess.

Still, he wanted that damned schedule. And he wanted Thraxton to bring it to him, neatly written, as any good governess would. When it was not forthcoming, he found himself peering out the windows, looking for her and the children, jotting down notes in a vain effort to see what activities were scheduled in the morning, and which in the evening. So far, he could see no sign that there was a schedule of any kind, and the thought irked him all the more. "Your granddaughter is quite unorthodox in her methods."

"That's why her fee is so high," Sir Phineas said with an agreeable nod. "If she were like everyone else, she couldn't charge such outrageous sums."

"For what I'm paying, I would expect more than just unusual methods."

Sir Phineas's white brows rose. "You sound disgruntled. Is something wrong?"

"I asked her to make a schedule for the children. She won't do it."

"Not one for the formalities, my Anna."

"No. But I have my hopes that she will soon see reason." One way or another.

"I wouldn't count on it myself. Stubborn woman. Takes after her grandmother, you know."

Anthony didn't reply. Just this morning he'd written a note to the stubborn Miss Thraxton, asking for a copy of the schedule by noon. Anthony cast a dour glance at the corner of his desk where her answer rested.

Greyley,

I am currently adjusting the children's program per your request. I am aware that you expect no less than perfection, and I wish it to be correct in every instance. I have also been mulling over the best location to place such a document.

At first I considered the wall of the nursery, but that might not be convenient for you should you wish to reread it. Then I thought perhaps your library would be suitable, but alas, there doesn't seem to be any room on the walls due to the shelving. After much thought, I believe I have hit upon a tolerably good idea of where I want to stick it.

In the meantime, I will continue to work on the "schedule" and sharpen it to my utmost ability.

Sincerely,
Thraxton

He'd read that damned note three times already. Just what did she mean by "sticking" it somewhere? Had the note come from one of his brothers, Anthony would have known for certain. Surely Thraxton didn't mean—

"Ah, I hear Anna now." Sir Phineas walked to the library window and looked out.

Anthony came to stand beside Sir Phineas. Anna sat in the middle of the garden, the children about her, all except Desford, who stood bouncing a ball a good ten feet away. She was reading aloud. If he leaned toward the glass, he could hear her velvety voice as she told the story of a princess, a gallant knight, and a horrible three-headed dragon.

Tucked in Anna's lap, Selena sat mesmerized, her doll clutched to her as Anna read of a marvelous battle. Marian stood to one side, a metal tray tied over her chest with a rope, a wooden sword clutched in her hand. Her skirts were tucked into her pockets, and every time Anna read a particularly horrifying description of the battle, Marian would mime the action, her face as fierce as any warrior's. Elizabeth seemed content just to sit at Anna's feet, her arms clasped about her knees, her eyes wide. Even Richard sat listening a short distance away, his gaze seemingly glued to Miss Thraxton's face as she read.

Sir Phineas gave a complacent smile. "Pretty picture, eh?"

"They seem content," Anthony said grudgingly. "They weren't so well behaved with the last governess.

"Oh, this is just a lull in the storm. There's still some fire in them. Just yesterday young Desford put a snake in Anna's chamber pot."

Anthony lifted a brow. "I daresay she put one in his in retaliation."

"She probably would have, if she'd found it. But I took the liberty to intercede on her behalf. Desford didn't know what hit him." Sir Phineas chuckled.

"Up to every row and rig in town, are you?"

"And then some. Still, I have to admire his spunk. Energetic young man. Never stops trying, though he has been more careful since Anna fell and bruised her arm."

Anthony frowned. "Perhaps I should speak to him."

"No, no, there's no need. Besides, Anna would see it as an insult. Daresay she just needs a few more weeks to settle them down a bit." The old man pursed his lips. "I worry about her, though. She seems a little wan, don't you think?"

Anthony looked at Anna once more. Sunlight dappled from the trees above, spilling a golden grid across her hair and touching lightly on the line of her nose and cheek. She read with great fervor, every line of her body engaged in the telling of the story, energy radiating from her in an almost visible glow. It was a pleasure just to watch her.

After a moment, he cleared his throat. "She looks healthy to me." Better than healthy. Radiant, even.

Sir Phineas sighed sadly. "She spends far too much time with the children. Even eats her meals with them, which is a mistake. We all need some time on our own."

That was true. Anthony himself knew how wearing the children could be. Yet Anna seemed to have cast some magic over them, for there had been remarkably little trouble since she'd arrived. Oh, there'd been one or two skirmishes—Anthony's shoehorn had disappeared and with it two of his best cravats, which later turned up hanging from a tree, made into a doll hammock of some sort. But nothing more daunting than that had occurred—at least, not to him.

"Poor Anna," Sir Phineas said, sending a sidelong glance at Anthony. "Daresay you haven't had the chance to see it yet, but she has a tendency to overdo things."

"I've noticed," Anthony replied shortly, his gaze falling on her missive once again. There was something to her grandfather's concerns. It could not be healthy for Anna to overextend herself with the children.

He flicked a careful glance at Sir Phineas. "Perhaps you should say something to Miss Thraxton about pacing herself."

"She won't listen to me." Sir Phineas rubbed his chin thoughtfully. "But she might listen to you."

"I doubt that."

"Nonsense. All you need to do is tell her the way things are, and don't let her argue. That's fatal."

Anthony eyed the old man uncertainly. "From what I've seen of Miss Thraxton, being confrontational only makes her argue louder."

"But she'll be listening, won't she? And that, my friend, is half the battle."

"Hm," Anthony said. It was an intriguing proposition, confronting Thraxton and winning his way. Very intriguing, now that he'd thought about it.

"If you want my advice," Sir Phineas continued in an expansive tone, "I've always found women more approachable outdoors. When riding, for instance. I don't know if it's the sunlight, or the benign effects of exercise, but women seem to be more receptive when you approach them in a natural element."

That was the silliest thing Anthony had ever heard. Still . . . he remembered Anna's frosty demeanor on his few trips to the nursery in the last few days and decided that Sir

Phineas was right; the sunlight and the ease of the situation might serve him very well indeed. If he managed to convince the infuriatingly reticent Miss Thraxton to go riding—just once—he might be able to discover how she was faring in addition to getting that damned schedule out of her. "Miss Thraxton seems to enjoy the mare."

"Lud, yes. She'd ride for days on end if she could arrange it."

Anthony hesitated. "If I invited Miss Thraxton to join me for a ride, she might refuse."

"She might," Sir Phineas said mildly. "Though I shouldn't think she'd pass up the opportunity to give her opinion on . . . your vestibule, for example." He leaned forward. "She thinks it needs a mural. Mentions it every time she walks through."

The old man's gaze landed on a wooden box that lay on the surface of the desk, and he brightened. "I say, are those—"

Anthony flipped open the lid and held out the cigarillos. "Have one. My brother Brand gave them to me as a belated birthday present, and I fear they are going to waste."

"You don't smoke?"

"No."

Sir Phineas's hand disappeared into the box. "Thank you. You are quite generous." A moment later he headed for the door with a wave over his shoulder. "Until later, Greyley."

Anthony looked down at the box of cigarillos. Almost half of them were gone. *That trickster.* He grinned reluctantly and then closed the box and set it on the desk. But Sir Phineas was right about one thing: He did need to keep a closer eye on both Anna and the children.

He found himself back at the window, the garden now empty. He stayed where he was, watching the retreating sun spill across the flowers to warm the bench where she'd sat, until Dalmapple returned with more matters to attend to.

Chapter 15

Some women—the good ones—are like a breath of fresh air, amusing and different and invigorating. The trouble is that it is damnably difficult to capture air and hold it for any length of time.

Lord Jessup to Mrs. Kemble, while playing faro
at a gaming hell off James Street

"There you are." Lady Putney's shrill voice cut through the large, sunny nursery.

Anna stiffened, glad her back was to the doorway so that the children didn't see her involuntary grimace. Every morning for the last five days Lady Putney had come to visit, a swath of silk, perfume, and poison, upsetting everyone and destroying whatever calm Anna had managed to instill.

Still, as noxious as Anna found Lady Putney, she preferred her presence to the earl's brooding company. He, too, came to monitor her progress in the nursery, though he rarely attempted to interfere except to ask for that ridiculous schedule.

But Anna knew that the second she put such a document into Greyley's hands, he would expect her to follow it to the letter. She valued her freedom too much for that.

As for Lady Putney, her purpose was far less benign.

"Miss Thraxton," Lady Putney said, her mouth thinned

into oblivion. "It's almost eleven o'clock. Aren't the children allowed some time to play?"

Desford immediately threw down his pen. Anna grit her teeth—it had taken her most of the morning to convince the stubborn child to begin his lessons, and now that woman had ruined all.

Some of her frustration must have shown on her face for Elizabeth leaned closer and whispered, "Are you well?"

Anna patted the child's hand before she turned to face Lady Putney. "How kind of you to join us yet again."

The older woman's frown deepened. "I have spent the last week watching you, and I must tell you that I dislike what I see."

Anna turned back to the table and silently conjugated the Latin word for "attack."

"You work them all morning without cease," Lady Putney complained. "Then you take them for rides for hours on end."

"Exercise is good for the children," Anna said. She often allowed them to do their lessons out of doors, which they seemed to enjoy. Even Desford was more manageable when sitting under a tree, his bare toes in the grass, the wind ruffling his hair.

Lady Putney sniffed. "I cannot believe you allow the children to spend such an inordinate amount of time in the sun. Poor Elizabeth has a sad tendency to freckle."

Elizabeth flushed a painful red, and Anna's temper slipped another notch. "Well, I think Elizabeth looks lovely with a little color."

The girl gave her a tremulous smile, which Anna returned with a firm one of her own.

"Color!" Lady Putney exclaimed. "She'll look like a milkmaid if you continue."

Anna's smile began to ache. "Lady Putney, if you will excuse us. We have lessons to do and—"

"That is another thing," Lady Putney said, wafting further into the room, her black hair in jarring contrast to her pale skin. "The girls are not improving in their watercolors. Just yesterday Marian was attempting to paint a flower and it looked more like a horse than else."

"It was a horse," Marian mumbled, her jaw set. "I don't like flowers."

Anna placed a hand on the child's shoulder. "Lady Putney, perhaps we should have this conversation another time, when—"

"No. We will discuss it now."

Anna stiffened. "Lord Greyley employed me. I answer to him and no one else."

"Lord Greyley feels exactly as I do," Lady Putney said, a narrow smirk on her red mouth. "We have discussed your inadequacies many times."

The wretch! For some reason, it hurt to think that Greyley had confided his disappointment to Lady Putney. "I'm sorry to hear that Lord Greyley finds my work so unsatisfactory."

"So am I," said a deep voice from the doorway.

Anna whirled to find Greyley's hard brown gaze fixed on Lady Putney. From the grim set of his mouth, he was far from pleased. Anna's heart lightened somewhat.

Meanwhile, Lady Putney turned a bright pink. "Greyley, there you are. I was just telling Miss Thraxton—"

"I heard what you were saying," the earl said, strolling into the nursery, his broad shoulders barely clearing the door. "I would appreciate it if you would stop speaking for me when you have no right. We have never discussed Miss Thraxton in such a manner and you know it."

Lady Putney's smile froze on her face. "Surely you would agree that her methods are unconventional and—"

"Miss Thraxton is the governess. You are not."

Lady Putney's eyes grew hard. "Do not speak to me like that. The children are always my concern."

"No, they're mine," the earl said in a suddenly silky tone. "And if you cannot reconcile yourself to that fact, then allow me to order your carriage."

Desford stood, his hands clenched into fists. "Grandmama cannot leave."

The earl flickered a glance his way. "She may stay as long as she respects the rules of the house."

The boy's jaw jutted. "What if I don't respect the rules? Will you toss me out on my ear, as well?"

Despite the tenseness of the situation, Anna had to repress a smile. Greyley and Desford stood staring at each other, and though their coloring was vastly different, they looked astonishingly alike.

Anna cleared her throat. "Pardon me, but perhaps we should continue this conversation elsewhere. The children have quite a lot to do today and—"

"Miss Thraxton," Lady Putney snapped. "Need I remind you that you are the governess. If the earl or I wish to speak to you, then—"

"Lady Putney," Greyley growled, glaring darkly. The sunlight that poured through the nursery windows glinted on his hair and turned it hard gold. "That's enough. I believe you should leave."

Lady Putney drew herself up, her crimsoned mouth trembling with outrage. "Very well. But I will be watching, and if I see Miss Thraxton engaged in even one impropriety, I will not be silenced." So saying, she turned and swept from the room.

His jaw set, Greyley turned to Anna. "I hope that harridan has not been bothering you an inordinate amount."

"No more than usual." Try as she would, Anna couldn't

help but wonder if there was some basis of truth in Lady Putney's allegations. "Lord Greyley, I wish to ask you a question and I would like a direct answer, if you would."

He regarded her for a moment, then shrugged. "Ask."

"Do *you* approve of the way I've been instructing the children?" As soon as the question left her mouth, she wished she could call it back. But her Thraxton blood was boiling and she'd be damned if she'd let even the implication that she was unworthy continue to stand.

He didn't answer, his dark gaze melting through her, turning her bones to jam. "No, I don't approve of the way you've been instructing the children. However, they seem to like you. And so far, they are behaving."

Anna glanced back at the children. It was true they had settled into a pattern of late, with Desford offering fewer and fewer tricks. Still, she had the distinct impression that something was brewing. She could tell by the way Desford was less vocal in his arguments, and from Elizabeth's guilty expression whenever Anna smiled at her. *Something* was about to happen.

But there was no need to mention it to Greyley. As soon as she discovered their plan, she'd overset it. Until then . . . She glanced back at the earl. "I should return to the children's lessons. Was there anything you wanted?"

"Yes. I came to see if you would join me for a ride this afternoon."

"Ride?" Her voice cracked in half and made her wince.

He smiled, his eyes crinkling in the most attractive way. "There are some paths that I'm certain the children know nothing about. We could explore those and you could see if they are suitable for your daily jaunts."

"A ride would be lovely. The children would enjoy it very much."

"Not the children," he said, a touch of impatience to his voice. "Just you and I. Alone."

Alone. With Greyley. The thought tantalized, beckoned. Anna swallowed with difficulty. "I don't think that would be wise—"

"You could tell me more about the mural you long to see in the foyer," he said. "And all your plans for instructing the children."

That was too much, even for her. "Lord Greyley, it would not be appropriate for us to . . ." To what? A thousand forbidden images flittered through her mind, most of them centered around the still-fresh memory of his mouth hot over hers. She quickly locked the door on her unruly imagination and cleared her throat. "Lord Greyley, it would not be appropriate for us to ride alone together. I am just the governess."

"Miss Thraxton, this is Greyley House. I make the rules here. Besides, I only wish to discuss the children. And the mural."

"We can do that here."

"Can we?" His gaze slipped past her to the room beyond.

Anna turned away and met the interested stares of the children. Elizabeth was even leaning forward, intent on catching every word, while Desford's brow was lowered. "Lord Greyley, I cannot go riding with you. That is the last I'll say on the matter."

Anna's expression was so much that of a martyr on the verge of being tossed into the flames that Anthony had to resist the urge to grin. "Come, Thraxton. I won't curse, bite, or spit. I promise."

She muttered something that sounded curiously like "I doubt that."

"What?"

"Nothing. If you'll excuse us, we have work to do." She turned back to the children and began calmly discussing the conjugation of a Greek word that Anthony only vaguely remembered from his youth.

Anthony raked a hand through his hair. Damn it, he wasn't suggesting anything improper, just a ride. What the hell was wrong with that? "Miss Thraxton, I—"

"Lord Greyley, while you are welcome here at any time, you must promise not to interrupt the children's instruction. It is only fair."

Anthony found that he disliked being corrected even more than he disliked being dismissed. "Very well," he said stiffly. "I will leave you to your work."

With a final nod, he left the impertinent wench where she belonged—tending the hellions in the nursery. Consoling himself with the thought that such duty had to be onerous and boring and massively unpleasant, he strode to the library where he methodically overindulged in a bottle of port.

What had he been thinking, anyway? Thraxton was the governess. In all his years, not since the legendary Matilda, had Greyley even once embarked on a flirtation with a member of his staff. He felt that to do so would be to overstep his boundaries as lord of the manor. Boundaries he took very seriously.

But with Thraxton . . . it was difficult to remember that she was not his social equal. She walked, talked, acted, breathed, and defied him like a born member of the gentry. Which was what she was.

A true gentleman would never invite one of his employees into taking long, lonely rides across his lands. Even though he had been acting on the advice of her grandfather.

Anthony silently toasted Sir Phineas for his forward-thinking ways. Now there was a man who knew how to deal with adversity. Having lived with Anna Thraxton, Sir Phineas was probably as close to being a saint as any man alive. Anthony toasted the old man yet again. By God, Anthony would heed the old man's advice and find a way to make Anna go for a ride. It would take wit and cunning, but Anthony was certain it could be done. He mulled over the possibilities as he worked his way through the rest of the port.

Later on, Mr. Dalmapple returned to the library only to take one look at the earl and then prudently closed the door and left. Shaking his head sadly, he went home early for the first time in almost twelve years.

Anthony awoke the next morning with a raging headache and a foul taste in his mouth. God, but he was too old for this. Too old for five children and far, far too old to deal with one cheeky governess.

The door to his room was unceremoniously opened. Anthony cautiously lifted one eyelid to see his brother Brand standing at the foot of his bed. Anthony groaned. "When the hell did you get here?"

"This morning. Aren't you going to welcome me?"

Anthony opened his other eye and then gingerly swung his feet out of bed. "Do you ever knock?"

Brand dropped into a chair by the fire. "You'd be surprised at the things you can discover by barging into someone's bedchamber unannounced."

"I'm going to start keeping my pistol more closely at hand. Perhaps if I shot you, you'd learn some manners."

"You can try." Brand leaned back in the chair and laced his hands behind his head. "I'm only here for a day or so."

"Oh?" Anthony eyed his younger brother with a bleary

eye. Brand appeared to be in amazing spirits. "Bastard."

Brand's grin widened. "I hate to bother you while you are busy being in such a foul mood, but I've a favor to ask. I wondered if you would mind if I left Satan here."

"Aren't you taking him with you?"

"Not this time. I've business to attend to and it won't wait."

"I don't like you disappearing for weeks on end. You should tell someone where you are."

Brand lifted his brows. "Worried about me, brother dear? I'm unmanned."

"Don't make me ill. I just don't want to be the one to tell Marcus his little brother is missing yet again. He's not the most pleasant of people when angry."

"No, he's not. He's too protective, which is one of his less endearing faults."

"He is the head of the family. That makes him responsible for you whether you like it or not."

"He takes his job far too seriously. But then, so do you." Brand frowned. "The Elliots are a difficult family to manage."

"There are some who show promise."

"Name one."

"Rupert could turn out well."

"Rupert Elliot is a rakehell of the lowest sort. You are the only one who sees any good in him. Even his own mother says he's uncontrollable."

Anthony gave a brief smile. "If Lady Putney says it is so, then it is a lie."

"I have to agree with you there. I've only been here half an hour and she has already banished me from the morning room for what she termed 'an impertinent and rude comment.'"

"Was it 'impertinent and rude'?"

"Oh yes." Brand stretched his legs before him. "Tell me,

Anthony, why do you stomach that woman's presence under your roof?"

"The children. For some reason I cannot fathom, they seem to like her, and I have no wish to make her a martyr in their eyes."

Brand shook his head. "If you kick her out, she becomes a saint and you, the devil. If you leave her here, she will continue to poison the minds of the children against you. You are well and truly damned."

Anthony rose and splashed his face with water from the basin on his nightstand. "Which is why I have employed Miss Thraxton."

Brand appeared impressed. "Ah, the delectable Thraxton."

Anthony turned to his brother. "Delectable?"

"Don't tell me you haven't looked at that woman. She's all leg and bosom, and that hair . . ." Brand placed his hands over his heart and sighed. "Delectable doesn't even begin to describe such beauty."

Anthony scowled. "I'd thank you to remember that Miss Thraxton is in my employ. I won't have you troubling her."

Every vestige of humor vanished from Brand's face. "I've never forced my attentions on any woman, much less one under your roof."

A strained silence filled the room and Anthony grimaced. "I'm sorry, Brand. I'm just a bit worn around the edges."

"Thanks to Miss Thraxton?"

"She's the most argumentative female I've ever met," Anthony said honestly, wondering why he also found himself wanting to grin. He ruthlessly suppressed the urge. "She's very forthright, as is her grandfather."

"That must be the elderly gentleman I spoke with in the breakfast room. He tried to convince me to purchase two hundred French sheaths."

Anthony frowned. "Damn it, I thought I had put a stop to that."

"According to Jenkins, he has been hawking them to the upstairs maids. Apparently they didn't know exactly what they were and thought they were caps of some sort." Brand chuckled. "Lord, I would have loved to have seen *that*."

"It's a wonder he hasn't begun advertising in the *Post*."

A soft knock came at the door. At Anthony's call, his valet entered the room, a coat carefully folded over his thin arm. "Your coat, my lord," Ledbetter said. "I took the liberty of brushing it." He deposited it on the edge of the bed, then stepped into the dressing room and came out with a deep red waistcoat.

Made of watered silk, it was heavily embroidered with black and gold thread. Anthony frowned. "Where the hell did that come from?"

"You purchased it last month, while in London."

"I must have been drunk." Anthony waved a hand. "Take it away."

Ledbetter managed a pained smile. "I believe you were a trifle to let, sir. However, it is still a very well made garment."

"I'll wear the blue waistcoat."

"But my lord, this is very fashionable—"

"I don't want fashion; I want comfort. Besides, I'll be damned if I wear something that sparkles. I'd feel like a Bartholomew boy." He glanced at the red waistcoat, then grimaced. "While you are fetching a new one, toss that one in the fire."

Ledbetter all but gaped. "My lord, the gold threading was very expensive! And the buttons are made of—"

"I don't care, just get rid of it."

Brand tsked. "Ledbetter, I apologize for my brother. He has no sense of fashion."

"No, all of the dandyism in our family settled on you, didn't it?" Anthony returned, casting a caustic eye over his brother. It was amazing, really, but Brand was never anything other than perfectly dressed. Anthony had seen him at five in the morning, completely besotted with drink, and yet he still managed to appear as if he'd just stepped from his dressing room.

"My lord," Ledbetter said in an imploring tone, "please do not ask me to destroy this garment. It is far too fine for such an ignoble end."

"Then give it to one of the footmen."

"But I—"

"I don't care what you do with it, just get it out of my wardrobe. It offends me."

"Yes, my lord." Ledbetter carefully picked up the waistcoat and disappeared into the dressing room. He returned very shortly with two more waistcoats, one a rather plain blue, the other an extravagant green creation.

He held out the green waistcoat. "If the red one is too uncomfortable, then perhaps you should try this one, my lord. It is quite fetching."

Brand sat up. "Good God, are those mother-of-pearl buttons?"

"I don't know and I don't care," Anthony said. "I'll take the blue one, Ledbetter. Put that other one away."

"But sir, I thought perhaps—"

"The blue one."

"Better listen to him, Ledbetter," Brand said. "He's in the devil of a temper this morning."

The valet hesitated, then glanced at his employer and nodded. "As you wish, my lord." He laid the blue waistcoat on the bed and then slowly left the room, his shoulders bent, his head down.

Brand watched him go. "I may attempt to steal Ledbetter from you. He'd get a good deal more joy from dressing a man of fashion than a country squire."

"Steal him, if you can. He won't go."

Brand's blue eyes turned his way. "Paying him through the nose, are you?"

"You wouldn't be enough of a challenge. Ledbetter has devoted his life to trying to improve me." Anthony took a cravat from the pile and carelessly knotted it about his neck. "I think he's vowed to reform me or die trying."

Brand winced. "At least attempt a decent knot." He indicated his own neckcloth, which was an intricate concoction of knots and ties that defied description.

"What the hell do you call that?" Anthony demanded.

"The St. John. It's my own creation."

"How long did it take you to tie it?"

"Two hours."

"That's half a day!"

"You know, Anthony, it would do you a world of good to get out more, see some of the world." Brand carefully smoothed his perfectly pressed cuff. "Might put some polish on you."

There were many in society who thought Brandon St. John was a useless fribble, more interested in fashion than else. Anthony suspected Brand's attachment to the cut of his new waistcoat and the turn of his cuff was simply his way to redirect attention from his private affairs.

And those, whatever they were, engrossed him an unusual amount of time. "When do you leave?"

"Don't you like my company?"

"Of course I do. Behind that outlandish waistcoat is a man I'm proud to call brother."

"My waistcoat is all the crack."

"I'm sure it is. Or it will be, once you flash yourself about town. I'm merely surprised you haven't raced off into the night as you so frequently do."

"One must play. And when one has a particularly succulent lady friend who also likes to play . . . well, the possibilities are endless."

Anthony wondered briefly if the reason Brand kept his lady friend such a secret was that she possessed a husband and thus they were required to be discreet. It was a possibility, for Brand had certainly been secretive of late. "Whatever you do, be cautious. I don't want to have to explain to Marcus how you got your head blown off."

"Marcus would draw my claret if I kicked up so much as a breath of scandal. He's gotten rather peculiar about that lately."

"That's because our youngest brother has been giving him trouble."

"Chase has been kicking at the traces again, has he?"

"And more seriously this time. Marcus wouldn't give me the details, but he was far from pleased."

"I'm glad I don't have such problems. You and Marcus can run your families any way you wish—I like my freedom."

"If you came here to gloat, then be gone."

"Actually, I wanted to know if you wished to go for a ride this morning. It's a lovely day."

Anthony glanced at the window. Bright sunlight crept through the curtains and brightened the whole room. A brisk ride might clear his head, too. "I would—"

Ledbetter burst into the room. "Pardon me, my lord, but your shoes!" He stopped and pressed a hand to his chest, panting heavily. "They cannot be—but they are! I cannot believe—"

"Damn it, Ledbetter! What about my shoes?"

"They have gone missing."

Brandon frowned. "Missing?"

The valet nodded. "All of them."

"Perhaps they have been misplaced," Brand offered.

"No, my lord. They were all there last night. I polish His Lordship's boots every night, and last night, when I brought them back, all of his shoes were right where they were required to be. I fear someone has stolen them."

"That's odd." Brand glanced at Anthony. "Who could possibly want your shoes?"

Anthony knew of at least five little somebodies who might think it amusing to steal his shoes. "I'll strangle every one of those little monsters."

"Ah, the children. I'll wager you are right. Unless . . ."

"Unless what?"

"Unless it was Miss Thraxton. Perhaps she harbors a secret passion for you and has taken your shoes and has built a shrine with them in some obscure part of this moldy house."

Anthony shot him a dark glance. "Aren't you needed in London?"

"No. And even if I were, I wouldn't miss this little play for the world."

Anthony made an exasperated noise. "If I've told you once, I've told you a thousand times that I—" He caught sight of Ledbetter's averted gaze. "Damn it, we'll discuss this later. Ledbetter, are there any shoes left at all?"

"Yes, my lord. One pair, but—"

"Bring them out."

"Yes, but—"

"*Now.*"

His mouth pinched with disapproval, the valet bowed and disappeared back into the dressing room.

"Why do you think they stole your shoes?" Brand asked, still looking annoyingly amused.

"To irritate me to death."

"You are quite red. Be careful or they will succeed."

"I'll be damned if I let a bunch of ill-mannered hoydens get the best of me. When I see them, I will calmly demand they return my shoes or—" Anthony bit off his thoughts.

"Or?" Brand prompted.

Or what? What could he take from them? The rides they enjoyed with their governess? He suddenly had a picture of Anna returning to the house, her hair tumbling from her pins, that ridiculous hat with the long white feather caressing her cheek. By God, that's *exactly* what he'd do. Maybe then she'd ride with him instead.

Ledbetter returned carrying a pair of red velvet slippers, ostentatiously embroidered with purple and gilt thread. The tips were slightly pointed and large gold tassels adorned the sides.

Brand choked. "Bloody hell!"

"They're from our beloved Aunt Delphi," Anthony said, eyeing the shoes with distaste. "She assured me they were all the rage in France."

"And to think I complained when she bought me that pair of spangled stockings," Brand said. "Pray tell me you aren't going to wear those monstrosities."

"I don't have a choice. I'm going to find Miss Thraxton and show her how remiss she's been at her position." Anthony yanked the slippers from Ledbetter's hand and threw them onto the floor, then rammed his feet into them. His heels hung a good inch over the backs. "Damn it!"

Brand winced. "I can't watch this. I'm on my way to the stables to see to Satan. Come and join me if you find your riding boots." Casting a last, laughing glance at his brother's feet, Brand left.

As soon as the door closed, Ledbetter sniffed. "If you don't mind my saying so, this isn't a matter for levity. Footwear is an important part of one's attire." He glanced at Anthony's feet and shuddered. "I will be waiting to hear what has occurred to your shoes. I only hope they have not been left in a moldy, damp place."

Anthony didn't answer, but turned and tromped out, gold tassels swinging with each step.

Chapter 16

The problem with gambling, whether it be for sport or profit, is that one rarely wins without also losing.

Mrs. Kemble to Lord Alvaney, commiserating with each other at the annual Huntington Charity Ball

"Elizabeth, will you read the next section? I wonder if our poor knight will ever find his way home," Anna said, her face tilted to the sun. It was a lovely morning—warm and sparkling, not a cloud in sight. In fact, it had been the lure of the endless blue sky that had drawn her forth with the children, a blanket, and a book.

Yesterday had been a complete waste. After Lady Putney and Lord Greyley had descended on the nursery, neither she nor the children had been able to refocus their efforts. Anna had been forced to end their session early.

But today would be different, she told herself. Today she would not spend a single minute thinking about Anthony Elliot. Not one, she vowed.

After settling the children on a large blanket on the velvety lawn, Anna leaned back on her hands and let the morning breeze ease her heart. The sun shimmered in the midmorning sky, the grass was green and lush beneath her toes. Above, the tree branches swayed and birds sang. The only jarring note in an otherwise perfect summer day was the stern, stark outline of Greyley House.

It was just like Anthony Elliot to own a house that cast a dark shade over the surrounding countryside. It reminded her far too much of his overbearing personality.

Normally, Anna would have been in more agreement with the earl on the need for a routine in the nursery. But for some reason she felt that the Elliot children needed something more than a routine—they needed warmth and sunshine and life. It was as if they were frozen, unable to be children. And she had a strong suspicion that much of the damage had occurred when their parents were alive.

In a way, that was a relief, for it meant that there was a chance that Greyley could find a way into the children's affections if he desired. It had surprised her to realize that the earl held the children in some affection already, though he denied it by calling them "devil's spawn" at every available opportunity.

She glanced beneath her lashes at the silent Richard, who sat on the very edge of the huge blanket, staring intently at Elizabeth as she read. It was amazing, really, the way he watched her form each sound, almost as if he were attempting to memorize them. Anna watched him for a while, satisfied that he was engaged with the story.

Elizabeth turned the page, her brow furrowed as she attempted to figure out some of the larger words, her childish lisp comforting. When she came to a word she couldn't decipher, she would glance at Anna. But Anna patiently waited for her to sound it out.

Selena and Marian hung anxiously on Elizabeth's every word while Desford sat staring out across the fields. To a casual observer he didn't appear to be listening, but Anna noticed the flicker of impatience that crossed his face every time Elizabeth's reading skill stumbled to a halt.

Anna stretched her legs to one side, keeping her skirts about her ankles. The sun warmed her shoulders, and she wished she had a morning dress made of lilac muslin. Or perhaps a lovely mint color, one that would bring out just a hint of green in her eyes. She sighed. She so loved pretty clothing. As soon as she received her payment, she'd—

A small, warm hand settled into Anna's, and she smiled down at Selena as the child climbed into her lap. Though Desford scowled at the action, Anna settled her chin in Selena's soft curls, and they sat comfortably as Elizabeth continued with the story. As peaceful as the scene about her was, Anna knew better than to trust it.

More than once this morning, she had caught Desford whispering to the others. They had immediately stepped apart when they noticed Anna watching. She rubbed her cheek against Selena's tumbled curls and thought about simply asking the small sprite what was afoot, but she abandoned the idea as soon as she thought it—she wouldn't set the children against one another. It would destroy what little peace of mind they had.

Selena squirmed around to a more comfortable position, her chubby cheek resting against Anna's arm. She remained there all of two seconds before she sat upright, her gaze fixed across the lawn toward Greyley House.

Anna glanced in the direction the child was staring. Stalking across the lawn was Greyley himself, broad shouldered and moving with a lethal, deadly intent. Judging by the dark cast of his expression, something was seriously amiss.

Elizabeth's voice trailed into silence, and all the children shifted uncomfortably as the earl came to a stop at the edge of the blanket.

Then Anna noticed his slippers. She had to bite her lip before she could speak. "I see that you're still wearing your slippers. Did you forget your shoes?"

"No," he said in a voice straining to find patience. "I have not forgotten anything. My shoes are missing."

"All of them?"

"Every damned one."

Anna clamped her hands over Selena's tender ears. "Please don't use such words in front of the children."

Desford snorted. "Why the hell not?"

"Desford!" Anna said, sending him a frown. "You may forget you are a gentleman when in the presence of your guardian, but not in front of your sisters, if you please."

He reddened. "Very well. But only if he'll do the same." He jerked his thumb toward Greyley.

Anna raised her brows. The earl sent her a withering glare, but she did not waver.

His mouth grew white at the corners, as if it took all of his self-control to keep from saying what he *really* thought. Finally he took a long, slow breath, then flicked a glance at Desford. "It's a bargain. I'll refrain if you will refrain."

Desford blinked. "You will?"

Greyley held out his hand. Desford looked from his guardian's face to the hand stretched before him. Anna held her breath, wondering if Greyley realized how important this moment was.

When Desford didn't move, Anna said softly, "It is only fair for the other children, Desford. They should not be subjected to such language."

After a long silence, Desford took Greyley's hand and managed a manful shake. "Done. I'll watch my language and so will you."

Greyley's expression softened slightly. "Done."

Anna had to give the earl credit. Before last week, he would have blasted them all with a spate of ill temper designed to cow them into obedience. But today he had met Desford on his own terms and they had both walked away the better for it. What was even more amazing was the fact that Greyley, even standing in silly-looking slippers in his own front lawn, his pride a tiny bit tattered, still managed to appear the prince.

Yes indeed, the earl was coming along quite nicely.

Greyley flexed his shoulders as if to rid them of a troublesome knot. "Now, Desford, where are my shoes?"

The boy shrugged. "I don't know. I voted against the idea."

"You *voted*?"

"We always vote," Marian said. "Robin's merry men did it."

"Desford says we're a democracy, like the colonies," Elizabeth added.

Greyley's mouth had dropped open. He closed it and then swallowed. "Sweet Jesus, you *voted* to steal my shoes."

"Oh no," Elizabeth said with an earnest expression. "No one said anything about stealing. They are your shoes, no matter what."

"That's true," Marian said, looking at the earl's feet. "We just moved them."

Anna rubbed a hand over her mouth to cover a grin. The earl looked so ridiculous wearing the small tasseled shoes.

"Where are my shoes?" Greyley asked again.

The children looked at Selena. Anna stooped down so that she could see into the child's eyes. "Selena, did you take the earl's shoes?"

Selena beamed pleasantly. "Richard helped me."

Anna glanced at the silent boy, who stared stoically ahead, his face pale and set. He appeared so rigid with fear and emotion that Anna could not find it in her heart to be angry. She sighed and turned back to Selena. "Where are the earl's shoes?"

Selena pointed vaguely away from the house. "There."

Seething, Anthony followed the direction of her pudgy arm, across the lush expanse of lawn to the spreading oaks that trailed down to the—His gaze halted, his temper flaring. *Damn it.* "The pond."

Elizabeth dropped the book. "Selena! You were just supposed to put them under something, where they couldn't be seen."

"We did put them under something," Selena said, frowning at what she obviously considered a silly comment. "We put them under the water."

Anna leaned toward the small girl. "Selena, you didn't throw *all* of His Lordship's shoes in the pond?"

Selena sucked on her finger, her brow wrinkled in thought. "Not *all* of them."

Anthony relaxed a little. That was something, at least, he thought.

"Where are the shoes you didn't toss in the water?" Anna asked.

The little girl pointed to Anthony's feet. "Marian said they were too ugly to borrow, so Richard and I left them in the closet."

Bloody hell. Anthony rubbed his neck. It was almost more than he could bear. Three months ago his biggest care had been the state of the south field. Now he was living in daily fear of waking up trussed and tied like a Christmas goose, his clothing stolen, his favorite horse sold to the gypsies.

"Selena," Anna said, "why did you throw the earl's shoes in the pond?"

"To see if his face would get red." She looked at Anthony. "It did."

Anthony thought of his new Hoby boots resting in the muck of the pond. Damn it, this was untenable! He opened his mouth to voice his anger, but found a soft hand laid against his lips, halting every thought in his head. Anna had moved to stand beside him. She was tantalizingly near, every feature emphasized by the brilliance of the morning sun.

Her skin was so soft, the faint scent of ink and paper lingering on her fingers. And he could feel where her breast pressed against his arm.

"Remember your bargain with Desford," she said softly. "No cursing."

Remember? How was he supposed to remember anything with those spectacular breasts pressed against him? He barely managed to nod, and she gave him a reassuring smile, then turned back to the children.

"How many shoes are we looking for?" she asked the children.

"Forty-two," Marian said. Richard nodded.

Anna straightened. "You must be teasing." She sent a questioning glance at Anthony.

He shrugged. "That sounds about right."

"I would have never thought it, but you, sir, are a dandy."

Anthony didn't know how to respond. He'd been called arrogant, and thoughtless, and intractable. But never had anyone dared call him a dandy. "I am *not* a dandy. In fact, I am as far from being a dandy as it is possible to be."

"Then why do you have so many shoes?"

He frowned, incredulous that she would even ask such a question. "Because they not only threw my shoes into the water, but all of my boots as well. They even tossed in my dress slippers." He glared down at his feet and said grimly, "All except these."

She bit her lip. "It is a pity they forgot those. I daresay they would look a good deal better in the pond."

Anthony stiffened. "Just what do you mean by that?"

She didn't appear the least put out by his harsh tone. In fact, there was a decided quiver to her lips, as if she were struggling to contain a giggle. "I've never thought of you as a tassel sort of man. But then one never knows, does one?"

Anthony promptly forgot that he had always hated the slippers. In fact, he'd been tempted to toss them into the fireplace when he'd first gotten them, but the realization that Aunt Delphi might someday visit made him think better of it. So he'd hidden them in his closet and forgotten about them until today. "You are supposed to get those children under control, Miss Thraxton."

"We cannot make angels out of them overnight," she replied easily. "After we have retrieved your shoes, we will discuss what is to be done with the children. Rest assured that they will pay for this escapade." She turned and walked toward the pond, never checking to see if Anthony followed or not.

He was tempted to stay right where he was. After all, since the children were under her care, she was in part responsible for this latest debacle. "They are already ruined," he said loudly.

"Perhaps. And perhaps not," came the reply, floating across her shoulder. She walked with long, purposeful strides, and Anthony couldn't help but admire the sway of her hips as she went.

Anthony glanced to where the children sat watching with curious gazes. "We will discuss this further once I've retrieved my shoes."

Selena took her finger out of her mouth. "I can throw very far."

"Can you?" he asked grimly.

"Farther than Richard."

The boy looked sullenly at his sister, and for an instant Anthony thought the child might actually say something. But the moment passed, and Richard hunched his shoulders and turned to stare at the banks of the pond where Miss Thraxton was now standing.

Anthony raked a hand through his hair. The way things were going this morning, he wouldn't be surprised to discover that his shoes were in the deepest part of that damned pond. Without another word, he turned and followed Anna to the water's edge.

By the time he reached her, she had already tossed her shoes to one side and was standing barefooted among the reeds that lined the edges of the pond. She didn't speak when he stood beside her, but stared out over the water with a wistful expression on her face that softened the line of her mouth.

She murmured, "It is quite lovely here."

Anthony followed her gaze. Deep green grass surrounded the crystal water. Dragonflies hazed over the water, while the wind touched the reeds and made them dance.

"Did you add the pergola yourself?"

He nodded. "Sara is very fond of the water. I added the pergola when she was staying with me."

She rewarded him with a brief smile. "You are a good brother. When we were in school, I was always jealous of her. She had all those brothers to write her letters and come and visit, while I had none."

"She didn't appreciate it."

"Only when you became overly bossy. Which was most of the time."

"We took care of her the best way we knew how."

"I daresay you did." She lifted her skirts and stepped neatly over the high grass toward a small skiff that was tied among the shallows. "Desford uses this boat to fish, so it must be sound."

"I wouldn't trust it."

"Nonsense," she said, nimbly scrambling into the boat, only the edge of her skirts getting wet. It tipped unsteadily, but she quickly sat and took the oars. "Stay where you are and let me see if I can find your shoes. They cannot have tossed them far from shore."

Anthony frowned. "Anna, wait—" But it was too late. She was already rowing from shore. Damn all independent women. "Come back here."

"In a moment," she said, holding the oars up so that she could peer over the side of the skiff. The boat tilted precariously with her movement.

"Miss Thraxton, if you do not give a care, you will fall in."

"Nonsense. I will be back to shore in a moment." She leaned over the other side, the boat tilting even more. "I can't see your shoes at all. I hope they haven't sunk into the muck."

"And I hope you can swim," he returned hotly, a curious weight in his chest. Bloody hell, but the pond was not a place for foolery. It was treacherously deep, the bottom covered with thick slime.

"Oh, I can swim," she replied cheerfully, her gaze still fixed on the water. "But it doesn't appear to be more than a few feet here, just like the pond at our old house in Milford."

"Row ashore now."

"And leave your shoes to rot in the water? Ledbetter would have my neck in a noose."

"Not even Ledbetter will be able to find you should you fall in. The water is deeper than it looks."

"Don't worry. I don't plan on overturning the boat so . . ."

Her voice trailed into nothingness, her gaze fixed on her feet. "Oh dear."

"What?"

"The boat is sinking."

"*What?*"

She pushed herself to her knees on the plank seat, and Anthony could see that a portion of her skirts was already wet. "The water's coming in quickly."

"Can you bail it out?"

"With what?" she asked, moving to one side.

"Row ashore," he snapped. "Quickly!"

She took hold of the oars and attempted to maneuver the boat around so that she could row, but one of the oars became entangled in a lily pad.

Anthony took a step forward, ignoring the way his slippers sank into the mud. From his vantage on the bank, he could see how quickly the boat was lowering in the water, the bow less than inch from the surface. "Anna, I'm going to—"

The bow dipped beneath the water. Anna gave a startled yelp as it tilted quickly to one side. "Oh dear!" she gasped, dropping the oars and scrambling to the high end of the boat.

"Stop that!" Anthony snapped. But it was too late. The small skiff flipped over, its sole occupant tumbling with it. Before Anthony's horrified gaze, his new governess disappeared beneath the water with an ear-piercing shriek.

"She said she can swim," said a voice behind Anthony. The children had gathered on the bank and stood not two paces behind him.

The water churned as Miss Thraxton surfaced briefly, then disappeared once more, her wet skirts pulling her under. Anthony muttered a curse, kicked off his tasseled slippers, and yanked off his coat.

"Maybe she's swimming under water?" Elizabeth offered. Desford shot her a disgusted glance. Even he knew better than that.

The earl apparently thought the same, for he didn't answer. He was already marching into the water, tossing his coat aside and muttering the whole while. "Damn that interfering woman! I warned her—" He dove beneath the surface.

Elizabeth stared at the spot where he disappeared. "I think he's angry at Miss Thraxton."

"I wouldn't be happy about having to swim. It's cold," Desford said, trying to sound calm when his throat was curiously tight. "Just like a girl, to get into trouble doing the simplest thing."

Elizabeth jutted her chin. "Miss Thraxton was trying to find the earl's shoes, which *we* lost."

"We didn't lose his shoes," Selena said, frowning in indignation. "I knew 'xactly where they were." She looked at the pond with a speculative air. "Miss Thraxton probably has them with her now."

Desford blew out his breath, his chest aching as the seconds passed. "Miss Thraxton is not getting the shoes. She's drowning because her skirts are holding her down."

Selena looked startled. "Will she die?"

"No," Desford replied almost fiercely. His stomach hardened into a knot. He hadn't meant for Miss Thraxton to be dunked in the water, but Greyley. Who would have known the governess would strike out on the pond without anyone with her?

The water by the boat churned. A red swath of hair appeared at the surface, followed by Miss Thraxton's pale face. She gasped loudly as she broke free, a strand of lily pad tangled in her hair and dangling across her face.

Her arms flailed wildly. "Help—" She disappeared beneath the surface once more.

Greyley reached her at just that moment. He dove under water and for an instant, silence once more filled the glen.

Marian sighed, her hands clasped to her chest. "He's going to rescue her, I just know it. It's like a fairy tale."

Desford eyed the water where the earl had just disappeared. He supposed it could be called a rescue. Still—it wasn't a very deep pool. If Miss Thraxton would just get two feet more to her left, she would be able to stand at ease. Or so Desford hoped. A faint ache throbbed in his throat. Surely Miss Thraxton would be all right . . .

A hand settled on Desford's shoulder. He looked up into the gently smiling eyes of Sir Phineas.

"I once played that very trick on my brother, Dickie. Rodgers, our head groom, had to jump in and save him." He gently squeezed Desford's shoulder. "Don't worry about a thing. My Anna's a strong woman and Greyley has her firmly in hand."

Desford's chest tightened even more and he thought for a moment about confessing all. But he had the feeling that he didn't need to say a word. He was still mulling this over when the water erupted once again and Miss Thraxton appeared once more, this time assisted by the earl. He was trying to hold her aloft, but she struggled mightily, her skirts tangled about her long legs, her red hair streaming about her. "Don't drop me!" she gasped, clutching him frantically.

"She's just like a mermaid," Marian said, her voice awed.

Elizabeth fingered the ribbon that tied her hair. "I wish I had red hair. Long, long red hair. Desford, don't you think Miss Thraxton's hair is pretty?"

He shot her a disgusted look. Since Miss Thraxton's arrival, Elizabeth had become the biggest *girl*. Not only that, but both Elizabeth and Marian had shown a regretful tendency to join the enemy camp.

Grandmama was right—the sooner they were all rid of the governess's influence, the better. Still . . . the comforting warmth of Sir Phineas's hand made him pause. When Desford really thought about it, he realized that he did not like his grandmother. As much as he wanted to believe her protestations of affection, they rang false.

"Look, Desford!" Marian said, pointing. "Miss Thraxton is trying to climb onto the earl's shoulders."

Sure enough, Miss Thraxton had managed to hook her knee over the earl's shoulder and was even now trying to climb atop his head.

"Oh no!" Elizabeth cried. "She's pushing him under!"

Before the children's interested gazes, the two disappeared from sight once more.

Selena sighed sadly. "I suppose we'll be getting another governess after all."

Desford snorted, desperate to prove her wrong. "It'll take more than a little water to get rid of Miss Thraxton." He found himself leaning against the old man, the faint scent of tobacco making his eyes sting.

"Lord Greyley has Miss Thraxton now!" Marian said excitedly.

Kicking free from the cold depths of the pond, Anthony was actively thinking of all the other, smaller governesses he should have hired. There was the Shropshire woman who was reportedly very well trained. And then there was the Kendalls' new governess, a linguist with an allegedly uncanny way of teaching watercolors.

If it had been anyone other than Anna Thraxton, he would not now be drowning in his own frigid pond. He untangled himself from her grasp and then grabbed her beneath the arms once again, and hauled her back to the surface.

As soon as she broke free, she began to cough and sputter, clutching his shirt frantically.

"Easy," Anthony admonished. "I'm treading water and—"

She grabbed his hair and attempted to climb him like a ladder. Water filled his mouth as she desperately attempted to get on top of him, her leg pressing down on his shoulder, her arm slung across his head.

It was true he'd dreamed of her in this exact position—of her thigh against his cheek, her womanhood enticingly near his mouth. Only in his dreams, she hadn't been screaming for help and he hadn't been drowning beneath the surface of a murky pond.

He yanked her leg from his shoulder and pushed her away, then grabbed the overturned skiff. "Good God, woman!" he managed to choke out. "Stay still or I'll let the fish have you!" He pushed the upended skiff forward at that moment, relaxing only when she clung gratefully to one corner. As soon as he got her back to shore, he'd be damned if he wouldn't exact a complete and thorough apology from her.

She clung to the boat, laying her head against the wet wood, her hair streaming over her shoulders and floating in a russet circle about her shoulders.

Anthony's irritation dissipated when he saw her pale face. "Are you hurt?"

A shuddering breath ripped from her lips. Her gray eyes appeared almost green as she panted her answer, "I thought . . . I thought I was . . . going to drown."

"So did I. You said you could swim."

"I can," she said, gulping air.

"You call *that* swimming?"

She frowned, her panting already lessened. "I never said I was good at it. And I've never had to swim with skirts."

He made a disgusted noise. "Hold on to the boat. I'm going to pull you ashore."

She did as she was told and he managed to get them back to land without further mishap. The children crowded around as Anna stumbled onto the bank and sank into a heap.

Sir Phineas bent to peer into her face. "Just breathe," he said helpfully.

Anna, struggling to do that very thing, silently wished him to Hades.

"Miss Thraxton?" Elizabeth said anxiously. She turned wide blue eyes to Anthony, who had come to stand beside her. "Maybe she needs a doctor."

"Or a horse," Selena offered.

"Why would she need a horse?" Desford demanded.

"To take her to the house," Selena said, obviously annoyed she had to explain such a simple idea. "She's too tired to stand and I don't think Lord Greyley could carry her. She's a very big woman."

"I'm not big," Anna said, lifting herself on her elbow and pushing her hair from her face. Of all the indignities, being called fat in front of Lord Greyley was more than she could handle. "I'm just tall. And I'm don't need a horse. Really. I . . . I just need to rest."

Anthony didn't comment. There was no denying that her usually pale skin was even whiter than usual.

An unfamiliar stir of sympathy made Anthony turn to Sir Phineas. "Could you take the children back to the house? I will bring Miss Thraxton as soon as she has regained her breath."

"We can't leave yet," Selena said, sucking on her finger. "She might throw up."

Five hopeful gazes fixed on the governess while Sir Phineas manfully struggled to hide a grin.

Anna moaned and turned on her side. Sir Phineas hastily took Elizabeth and Selena by the hand and led them away. The other children followed, glancing back with regret. Only Selena voiced an objection, and that was to ask for someone to call them back immediately if Miss Thraxton fell ill.

Anthony waited patiently. After a moment, she sat up, her breathing more controlled. Her hair was knotted and tangled and a lump of lily pad hung over one ear. The water had darkened her red hair to a deep, rich auburn.

Anthony watched her, reluctantly admiring her. She'd been so damned determined to find his shoes and spare the children that she'd put herself at risk. He suddenly wondered if this was how she'd managed such success as a governess, by protecting her charges as if they were her own. "Are you better now?"

She managed to nod. "I think so."

He stooped down so that he could see her face. Her dark brown lashes were splayed across her cheeks in perfect, pointed crescents. He reached out and slid a finger over them, disturbing the collected moisture on her cheeks.

Anna jerked away as if burned. "What are you doing?"

"Wondering how you can see through such thick lashes. They tangle at the corners, you know."

"So do yours," she replied, then flushed a deep, delightful pink.

Anthony's groin tightened. God, but she was a magnificent woman—more woman than he'd ever known.

She pushed herself to her knees. "I really can swim, you know. It has just been a while."

"How long?"

"I think I was ten. Somehow, I was better at it then."

"I daresay you'd remember how if you had more practice." He stood and held out his hand.

Without demur, she placed her hand in his and let him pull her to her feet. "I don't know what to say. This is quite awkward."

"Drowning usually is." He watched her mouth press together in a most delightful manner. Though she was thoroughly wet and beginning to sniffle, she still managed to possess an innate elegance. She would make a commanding countess.

Good God, where had that come from? She might have the air one expected from a countess, but not the manner.

As if to confirm his thoughts, she pushed her hair from her face, succeeding only in shoving the lily pad to a more prominent position on the top of her head, then said in an ungracious tone, "I suppose I should thank you."

"I suppose you should," he replied. After all, he'd lost his slippers, and his new coat lay in the damp grass. "You should also inquire as to whether I'm injured. You left a footprint on my neck."

She bit her lip, though it appeared as if she were more amused than sorry. "I don't know what came over me—I rarely frighten."

"Hm. You didn't happen to climb trees when you were a child, did you? You have quite a grip for a gently bred lady."

Color again bloomed in her cheeks, contrasting with her red hair and the cream of her skin. Anthony thought he'd never seen a more beautiful woman.

She sniffed. "No, I did not climb trees as a child. I did, however, excel in scaling the trellis outside my window in an attempt to be near the barn at all times. I like to ride and my father was adamant that it should not interfere with my studies."

"Ran from the governess, did you?"

She grinned, her teeth flashing whitely. "Like a hoyden. But it was worth it. I'd have done anything to be with my horse, Princess. She was a beauty."

"And yet you refuse to ride with me. I begin to feel slighted."

"Only because it would be unbecoming for me to be seen about the countryside with my employer."

"Ungrateful brat."

"I am not ungrateful, Greyley. In fact, I am fully aware of what I owe you for this morning's efforts. Thank you for coming to my rescue."

"Don't think about it. Some aspects were quite pleasing." Like the way her thigh had been so delightfully close to his mouth. The thought sent a pang of heat to his nether regions, and he was damned glad they were in full view of the house, or he might have been tempted to do something about it, to hell with propriety.

"If there is anything I can do to repay you, I hope you will not hesitate to ask."

"You can thank me by going for a ride with me tomorrow morning." He wanted her alone and in his arms, he realized with sudden clarity. Not that he was searching for a dalliance. Good God, he hoped to be married in three months.

But still . . . his gaze slid slowly over Anna. Her wet gown clung lovingly to every curve, making him think of a dozen reasons that he might want to reconsider his "no dalliance" rule.

She was a sight indeed—tall and slender, with generous breasts and rounded hips that made his groin tighten. Better yet were the long legs he could see clearly outlined by the white muslin—the length and curve of those legs far exceeding even his active imagination. By Zeus, but she was a woman made for passion.

Anna pulled her skirts to one side and began squeezing water from them, the gesture unintentionally outlining one leg and hip in stark relief. "I am in your employ, Lord Greyley. It is never a good idea to mix with the help."

"I will mix when and where I will, thank you."

"Earls and governesses do not go for rides together."

"According to what rulebook?"

"According," she said in a voice he was sure she normally reserved for her pupils, "to the rules of society. I seem to remember you preaching them to your sister not so long ago."

"My expectations for my sister and for myself are quite different."

"Spoken like a true man." She shivered as she spoke, and for the first time, Anthony noticed how very transparent muslin became when wet. He could see the outline of her breasts so clearly that his breath thudded to a halt for a moment. Her nipples appeared faintly through the layers of drenched material—large and dark and desirable, perfectly made for his mouth.

Anthony discovered that it was possible to lose both the power of speech and thought all in the same instant.

Anna lifted her arms to push her hair back from her face, and Anthony was presented with an even clearer image of what lay beneath the layers of cloth. His body ached with the images and he had to swallow a groan.

Her hair secured behind her ears, she turned to the house. "I need to return to the nursery. The children must answer for this latest escapade. I've decided that they will write a letter of apology to both of us and then will do chores to help pay for the replacement of your shoes."

Anthony could have told her that it would take the children several years to do that, but he refrained. She was right; the children should be punished and he had to admit she'd thought of a fair method.

He cleared his throat. "While the children are doing chores, I suppose I will be off riding alone somewhere." He stared into the distance with what he hoped was a sad expression.

Anna frowned, her bad mood worsening. She'd been mocked, had almost died, and now had been forced to stand in front of Greyley and pretend she didn't look like a drowned rat. She pulled her hair to one side and again attempted to twist some of the water from it, only to discover a huge lily pad on her forehead. She pulled it free, embarrassment heating her cheeks. "I am returning to the house."

"Don't you think you owe me something? After all, I saved you, and at great personal cost, too, for I nearly gave up my own life in the process. The least you can do is ride with me."

"No rides."

"Then I'll settle for a kiss."

It was infuriating the way this man could turn a simple sentence into a lazy challenge. And Anna was not good at passing up a challenge.

It would be nice to ride with an adult for a change. Lovely, actually. The children were prone to go in different directions, and she spent most of her time trying to keep them all together.

Anna peered at Greyley from under her lashes. He *looked* harmless enough. Oh, he was handsome, and charming when he put his mind to it. But he had none of the polished address of the other wasted fribbles she knew. Perhaps it wouldn't hurt to go for just one ride. "Oh, very well. But only for a half hour."

"Half an hour is hardly long enough to give the poor horse a stretch."

"Forty-five minutes and not a moment more."

"An hour. I won't settle for less."

Heavens, but the man did not know the meaning of the word "no." Anna sighed. An hour wasn't that long, she supposed. She had just opened her mouth to agree, when he added, "Every day for a month."

She gaped at him. "You must be joking."

"I saved your life," he reminded her yet again, a very smug grin on his face. His gaze wandered over her face and down to her breasts. Something about the intensity of his expression alerted her, for she followed his gaze and gasped to see how little her wet gown hid. She hurriedly crossed her arms over her chest, but not before Greyley's grin set her face aflame.

How she disliked arrogant men. They made for beastly earls and horrid employers. "I will ride with you for half an hour every morning, for one week only. I can't spare more time than that."

He reached out and brushed the backs of his fingers over her wet cheek. "What's wrong, Thraxton? Afraid to be alone with me?"

She sniffed. "I'm not afraid of anything. Just don't expect me to speak. I'm not a witty conversationalist before I've had my breakfast."

"Of course," he replied smoothly, as if he didn't care if she bothered to speak at all. "May I add that I hope you teach the girls how to accept an invitation with better grace than you have shown today?"

Drat the man! She plopped her hands on her hips. "Lord

Greyley, rest assured that the girls will benefit from the time they have spent with me."

Too late, she realized that she'd forgotten to cover herself, for his dark brown gaze was once again fastened on her chest. Her temper snapped. "Damn it, Greyley, pay attention! *I* am speaking, not my breasts."

His gaze rose to her face, his eyes hot and brown, his mouth strangely soft. "You may not be able to hear your breasts speaking, but I can."

Anna gasped and covered her chest. "That is quite enough."

"Indeed it is," he agreed, taking two swift steps and closing the space between them.

Anna instinctively moved to retreat, but Greyley reached past her and picked up his coat from the grass. He shook it out, then swung it over her shoulders and pulled it closed.

"You can't walk into the house like that. I'd have to fire every footman we've got, and Jenkins would not be happy. He's just trained them."

His fingers brushed her chin as he fastened the coat up the front. The gesture was so quixotic, so unlike Greyley, that Anna neither moved nor protested.

He fastened the last button, then chucked her under the chin as if she were a child of six. "There you are, sweet. That should get you indoors without too much of a bustle."

"How chivalrous," she said, then moved to step away, but Greyley's notion of chivalry included imprisonment, for he gripped her shoulders and held her fast. She scowled. "Let me go."

He smiled then, that indolent smile that was all his. The smile that crinkled his eyes and made her heart flutter in the most uncomfortable way. "Miss Thraxton, your hair is incredibly fetching when wet. I had no notion it was so long."

She wondered warily what he was up to now. "I daresay I look well slathered with mud, too."

His gaze traveled from her face to her throat. "I believe you'd look fetching no matter what you did, or did not, wear. There are few women who can say that with any measure of truth."

His voice rumbled low and intimate, almost hypnotic. Truly, the man was a conundrum—one moment insulting her, and the next complimenting her like a courtier. Her confusion must have shown in her face, for he grinned and then turned her toward the house and gave her a little push, as if she were a recalcitrant child. "Go and don some dry clothes. We will meet in the morning for our ride."

Lord help her, but when had Greyley turned into such a captivating man? She caught sight of his bare feet. "How can you ride without boots?"

His gaze followed hers. "I'll borrow my brother's while I send to London for some new ones. Never fear, I'll be properly clothed when we go for our ride."

Anna met his warm brown gaze with a sinking feeling. She didn't dare ride alone with him, for her own safety as well as his. Gathering her rumpled composure, she turned and marched toward the house, all too aware of Greyley's silent company as he followed behind. She could almost feel his gaze on her shoulders, her hips, her legs.

She couldn't tell what he was thinking, yet when she caught his gaze just as she reached the house where Jenkins stood waiting, she thought she detected a surprising blaze of warmth. A look so fraught with promise that she barely managed to curtsy before she mumbled a disjointed thank you and then unceremoniously fled.

Later, dressed in a fresh gown, drying her hair before the

fire in the nursery while the children wrote their apology letters, Anna remembered in vivid detail her conversation with the earl. Something had changed. He was no longer chasing after the elusive schedule, but her. She could see it in his eyes, in the way he watched her. Some part of her thrilled at the thought. He was incredibly handsome. And she was beginning to realize that there was more to him than she'd thought—the way he took such care of the children, for instance.

That made him all the more dangerous. She would go riding with him—she'd promised. But she'd take her own protection, one destined to end Greyley's desire to ever go riding with her ever again.

Chapter 17

Nothing is quite so satisfying as a brisk ride in the park. Except, of course, eating, sleeping, drinking, and playing cards.

Lord Alvaney to Sir Rotherwood,
while sharing port at White's

"The *brown* waistcoat, my lord?" Ledbetter's voice resounded with disbelief.

"Yes, damn it. And be quick." Anthony was to meet Anna in ten minutes and he was running late.

Yesterday, after the incident at the pond, Anthony had changed into dry clothing and then retired to the library. Instead of being greeted by the faithful Dalmapple, he found Brand waiting. From his vantage point of the library window, he had apparently witnessed a good bit of Anthony's conversation with Miss Thraxton and was brimming with an inappropriate amount of curiosity.

Anthony had brushed aside Brand's insinuations that there was more between him and Anna Thraxton. But still . . . he couldn't forget the heat that flared between them. It was the damnedest thing.

His marriage to Charlotte was to be the usual arranged affair—once she'd given him the children necessary for the continuation of the Greyley line, she'd go about her amusements just as he planned to go about his. Like many men of the *ton*, he'd probably have taken a mistress once the patina of wedded bliss wore thin. After the first year, of course; he was a gentleman, after all.

All that had changed once he'd seen Anna Thraxton in a dripping wet gown. He'd be damned if he'd wait another moment. Though he'd been born an Elliot, he'd been raised a St. John. When he wanted something, he obtained it. And he wanted Anna Thraxton. She would be the perfect mistress; he was certain she would be as passionate in bed as she was out of it. All he had to do was awaken that passion and fan it to heights she couldn't ignore.

The idea played through his mind over and over. The end result was that he had stayed up far too late planning his stratagems, imagining the ultimately pleasurable outcome of his success. He would make sure the alliance would be to her advantage as well. It bothered him to see a woman of her station laboring away, regardless of the fact that it was becoming more and more plain that she had a gift for taking care of people.

She deserved silks and sapphires, a lovely home and the safety of knowing she'd never have to labor again. And he was going to give her all of that, and more.

The tantalizing thoughts followed him to bed and he'd dreamed of winning Anna in ways that left him hot and ready. It was the early hours of the morning before he finally fell into a mercifully dreamless sleep that lasted well past the time he usually rose.

He glanced at the clock, cursed loudly, then yanked on Brand's riding boots. They were a size too small and pinched like the devil, but he didn't care. The intractable Miss Thraxton would not wait a second past the appointed time.

Ledbetter appeared with the brown waistcoat. He ventured to say, "You've never worn this before. You said it was 'overly ornamented.'"

"Hand it to me," Anthony growled. If Anna decided not to wait on him and had returned to the nursery with the children, she'd be as safe as a nun locked in a cloister.

He buttoned the waistcoat, yanked his coat in place, and strode out the room. He reached the foyer and was relieved to see his quarry standing at the bottom of the stairs before the wide cheval mirror, adjusting her collar. "Miss Thraxton."

She peeped at him from beneath the brim of her hat, an almost mischievous expression in her light gray eyes. "Lord Greyley, you are late. I was just going to ask one of the footmen to send you a note."

"I'm afraid I overslept."

"Did you?" Anna gathered her skirts and walked past the footman who held the door open, the white feather on her hat bouncing cheerfully. "I've been ready for hours."

Anthony frowned. She should be wary, if not irritated, he'd foisted this ride on her. He was halfway down the steps when he realized what had left his future mistress in such good spirits.

Not two, but seven horses were saddled and ready for the ride. At the front sat Selena astride a very fat old pony that appeared none too pleased to be awake at this time of the morning. "We're going riding," she piped up, her voice breaking the chill morning silence. "With the sun!"

The other children broke into burbling talk, annoyingly eager to be off. Even Desford seemed less filled with scowls.

Anthony caught Anna's arm and brought her to a halt before him. "This was not part of our bargain."

She pulled her arm free and tugged on her gloves. "We

had no bargain. You invited me to go for a ride and I accepted." She turned a calm gray gaze his way, her lashes casting shadows over her cheeks, her wide mouth curved in a smile. "What difference does it make, Greyley? The children won't slow us down. They are capital riders, even Selena."

"Perhaps I wished for the opportunity to speak with you without interruption."

"If we ride two abreast, we will be able to do just that," she returned, then sailed down the remainder of the steps and allowed a groom to assist her onto her horse.

Anthony watched her with reluctant appreciation. The minx had outmaneuvered him. So far. A ghost of a grin soothed his irritation. His success might be delayed, but only that.

He followed her down the steps and mounted his own horse. Soon they were under way, the wispy morning fog lifting as the sun heated the day.

Anthony led them to a wide, leafy pathway that led to a small, gurgling river. He'd originally intended to take another route, but there would have been no opportunity to ride two abreast on such a narrow path.

But Anna still managed to avoid him, riding forward to check on Selena, whose stubborn pony showed an annoying tendency to stop walking and take a nap, or to quell Desford and Richard, who wanted to race at breakneck speed.

Content for the moment just to watch her, Anthony let her have her way. She was amazing with the children, speaking to them as if they were adults. She calmed Elizabeth, who had developed a fear of Marian's pony because it tried to nip at her, convinced Selena to be firmer with her stubborn mount, and then adroitly soothed Richard's wounded feelings when Desford decided to ride ahead.

Finally, there was nothing more to be done—the children were settled, enjoying the ride and the feeling of the crisp air and the bright sunshine. Anna returned to ride by his side.

Anthony nodded toward Desford, who rode just ahead. "I remember very little about being that age."

"Even if you did, it wouldn't help you to understand Desford. Poor child, he doesn't have anything of his own. Not really." At Anthony's surprised look, she waved a hand. "Oh, I don't mean clothing and such. I mean personal items. I, for example, have a locket that belonged to my grandmother. It isn't very valuable, for Grandpapa bought it for her at a fair. But it is dear to me all the same and gives me the feeling of belonging somewhere."

"Surely he has something of his father's?"

"No. Not a thing. I gather the children were collected from their home and brought here in a rather abrupt manner."

Had they? Anthony'd sent Dalmapple to bring the children to Greyley, but he couldn't remember telling anyone he was in a hurry. Oh, he *might* have told someone not to dawdle, but surely— He caught Anna's accusing stare and frowned. "I never intended that they leave anything behind."

"That's not the impression they were given."

"I shall remedy that as soon as possible." Ahead, Desford was engaged in a loud argument with Marian about the quality of their mounts. It reminded Anthony so much of himself and Sara at that same age that he almost smiled. "I was about Desford's age when my stepfather gave me my first knife. I have it still. Perhaps I should pass it on to him."

She slanted him an interested glance. "Your sister once told me that you were fond of your stepfather."

"I try to live up to his name every day.

Anna tilted her head to one side, a fat red curl coming to

rest on her collar. "I think you are far more St. John than El-liot."

"Miss Thraxton, you unman me."

"If it were that easy, Lady Putney would have done it long ago."

He had to laugh. "Indeed she would."

Anna smiled and they rode in silence for a way. The sunlight dappled her hair with a lacy pattern and caressed the white line of her cheek. She had the smoothest, most perfect skin of any woman he'd ever seen, white as cream and silken to the touch.

The increasingly loud sound of rushing water interrupted his thoughts and they came to a large clearing beside a stream. "We should stop here," he said just loud enough for the children to hear him.

"May we swim?" Marian asked, already sliding off her pony.

"Not in those clothes," Anna said.

"Oh," Marian said, disappointment in her tone. She looped her pony's reins over a bush and looked longingly toward the stream. The other children did the same, Desford helping Selena down as soon as his own mount was secure.

"Maybe we can just wade," Elizabeth said hopefully.

"There is a path you can explore," Anthony offered as he dismounted. The children were off down the path in a trice, talking excitedly. Desford followed at the rear, casting one or two curious gazes behind him as he went.

Anthony glanced at Anna. "The path only goes a short distance and leads them away from the water. They will be back within thirty minutes, depending on how long they tarry." He looped his reins over a branch, then returned to Anna. "It appears we will have some privacy after all."

Anna's fingers curled tightly about the reins. For some

reason she was finding Greyley's dark glances even more disturbing than usual. "That was devious."

"Surely not."

She ignored his outstretched hand. "I don't like the children wandering through the woods. They could get hurt."

"They are within shouting distance. Once you dismount, we could wander in their direction. I daresay we'll meet them coming back."

She looked down at him, at the way his dark gold hair fell over his brow, softening his stern features. There was a hint of humor about his mouth, and in his dark brown eyes. "You wish to discuss that damnable schedule."

"Among other things."

She really didn't have a choice. To remain on horseback put her at a distinct disadvantage in locating the children. With a barely repressed sigh, she dismounted. Instead of stepping away, he moved closer, clasping her waist with a strong grip. Anna was used to being as tall as, if not taller than, most men, and she noted the strength of him with approval.

Once her feet touched the ground, she glanced up at him. "Thank—"

His mouth descended on hers, warm and commanding. For a startled second Anna did nothing, but savored the feel of a man's arms about her, of being possessed and cherished. His hands tightened, then moved to her hips, and suddenly it was as if her senses exploded in a flame of searing heat. She forgot where she was, forgot who she was, and melted beneath his kiss.

The kiss deepened and Anna moaned restlessly. She was afire, hot and restless, drained of the will to protest. She didn't want to protest—she wanted this man in a way she'd never wanted another. The realization shook a path through her bemused senses and she broke free, stepped away, trembling. "You cannot do that."

His eyes glowed with heat. "Why not?"

"Because you are an earl and I am a governess."

He smiled then, and captured her against him, his warm body sparking a response deep within her. "You are also a Thraxton while I am a mere Elliot. Your family is far more respectable than mine."

It was madness. It was folly. It was also unaccountably delicious. *So long as I keep my heart in my possession . . .* She found herself leaning forward, her lips brushing his with the faintest of touches.

The simple touch was lost in an avalanche of emotion. They were not just kissing, they were tasting, devouring, their hands pulling each other closer, harder. Anna moaned as Greyley's hands cupped her bottom intimately, pulling her against his erection. She tilted her head back and his lips traced an impassioned line down her throat.

"Miss Thraxton?" came a childish voice.

It broke over Anna like a wave of icy water and she took a stumbling step away from Greyley.

There, not ten feet behind her, stood Selena. The little girl eyed her warily. "Are you sick?

Heart thudding, Anna managed an uncertain laugh. "Sick? No, no! I'm fine."

"You were moaning like your tummy hurt."

"It wasn't her tummy," Greyley murmured, his voice low and indecently husky. "It was her—"

"Eye," Anna said sharply, glaring at him.

"That's what I was going to say," he replied, a dangerous quirk to his mouth.

Anna conjugated the Latin word for "kick" before she managed a smile at Selena. "We were just looking for something that was stuck in my eye."

"A large piece of bark," the earl offered.

"Exactly," Anna said, a little mollified the blackguard was finally assisting her.

"A large, *hard* piece of bark," he added.

Anna snapped him a look. "I'm sure Selena does not need to be told every *little* detail."

His smile disappeared. "Little?"

"*Little*," she repeated firmly.

"There you are," Desford said, coming down the path, his gaze on Selena. "Where have you been?"

"Talking to Lord Greyley and Miss Thraxton. She had a piece of bark in her eye and he was kissing it out."

Anna made a distressed noise while Desford's gaze narrowed thoughtfully. "No, no," she said. "It was nothing like that."

The boy's mouth pursed, but to her surprise, he made no further comment. Instead, he took his sister's hand and led her back down the path. "We found a waterfall," he said as he went, disappearing behind the curve of the trees.

"Oh no," Anna said fretfully.

Greyley's warm hands encircled her waist again, but Anna moved away. "That's enough of that."

"You didn't enjoy it?"

"On the contrary," she said bluntly. "I enjoyed it far more than was suitable."

His gaze flared and he took a step toward her, then stopped, his hands fisted at his sides, a smug expression on his face. "What are we going to do about this, Thraxton?"

"About what?" she asked, desperately bidding for time.

"This attraction we have for one another."

"Nothing, of course," she said, smoothing her hair and trying to appear sane and sensible. "We have responsibilities. And treading down this path would be very dangerous for both of us."

"I like danger."

Good Lord, so did she. But not here. And not now. She knew the ending of this story, and it was nothing but heartbreak and the loss of her self-respect. "Not possible. We, Lord Greyley, are going to forget this ever happened." Anna turned on her heel and walked down the trail where Desford and Selena had just disappeared. "I'm going to see to the children."

He made as if to follow her, but she held up a hand. "Stay here and watch the horses."

His face darkened. "Anna, I—"

She left, almost running in her determination to get away. Once she was out of sight, she stepped off the path and leaned against a tree, pressing trembling hands to her heated cheeks. Ahead she could hear the children laughing, the sound calming her somewhat.

Damn Greyley for kissing her and making her forget herself and her responsibilities. She might be a Thraxton, but she was also the governess, and if anything were to develop between her and Greyley, it would be heartache of the first order. And for what? A few moments of passing pleasure? He couldn't possibly want more than that. And neither, Anna decided with a loud sniff, did she.

That decided, she gathered the children for the ride home.

Chapter 18

Marriage is a fine institution. Fine for women and an institution for men.

Sir Rotherwood to Edmund Valmont, while discussing the merits of remaining single

Anthony awoke to the sounds of rain. It thrummed on the overhang of his window and slapped the glass panes. He sighed and rolled onto his back, staring up at the red curtains that hung around his bed. The rain put an end to his hopes of another ride with Anna, even if he did have to take those blasted children along.

Actually, though, he hadn't really minded the children. As they'd ridden back, they'd stopped along the way to enjoy the sight of a cow rubbing its back against a tree and then again later, to enjoy a lively discussion over which thicket hid a particularly large rabbit that had frightened Desford's horse by running across the road in front of him.

To his surprise, Anthony had enjoyed himself immensely. He'd also discovered things he'd never known. For example, he'd never realized what a talent Marian had for riding, but she was amazingly adept, far too much to be riding such a slug. He would look for a new horse for her today.

Then there was Richard. Though the boy'd remained silent, once or twice Anthony thought he'd seen just the hint of a smile, which was indeed something new. Perhaps it would just take some time and the warmth of the sun to bring the child back to life.

Anthony had enjoyed the antics of Selena and Elizabeth, too, as they shamelessly vied for Miss Thraxton's attention. He didn't blame them for their efforts—the governess showed to advantage in her sapphire blue habit, that ridiculous hat pinned to her red tresses, the long white feather caressing her cheek every time she turned her head.

It was enough to drive a man to drink. Worse, she had been noticeably cool toward him after their kiss, keeping her attention focused on the children.

Anthony tossed the sheets aside, then stood, the cool morning air brushing over his naked body. The wind moaned against the outside of the house, rattling the windows. Anthony dressed and had just begun to knot his cravat when a brisk knock heralded the entrance of Jenkins, who carried a crisply folded note. Anthony recognized the elegant script immediately.

Greyley,

After careful thought, I realize that we cannot continue our rides. However, the children are more than eager for the exercise and thus await your pleasure once the weather has cleared.

Sincerely,
A. Thraxton

Anthony wadded up the note and sent it sailing toward the fireplace. Damn the woman. He returned to knotting his cravat, meeting his own gaze in the mirror. Anna Thraxton was not making his quest easy and it didn't surprise him the least bit.

What was it about her, he wondered, absently noting the St. John talisman ring where it sat neglected among the fobs on his dresser. He pushed the ring aside and selected a ruby cravat pin. Perhaps it was the challenge of the chase—he hadn't been so amused in some time.

Just being with her made him feel . . . He shrugged. It was the excitement of something new, something different from the ordinary. Something to be savored, for it would not last long.

Ignoring Ledbetter's plea to wear a more significant pin on his cravat, Anthony left his room and made his way to the library. Mr. Dalmapple awaited him there, a list of pressing decisions carefully scripted on a neat sheet of vellum.

Anthony listened to his man of business with half an ear, his gaze fixed on the streams of rain that cut across the library windows. He rubbed his mouth thoughtfully, smiling a little to himself. All he had to do was find a way to get her alone again.

Going to the nursery was out of the question. Somehow, some way, he had to get the lovely Miss Thraxton to come to him.

Excitement stirred in his stomach and quickened his blood. What would tempt a woman bent on remaining within the strict boundaries of propriety? What would lure her from the safety of the nursery?

Perhaps . . . perhaps a simple game of billiards. What could be more innocent? For an instant, he imagined the sight of Thraxton's pale skin against the green felt of the table, her auburn hair splayed like a fan about her face. Hell, nothing was innocent with a woman like her around. Still . . . the word "billiards" would conjure no such indecent thoughts in a woman with such strenuous notions of propriety.

Grinning, Anthony reached for a sheet of vellum. He ignored Dalmapple's running commentary on the state of the west fields and dipped his pen in ink.

Thraxton, he wrote with a nice flourish.

I hope this note finds you well and none the worse for yesterday's—

Anthony paused. Yesterday's what? Sensual kisses? Forbidden touches? He chuckled and then wrote:

—vigorous activities. As the rain appears to have ended our hopes for a ride, a game of billiards will have to do as a substitute. I will be in the billiards room at ten. I trust you will be there when I arrive.

Yours,
Greyley

He silently reread the letter. Dalmapple had by this time noticed his inattendance and was now morosely scribbling in his account books, casting dark glances his way.

Anthony sanded the missive. It was abrupt and very commanding. He was certain she'd hate it. She didn't have the nose of a Roman emperor for nothing.

He rang for the footman, pleased with himself. He was baiting her, teasing her for amusement's sake alone. It was childish in a way, he supposed. But it was also the most fun he'd had in a long, long time.

A discreet knock on the door heralded the footman. Anthony gave the man the missive and sent him off to the nursery. Then, satisfied, he settled back in his chair and waited. Dalmapple decided to take the opportunity to redirect his attention to the affairs of the estate, but Anthony waved him out, telling him that he'd meet with him on the morrow.

As Dalmapple left, sniffing as if in a huff, Anthony imagined Anna's hair curling over her bared shoulders, caressing the line of her naked breasts and the flat plane of her stomach. The image heated him instantly and he had to shift in his chair to accommodate his reaction. He did indeed want Thraxton in his bed. Unclothed and ready for some sport. An hour or two should do it, he decided charitably. Maybe three.

Anthony glanced at the window where the rain lashed against the pane. It would have been pleasant to have awakened with Thraxton in his bed this morning, where their passion would have brightened an otherwise dreary day. Did she wear a gown to bed? He would bet his last penny she did—a long, overly frilled and heavily ribboned monstrosity of a gown, no doubt. One that hid her figure thoroughly.

Perhaps he would buy her something scandalously filmy. The thought took root and he sat musing over the merits of pale pink silk and gossamer white lace until a polite knock on the door interrupted his musings. The footman returned, a crisply folded missive on his tray. Anthony tried to still his disappointment that the intemperate Miss Thraxton had not stormed into his library, her passions in an uproar.

He took the note from the footman and gestured for the man to wait.

Greyley,

While I was charmed to receive such a politely worded invitation, I feel I must decline. I have many duties to see to today and you, my lord, are not one of them.

Sincerely,
Thraxton

Anthony leaned back in his chair and propped his feet on his desk. Perhaps he'd been wrong—maybe he should use softer, gentler language, like Brand would use. Anthony snorted. Anna would scoff at such nonsense. No, a woman like Thraxton responded to direct handling and nothing else, like a wild horse that needed taming.

After a moment, he removed his feet from the desk, took pen in hand, and began to write.

Thraxton,

Not only do you owe me your life, but you are also in my employ. Meet me in the billiards room at ten or I will come and get you.

Yours,
Greyley

Anthony sanded the missive, then handed it to the waiting footman. Arms crossed behind his head, Anthony sat back in his chair and waited, whistling a refrain from a colorful song he suddenly remembered from his youth.

Within moments he heard the snap of a determined pair of slippers approaching the library. He barely had time to loosen his cravat and prop his feet on his desk before the door was thrown open and Anna sailed in, her chin high, her air that of an offended goddess.

She slammed the door closed so hard that a book fell off a nearby shelf. Anna stepped over the book and then marched to his desk. Once there, she placed her hands palm down on the wide surface and leaned forward, her face flushed a becoming pink. "I cannot believe you would be so rude as to demand my presence based on the fact that I am in your employ!"

"You have no idea how rude I can be," he said affably, admiring the proud line of her nose. She really was a magnificent woman, all fire and spice.

"I am not a scullery maid, Greyley, and you'd do well to remember that fact."

The way her eyes sparkled silver when she was angry was also something to be admired. "I would never invite a scullery maid to play billiards. In fact, I wouldn't invite a scullery maid anywhere."

"But you would invite a governess."

He removed his feet from the desk and stood, leaning forward until his face was even with hers across the wide desk. "I can invite you, Anna Thraxton, to play billiards, ride, even dance with me. I am, after all, master of this house."

"You are an arrogant bastard, Greyley."

"True," he agreed with a faint smile. "But I'm also an excellent host." Outside, thunder rumbled across the sky and the rain increased to a torrential pour. Anthony gestured toward the window. "I would rather ride, as I'm sure you would, but the rain has prevented it. I simply thought to exchange the one pleasure for another."

She had to bite her lip to keep from returning his smile. Greyley outraged, anger sparkling in his dark brown eyes, was incredibly handsome. Greyley amused, his firm mouth curved in a smile, was simply devastating. Anna's resistance was melting by the second.

As if he could read her mind, his smile widened to something slow, easy, and intimate. "Perhaps after lunch you will find the time for *two* games of billiards?"

Despite her irritation, Anna was no match for his warm brown eyes. She sighed. He looked just like one of the children begging for someone to play Jack Pole or Rough 'n

Tumble. "It would be highly inappropriate for me to do any such thing and you know it."

"You are at my house, Miss Thraxton. Within these walls, I decide what is appropriate and what is inappropriate."

Anna almost laughed. He was so determined to bend everything to his will. "Nothing will make me agree to *that.*"

"Then what would be acceptable to you? I cannot allow you to languish in the nursery. My sister would consider me a poor host indeed, and she's not shy in berating me."

"I'm not a guest and I'm not languishing. I like being with the children. Unlike you, I actually enjoyed the ride yesterday."

His hot brown gaze rested on her, stroking her face, lingering on her lips. "So did I," he murmured. "Far more than you realize."

His tone was so intimate that Anna moved away from the desk, her heart thudding in the most uncomfortable way. "Lord Greyley, I cannot be alone with you again. Last time . . . last time was a mistake." One that left her lying awake long after she'd gone to bed, her thoughts far, far from those of a respectable governess.

His gaze heated from brown to black in the space of an instant. "Last time was magnificent and you know it."

"It was pleasant," she said, wiping her damp palms on her dress, hoping that lightning did not strike her where she stood. Calling Greyley's kisses pleasant was tantamount to calling Hampton Court Palace "nice." "But we cannot allow ourselves to be so lost to propriety again, or—" She blushed, thinking of what that "or" portended.

"Oh, but we can," he said in a reasonable voice, coming out from behind the desk, his movements as smooth and sure as a lion on the hunt.

"I should leave," Anna said, suddenly breathless as she watched him approach. She took a step back.

He followed her. "You'd abandon the field of battle, just like that?" He shook his head sadly, though a gleam of humor lit his eyes to gold. "Thraxton, you disappoint me."

She eyed him narrowly. There was something different about the earl today. Something . . . lighter. And infinitely more dangerous. "You wrote that horrible note just to infuriate me, didn't you?"

He grinned, his teeth white.

Damn the man! "Just what do you hope to accomplish with such mischief?"

"I just want to talk."

"Talk?" she scoffed. "I don't think talking was what you had in mind."

"Hm." He lifted a finger and traced the line of her cheek, the touch exquisitely gentle.

Anna's heart beat such an erratic rhythm that she was surprised he didn't comment on it. "Greyley, we shouldn't do this." But oh, how she *wanted* him to do this. She *wanted* Greyley to kiss her. Kiss her, and more.

It seemed to Anna as if her entire life was to be bound forever by the strict rules of being a governess while some wild, lonely part of her hungered for something more. Something passionate. And Greyley represented that passion.

It would mean nothing, of that she was sure. But still . . . She looked up at the line of his mouth, her body softening at the sight. He was magnificent. Anna couldn't imagine allowing herself to experience the forbidden with anyone else.

"Anna," he whispered, his fingertips brushing her lips. "What do you want?"

"I don't know, but I think . . . I think I want you." Anna closed her eyes as she heard herself whisper the words. He would think her such a fool. A woman of no principles. She opened her eyes and saw the answering blaze in his.

"I want you, too."

Anna swallowed hard, her feelings tied into knots so tight that she couldn't imagine how to begin untangling them. She glanced up at him through her lashes, wishing he wouldn't stand quite so close. At the same time, she wished he'd just reach out and sweep her into his arms and end her agony.

He leaned forward so that his lips were but a whisper from hers. "We can be very good for each other." His breath brushed her face, hot and possessive.

She shivered. "Can we?"

Anthony's hands slid around her waist. "You are a very attractive woman, Thraxton. Beautiful, even."

If she leaned forward just the tiniest bit, she'd be against his chest. To Anna's horror, she found the thought fascinating. Engrossing. Wonderful beyond description. Agitated, she stepped back as far as his grasp allowed. "If you are doing this just to get that damned schedule out of me, then you're wasting your time. I don't like schedules and I don't intend to use one."

His lids lowered slightly and he regarded her for a long moment, his eyes shadowed by his thick lashes. "You can't elude me forever. There's fire between us, Anna. And you know it."

"I'm sure Hades tempted Persephone with those exact words."

"And look what a pleasant interlude they had."

And an interlude would be all it was, Anna decided, her thoughts clearing miraculously. A pleasant interlude to be enjoyed, something to keep with her as she went about her business being a prim and proper governess.

Some of her feelings must have shown on her face, for in one sharp movement, he pulled her hard against his chest and kissed her. As his mouth opened over hers, all sane thought left her. Emotions swirled in a wild dance that sent ripples of hunger through her, making her move in restless abandon. In some distant recess of her mind, she recognized that Anthony Elliot was a trained specialist when it came to delivering soul-searing kisses. Kisses that stole her breath and melted her into a mindless puddle of desire. His passion ignited hers, and she returned the kiss so wantonly that he moaned her name against his lips.

Anna was a woman who loved the feel of raw silk on her bare skin. A woman who lusted after the better things in life. She dreamed of diamond and ruby necklaces, their weight decadent against her naked throat. And now she discovered even more wanton dreams—of being held in a man's arms as he kissed her into madness and beyond.

Anthony's mouth trailed a hot, damp line to her throat. "Anna," he murmured against her skin. "Do you know what you taste like?"

She took a shuddering breath, her hands unconsciously twining in his hair as she offered herself to him. "What?"

He lifted his head and smiled down into her eyes, his hand cupping her face, his thumbs tracing the line of her cheeks. "Rice pudding."

She laughed, and his smile faded, replaced by a sudden hunger. He kissed her again, fierce and passionate, as if her laughter had sparked some new response, something blazing hot and possessive.

She forgot she was a governess, forgot she was bound by propriety, forgot everything but the delicious feel of being with him.

Anna leaned into him, soaking in the heat of his hands as they slid over her shoulders, her back, her hips, molding her gown to her skin. Whispering her name, he slid a hand over her hip to her thigh, then to her bottom, where he held her tightly against him, letting her feel his response to their nearness.

She caught her breath, then tugged on his cravat, pleased when the loose knot fell free and left his neck open. The bronze strength of him shone where his corded neck muscles rose to his strong jaw. Anna traced the line of his throat, savoring his deep groan when she nipped his ear. She felt wanton and free, and it was a heady experience.

He eased her back, placing hot kisses on her forehead and feathering her lashes with his caresses. The hard edge of the desk met the backs of her thighs, and Anthony easily lifted her in one smooth motion so that she sat on the edge. He deepened his kiss, gently thrusting his tongue into her mouth in a pulsating rhythm.

Anna gripped his shirt, pulling him closer, losing herself in his strength. Anthony responded hotly to her fervor. He traced the line of her hip, down her thigh and leg. Then, slowly, ever so slowly, he placed his hand on her bare ankle, lifting the caress to her calf, then her knee. His long fingers splayed over her bare skin, touching, smoothing as he pushed her skirts up with each move.

Jolts of searing exhilaration coursed through her. Anna reveled in the feelings he provoked. For the first time in over a year, the small part of her that resented being relegated to a mere governess slipped free. She pressed herself against him, inhaling his spicy male scent and letting his hands roam as they would.

His hand slid beyond the delicate skin of her knee to her thigh. There he hesitated, pulling back to look at her, a question in his dark eyes. A question Anna didn't want to answer. She pulled his mouth back to hers as she arched against him, wanting something . . . more. Anthony moaned, and for an instant Anna knew she had complete power over the moment. If she closed her thighs, he would stop. But if she opened them . . . it was sweet madness.

She ran her hands over his broad shoulders and moved her thighs apart. It was a sweetly abandoned movement, and Anna shivered with desire, the knowledge that what they were doing was forbidden making it all the more powerful.

Anthony was lost. With every kiss, every touch, he was a welter of desire. He'd never been so close to being out of control, but then he'd never been with Anna before, either. There was something about her that awakened feelings he never knew he possessed. And now, sitting on the edge of his desk, her legs splayed in the most wanton manner, her hair falling about her shoulders, her silver eyes luminous with desire, he decided she was the most sensuous woman he'd ever met.

Fighting for control, he buried his face in her neck, breathing in her scent. It was lemon and rose, the freshness of a spring breeze and something more exotic. The desire to experience life, to make everything about her as beautiful as she was, overwhelmed him. Anthony's chest tightened and he took a shuddering breath. She was intoxicating and she was in his arms. All his.

Until he wed. Every St. John principle he'd ever learned came rushing to the fore and it was with exquisite agony that he attempted to recall his traitorous body to order. He couldn't do this. Not to himself. Not to Anna. Not unless she agreed to allow him to become her protector.

He lifted his head and looked down into her eyes. "Anna, you have to—"

She kissed him. Not the tentative, feather-soft kisses of an ingénue, but with blinding white passion. Every thought Anthony possessed was consumed in a single flame and he kissed her back, drinking from her as if he were dying of thirst.

He teased and taunted her with his tongue even as his hand went back to her exposed legs. Without breaking the kiss, he ran his fingers up her thigh and then gently parted the slit of her silk drawers. She gasped sharply when he slipped his hand inside, his fingers finding her most secret part, but Anthony did not abate. Instead he trailed his mouth down her throat and increased the pressure of his fingers.

She moaned, shifting restlessly on the edge of the desk. Gently but firmly he caressed her, capturing her mouth with his and drawing her to him. She slowly relaxed even as she became hotter, wetter with need, her hands clutching his shirt in desperate wonder.

He increased his ministrations, feeling her swell with heat. She moaned hotly, then stiffened, "Anthony!" she gasped.

He lifted his head so that he could watch her, see the flood of wonder in her pale eyes. She clutched at his shirt as she climaxed, and pressed her face against his neck. Anthony held her close as the tremor subsided, wrapping his arms tightly about her, gritting his teeth against his own burgeoning passion.

He'd never wanted a woman this badly before, and never an innocent. He closed his eyes and rested his cheek against Anna's silken hair, fighting to contain the remnants of his control. As much as he wanted to, he couldn't take her on his desk. No, at their first union she would have every comfort available. Every pleasure he could think of. He was a St. John, damn it. And he would do his best to take care of Anna from this day forward.

Slowly, as Anna's breathing returned to normal, the raging heat that roared through Anthony subsided as well.

He took a last, shuddering breath, then stepped away. Anna looked up at him, her mouth kiss-swollen, her pale skin glowing with the flush of passion. God, but she was beautiful. Beautiful and innocent. Anthony realized how close he'd come to ravishing a complete innocent, and one who was his own sister's best friend. The thoughts cooled the last remaining touch of ardor from his blood.

Anna passed a trembling hand over her eyes. Something tender welled inside Anthony and he took her hand and pressed a kiss to her fingers. "You are amazing."

A smile trembled on her lips. "No wonder men are so enamored of it," she said in a husky voice.

Anthony chuckled. "And women, too, sweet. Don't let anyone tell you otherwise."

She turned an adorable pink, her gaze dropping to her lap. The blush deepened to a fiery red as Anthony's gaze followed hers. Her skirts were still rucked up about her thighs, her drawers parted to reveal the slightest hint of the dark red curls that lay hidden.

Anna made a convulsive move to yank down her skirts, but Anthony captured her hands. He pulled her from the desk and stood her on her feet. Her skirts dropped gracefully to the ground. Though modestly covered, she looked anything but normal, her mouth still red from his kisses, her hair mussed. Anthony's body stirred at the sight and he reluctantly moved away, silently chastising himself.

Strange as it seemed, he realized the reason for his unease. He actually liked Anna Thraxton. Liked her better than any woman he could think of. She was intelligent, beautiful, capable, held fiercely to her opinions, and was loyal to a fault.

And she liked him—he could see it in her eyes, in the

way she grinned so quickly when they talked. As ludicrous as it was, Anthony had no wish to destroy the glimmer of respect he saw in her gaze. He sighed and rubbed a hand over his face, wondering what he was supposed to do now.

Watching him, Anna's throat tightened. He might be sorry for their impetuous actions, but she wasn't. She set her shoulders and pretended to smooth her skirts so she wouldn't have to meet his gaze. She was glad this had happened. Faint tremors of pleasure still echoed through her and her breasts felt full and tight. For the first time in over a year, she felt alive and free and . . . happy.

A smile quivered at her lips. Anna tried to smooth her hair back into a semblance of its usual style, knowing as she did so that it would take a handful of pins and a mirror to do it correctly. Her hands still shook and it was all she could do to replace the pins she found scattered on the desk. She stifled a giggle when Greyley made an impatient sound and tucked one of her loose curls behind her ear.

She glanced up at him and froze—it was as if he wished to devour her. His gaze was hot, possessive, a furious passion deep in the brown depths.

The silence grew and stretched. Anna cleared her throat, desperate to find a way to ease the tension. The children . . . yes, she would talk about them. "Since we are here, Greyley, there is one thing I wanted to ask you. Mrs. Stibbons has allowed the new maid, Lily, to assist me in the nursery."

The change of topic did not seem to be to his liking, for he frowned. "Anna, we cannot—"

"You know Lily, don't you?"

He was silent for a long moment. Then he sighed. "No. Who is she?"

"She is serving as lady's maid to Lady Putney. But Lily has taken so well to the children and seems so nervous when not in the nursery, that we thought we might hire a new lady's maid for Lady Putney."

"Do as you deem necessary."

"It might make Lady Putney angry."

"Then I shall like the plan all the more," he replied shortly.

Anna had to fight a sudden impulse to lean over and trail her lips along that tight jaw. She wanted to taste him again, to feel his touch. Even more, she wanted him to finish what he had started. She knew from his expression what it had cost him to stop when he had.

Good heavens, but she was in a coil. She was in more danger with Greyley than she thought possible. The more she saw his attention to the children and his service to the Elliot family, the more she'd come to value him. And that was the last thing she wanted to feel for a man bent on seducing her.

Not that she minded being seduced; it was quite the opposite, in fact. But she knew the pain that would come if she were to succumb to other, more serious thoughts and feelings. If she began to believe that there was a happy-ever-after for her, a governess. And therein lay the danger.

The silence in the room grew until it felt oppressive. Anna forced a brittle smile to her lips. "Greyley, I know this is awkward. We'll just pretend it never happened—"

She was in his arms and pinned against his chest before she could blink. "No," he said gruffly, looking down at her with a blazing look that vanquished the pain in her heart. "We won't pretend anything. I want you, Anna. But only if you want me, too. I just didn't mean for us to go so far." He glanced around the room and shook his head. "Not here, anyway. I want us to have something more special, something more permanent."

Anna's breath caught in her throat. "Permanent?" She hated the way the word sounded so hopeful, but Anthony didn't seem to mind.

He looked down at her, a gleam in his eyes as he ran his hands over her back and hips, over and over again, the movement sending ripples of pleasure through her. "Yes. I have a small house not two miles from here and—"

"A house?"

"Yes. For now. Later . . ." He shrugged. "If you wish something more grand, I can have something built here, on Greyley lands."

"Later?"

His jaw tightened at her expression. "Anna, I will take care of you always. I swear it."

The brief flash of hope was incinerated by searing anger. She pushed herself away. "You—"

"Well!" came a voice from the doorway. "There you two are."

Anna whirled to see Lady Putney standing just inside the library. *Oh no. How long has she been there?*

Lady Putney's gaze narrowed on Anna, seeming to take in her flushed checks. "I can see that I'm interrupting something."

"Nonsense," Anthony said shortly.

Anna managed a brittle smile. "Lady Putney, how nice to see you. Have you come from the nursery?"

"Yes, which you would know if you had been where you belonged," the old woman said coldly.

Anthony frowned at Lady Putney. "That's enough of that. I'm glad you've come."

She raised her thin brows, suspicion on her face. "Why?"

"A girl named Lily has been serving as your lady's maid."

The change of topic unnerved Lady Putney, for she blinked. "Lily? She is a clumsy child, but with a little instruction, I daresay she'll do."

"Her clumsiness is about to become someone else's concern," Greyley said without any show of emotion. "She has shown herself to be adept at working with the children so I am assigning Lily to Miss Thraxton. You will find another maid."

Anna winced. Why did Greyley have to be so preemptory in his speaking? He barked orders as if he were the general of a very uncooperative army.

Lady Putney's jaw tightened. "I just got that stupid girl where she could do my hair with some talent!"

"What a pity," Greyley said. "Lily is going to the nursery and that is that."

Anna rubbed her forehead. *Sweet heavens, but the man is insufferable.* Greyley stormed his way through life, stepping on toes and tromping on other people's pride without the slightest regard. She said smoothly, "Lady Putney, Lily will come to the nursery only if you don't mind."

Greyley waved his hand. "Lady Putney will not be discomfited. I will send to London for a suitable replacement. Someone more practiced in being a lady's maid."

Anna could see the elder woman grappling with the decision. Since it was obvious that Anna wished for Lily's assistance, Lady Putney did not wish to relinquish her claim. But if she did not, she would lose Greyley's generous offer of a London-trained maid.

"Perhaps I should simply find another servant," Anna interjected, keeping a narrow watch on Lady Putney. "I'm sure there are a dozen or more who would do."

Anthony turned to Anna. She met his glance with a meaningful stare.

After a moment, he smiled, then said, "I'm sure you are right, Miss Thraxton. There are probably two dozen persons capable of dealing with the children in the nursery. And I'm sure that Lily is a more than proficient lady's maid for Lady Putney. Besides, I'm not sure what it would cost me to procure the services of a London trained maid, but I'm certain it would be outrageous and—"

"Wait," Lady Putney said, her mouth pinched. "Surely you would not count pennies when talking about my comfort. I will tell Dalmapple to see to the hiring of a maid from London as soon as possible." She turned a bitter glare at Anna. "As for Lily, Miss Thraxton is welcome to her. She has clumsy hands and has pulled my hair I know not how many times during the past sennight. I am forever boxing her ears for her lack of attention."

Anna decided it would be very satisfying to box Lady Putney's ears, but only if she could use a boat oar to do so. She managed a credible smile. "Lady Putney, you are too kind to allow the children to have your maid."

That seemed to mollify the woman, for her face softened slightly. "Yes, well, anything for the children. They are my only joy." She sent a bitter glare at Greyley. "That is the reason I came looking for you. The children have not been to Chawley House in some time. I would like to take them for a visit."

"Chawley House?" Anna asked.

"Lady Putney's home in Somerset," Anthony said grimly. He glanced at Lady Putney from beneath his brows. "We have spoken of this before, and we agreed that the children would stay here for at least a year."

"I only wish to take them for a week or so. They would benefit from it, especially poor Desford. He is wilting away in this moldy pile."

"Greyley House is not a 'moldy pile.' "

Lady Putney shuddered. "This house is a mausoleum."

"Then leave," Greyley said, reaching out to pull the bell rope. "I'll order a carriage."

Lady Putney seemed to realize she'd gone too far, for she tittered nervously. "I cannot leave while the children are here."

"Yes, you can." But he removed his hand from the bell pull. "And it is time you realized that."

The tension in the room was so taut that Anna cleared her throat. "Lady Putney, perhaps you would like to go to the nursery with me now, to visit the children." It seemed imperative to get the interfering woman out of the room before Greyley burst into flames.

Lady Putney's face tightened. "Miss Thraxton, it is not your place to tell me what to do."

"She didn't tell you to do anything," Greyley replied. "She asked you. And much more nicely than I would have."

Lady Putney looked from Anna to the earl and back, dawning disgust on her face. "Well! I see how things are."

"I doubt it," Greyley said. "But that is nothing new."

"I don't have to listen to this," Lady Putney replied. She turned to Anna. "Miss Thraxton, I hope you enjoy the services of *my* maid. I'm sure you've earned it." Sniffing rudely, she turned and left, slamming the door behind her.

Anna whirled to face Greyley. "Must you be so offensive?"

"You don't know the half of what that woman has done."

"It doesn't matter. Setting up her back will do no good at all."

"Listen, Thraxton, I don't need anyone telling me how to act."

"I beg to differ. Your manners are harsh and unfair. Worse, you allowed Lady Putney to think that we were—" Her anger threatened to boil over. "Lord Greyley, our involvement is at an end." She turned toward the door.

He stepped forward as if to stop her, but Anna was too quick. She made sure she slammed the door behind her, the sound echoing in the hallway.

The nodcock! The arrogant, ill-mannered ass. She fumed all the way back to the nursery, throwing the door open with such force it bounced against the wall.

The children all looked up, as did Mrs. Stibbons, surprise on their faces. Anna cursed her own ill temper. "Sorry. Must have been a draft."

Mrs. Stibbons set Selena off her lap and stood. "I was just tellin' the children a story."

Selena nodded, her curls bouncing along. "It was about a giant."

"And a magic arrow," added Marian, who was pink with excitement.

Anna's mouth softened, though she couldn't quite manage a smile. "You must be quite a tale spinner, Mrs. Stibbons."

"I've heard it before," Desford said sulkily.

"There now," Mrs. Stibbons said, smiling merrily. "That's why I brought some of Cook's finest apple tarts, for those who'd be bored to tears by my poor rendition of the Tale of Chatswith." She leaned toward Anna and said loudly, "Master Desford was very polite and did not once offer to tell the surprise ending."

"Excellent," Anna murmured, noticing that Desford was keeping his gaze fixed on an apple tart. "I've already noticed that he is a man of his word."

His gaze jerked up to her, and he frowned, and then looked away.

Mrs. Stibbons noted it all. Once she had settled the children back to their tasks, she said quietly, "Don't let Master Desford set you off, miss. He's a good boy, but full of the Elliot pride. If Lord Greyley would just imagine himself at that age, they'd get along like Flick and Flin."

"I fear that Lord Greyley lacks the delicacy of thought such a concept would take. He has all the charm of a violent explosion."

Mrs. Stibbons chuckled. "There you have it, miss. I'm glad to see you know him so well already."

"He isn't very difficult to decipher."

"Oh, he's the salt of the earth, he is. As good as they get, but—" She blew out her breath in a gusty sigh. "There are times I could wring His Lordship's neck. He's a good master, but he doesn't understand the need for a soft word now and again."

"He's gotten his way far too much for his own good."

"Lord, yes. What he needs is a good wife. A pity Miss Melton's grandmother died and she had to go into mourning. I think they'd have already wed if it wasn't for that."

Anna's heart jerked to a halt and she slowly turned toward the housekeeper. "Miss Melton?"

"His Lordship's betrothed."

A roar pitched forth, echoing in Anna's ears. She thought of Greyley's mouth on hers, of the warmth of his arms about her and she took a long, slow breath. "Miss Melton?" she said again, as if in repeating the words, they might disappear like a wisp of troublesome smoke.

Mrs. Stibbons seemed blithely unaware that the air had turned to dark gray and was too thick to breathe. "Barely eighteen if she's a day, and as pretty as they come, not that I think that had anything to do with it. His Lordship knows his responsibilities and he has to provide an heir else the entire estate will revert to the Elliots, and there's not a one who's worth a thimbleful of His Lordship's spit."

"Then Greyley's engagement isn't a love match?" Anna said, unsure why such a trivial thing made her lungs work again.

Mrs. Stibbons laughed merrily. "Lord love you, child! The gentry don't do things that way. Besides, I don't think His Lordship loves anyone."

"Except his sister."

"True. And his brothers—you can tell he's fond of them. His marriage to Miss Melton was arranged between her father and His Lordship. The Melton land marches along Greyley's and I daresay His Lordship thought to increase his holdings." Mrs. Stibbons took a handkerchief from her pocket and wiped a smudge off Selena's cheek. The little girl didn't even look up from where she was trying to make an "A" on a chalkboard. "A pity you'll never meet Miss Melton, for I daresay she'd benefit from the experience."

Anna leveled a look of disbelief at the housekeeper. "Why do you say that?"

Mrs. Stibbons tucked the handkerchief back in her pocket. "Miss Charlotte Melton is as sweet as they come, but she's a mite short on spirit, if you know what I mean."

Greyley *would* choose a bride with the character of a limp rag, Anna thought, seething at the thought that the bounder had been trying to make love to her while he'd been engaged to another woman. Not that Anna had thought for one second that Greyley's intentions were anywhere near honorable. He couldn't spell the word, much less serve as a definition.

Still, tears gathered at the thought of how intimate they'd already become. It was maddening, but she cared about him. Cared more than she wanted to admit.

To take her mind off her unruly emotions, Anna turned to the children and said in a brittle voice, "Perhaps we should make shadow puppets today."

For the rest of the afternoon, Anna kept the children busily engaged, making puppets to go with their lessons on Queen Elizabeth and the glorious battle with the Spanish Armada. While assisting Desford in flipping tiny paper cannon balls at the large ship cutouts, Anna realized that perhaps it was all for the best. Her feelings for Greyley were growing far too quickly for her own comfort—just witness what the news of his betrothal had caused. A dull ache still reigned in the region of her heart.

If it weren't for the fact she needed her pay to take care of Grandpapa, she'd be tempted to pack up and leave. Anna fingered a paper cannon and wondered what Sara would think of her brother's betrothal to an eighteen-year-old miss who was still wet behind the ears.

Of course, that was just Mrs. Stibbons's opinion. It was entirely possible that Miss Charlotte Melton was a very competent and knowledgable young woman. Perhaps she was even mercenary, or cruel. Anna's arms tightened about Selena, who had come to stand at her knee. Anthony was just like any other man, susceptible to flattery and a pair of thickly lashed eyes.

Well, Anna would meet this paragon and see how the wind blew. And if Miss Charlotte Melton was anything less than the purest driven snow, Anna would immediately send word to Sara. It was the least she could do.

That decided, she picked up a pair of scissors and furiously chopped out a new cannon for the children's amusement.

Chapter 19

The man owes me twenty pounds and what does he do but stick his spoon in the wall and die without so much as a by-your-leave. There's nothing left for it now, unless, of course, I were to nip a few of those silver buttons off the corpse, which I'd never do, there being so many people about and all.

Edmund Valmont to his friend, the Duke of Wexford, at the funeral of Lord Dunsmore, who died while eating a sausage at his lodgings on St. James Street

The next morning brought an end to the rain and a general increase in Anthony's surly spirits. Brand left immediately after breakfast, saying he had urgent business in Devonshire to attend to. Another amorous adventure, Anthony decided sourly. He supposed he could sympathize; there was something intriguing about an elusive woman. Especially one who managed to avoid him even while employed under the same roof.

Since their meeting yesterday, Anthony had seen no more of Anna than the trail of her skirt as she whisked around the corner, always just out of sight. Every time she eluded him, he became more determined to seek her out. He'd even attempted to visit her in the nursery, but she'd recognized his tread on the stairs and had escaped out the narrow servants' passage, leaving her teacup still gently steaming on a table, and a red-faced Lily stammering unintelligibly.

This morning had been no better—he'd ridden after the children who'd left for their morning ride, thinking to catch her there, only to discover two harassed grooms and a footman in attendance rather than Miss Thraxton. Robbed of his quarry, Anthony had stormed home and closeted himself with Dalmapple for the rest of the morning, taking care of matters of the estate and immersing himself so completely that he only occasionally thought of Anna. Once every two minutes or so.

He was just finishing a particularly thistly problem concerning the purchase of a rundown estate in Lincolnshire as a potential future home for Desford once he reached his majority, when a noise drew Anthony to the window.

He pushed back the edge of the curtain and looked into the garden below. On a low bench by the path sat Anna, dressed in a gown of soft blue that made her look as cool and refreshing as a spring breeze. She seemed engaged on some needlepoint, her hands steadily drawing a needle and thread through a bit of cloth.

On the bench across from her sat Desford, a book lying open on the ground at his feet. The boy was obviously on the defensive, his narrow shoulders hunched.

Careful not to make a noise, Anthony opened the window just a bit.

"I don't have to be here," Desford said.

Anna calmly took another stitch. "Yes, you do. If you cannot complete your lessons in the morning like the rest of the children, then you will give up your free time and do them now."

Desford mumbled something that sounded suspiciously like a curse. Anna lifted her brows. "Pardon me?"

The boy turned bright red and burst out, "The last governess we had never made us finish anything. She was much nicer than you."

"Then you shouldn't have chased the poor woman away. I daresay she would be here still if you hadn't put glue and feathers on her pillow."

"She deserved worse," Desford said darkly.

"I agree, especially if she allowed you to leave your lessons unfinished." Anna slid the needle into the cloth once more. "But now I'm your governess and you must finish your work."

"And if I don't?"

"Then you'll sit there until you've finished. You've already missed your morning ride, and you are about to miss your lunch."

As if on cue, the door from the morning room opened farther down the garden, and two footmen carried out a small table. Mrs. Stibbons followed with a maid and as soon as the table was in place, they draped a white cloth over it, fussing at the wind as they did so.

Anthony raised his brows. So the children were eating outside, were they? And in full view of Desford. Anthony had to give Anna credit—she was a formidable opponent.

Desford watched the preparations with a stubborn glare. Anthony could imagine what he was thinking—there was an almost festive air to the scene as the servants whisked about setting the table, the china clinked like chimes while the silver sparkled in the sun. Above, the swaying trees sprinkled sunlight over the whole.

Anthony shook his head at the grim look on the boy's face. It was amazing, the amount of stubborn pride contained in that small body. In fact, there was a good deal about Desford's expression that reminded Anthony of himself at that age. In a way, they were the same—both left alone at an early age, though Desford had no stepfather to guide him.

The thought held Anthony for a full moment and he frowned down at the boy's bent head. He remembered his own struggle to feel accepted, even with a stepfather who had taken pains to make him feel included. Perhaps he'd been too harsh with Desford. It hurt to admit it, but perhaps Anna was right. Maybe he did owe the children more gentleness.

He grimaced. In another week, that blasted woman would have him playing the harp and wearing skirts.

Anna's chuckle drifted up to the window. "Don't look so glum, Desford. You'd better pick up your book. It's almost noon and luncheon will be ready soon." She turned her head. "Ah, here come the others now."

The excited murmur of children's voices grew near and Elizabeth burst onto the path, followed by Selena and Marian. Richard trailed in the rear, a faint smile on his now-tanned face. Every day the boy seemed taller, somehow.

"There you are." Anna set her sewing aside and smiled. "How was your ride?"

"I falled off and hurted myself," Selena said, rubbing her seat, her face puckered. "But I didn't cry."

Marian snorted. "Then who was it that made such a racket that Miss Tateham pulled over in her curricle and offered to get a doctor?"

"That's because I screamed," Selena said. "But I didn't cry." She sent a pleased look at Anna. "I screamed very, very loud. Lots of people came to see my hurted bottom. Would you like to see it?"

"I'm sure it has already been thoroughly examined by now. Are you feeling better?"

Selena nodded regretfully. "It only hurts if I sit."

Mrs. Stibbons bustled up and clucked her tongue. "Poor thing! I'll fetch a nice soft cushion for you to sit upon. You'll be just like a princess."

"Princesses have hurted bottoms, too?" Selena asked, impressed.

"All the time, on account of their being so delicate." Mrs. Stibbons gathered the children. "Come and eat, loves."

Elizabeth started to scamper off, then paused. "Are you coming, Miss Thraxton?"

"Not right now. Desford is still working on his morning lessons."

"Des, you haven't finished yet?" Marian asked, incredulous.

Desford straightened his thin shoulders. "No, and I told Miss Thraxton I'd be damned if I would."

Elizabeth gasped. "You said 'damned' to Miss Thraxton? And she didn't wash your mouth out?"

Desford smirked. "No."

"That's because I didn't hear you say it," Anna said calmly, pinning the child with a no-nonsense look that made Anthony grin. "Furthermore, you gave your word not to curse in front of your sisters. Have you forgotten?"

Desford flushed. "No."

"Don't forget again," Anna said in a milder tone, as if recognizing the boy's honesty. "Children, go ahead and eat. Desford will be along when he finishes."

With Mrs. Stibbons leading the way, the children moved on down the path, chattering loudly and leaving Desford to glare after them.

The housekeeper settled them at the table, made sure everyone was served, then returned down the path to Anna. "What about you, miss? I'm sure you're hungry."

"Desford is, too. Perhaps you could bring us a tray in a few moments? We'll just eat here."

"Yes, miss," Mrs. Stibbons said cheerfully. "I think you're going to be very happy with lunch today. We have shepherd's pie, one of Master Desford's favorites." She offered a warm smile to the boy, then bustled off.

Silence reigned once more, broken only by the low talking and the occasional outburst of laughter from the table on the terrace. Desford kicked at his fallen book, his mouth turned in a sullen frown. Anna sewed quietly, occasionally lifting her face to the gentle summer breeze.

Anthony watched her, aware of a deep ache of dissatisfaction. She was a conundrum, fire one moment, then sitting contentedly in the sun the next, completely at peace with herself and her surroundings. He wondered what she would do if he joined her in the garden, sat with her on the bench, discussed the day's events with her . . . A strange peace stole over him.

He wanted more than a short *affaire de coeur* with her. He wanted her all to himself—days, nights, afternoons, mornings . . . perhaps if he were patient, she would agree to take a house nearby. That would serve them all the better.

The door from the morning room opened once again and Mrs. Stibbons reappeared, followed by a swarm of servants that descended on the alcove where Anna sat with Desford. Within a short time, a small table had been placed on the flagstones, shaded by a huge oak tree. Two covers had been laid and large plates of food sat under shiny metal domes.

Anna thanked Mrs. Stibbons and waited for the last servant to leave before she rose and took a chair at the table, leaving her sewing on the bench. She opened her napkin and sighed happily. "I don't know about you, but I'm famished."

Desford brightened and started to rise. "I—"

"No, Desford. After you've finished your lessons."

He blinked, astounded, and sank back onto the bench. "You would withhold my lunch?"

"And your dinner. And your breakfast tomorrow morning. We both have jobs to do, Desford. Yours is your lessons, mine is to see to it that you do them."

"I won't do them."

"Then you will go hungry." She picked up a piece of bread and spread marmalade across it, then took a generous bite. "Hm. I do so love orange marmalade."

Desford stared resentfully as his governess took a bite of shepherd's pie, the savory scent reaching even Anthony in the window far above. Anna commented on each bite, whether it was about the tenderness of the meat, or the excellent sauce Cook had poured over the potatoes.

Anthony almost chuckled aloud when Desford wiped his mouth with his sleeve.

It was amazing the way Anna approached her charges. She never spoke to them as if they were children, but rather as if they were little adults, capable of understanding the most obscure reasoning. Anthony was suddenly a little jealous of Desford. Certainly Anna had never gone to such lengths of trouble for *him*. Not yet, at least.

Anna pulled the cover off a dish. "Rice pudding. Isn't that your favorite?"

Desford looked at the rice pudding with a longing expression. "Does it have sultanas?"

"Lots," Anna said, scooping up a huge bite and putting it in her mouth. She chewed slowly, such a blissful expression on her face that Anthony chuckled. "Mmmmm." She swallowed. "I must tell Cook that she's outdone herself."

The gentle breeze lifted a tendril of Anna's hair and wafted the scent of cinnamon through Anthony's window.

He leaned against the window casement and watched as Desford slowly, slowly reached for his book and paper.

Anna ignored the child, merely refilling her dish when she finished the rice pudding. "You'd best hurry," she said, looking at the bowl thoughtfully. "There's not much left."

Desford swallowed, then looked down at his paper. His brow creased. Slowly, by degrees, he began to work. Anthony noticed that Anna didn't eat anything else, but sat quietly, her face lifted to the sun, a slight smile on her face.

Moments passed and finally Desford shut his book. "There. I finished."

"Excellent! Now come and eat. Here is some pie. And look, I saved two tarts for you."

He stood by the table, but didn't take his seat. "Don't you want to look at my work?"

She appeared surprised. "Why?"

"To see if I did it correctly."

"Did you try to do it wrong?"

"No, but . . . I don't know. I just thought you'd want to see it."

"Desford, if you said you did your work, then you did it. And if you made a mistake, I'm sure it was an honest one. We'll look at it together, once we've eaten." She flashed a smile. "I'm not sure I can vouch for the tarts if you don't hurry. It was difficult enough to resist the rest of the rice pudding."

A slow grin broke out on Desford's face and he joined Anna at the table. Soon they were passing dishes back and forth. Anna said something in a low tone and Desford broke into a rusty laugh. Anthony leaned further out the window to hear their conversation and hit the casement with his shoulder. It creaked in an annoying fashion and Anna's silver-gray gaze lifted to the window.

Instinct made Anthony step aside. He found himself pressed flat against the curtains, the wall at his back. Feeling like a fool, he stepped away and toyed briefly with the idea of closing the window, but the memory of Anna's bright gaze made him hesitate. She wouldn't appreciate any interference from him, not after the way he'd snapped at her yesterday.

The memory made him wince. He'd reacted like a beast, but he hadn't liked to hear her say that he was wrong in his dealings with Lady Putney. That harridan was damned lucky he didn't toss her out on her ear. Anna's belief that he should actually be polite to such a constant thorn in his side was ludicrous.

Of course, he had been wrong to allow Lady Putney to believe that there was something more between him and Anna . . . he should have put a stop to that nonsense right away. But somehow, it had annoyed him the way Anna had immediately denied the association. She was the most insufferable female he'd ever met.

Desford's laughter drifted through the window again and Anthony wondered if it was safe to look outside once more. He tiptoed to the window, then stopped.

Bloody hell, what was he doing hiding in his own library curtains like a thief? Greyley House was his, damn it, and if he wanted to look out of the windows, then he could.

He was still standing to one side of the window, debating the merits of joining Anna in the garden or sending a note for her to come to him, when a voice rang out from behind him. "Do you always make it a habit to spy on your employees?"

Anthony closed his eyes and sighed. "Only when they have red hair," he said, before turning to face the very person he thought was still sitting in the garden below him.

But Anna was much closer than the garden; she stood in his library, arms crossed under her chest, a stern frown on her face. "Greyley, what are you doing?"

The prudent thing would be to retreat to his desk and tell Thraxton he'd talk to her another time. Neither of them were in any temper to discuss anything. Instead, he took the few steps it took to bring him to her. "I was watching the children, not you."

Just to tease her further, he reached out and captured a tendril of her silky hair. "But if you want me to watch you . . ."

She pulled away and whisked herself behind a chair, an irritated flash in her eyes. "Don't."

"Don't what?"

"Greyley, you must stop this nonsense."

"You, my love, are not nonsense. You are a passionate, caring woman. And I want you. What's wrong with that?"

She sighed impatiently. "Damn it, Greyley! I cannot concentrate with you—" She bit her lip as if to stop her words.

Anthony raised his brows. She could protest all she wanted—he could see the truth in her eyes. "You like me, Thraxton. Admit it."

"Of course I like you!" she burst out. "But this . . . this is highly inappropriate. Not only am I the governess, but you—you are engaged to another woman!"

Anthony hid a wince at the outrage in her voice. "If Charlotte doesn't mind, why should you?"

"How do you know Miss Melton wouldn't mind? Have you discussed it with her?"

"No, but she has no illusions about our marriage. It's all part of the arrangement."

Anna's eyes widened. "Arrangement? You call your engagement an arrangement?"

"That's exactly what it is. A contract. Come, Thraxton, you aren't a naive child. It's the way things are done every day."

"Not in my family. And not in yours."

"You seem to forget that I am not a St. John. When my mother married my father, my real father, they had met only once before. Their parents arranged it all. Later on, after my father died, my mother met my stepfather and she began again."

"If you had your choice of which you'd rather follow, your father or your stepfather, which would you choose?"

"Anna, not one drop of St. John blood flows in my veins. However much I wish it otherwise, I am an Elliot."

"And that gives you the right to sin at will."

Was it sin to want to care for and protect a woman? Was it sin to yearn to discover what she thought about and why she laughed? To want to vanquish the shadows in her silver eyes and to provide her with the best of everything?

Everything, that is, but marriage. He'd made promises to the Meltons, to Charlotte, and he could not renege on them. The small part of him that longed to be a St. John refused to accept that possibility. "Thraxton, I don't want to argue. Let's talk about something pleasant." He rubbed a hand along his jaw, watching her intently. "You are doing miracles with the children, especially Desford."

"He's a good child, which you would know if you would give him a chance."

"Give him a chance? What about him giving me a chance? He's been against me since the first day he arrived."

"Yes, and your answer has been to bark orders at him like an ill-tempered general."

"Bribery, cajolery, starvation," he said, approaching the chair she hid behind. He set his knee in the seat and leaned closer. She smelled of the fresh breeze of the garden with just a hint of the cinnamon from the rice pudding. "Which of your methods do you suggest I use?"

She met his gaze evenly, her fingers turning white where they clutched the chair back. "How about respect, concern, and consideration? Any of those should do, I would think."

Anthony thought he'd never seen such tantalizing lips. They were perfectly sloped, drawn by a master hand. "I respect Desford. He's had a difficult time, losing his parents in such a way. I admire the way he's tried to protect himself and the others."

Anna placed a hand in the center of Anthony's chest and pushed him away in a none-too-gentle manner. "Have you ever told him that?"

"Well . . . no. Not yet." Damn it, he thought, disgruntled that she'd distanced herself from him. Did she think chatting with children came easily for him? He hadn't been around children, except Sara's baby who was too young to talk back.

"Perhaps if Desford understood why you act as you do, then he would be more accepting when you express your opinions."

More than likely, Desford would laugh to hear any such thing coming from someone he disliked so. For all her grasp of the rudiments of childhood behavior, Anna Thraxton didn't understand the first thing about men. Males didn't just walk up to one another and spout such mealymouthed platitudes.

Still . . . Anthony supposed it wouldn't hurt to tell Desford *something*. Perhaps compliment the boy. Or maybe they could just go fishing. Desford would understand the meaning of that gesture. "I'll try to speak with less—"

"Of a bark."

"I don't bark," he said, then ground his teeth at how harsh his voice sounded.

Anna tilted her head to one side, a thoughtful look in her gray eyes. "How old were you when you came into your title?"

"Three months. But I didn't assume responsibility for the family until I was seventeen."

Her brows rose. "You assumed responsibility for the *entire* family?"

"Every last one," he said grimly. He didn't like to remember those early months. They had been hellish. He'd been a stubborn young man, determined to bend a family of shysters to his will. The effort had almost killed him, but it had been worth it. The Elliot name, while not as pure as some, was no longer so reviled. It would take years to completely undo the damage the lower portions of the family had inflicted. Still, they were on their way. He caught Anna's disbelieving gaze and said tersely, "You would have done the same."

"I would never have used your methods—bullying and shouting and ordering people about."

He smiled, slow and sweet. "Oh, I've used one or two of your methods, too, my love. There is very little that money will not accomplish, if wielded in a judicious manner. I lured them to me, offering to pay their bills, to set their accounts to order. A little like you and Desford with the rice pudding."

"Bribery."

"For most, it was enough. For the rest . . ." He turned to his desk and sat on the edge of it, gently swinging his foot as he watched her. "An amazing number of Elliots are addicted to gaming. A family weakness, I suppose. I merely bought a number of their vowels, which they could not repay, of course, and threatened to send them to gaol if they did not change their way of life."

"And that worked?"

"To a great degree, yes. Gaol is not something men and women of fashion long for."

Anna could only guess at the amount of determination it had taken for one man to bring an entire family of wastrels to heel. She looked at Anthony with new eyes, noting the tiny laugh lines that creased the edges of his eyes and the firm set of his mouth. He'd fought hard for his family honor. Fought and won.

He met her gaze with an easy lift of his brows that sent her heart thumping wildly. "And you, Thraxton? What challenges do you face?"

"Grandpapa. Trust me, that is quite enough."

"He is a very interesting man. He comes to visit now and again. I lend him books and we discuss shipping, investments, reform work, classical literature—he can converse about any topic you wish."

"At one time, he had investments in over twenty different ports. Unfortunately, his last ventures were not so successful."

"Ah, yes. So he told me, though he seems hopeful of making a recovery."

It was nice, standing there, talking to Greyley about their families. But it was just an illusion of intimacy, a hint of what could have been, if circumstances had been different for them both.

Anna swallowed a sudden lump of hurt. "I really must be going. The children are working on a play."

He quirked a brow. "I'm not going to have to sit through it, am I?"

"Every minute. Furthermore, you will applaud wildly when the time comes and you will even ask for an encore."

"I'll do it," he said, his eyes glinting warmly. "But just for you."

"No. You'll do it for the children. Because it will make them happy."

"For the children, then," he agreed with amazing alacrity. His gaze softened, caressing and exploring until a shiver wracked her spine. "I'll have you to bed, Anna. And when I do, you'll see why we are meant to be."

If she were to walk to him right now, he would enfold her in his arms and kiss her senseless, which sounded perfectly and absolutely wonderful. She yearned to throw caution to the wind, to ignore her obligations, to ignore the fact that he was promised to another, but she couldn't. "Good-bye, Greyley."

Gathering her tattered resolution, Anna left. As soon as the door was securely closed behind her, she paused to regain her breath and restore peace to her thudding heart.

"What a surprise to find you here."

The shrill voice made Anna sigh. Lady Putney faced her in the narrow hallway, her painted face garish in the harsh afternoon light.

"Well, if it isn't Miss Thraxton," Lady Putney said, her gaze drifting to the closed door beyond. "Yet another tête-à-tête with His Lordship, hm?"

"Lord Greyley and I were discussing the children."

Lady Putney smiled, a tight, nasty smile. "A word of warning, my dear. I wouldn't be quite so familiar with His Lordship, if I were you. It could start some nasty rumors, and that would be fatal to one in your circumstances."

"Thank you for your advice, Lady Putney. I'll consider it thoroughly." With a stiff curtsy, Anna turned on her heel and left.

Lady Putney watched her go, her brow drawn in thought as she stared down the hallway. Somehow she'd lost her power over the children and she was just beginning to realize why. "Jenkins!" she called shrilly.

The butler appeared. "Yes, my lady?"

"Send paper and pen to my room. I wish to write a letter."

"Yes, my lady." He bowed and left and Lady Putney made her way to her room, her mind working furiously.

Chapter 20

*If Edmund Valmont is invited to my funeral, promise
you'll bury me in a plain coat with no buttons.*

The Duke of Wexford to his friend, Viscount Hunterston,
on the way home from Lord Dunsmore's funeral

Three days passed in which Anthony was kept busy by
the disgruntled Dalmapple with a number of items,
two of which had to do with Elliot cousins who were on the
verge of ruin. Anthony looked through the papers Dalmapple
had collected, his mind wandering. He'd only managed to
spend a very small amount of time with Anna and the children and he was unaccountably irritated by that fact.

He rubbed a hand over his face. What was he going to do?
Anna was making it more and more clear that she would
have nothing to do with him without a more substantial relationship. And Anthony couldn't blame her; she was a
woman who expected and deserved more. Still, he was
locked into a course of action from which there was no retreating. He'd made a formal offer for Charlotte and there
wasn't a damned thing he could do about it. God, what a
coil.

It was late, the light guttering in the lamp, the fire sputtering weakly. Weary in heart and soul, he decided to go to bed now, before he fell asleep in his chair.

Anthony rose and stretched, then left the library. As he crossed the foyer, he came to a sudden halt. Rupert Elliot stood in the entryway, handing his hat to the waiting Jenkins.

"Rupert!" Anthony said, coming forward. "What an unexpected surprise."

The young man turned, an immediate grin lighting his face. "I thought to sneak in and surprise you tomorrow at breakfast, but you have found me out."

"Breakfast? I wasn't aware you ate that meal. I've never seen you up before noon."

Rupert chuckled. "Luncheon, then. Either way, my surprise is ruined."

"So it is." Anthony sent a shrewd look at the young man. "What brings you to Greyley at this time of the night?"

"I was grasped with an immediate need to visit the country. And since I was in the neighborhood . . ."

"Rusticating, are you?"

Rupert grimaced. "You know me, it's devil to dare or nothing. I'm on my last legs and my next quarter allowance isn't due for another sennight. Thought I might as well come and visit you while I wait."

"And your mother."

"Her, too, I suppose. Is she giving you fits?"

"No more than usual."

"That, at least, is good news," Rupert said with a false smile, a faintly sick feel to his stomach. Greyley House was the last place he wanted to be. "How are the brats? Have they driven you to distraction?"

"Not yet, but they are still trying. How long can you stay?"

"As long as you can bear to have me."

Anthony glanced at Jenkins, who hovered discreetly in

the background. "Ready the green bedchamber for Lord Rupert."

The butler bowed, then left.

"Rupert, shall I have a tray sent to your room or have you eaten?"

"I never eat after midnight. Now if you wanted to send a bottle of port . . ."

Anthony laughed. "I'll have Jenkins see to it. Now off to bed with you. Your mother's in the east wing, if you wish to see her."

"Oh, I'll wait until tomorrow," Rupert said casually. "I just want to fall into bed. The ride here was hellish, with me thinking the dun men were hot on my heels."

Concern darkened Greyley's brow. "Is it as bad as that?"

"Lord, no," Rupert said with a bravado he didn't feel. "Not yet, anyway. My allowance is coming soon and all will be right."

"Very well. If you need something to tide you over—"

"*Don't*," Rupert said, more harshly than he intended. He managed a twisted smile at the earl's look of surprise. "I don't have it in me to say no, though I know I should."

"Don't be ridiculous," Anthony said. "We'll talk tomorrow, and you can tell me how things go on. I want to hear all of the latest news from town."

"I'm a veritable fount of gossip," Rupert said, sweeping a dramatic bow.

"You've never said anything truer." Greyley nodded to a footman who stood patiently to one side, waiting to take Rupert to his room. "Good night, then, Rupert. Sleep well."

Rupert watched Greyley's broad form as he left. Damn it, it was just like Greyley to offer to assist him. There were times when Rupert believed the earl would be a good friend, if Rupert were capable of possessing such a thing.

Sighing tiredly, he followed the footman to his room where he found his portmanteau already unpacked, a fire flickering steadily in the grate and fresh water on the stand. He tested the water in the basin with a cautious elbow. Finding it warm, he quickly undid his cravat, pulled off his shirt and washed away the travel.

Refreshed, he picked up his dressing jacket where some knowing maid had unpacked it and then slipped it on, gathering a lamp as he left his room. He walked down two halls, turning once until he was in the older part of Greyley House. There he found a wide oak door and knocked softly. On being bidden to enter, he opened the door and softly closed it behind him.

Lady Putney stood before her dressing table. Encased in yards and yards of ruffled silk that would have suited a far younger woman, she turned her perfumed and powdered cheek for his kiss. "Ah, my dearest Rupert! What took you so long?"

"Hello, Mother," Rupert said, ignoring her invitation for an embrace. "Why the hell did you send for me?"

She frowned. "Perhaps I just wished to see you, my last remaining son."

"Playing it a bit deep, aren't you, madam?"

"You are just like your father. Not a sensitive nerve in your body."

Rupert stifled an impatient sigh. "Come, Mother, what do you want? I happened to be in deep pursuit of a certain ladybird when I got your missive, and I'm anxious to return to London."

"I don't know why I let you speak to me that way. You are unkind."

"You didn't raise me to be kind. You raised me to be wealthy, frivolous, dashing, and a complete wastrel. All the things James was not."

"Leave your brother out of this. He is dead now and nothing we can do will ever bring him back."

"As if you'd want to. As if anyone would want to." Rupert perched on the edge of her dressing table and lifted a gold-topped bottle. "Spare me the histrionics. I'm not in the mood."

She snatched the bottle from his hand, her blue eyes blazing. "Are you in the mood for starvation, then? For complete ruin?"

"What do you mean?"

"I mean we are a feather away from losing everything we own."

Rupert frowned. "How can that be? Father left—"

"Your father didn't know the first thing about money. I was the one who made all our investments. Had it been up to him, you'd never have your horses, nor that high-perch phaeton you were so hot to purchase, much less those pretty clothes you demand."

Rupert had few illusions about who and what he was. "My blood is no worse than yours, Mother. We are both whores."

Her lips thinned. "Don't talk to me that way, Rupert. I am your mother."

"But not my guardian. Father knew you too well to allow such a thing. He left his friend Mr. Mills to see to it that I was taken care of."

She smiled then, tightly and without humor. "Mr. Mills will do as I tell him."

Rupert's heart chilled. "Explain yourself."

A simper crossed her round face. "Let's just say that Mr. Mills and I have come to an understanding."

"Did you prostitute yourself to that little worm, as well?"

"Don't press me, Rupert. I cannot converse with you when you are towering over me. Sit."

Seething inwardly, Rupert sank into a chair by the fire. "Well?" he asked rudely.

"There is no nice way to put this, Rupert, so I'll just say it bluntly—we have no more money."

"But I get my allowance in a sennight and—"

"There will be no more allowances."

"Good God. What's happened?"

"Last year was not kind to us. I had the opportunity to recoup some of our losses and I took it. It was risky, but I thought . . ." She shrugged. "It doesn't matter. It didn't pay off and we are lost."

"All of it?"

"There is some nominal amount left, but not enough. That's why I need you here." She looked at him with a speculative gleam. "Greyley has never cared for me, nor I him. But he's always seemed fond of you."

"I will not ask Greyley for assistance. He would never agree to—"

"Don't be a ninny. Of course he won't give us money. He despises the entire Elliot family, even though he is one himself."

"Can you blame him? Look at the hell we've put him through. Every time he turns around, he has to rescue yet another of us from the clutches of our own foolishness."

"That's his duty as the head of the family. Why he should complain about such trivialities is beyond me. Nevertheless, what I need from you has very little to do with Greyley. Almost nothing, in fact."

A warning flickered deep in his stomach. "What does it have to do with, then?"

"James's children." A sly smile curved her mouth. "They inherited the deed to a diamond mine."

"A worthless diamond mine. I remember when James

bought into that. You said it was all folly, that he'd lost his shirt on that one."

"He did. They began mining, but didn't find any diamonds. James was furious, for he'd invested a lot of money in verifying the site, but something went wrong. All of the other investors pulled out, but by that time, James had no more money and he couldn't afford to just walk away. He was left holding the deed to the entire operation."

"He was an obstinate fool."

"This time it paid off. The week before James died, I ran into him at the Havershams' musicale and he was looking more pompous than usual."

"They found diamonds after all?"

"Something almost as good." She picked up a small heart-shaped box on her dresser and opened it. A velvet bag lay inside. She lifted it free and tossed it to Rupert. "See what your brother did with his last few shillings."

Rupert opened the bag and poured the contents into his hand. Three large, perfectly cut rubies lay in his palm. "Good God."

"I've already had them evaluated and they're almost perfect." She sat on the stool by Rupert's chair and patted his hand. "The only way I can get my hands on that mine is to convince Greyley to let me have the children. According to James's express instructions, any funds or investments he possessed are to be held in trust for the children by whoever takes care of them."

Rupert could not seem to look away from the gems.

Lady Putney's glitter-hard smile widened. "If Greyley chooses to send the children elsewhere, he can, but he will have to relinquish their funds as well."

"We are lost, then. Greyley would never turn those children over to someone else."

"He will if his new wife refuses to countenance them."

Rupert pulled his gaze from the rubies. "Greyley is getting married?"

"Soon. He's engaged to Charlotte Melton, a bread-and-butter miss who is scared of her own shadow. There's no way the shy and retiring Charlotte would be able to handle those troublesome brats." Lady Putney rose, smoothing her hair as she did so, her arms pasty in the firelight. "I've become quite close with her mother and I've made sure they know all about the children."

"I daresay you haven't helped their behavior here, either."

"Oh, I've been busy. And soon it will all pay off. Pretty little Charlotte will cry and Greyley will be forced to give the children up. And there I'll be, their adoring grandmother, ready to welcome them home."

"It sounds as if you have everything under control."

"I did." Lady Putney's smile slipped. "Until Anna Thraxton arrived."

"The governess?"

"Yes. She's managed to do some remarkable things with the children, but what concerns me more is the fact that she has become close to the earl. Too close."

"Greyley with a governess? I cannot see it."

"You forget that we are talking about Anna *Thraxton*. She is a member of the *ton* in her own right. It is nothing more than a flirtation at this point, but if Thraxton convinces Greyley to wed her instead of Charlotte Melton, we will never get our hands on that mine."

"Is Thraxton such a threat?"

"Greyley is fascinated. I can see it."

"What do you need from me?"

Lady Putney flashed a brilliant smile. "I want you to use that considerable charm of yours and win Miss Thraxton for yourself."

Bloody hell, what a tangled mess. Rupert raked a hand through his hair. "I like Greyley."

"More than your handsome allowance?"

Rupert's heart thudded a sickening beat. All his life he'd been taught to demand the best and to do whatever was necessary to procure it. And some part of him had seen that Anthony was not that way. He was honest, and generous in a way, and as strong as they came. Rupert admired those traits, but looking deep into his own soul, he knew he wasn't that kind of a man. He was an Elliot born and bred and there was no way to escape it.

Despising himself all the more, he dragged himself upright, then stood staring down at his mother. God how he hated the fact that he was her offspring, that he shared her blood and her vanity and every other ugly thing about her. "I'll do what I can to attach Miss Thraxton's affections. But I warn you, if Greyley protests even once, I will cease."

Lady Putney smirked. "He won't. His pride won't let him."

"I wish I had that same pride," Rupert muttered, turning toward the door.

She placed a hand over his arm, her eyes gleaming with avarice. "You never will. You are an Elliot and there is nothing you can do to change that." Laughing lightly, she returned to her dressing table, where she began applying a thick green cream to her face. "Miss Thraxton rides every morning. Perhaps that would be the best time to begin."

Rupert nodded tiredly. "I'll do this one thing, but that's all. Once the mine is yours, you must promise to reestablish my allowance and never again interfere in my life."

She looked at him, amusement darkening her blue eyes until they were the same color as his. "Rupert, my dear, sweet boy, never fear. Once I have that mine in my name, why would I bother with you?"

"And Mr. Mills?"

"I will leave him alone, too." She made a face through the green cream. "And gladly, for he sweats like a pig."

Rupert gave her a derisive smile. "You have always been a woman of great discrimination, Mother. I will leave you to your fond thoughts." With a mocking bow, he left, his head aching fiercely, a sick weight in his stomach. Once he reached his own room, he immediately crossed to the window and threw it open. He leaned out and took deep, gulping breaths of fresh air, trying to calm the need to retch.

He looked down at the window ledge where his hand rested, a heavy gold ring on one finger. He'd never had to fend for himself and he wasn't quite sure how to do such a thing. Without his quarterly funds, he was nothing.

As distasteful as it was, he had no choice. Beginning tomorrow, he would begin his seduction of Anna Thraxton. He only hoped Anthony's affections were not strongly engaged. Rupert closed the window and went to drink himself to sleep.

Chapter 21

Women prefer to draw blood using words. It can cause just as much havoc, but it doesn't stain the carpet.

Viscount Hunterston to Lord Burton, while waiting on their wives outside a meeting of the Society for Wayward Women

Sir Phineas found Anna in the courtyard early the next morning. "Where are you off to?"

She barely spared him a glance as she allowed the groom to assist her onto her horse. "For a nice, quiet ride."

"You just returned from a ride not an hour ago."

"That was with the children. It was hardly quiet."

Sir Phineas leaned on his cane. She was up to something, he could tell from the gleam in her eyes. "When will you be returning?"

"By noon. Maybe sooner."

He didn't at all care for the way her hands clenched about the reins. The horse must not have liked it either, for it snorted uneasily. "What about your charges?"

"They are practicing their play this morning. Lily has them well in hand."

Sir Phineas reached up and placed his hand on her knee. "Anna, is all well?"

"Of course," she said lightly, though her cheeks pinkened. "I've just not been sleeping well, that's all."

Hm. This was getting more and more interesting. Sir Phineas made it a habit to wander down to the library late at night. He liked being up and about when no one else was, though for the past two days, his solitary sojourns had been interrupted by Greyley. Apparently the earl was having a difficult time sleeping as well.

Whatever was bothering Anna and the earl, Sir Phineas only hoped it was the same ailment. In the meantime, a little exercise couldn't hurt. Perhaps it would take some of the pinched look from her face.

He patted her knee and stepped back. "Have a lovely ride, dear." She managed a quick smile, though Sir Phineas could tell her heart was not in it, before turning her mount and galloping across the park as if the hounds of hell were in pursuit.

He watched her for a moment, admiring her command of the horse and her excellent form.

"She's quite a horsewoman, isn't she?" came a voice from behind Sir Phineas.

He turned and found himself facing a tallish young man dressed in the height of fashion, his blue riding coat perfectly fitted to his slender form. Sir Phineas recognized the dark brown hair and the blue eyes of the Elliots. "My granddaughter has always been able to ride."

"So I can see."

Sir Phineas frowned. There was something familiar about the man. "Pardon me, but have we met?"

The young man pulled his gaze from where Anna's figure disappeared in a thicket of trees. "I'm sorry; I should have introduced myself. I'm Rupert Elliot. I came from town last night to see my mother, Lady Putney."

Ah, so this was one of Lady Putney's spawn. Sir Phineas

bowed his own greeting. "Delighted to meet you. I'm—"

"Sir Phineas. Greyley told me you and your granddaughter were staying here." The young man flashed a rueful smile down at his clothes. "I thought to see if Miss Thraxton might like some company, but I was a little late rising."

Phineas noted the circles under the young man's eyes and came to his own conclusions. Still . . . perhaps there was some information to be gleaned. Sir Phineas smiled in his most winning manner. "A pity you missed Anna. Fortunately, I'm going for a carriage ride in a half hour, if you'd like to join me."

"Some other time, perhaps. I think I'll just go back to bed."

Sir Phineas gave a polite nod and watched the young man wander back toward the house. Before he reached the top step, the front door opened and Lady Putney emerged. Sir Phineas lifted his brow at that—it was rare to see the virago up before noon. As he watched, Lady Putney and Rupert engaged in a quiet, intense argument, the end result being that Rupert, now flushed a deep red, turned on his heel and strode inside. Lady Putney, her eyes narrowed in a cold, calculating manner, turned to stare at the point where Anna had disappeared.

As Sir Phineas stood, stroking his chin, Lady Putney caught sight of him. Her lips folded into an instant false smile before she, too, turned and went back into the house. Sir Phineas's gaze remained fixed on the front door of Greyley House. After several moments, he gripped his cane anew and went in search of the earl. Something was afoot and he was not about to let someone ambush his future son-in-law.

A warm morning breeze stirred the bushes. Anna's horse shied, rolling her eyes and snorting. "Easy, girl," Anna said, bringing the spirited mare under control. She loved Majesty and would miss her when the time came to leave Greyley.

The thought sent an unexpected lump to her throat. Damn it, what was she doing? she asked herself as she guided the horse out of the woods and into a wide field sprinkled with yellow flowers. *Being silly,* she instantly answered, then grimaced.

She hated it when she was honest with herself. Most people managed to evade home truths with astonishing ease, but her conscience was louder than necessary. Still, she had to admit that it was madness to seek out a woman who was, in a very vague sort of way, her own rival.

No, not a *rival,* really. Charlotte was apparently the type of woman Greyley wanted for a countess, while Anna was . . . well, she wasn't sure what she was. A prime candidate to mess up her life by falling in love with a man she couldn't have.

Not that she was in love, of course. She just had a very sincere liking for Greyley. Despite his offer to make her his mistress, she had to admit that there were things about him that nearly redeemed him. He was kind to the children, took care of his troublesome family, and worked hard to provide for everyone around him. Plus he had a wicked sense of humor and could kiss a woman until her bones melted. Anthony Elliot was a very disturbing package indeed.

And that was why it was so important that she meet Charlotte Melton. It wasn't because Anna was necessarily jealous of the woman, it was just that she wanted to be certain that Charlotte was everything she should be. Greyley was, after all, the brother of Anna's best friend. And he deserved something better than a hard-hearted adventuress. So here Anna was, on her way to assess the nature of Greyley's betrothed.

It was the least she could do, considering the circumstances. Besides, if she had a brother who might be on the verge of making such an error, Anna was certain that Sara would make the same effort on her behalf.

Anna rounded a corner of the path and found herself alongside a low stone wall that encased a large, well-laid out garden. This was it. Anna unhooked her knee from the pommel and slid to the ground. She tied Majesty to a tree limb, then entered the gate, glad to see the outline of a lovely house not far down the path.

She took a moment to smooth her skirts and tuck a stray strand of hair behind her ear. She was just dusting a smudge of mud off her skirt when she saw a young girl walking down the path.

Dressed in a morning gown of white muslin, her blond ringlets bouncing with each step, her blue eyes wide, she appeared annoyingly young and innocent. She was holding a small book in one hand, though she seemed far more interested in humming a waltz and dancing over the stones in the path than else. The girl appeared all of sixteen and was obviously Charlotte Melton's younger sister or a house guest of some sort.

Anna coughed and the girl came to an abrupt halt, gasping as if frightened.

"I'm sorry to bother you," Anna said with a friendly smile, "but I'm afraid I've lost my way. Could you give me directions?"

The young lady's startled expression did not abate. "Who . . . who are you?"

"Anna Thraxton." She gave a perfunctory curtsy. "I'm the governess at Greyley House."

The girl brightened. "Oh! Greyley House! I'm very pleased to meet you, Miss Thraxton. I'm Charlotte Melton. I—"

"You can't be!" Anna burst out. "*You* are Greyley's fiancée?"

Deep, rich color flooded Charlotte's cheeks. On many women, a blush enhanced natural beauty, bringing a lovely color to normally pale skin. But on Charlotte's ultra white countenance, the deep color made her appear overheated. "W-we have not yet announced the engagement," she stammered, a panic-stricken look in her face.

"No, but everything is understood, isn't it?"

"I-I suppose so." The girl wrung her hands, appearing absolutely wretched.

Anna abandoned all thoughts that Charlotte Melton might be a hard-hearted adventuress. The poor thing looked ready to faint. "Do you mind if we sit in the shade awhile?" Anna smiled kindly. "I'm a bit tired."

"Oh! Of course." Charlotte led the way to a bench nestled among some trees and surrounded on one side by lovely red flowers. She perched uneasily on the edge of the bench and waited for Anna to seat herself. "Perhaps I should send someone to fetch something to drink."

Anna lifted her hat, brushing her hair from her damp face. "No, thank you! I don't wish to be any trouble. I just need a moment to rest."

Charlotte glanced around. "Where is your groom?"

"Didn't bring one." Anna waved a hand. "I wasn't about to wait for some footman on a slug. Not with weather like this." She glanced up at the blue sky that peeped between the trees. "I don't think I've ever seen a lovelier day."

"Except the heat. It made me feel ill. I'm supposed to be sitting quietly on the terrace, but I got tired of the quiet. Besides, I thought it might be cooler in the garden."

"I daresay it is. Greyley House is somewhat frigid indoors, but then it is built like a tomb."

Charlotte looked shocked. "Do you really think so?"

"Who wouldn't? Have you ever seen the place?"

"Yes, I have." Charlotte swallowed with a visible effort. "It is not very hospitable, is it?"

Anna laughed. "Go ahead and say it—it's a dungeon! When I first saw it, I half expected a horde of angry prisoners to come swarming up out of the bowels of the place, intent on vengeance."

Charlotte had to smile. "That's exactly what I thought when I first saw it, but Mama said I was being fanciful. She told me not to say anything except that I thought it was lovely."

"As ugly as the outside is, I have to admit that the earl's done wonders with the inside. Have you seen the furnishings in his library?"

"No. I mean, yes." Charlotte sighed unhappily. "I'm sure I did, but I was too nervous to pay much attention. Mama told me that it was very important that I learn to feel more at ease about the earl. I do hope I can."

Anna wondered if Charlotte bleated about "Mama" in every sentence when talking to Greyley. "The earl is quite taken with that pile of rocks. He was not happy when I suggested the foyer needed a mural."

Charlotte's blue eyes grew wide. "Was he angry?"

"I daresay, but he doesn't bite. At least not that I've ever seen. And if he had the least inclination to snap at someone, it would be me."

"Doesn't he like you?"

"No. In fact, I'm quite certain he detests me." Or he did whenever he wasn't trying to lure her to his bed. She sent a guilty glance at Charlotte. "I daresay it's a good thing I'm leaving soon."

"Because he frightens you?"

"Heavens, no. Greyley doesn't frighten me in the least. If anything, his high-handed manner makes me want to provoke him even more."

Charlotte sighed. "I wish I had your spirit. Mama says I

mustn't act frightened when Lord Greyley calls, but he's so large and he . . . he *growls*."

Anna had to laugh at that. "Yes, he does. Rather like a bear." She took Charlotte's hand and patted it just as she would have done Elizabeth's. "Don't let Greyley frighten you. Give him some time and you'll get used to his ways."

"Do you think so?"

"Absolutely."

Charlotte squeezed Anna's hand. "I'm so glad I met you! You are the first person I've been able to talk to about—" She reddened. "I'm glad you came."

So was Anna. Charlotte wasn't anything like the hard-faced fortune hunter she'd expected. Anna tried to picture Charlotte at Greyley House, facing down Anthony's over-bearing manners, Lady Putney's acid tongue, and the children's rambunctious manners. It simply would not do.

Still . . . Anna looked carefully at Charlotte. At least the girl *seemed* kind-hearted and though she was obviously naive, intelligence shone in her soft blue eyes. "Charlotte, may I ask you a question?"

"Of course."

"What are your expectations for this marriage?"

"I'm honored that Lord Greyley has chosen me as his future countess." Charlotte's answer sounded as if she'd rehearsed it for hours.

Anna frowned. "So you want a title."

"Mama says having one will be the nicest thing. And then there's Lord Greyley's standing."

"You mean wealth?"

"I'm not supposed to talk about—"

"Yes, yes. What else?"

Charlotte blinked her eyes. So blue they made the sky look pale, and fringed with thick lashes, they made Anna uncomfortably aware of her own rather colorless gray eyes.

Charlotte frowned. "Besides the title and the standing, what else should I expect?"

"Children, respect, love . . ." Anna waited, staring intently at Charlotte's face.

"Mama says one should never mention such vulgar things as love. As for children . . ." The younger woman cleared her throat, her face blazing red once more. "Of course the earl will expect me to produce an heir for the continuation of the family line. One can only hope that will be all."

There was such a strain to her voice that Anna impulsively hugged her. "There, I'm sure Greyley would be more than happy with only one child." Anna suddenly felt sorry for Charlotte. She seemed to genuinely fear Greyley and no matter how silly that was, it could not be comfortable for her.

Charlotte managed a shy smile. "It's nice to have someone to talk to. I hope you will visit often?" There was such a look of entreaty in the girl's eyes that Anna's heart expanded.

The poor thing—all alone with no one to advise her but her mama, who sounded like quite a ninny. If Greyley wished these nuptials to prosper, then there was serious work to be done. Suddenly Anna knew what she would do. For Sara's sake, and Greyley's as well, she would help Charlotte become the perfect countess.

Why yes . . . it wouldn't take much, really. Charlotte had a large heart, that much was certain. All Anna needed to do was help Charlotte realize her own potential. Her own strength as a woman.

The idea took hold and Anna's heart eased. It was a simple plan and bound to help Greyley. If he thought he could be happy with a bread-and-butter miss, he was sadly mistaken. The relationship would pale within a fortnight. He needed someone stronger, someone who could stand on her own.

Anna eyed the girl thoughtfully. As shy as Charlotte seemed, there had to be some spirit in her. Someone just needed to coax it out of her. Anna decided that that someone would be she.

She took Charlotte's hand and smiled reassuringly. "I'd love to come and visit. I daresay I'll be riding this way several times a week. More, if I can arrange it."

"That would be so nice! I have only Mama and Papa for company and while they are quite pleasant, I sometimes wish for someone closer to my own age."

"I don't know how close I am in age, but I'd be glad to visit. We can talk about all sorts of things, too. Books, poetry, household management. Greyley."

"Perhaps you can tell me more about the house. Maybe then it won't seem so . . ." The girl bit her lip, sudden tears welling in her pretty blue eyes.

Heavens, but the child was easily moved to sniffles! Stifling her impatience, Anna stood. "I suppose I should be going. It was a pleasure to meet you, Miss Melton."

Charlotte stood, clutching her book in front of her. "Must you go already? I've enjoyed talking with you so much."

Anna caught the title of the book as the sunlight glanced off the gilt lettering. "Ah, Shakespeare's *Henry V*. Do you like it?"

"No. I don't really understand it at all. But Mama promised Lord Greyley that she would make me read in an effort to improve my mind." Charlotte mournfully regarded the small book. "I don't think it's working."

"That's because you have the wrong book. The least they could have done was allowed you to read *Romeo and Juliet* or *Midsummer Night's Dream*." Anna frowned for a moment, then grinned. "Come! I have just the book for you." She went to where Majesty stood outside the gate and reached into the bag that was tied behind the saddle and pulled out a nicely bound book. She always took a book with her when riding with the children to while away the time whenever they stopped to rest. "Here. It's Byron's *Childe Harold.*"

Charlotte's face fell. "I'm not sure my mama would approve. She said Byron is dreadfully wicked."

"What a pity, for the book is one of Lord Greyley's favorites." That was stretching things a bit, but Charlotte would never know.

The girl looked down at the thin book, her worried expression melting into a determined one. "If it is one of Greyley's favorites, then I shall read it regardless of what Mama thinks."

"Good for you," Anna said, applauding this harmless bit of rebellion. Greyley needed a wife who had more than two thoughts in her head. He needed a wife who would meet him argument for argument, thought for thought; one who was well educated and aware of the world. And Charlotte was none of those things.

Yet. Anna smiled to herself as she saw Charlotte reading the opening of *Childe Harold*, her lips moving soundlessly with each word. "Charlotte, why don't you read the first part and we'll discuss it the next time I come to visit."

"When will that be?"

"Within the next few days," Anna promised, her mind racing as she made a mental list of all the things Charlotte would need to know. "Perhaps next time, I will bring the children with me."

Charlotte took a wary step back. "Mama would not like that. Lady Putney says they are wild."

Anna frowned. "When did you meet Lady Putney?"

"Oh, she comes to visit Mama all the time. They are great friends, you know."

Anna was developing a healthy dislike for the unknown Lady Melton. "How lovely for your mother."

"Did the children really catch one of their governesses on fire?" Charlotte asked, her eyes wide.

"No, they just tarred and feathered her dog, which was a nasty creature from what accounts I've heard."

"And the frogs? Did they really let hundreds of them loose in His Lordship's chamber?"

"More like a dozen," Anna said in a cheerful voice, determined to undo whatever harm Lady Putney had done. "They didn't cause much harm, except to frighten the upstairs maid."

Charlotte shuddered. "Frogs are such slimy creatures. I'm certain I would have screamed, had I found one in my room."

Anna settled her hat more firmly on her head. Damn Lady Putney. "I hope you enjoy *Childe Harold*."

"I'm sure I will. Should I ask one of the footmen to take you home? You don't want to get lost again."

"I don't think it will be necessary. Now that I can see the woods from this angle, I can see the path quite clearly." She smiled at Charlotte. "I look forward to visiting you soon."

"Don't wait too long," Charlotte said with a shy smile. "All of my friends are in London, having their season." Her face darkened momentarily. "I'd be having my season, too, but Grandmother died and we are not yet out of mourning. I do so like London."

"I'm sure you will go often enough with Greyley once you marry."

Charlotte's lip quivered a moment before she gave a mournful shake of her head. "The earl isn't fond of London, so I daresay I'll be staying here most of the time."

"But Charlotte, if you like London, you should tell Greyley. You deserve some happiness, too."

"I'm sure I will not miss it much. Mama thinks it would have pulled horribly on my nerves to stay more than a week, though I do not think so. I never felt more alive than when I was there before."

Try as she might, Anna simply could not picture Greyley with this child. What was wrong with the man? He must have been swayed by Charlotte's blue eyes, golden ringlets, and sweet, biddable nature; the child really was the exact opposite of the hardened, scheming Elliots. Unfortunately, Greyley's troublesome family would eat a tender morsel like Charlotte alive and spit her bones into the sand without a single thought.

Well, that wouldn't happen if Anna had anything to say about it. She'd teach Charlotte all she needed to know to be a good countess, and Charlotte, in return, would be the perfect wife for Anthony.

A dull pressure grew somewhere in the region of Anna's heart, forcing an ache to her throat. She pressed a hand to her chest, but it did not go away. Instead it grew until Anna finally cleared her throat. "I must be going. I had best take a hot bath before I stiffen from riding so far."

"But how will you get on your horse? There's no mounting block."

"I don't need one," Anna said briskly. "I can use this bench."

"Aren't you afraid you'll fall?"

"Oh no! I was the most dreadful hoyden when I was a child, and I was forever sneaking off on the horses. I quite detested the sidesaddle, too, and refused to use one unless forced."

"I don't think you should—" Charlotte broke off as Anna led Majesty inside the gate. Charlotte scrambled back several paces while Anna placed a foot on the bench and stood, then mounted without trouble.

Anna arranged her skirts, then grinned down at Charlotte. "Good-bye. I shall return soon."

Charlotte nodded and then watched as Anna eased Majesty through the gate. The wind lifted the long white feather that fluttered from Anna's hat and for an instant, Charlotte thought her new friend appeared exactly like a warrior goddess. Certainly she had the bright coloring and the bold nose of one.

The image was almost destroyed when the restive horse shied at a shrub. But after a tense moment in which it appeared that Anna was addressing some strong words to the air about her, she managed to settle the horse back into a trot. Soon, horse and rider crossed the field that bordered Greyley lands.

Before Miss Thraxton had appeared on her horizon, Charlotte had been wandering the gardens in a state of unrest. When she'd first agreed to the wedding, it had seemed far, far away. Mama had assured her that her timidity would disappear as the time approached. Swept away by the excitement of the earl's professed affection and the magnificence of his person, Charlotte had readily agreed to the match. He was wealthy, her father thought very highly of him, and she liked the thought of being a countess.

But as the months progressed, she felt less and less at ease with the earl. And now . . . Charlotte hugged the book to her breast and watched as Anna jumped Majesty over the small stream, horse and rider moving as one. There was something regal about Anna Thraxton. Charlotte imagined herself nine inches taller and with long, flowing red hair.

The picture kept her agreeably entertained until Mama's sharp voice drifted from the terrace. Startled, Charlotte tucked the book into her skirt pocket and pressed her lips into a straight line. She would learn to become a good countess.

Fortune had already smiled on her by providing such a ready tutor.

Feeling more hopeful than she had in months, Charlotte hurried up the path toward her mother's voice.

Chapter 22

Women should learn to leave men alone. We can stumble along just fine without you, providing, of course, you leave a well-marked map.

Lord Burton to Lady Burton, while attending a lecture on reform

"**M**iss Thraxton, look!" Elizabeth twirled before Anna, her gown of blue satin spinning about her legs. A wreath sat on her hair, blue and white ribbons streaming across her curls. "Mrs. Stibbons put new lace in the insets."

"How lovely," Anna said, smiling. They were working on the costumes for the play. Mrs. Stibbons was so excited about the production that Anna decided that the housekeeper hid a secret aspiration to be an actress.

Not that the children were any less excited. Assisted by Grandpapa, Desford and Elizabeth had written most of the scenes, which offered a very colorful and highly fictitious rendition of the first Earl of Greyley and his exploits in securing the family lands. Desford seemed to enjoy writing, for he'd asked permission to add a few additional scenes to trace the family through the ages. Anna was amazed at how enthusiastic he seemed. The other children gathered props, painted scenery, and squabbled with great vigor over the various parts.

All told, the production should be a huge success. It was to be her crowning achievement and a clear sign that perhaps it was time for her to move on. Desford hadn't played a trick in weeks, and while he still had his moments, he was slowly coming around. Soon the children would be ready for a new governess. Perhaps Lily, who enjoyed the children as much as they enjoyed her.

The children chattered excitedly about the play, but Anna's thoughts drifted to her meetings with Charlotte. Since last week, Anna had composed a list of all the books suitable for bringing a young lady's intellectual quota up to standard. She particularly looked forward to sharing Mary Wollstonecraft's *A Vindication of the Rights of Women.*

Anna imagined Charlotte discussing such a topic with Greyley and she had to hide a smile. He was going to be astounded to see the changes in his gentle bride.

Of course, even with an eager pupil, it would take months before anyone would see any lasting changes, especially in someone with such a naturally timid nature. Still, Charlotte had promise. Every day she seemed to grow before Anna's eyes.

"My lady?" Jenkins stood in the doorway of the nursery.

"Yes?"

"Lord Greyley would like to see you in the library."

Selena looked up from a pile of purple ribbons and pulled her finger out of her mouth. "Lord Greyley wants to see Miss Thraxton all of the time."

Though his lips never moved an inch, Anna had the feeling the butler smiled. "Indeed," he said pleasantly.

Anna sniffed. "Please inform Lord Greyley that I'm not

available at the present time." She was due at Charlotte's house at ten.

"His Lordship seemed *most* insistent."

"I daresay he was also *most* rude."

Jenkins's mouth twitched. "He was a bit . . . commanding."

"However much I wish to answer such a delightful summons, I cannot." She had better things to do than pander to His Lordship's overinflated sense of grandeur. Besides, she had no wish to be alone with Greyley, especially not in a room with a lockable door. Her feelings still threatened to bubble up and scorch her every time she thought about him.

The butler bowed, then left. His footsteps had barely receded when Anna heard Grandpapa limping down the hallway, his cane thumping along with each step. He entered the room and smiled brightly at the children, who immediately clamored to show him their costumes. Even Desford, who looked dashing in a hat festooned with a large feather, managed a glimmer of a smile.

After admiring the children's costumes, Grandpapa took the seat beside Anna. His glance lingered on her clothing. "Going riding yet again?"

Since she was to leave shortly, she'd already donned her habit. "Yes. I'm meeting Mr. Elliot at ten. He's escorting me."

"Hm."

Something about that "hm" didn't sit well with Anna. She sent a black look at Grandpapa, which did no good at all, for he merely returned her look with a bland one of his own.

"Well?" she asked.

"Well what?" He picked up two spare feathers from a pile on the table and sat twiddling with them.

"You have something to say, so you might as well go ahead and say it."

"Oh, I don't have anything to say." He took the tip of the

feather and leaned over the table so that he could tickle one of Marian's ears. "Nothing of interest, anyway."

"Out with it. You'll burst your spleen if you keep it all inside."

He smiled at Marian, who giggled and slapped at his feather. "No, no. I couldn't possibly intrude on your life in such a manner."

Anna snorted.

Grandpapa sent her a shrewd look. "You tense up like a statue every time I mention Greyley's name. Makes me a bit shy to bring up the topic."

"That's because I find the man impossibly overbearing."

"Oh? And what about this Rupert Elliot? He seems to be hanging about quite a bit this last week."

"I find him charming." And necessary. It was only a matter of time before Greyley suggested that *he* accompany her on one of her morning jaunts, something she could not allow to happen. To avoid that possible event, she'd invited Rupert to join her. She was certain she could win his silence, for she had the impression that he was more than willing to thwart Greyley.

Anna took the feathers from Grandpapa and laid them back on the table. "Rupert has been nothing but a gentleman."

"Just remember who his mother is. I don't trust that harpy and neither should you."

"I don't trust anyone at Greyley House."

"Not even the earl?"

"Especially not the earl."

Grandpapa's gaze sharpened. "Did something happen?"

"Of course not," Anna said stiffly. Unwilling to pursue the conversation further, she turned away and scolded Selena, who was using one of the feather quills to poke Richard in the behind every time he bent over to tie his shoes.

Sir Phineas wisely let the topic drop, though he watched the play of emotions on his granddaughter's face with interest. He picked up the feathers once again, then waited until Marian looked elsewhere before he tickled her ear with the feather.

While she giggled, he said to Anna, "You know, my dear, I've been watching. I know more than you think."

Her cheeks flared. "Good God, I hope not," she muttered.

"What's that?"

"Nothing," she said hastily, taking the feather from his hand and replacing it on the table. "If you'll excuse me, I'm off for my morning ride."

Sir Phineas waved her on. "Have a lovely time, dear. I think I'll stay here with the children."

She bade the children to mind Lily before sweeping out the door. As soon as she was gone, Sir Phineas reached over and pulled Selena into his lap. She nestled there, snuggling against him contentedly, chattering about her part in the upcoming play.

Sir Phineas listened with half an ear, nodding when necessary and smiling at Selena's animated expression. It appeared as if Anna and her earl were not yet out of the woods.

It was a pity his granddaughter was born with such a stubborn disposition. He was wondering from which of his wife's many relatives Anna could have inherited that unfortunate tendency when a crumpled bit of paper on the floor caught his eye. Shifting Selena to one leg, he used his cane to pull the paper closer, then bent and retrieved it.

Silently he perused the sheet. It was much crossed through and overwritten so it took him a moment to realize what he was reading. When he did, a slow smile tugged at his mouth.

"What is it?" Selena asked, staring at the letters with an uncomprehending gaze.

"A part of your play, but somehow I don't remember this scene."

Selena took the paper, beaming. "This must be the secret scene."

"The what?"

She glanced at the other children, but they were all busy with their costumes and no one seemed to have heard a thing. She leaned closer. "We have a secret scene, but Desford says we mustn't tell or it won't be secret."

"I see," Sir Phineas said. He leaned forward and whispered into her ear. "If it's a secret, then you need not say another word."

She nodded wisely, then folded the paper in half and stuffed it into the pocket of her dress. It didn't fit, but her attention was already on the feather that lay on the table and the page soon fluttered back to the floor.

Sir Phineas glanced across the room at Desford, who was pretending to sword fight with Richard. *Well, well, well. Perhaps I'm not alone in this thing, after all.*

Feeling better than he had in days, Sir Phineas stayed in the nursery and played with the children until lunch.

Anna lightly ran down the steps to the foyer, her mind already busily engaged in all the home truths she could deliver to Charlotte in the space of an hour.

They rarely had more than that, for Charlotte's mama was not at all thrilled to see her daughter becoming friends with a mere governess. But the Thraxton name, along with Anna's intimate knowledge of Greyley House, had kept Lady Melton from preventing the visits. Had the woman any idea what things Anna was teaching Charlotte, Anna

was certain the older woman would have done so immediately.

It had taken some doing, but Anna had been able to make
Charlotte see the wisdom of keeping dear Mama in the dark
about the exciting books and treatises Anna gave her to
read.

Anna turned the last corner of the stairs and came to an
abrupt halt, her skirts swinging forward to brush her ankles.
Anthony stood at the bottom of the steps, leaning against the
railing. The intensity of his expression made her heart leap. It
was as if only a thin, thin web of civility prevented him from
swooping her up and carrying her to his bedchamber to have
his way with her.

"I've been waiting for you," he said, his deep voice so
warm Anna felt she could touch it. "Where are you going?"

"Riding."

His gaze flickered over her habit. "With whom?"

"I don't answer to you for what I do in my spare time."

"No, you don't," he agreed pleasantly enough. He moved
around the banister and climbed the steps toward her.

She was struck by the lethal grace that accompanied his
every move. Anna took a nervous step back, halting when she
realized the landing was right behind her. Somehow it
seemed more prudent to stay on the steps. "What do you
want?"

He stopped on the step just below her, his face at a level
with hers. "You seem to be riding a lot lately."

"Have you been spying on me?"

A smile lifted the corner of his mouth, his eyes traveling
across her face, lingering on her lips. "I wasn't spying. I was
admiring."

A pleasant trill danced along Anna's spine. She found herself wishing that his eyes weren't at a level with her own, but she couldn't look away without finding herself staring at some other, more dangerous part of him.

"I spoke to Desford last night," Anthony said unexpectedly. "He and I are going fishing."

Anna's heart warmed. He was so capable of giving. "That's quite a step forward."

"You can congratulate me if I manage to return without being pushed into the pond. He didn't look too thrilled with the idea."

"I'm sure he was overjoyed. He's just not one to show his excitement."

"He wouldn't have gone at all except that Elizabeth jumped up and said she'd go if Desford didn't want to. He wasn't about to give up his place to a mere girl."

"It's still a beginning." A huge one, considering the fact that Greyley had sought out the child himself. It was gratifying to know that she had managed to help him at least a little. Anna would write Sara a letter this very afternoon and explain how Greyley was improving before her very eyes. Sara would also want all of the details about her brother's betrothed.

The thought of Charlotte made Anna aware of the time. The girl would be waiting and they had important work to do. "I really must go."

He leaned his hand on the banister beside Anna, the movement bringing his shoulder within inches of her chest. "You look very fetching in blue. The color enhances the whiteness of your skin."

She tried to inch away, but couldn't. "Mr. Elliot will be waiting on me."

Anthony's mouth thinned. "Rupert is going with you?"

"I invited him to accompany me and he—" Anna gasped as Anthony hauled her against him. Her hat tumbled down the stairs and rolled into the center of the foyer, where it came to rest at the feet of one of Greyley's suits of armor. "I paid a lot of money for that hat."

"I've never liked it," Anthony growled, aware of a malevolent heat burning in his throat. "I don't like you riding with Rupert. He is a bounder and worse."

Her eyes blazed with disdain. "Oh, you fear he might show me some sort of disrespect? Like asking me to become his mistress, perhaps? The way you did?"

"Damn it, Anna! You don't know him as I do."

"I know that he is more of a gentleman than you. He has never offered me any insult, while you—" She snapped her mouth closed, her contempt clear for him to see.

"Anna, don't," he said, his chest aflame with the agony of thinking of her with another man. He splayed his hands over her back, molding her closer. "You are so beautiful."

A flush of color touched her cheekbones. "No, I'm not. I'm too tall, my nose is huge, and I have large feet."

He leaned his forehead against hers. "You are the perfect height for me, your nose is adorable, and your feet are lovely. I promise to kiss every one of your toes the second I get you into my bed."

To his surprise, she didn't move away. "I'm not going to bed with you."

Was there just the tiniest hint of regret in her voice? "I want to kiss you."

She looked down, her lashes resting on the crest of her cheeks.

Anthony cupped her face and kissed a trail along her cheek, to her neck. She tasted like spring and cinnamon and forbidden heat. His body reacted immediately.

"Greyley . . ." She pushed him away, her breath loud in the silence. "My hat is on the floor."

He nuzzled the heat of her skin. "I hate that hat. It hides your eyes."

"I don't care if you like it or not. I don't want it ruined."

"It will be fine," he murmured, kissing her neck to the delicate line of her ear. "And if it isn't, I'll buy you a new one."

She shivered and he increased his efforts, breathing across her smooth, white skin. "Greyley," she said, her hands flat against his chest, though she made no move to push him away. "You must stop this at once. Someone might come . . ."

"We can go to the library if you'd like—"

"No," she said quickly, her breath ragged in his ear. "I cannot be alone with you."

He trailed a kiss from her ear to the corner of her mouth. "I must have you."

A deep, shuddering sigh wracked her before she pushed her hands lightly against his chest. He stopped immediately and smiled down at her. "We cannot ignore what is between us, Anna."

"There can never be anything between us. I've already told you that."

"You are wrong. I will have you—"

"As what? Your mistress?" She laughed and the bitterness of it wrung his heart. "I will not be made a laughingstock and that is what would happen. I've been mocked enough, thank you."

He tilted her face toward his, admiring the proud way she met his gaze. "No one would dare mock you if you were under my protection. I will take care of you and your grandfather if you'd only let me."

Her hands clasped his wrists and he saw tears glistening in her eyes. "You know better than that," she whispered.

God, but it was bittersweet to see the longing in her eyes. "Since when do you or I care what other people think?"

Anna didn't answer for the longest time, her hands warm on his wrists. Finally, she said, "You don't know what it is like being a governess. I've lost everything; my friends, my position in society, my future. But I still have Grandpapa, and I still have my pride. I will not give up either."

"I didn't ask you to. I just offered—"

"You offered an exchange—security and a home for my virtue and honor." A slow, wracking sigh shook her. "Anthony, I cannot. Please do not ask me again."

"I *will* ask you again," he said fiercely, holding her once more, feeling her slender body firm against his. "And again and again, until you agree. Anna, I want you with me."

"But not as your wife."

He closed his eyes, his jaw aching with the hollowness that seemed to grow by the moment. "I can't. I gave my word and I cannot renege. Anna, please. If you would just listen to what I have to offer—"

"I don't want what you offer. I've taken care of myself and Grandpapa for over a year now, without any help, too." Her chin firmed and he marveled at the strength that shone in her eyes. "I don't need you, Greyley. Go and marry Charlotte."

"Damn it, Anna! I've already explained the nature of my relationship with Charlotte and it has nothing to do with us." He reached out and captured a tendril of hair that had escaped her pins. "We will be together, Anna."

"No, we won't. I can't allow it to happen."

"We can't stop it. It was meant to be." He wrapped the strand of her hair about his fingers and pulled her face to his. He placed a soft, light kiss at the corner of her mouth.

The touch was so tender, so soft that if Anna closed her

eyes, she would have wondered if it had been real or just the remnants of a heated wish.

His eyes glinted darkly. "We were ordained by the stars. Foretold in days of old." He kissed her, his lips brushing softly across hers, this time sending tremors through her.

Anna had to clench her hands into fists to keep from leaning into him. Waves of heat seemed to rise about her, obscuring her vision, making her shift restlessly. She already knew the delight that was held in his hands.

It was sad to realize that once she left Greyley House, she would never again have the opportunity to know those pleasures. For there was only one man she'd ever allow this close to her—and he belonged to another woman.

"Anna, please," he whispered against her cheek. "I can't eat, I can't sleep. I need you with me." He nipped at her ear, his breath sending delighted shivers through her.

She forced herself to remain still. "If you have trouble sleeping, then try a glass of warm milk."

He lifted his head and looked into her eyes, a sardonic quirk on his lips. "Is that what you do each night? Drink glasses and glasses of warm milk?"

"Heavens, no. I never dream of anything more disturbing than falling out of my window. But then, my conscience is fairly clear." Except for the fact that she lusted after her host and employer.

"I suppose I deserve that," he said. "I should never have allowed our passion to go as far as it did in the library."

In his own way, Anna realized that Anthony was apologizing. It wasn't what she wanted, but it was something. "Especially since you are engaged."

"I've told you that Charlotte would not care. In fact, I daresay she'd be relieved to know that I had made arrangements to take my pleasure somewhere else."

Now that she knew Charlotte, Anna had to agree. The girl's visions of love did not include hot, passionate kisses that left one feeling as if all her bones had been seared to ashes. Young and less earthy than Anna, Charlotte believed in courtly love, in poetry and flowers, in soft words and meaningful glances—none of which had to do with base passions.

Anna closed her eyes. It was a pity she was not to wed Greyley; she would have been able to deal with his passions *and* his ill-tempered moods, both of which were sure to put the innocent Miss Melton into a tizzy of fear. If only— She stopped. No. She would not think of the "what ifs." She couldn't afford to. Blinking away a sudden tear, Anna tried to free herself from Greyley's grasp.

"I have to go." Quickly, before she made a fool of herself.

"Anna, don't. Perhaps I can—"

Her tenuous control broke, and suddenly the unfairness of it all poured across her until she stood drenched in outrage. "You can do what? Explain the reasons why you cannot marry a lowly governess?"

His hands fell free of her arms. "Lowly? I have never considered you thus. I spent the last eighteen years of my life trying to convince everyone, including myself, that the Elliot name is worth honoring. I have given everything I possess to make it so, and I cannot walk away from that. I gave my word to marry Charlotte. A man is only worth as much as his word, Anna. You wouldn't want it any other way."

Anna took a shuddering breath. He was right—she wouldn't have him be any less honorable, any less true to his St. John heritage than he was. "Do what you must, Anthony. And so will I."

She stepped around him, then walked slowly down the stairs. Her heart lurched with each step but she didn't falter. She stopped to pick up her hat, and then she walked out of the house, too numb to feel anything other than the roar of emptiness.

Chapter 23

It is not enough to simply remove temptation. We must beat it away, burn it, suppress it, combat it with as much ruthless intent as we can muster.

Lady Burton in a letter to the Countess of Bridgeton, asking for sponsorship of a new effort to remove the sad effects of gin from the slums of London

The next week was an agony for Anna. Though Greyley did as she asked and stayed away, she was aware of his dark gaze on her. And she yearned for him, longed for him, even as she knew it was impossible. Lady Putney seemed aware that something was amiss and she made no secret of her disapproval.

Once Anna came upon Anthony in the morning room and they had stood transfixed, not speaking, but neither of them making an effort to leave. It was as if a secret thread tied them together. Thin, but as strong as steel, it bound them even as it separated them one from the other.

To protect herself from the yearnings in her heart, Anna'd taken to keeping the children near and, when they were not, she found someone else to serve as impromptu chaperone.

Fortunately for her, Greyley's cousin, Rupert, seemed more than willing to be her constant companion. Anna found him an unexpectedly merry cohort, willing to assist her with all manner of projects. She even took him to visit Charlotte, though she made him wait in a copse of trees a small distance from the house. As much as she enjoyed Rupert Elliot's company, he was not the type of young man she would introduce to an impressionable girl like Charlotte.

Anna also did what she could to stay busy, though all the while she lusted for Greyley, dreamed of his hands on her, imagined his body against hers until she knew that she could not remain at Greyley House much longer. As soon as the children were more established with Lily, and Charlotte was more confident, then Anna would leave.

The thought made her teary-eyed. Why did this tension have to exist between her and Greyley? "I have the self-control of a pat of butter," she muttered to herself as she sat in the nursery, working with the children on their Latin.

"What's that, miss?" Mrs. Stibbons asked. She was sitting in one corner of the room, assisting Lily in hemming a cape for Richard's part in the play.

"Nothing," Anna said, returning to her work, her face red.

Selena leaned toward Mrs. Stibbons. "She said she had the butt of a sheep herd."

"I did not," Anna said, casting a harried glance at the housekeeper.

"Did, too. I heard you." Selena peered at Anna's behind, her brow crinkled in thought. "It's not that big."

Anna narrowed her gaze. "That's enough from you."

Selena grinned and returned to her work while Mrs. Stibbons chuckled. "That child is a merriment unto herself."

"Indeed she is." Anna caught sight of Rupert in the doorway. "Ah! Have you come to visit?"

The children immediately clamored out of their chairs and swarmed the young man.

He laughed, holding out his hands to fend them off. "Back, you little fiends!"

"Uncle Rupert!" Elizabeth cried, her cheeks red with pleasure. "Did you bring us anything?"

"You said you'd bring us candy," Marian said eagerly.

"I want some candy, too," Elizabeth interrupted.

Rupert laughed and held out his hand. Five sparkling candies lay in his palm. "Selena first. She's the youngest."

"Ohhh," Selena said, staring at the candies with great concentration. "I like red candies."

She started to take it, but then hesitated. "I like yellow ones, too."

"Oh for heaven's sake," Marian said, hopping up and down. "Just pick one."

Selena acted as if she hadn't heard her sister. She touched the orange candy with a grubby finger. "I've never had an orange candy before."

"Then take the orange one," Desford said, frowning.

"But I might not like it." Selena's brow cleared. "I know. I'll take the yellow one. It's a sunny day and this candy looks like the sun."

"Good," Elizabeth said, elbowing Richard aside so she could see the candies better. "Now it's Marian's turn to—"

"But perhaps," Selena said thoughtfully, sucking on one of her fingers, "perhaps I should get the red one because I do have a red dress and it is my favorite."

The children groaned while Rupert laughed. "I'll tell you what, princess. You take the red one and I'll bring you an orange one tomorrow."

Sighing reluctantly, Selena took the red candy. The rest was distributed without mishap and Anna soon had everyone settled back into their seats and doing their work, the candy making them all pleasantly quiet.

She turned to Rupert. "That was very nice of you."

He shrugged. "They are my family. Some of the few I can stand." His gaze flickered to Anna and he smiled. "You certainly have a way with them. I don't think I've ever seen them this orderly."

"They are good children." Better than good children—they were wonderful. Her throat grew tight and she had to clear it before she could speak. "They are creative, too. You should see the play they have planned."

"I'm sure it's delightful." He leaned forward and took her hand in his. "As are you."

When Greyley took her hand, her whole body tingled as if afire. When Rupert took her hand, it was all she could do to keep from snapping at him. She freed her fingers. "That's enough of that, Rupert."

"Not for me, it isn't," he said, his voice low. "Anna, I feel—"

"Indigestion, most likely," she answered easily. "The roast was not well cooked last night and it has made even me uneasy." Why was it so simple to turn aside this perfectly charming and handsome man, yet she could not make herself walk away from an arrogant, domineering ass like Greyley?

Rupert sighed. "You are making this very difficult for me, aren't you?"

"As much as possible."

A reluctant smile touched his lips. "Anna, I hope you don't think I'm too forward, but I couldn't help but notice that my cousin seems rather taken with you."

"Oh, he's quite decided that I'm to be his mistress," Anna said without thinking.

Rupert barely managed to keep his mouth from dropping open. For some reason, such openness was disturbing in a woman. Of course, Anna Thraxton wasn't an ordinary woman. In the past two weeks, Rupert had come to realize exactly what it was that had Anthony in an uproar.

He felt a momentary twinge of guilt. It was quite unlike Greyley to pursue an honest woman, and Rupert had little doubt that Miss Thraxton was every bit as virtuous as she seemed. That left only one possibility—that there was a genuine attraction between the two.

His mother had been right after all. "I hope my cousin hasn't made things awkward for you."

"Heavens, no! Greyley is rude, perhaps, but never awkward. I've told him I'll have none of him."

"He doesn't seem to have heard you."

"Yes, well, he's a wretched listener. Quite impossible."

Rupert had to smile. "I've never heard it said quite like that, but yes, he is a wretched listener."

Anna glanced at the children. "Yet he has done a great deal for your family."

Indeed he had. More than Anna could guess. Rupert's twinge of guilt grew. "I don't know if you are familiar with the particulars of the Elliot family, but suffice it to say that we are singularly lacking in decorum, grace, and quality."

"That's rather harsh."

"But true. Before Anthony took the family in hand, we were on the brink of ruin, both financially and socially. My uncle owed money to almost every peer in the realm, even the prince. And as you know, that is not an enviable position for anyone."

"I should say not. But Greyley seems to have prospered despite it all."

Rupert leaned a shoulder against a wall. "I don't know about that. He was only seventeen when he took the family reins. He's more somber now. He doesn't laugh as he used to."

A shadow darkened her eyes. "He takes on a lot, doesn't he?" she said softly.

"As he was taught. He was a St. John, you know."

"Where he learned his principles."

"And no one is quite so stubborn as a St. John."

"Except an Elliot?"

"We aren't nearly as stubborn as we are selfish, disloyal, and spendthrift."

"Lovely qualities for an entire family."

"You cannot change the way you were born," Rupert said with a shrug.

"Nonsense," she said briskly. "You are what you decide to become, Rupert."

"So Anthony tells me. He's becoming impossibly dictatorial."

Anna sighed. "I know. I've done what I can. But it's going to be up to Charlotte—" She broke off.

"Charlotte?" Rupert asked. "Ah, yes. Charlotte Melton. I've been escorting you to her house every morning."

"I was hoping you wouldn't know her."

"I've never had the pleasure of meeting her, but I'd heard—" He shrugged. "I know far more than you realize."

"I didn't realize you knew of the engagement. I would have introduced you, but—" She looked at him.

Rupert gave a rueful grin. "I'm not a proper man for a Miss Melton, eh?"

"She's a very gentle creature, almost half his age, and painfully shy. Makes me positively ill to think of what living with a man like Greyley could do to a gently raised child like that."

"I see," Rupert said. He watched Anna for a moment, noting the way the sunlight lit the deep auburn lights of her hair to the richest red. She was a beautiful woman, he realized with some surprise. Even with that bold nose. Strange he'd never noticed it before, but something about her manner made one shy away from really looking at her.

But perhaps it was no wonder. Any normal man would cringe from the directness of her opinions, the forthright way she had of speaking, and the annoying way she had of looking at one as if she could see right through you. All told, she was a formidable package. To everyone but a man like Greyley.

And perhaps to a man like Rupert. He leaned forward and smiled. "You have lovely hair."

She sent him a flat look. "Pray do not start that nonsense with me. I have a very low tolerance for drivel."

Rupert's pride was piqued. No wonder Greyley was so determined to have her. "Are you ready to go for a ride?"

"Only if you will promise not to make a cake of yourself. I'm quite immune, you know. And I rather like you—I'd hate to have to avoid you for the rest of your stay."

"Oh, very well, wretch," he said, feeling unaccountably cheered. He offered her his arm. "Shall we go?"

"I need to change. Can you meet me in front of the house in ten minutes?"

"No woman can change her clothes in ten minutes."

"I can," she said. "Lily, will you and Mrs. Stibbons watch the children? I'm going for a ride."

Lily beamed her agreement and Rupert watched as Anna walked from the room. He made his farewells to the children and went downstairs to wait. A scant ten minutes passed before she sailed down the steps, her habit neatly buttoned as she pinned her hat to her curls.

They were up on their horses and riding through the woods before Anna smiled at him. "I hope you don't mind, but I promised Charlotte I'd stop by." She shot him a hesitant glance. "I hope you won't tell Greyley that I've become acquainted with his betrothed. I don't think he'd like it."

Rupert flashed a boyish grin. "Oh, I'll keep your secrets, if for no other reason than to discomfit Anthony."

"Excellent! I've been lending Charlotte some books."

"What books?"

"Wollstonecraft, Byron, and some others."

"Good God," Rupert said, awe dripping from his words. "Anna, what are you doing?"

"Protecting an innocent girl from future unhappiness."

"And creating unhappiness for Greyley."

"Anthony needs a woman who understands her own value. With a few improvements, Charlotte will be perfect."

Rupert's grin widened. "Greyley will be furious."

"Oh, he's always upset about something."

"Good God, what I would give to see the first time she opens her mouth to refute him. He'll be livid."

Anna sniffed. "No man knows what's good for him. Look at Greyley—with all the capable, competent women out there, he chooses the most unsuitable child for his bride. Why, one week with your family and she would be torn to shreds and—" She glanced at him. "I'm sorry. I didn't mean to malign your relatives."

"If she's an innocent, I daresay you're right." He glanced at her curiously. "Why do you care so much about Greyley's intended?"

"Because Charlotte has no one to help her."

"You are a kind person, did you know that?" His lips twisted into a self-derisive smile. "The opposite of me."

"You are what you want to be. And you want to be naughty."

He grinned but made no further comment, and they rode for a short time without talking.

"Here we are," Anna said as they pulled up to the garden gate at Melton House. She easily dropped to the ground without waiting for Rupert to dismount. "I'm a bit late. Charlotte will be worried something happened."

He lightly leaped down from the saddle and came to stand beside her. "Worried? About an Amazon like you?"

"Charlotte doesn't have my hearty constitution. I daresay a ride in the sun would quite exhaust her."

"She sounds like a paltry woman."

"Oh no. Just delicate." A mischievous grin crossed Anna's face. "And very pretty."

Pretty? "Is she?" Rupert managed to say without too much inflection.

"Just wait until you meet her." Anna looped the reins over the fence and opened the narrow iron gate.

Rupert followed, closing the gate and looking about him with interest. The garden was beautiful—lush and heavily grown, with splashes of color that almost hurt the eye. The lazy sun warmed everything and sent the heavy scent of flowers spilling into the air.

Anna frowned. "Charlotte is usually waiting. Rupert, stay here. I'm going to see if she's on the other path." She disappeared down a narrow stone walk.

It was quiet in the little clearing, the heavy drone of a bee the only sound. A faint breeze stirred his hair. The minutes stretched and he sighed, feeling a little sleepy in the heat. He wandered to the rose garden and plucked a large, pink blossom. A sound behind him made him turn.

Expecting Anna, he was already smiling, a quip ready. But the words died on his lips. Before him stood a tiny, exquisite creature who looked like a nymph. Her skin was perfect cream, her cheek smooth and round. Her mouth, naturally red, parted as she gasped in surprise. She took an uncertain step back and the sunlight gilded her golden hair to silver.

Rupert stared, his breath suspended, his heart thudding loudly in his ears. He met her gaze, and his chest contracted. She had cornflower blue eyes, as innocent as a fawn's, with long, thick lashes that made his heart swell. The sunlight seemed to shimmer and expand, filling his heart, his soul.

Rupert took a step forward.

She turned as if to fly.

"Wait," he said softly. "Don't leave. Please."

She paused, though her body was still tense. "Who are you?"

He managed a bow, smiling up at her as he did so. "Rupert Elliot. I'm here with Miss Thraxton and—"

"Oh!" The nymph's face glowed. "I knew she would come today."

Realization dawned. "You are Charlotte Melton," he said in a strangely hollow voice.

She nodded shyly, her blond ringlets framing her face. "I should go and find Miss Thraxton."

"No!" He glanced wildly around, desperate for some reason to keep her with him. "We should sit and wait for her together."

Charlotte glanced at him uneasily. "I shouldn't stay in the garden alone with—"

"But we are not alone," he said promptly, moving to a nearby bench and dusting the seat. "Miss Thraxton is on her way here now."

"That's true."

"Here, you can put your books between us, to make sure there is no impropriety."

She hesitated yet again, and some bit of mirth made him say, "Anna would not hesitate."

That did it. Charlotte's chin lifted and she perched on the edge of the bench, setting the book between them.

"Is that one of Miss Thraxton's books?"

"Yes. I was going to return it to her, though I hate to give it up."

"What is it?" he asked, entranced by the enthusiasm that shone from her face.

"*Childe Harold*. It's the most wonderful book I've ever read," she said with so much sincerity that his heart caught again. She turned her wide gaze on him. "Have you read it?"

"Yes," he lied without the slightest remorse. "It is one of my favorites." And from this day forward, it would be. "In fact, I've told Lord Byron several times how much I enjoyed it."

"You know Byron?" she said, obviously awed.

He did, though Rupert had never met a more boorish individual in all his days.

"I've heard that he is excessively romantic." She gazed up at Rupert with an adorably shy smile. "Could you tell me about him?"

Anna came around the corner just in time to see Rupert take his place on the bench beside Charlotte. The two made a charming pair—the one small and fair, the other tall and dark. And there was a certain something about them, the way the air was charged with tension. The way Charlotte's head dropped as if she were fighting the desire to rest her head on Rupert's shoulder. And Rupert—Anna almost cursed aloud. He was thoroughly smitten. It showed in the way he stared at Charlotte as if he thought she might disappear at any second.

Though Anna hadn't disguised her footsteps, the two seemed oblivious to her presence. She managed to listen to Rupert give a very inaccurate account of Lord Byron, describing that debauched lord as "fiery" and "bold," and winning Charlotte's excited responses in return.

The conversation soon turned to other topics, and Anna learned that Charlotte had not been still in her pursuit of knowledge. She'd not only read *Childe Harold,* but had memorized entire passages and was perfectly able to discuss them with enthusiasm, if very little understanding.

Not that it mattered—to judge by his rapt expression, Rupert thought Charlotte's every utterance brilliant.

Good God, what had she done? Best to halt this little flirtation before it progressed into something more serious. Anna cleared her throat, immediately gaining the attention of the two on the bench.

They sprang apart, looking amazingly guilty. Anna frowned. She didn't like this at all.

Charlotte stood, nervously fidgeting with her book. "There you are, Anna!" she said in a breathless voice. "I was looking for you."

"Were you?" Anna said, pasting a smile on her face. "And now you've found me. Rupert, perhaps you should go and check on the horses. They might wander off."

He stood. "Of course. Miss Melton, it was a pleasure to meet you." He took her hand and placed a kiss on the back of it.

Anna watched as Charlotte's face pinkened with pleasure. "Rupert," Anna said ominously, "you had better hurry. I think I heard a dog barking and you know how skittish Majesty can be."

Rupert nodded, though he didn't take his eyes off Charlotte, his hand still holding hers. "Of course."

They remained where they were, hands clasped, staring into each other's eyes until Anna was certain she'd explode. "Oh for heaven's sake," she finally exclaimed, tromping forward and taking Charlotte's hand out of Rupert's grasp. "Go and tend the horses."

He reddened and with one last lingering glance at Charlotte, he turned and hurried up the path.

Anna stayed only another half hour, and all in all, it was a wasted trip. Charlotte was distracted, her gaze straying far too often in the direction Rupert had disappeared. Frustrated, Anna had abruptly said her good-byes and left. But the worst was yet to come, for on the way home, she had to listen to Rupert's gushing admiration for the "nymph," as he called Charlotte. By the time Anna reached Greyley House, she was so disgusted with the whole thing that she dismounted her horse and marched up the stairs without saying a single word to Rupert or anyone else.

She reached her room only to flounce upon her bed and lie staring up at the ceiling. Anna was certain Rupert's interest in Charlotte was only a passing attraction, something that would burn out as quickly as it began. Or so Anna hoped. She could just imagine Anthony's fury on discovering that his intended had fallen in love with Rupert—and she knew full well whom Anthony would blame.

Chapter 24

I can't help but think Anna harbors a secret resentment for Miss Melton. Every time she wrote the girl's name, her pen struck through the "t" with such force that it ripped the paper.

The Countess of Bridgeton to the Earl of Bridgeton,
while sitting at breakfast at Hibberton Hall

Rupert stared at the list on the desk before him. A man of twenty and four years should possess far more than six horses, a curricle, a high perch phaeton, a wardrobe of fashionable clothing, and a run-down cottage set on some lonely acreage in Derbyshire. Disgusted, he threw down the pen, ink splattering across the paper.

There had to be more, or Charlotte was lost to him forever. The last two weeks had been an awakening. For the first time in his frivolous life, he cared about someone else more than himself. Cared with a purity of passion that both frightened and exhilarated him.

Each day brought him closer to Charlotte and they'd taken to meeting secretly, talking for hours on end, finding each other as delightful as their first meeting had promised. Rupert closed his eyes, imagining the warmth of Charlotte's arms about his neck, the feel of her cool lips beneath his. He would never presume to so much as kiss her hand without having some understanding, and her relationship with Anthony held them apart.

But soon . . . if he could find a way to prove to her parents that he could support and cherish her, perhaps then he would have her.

He raked an impatient hand through his hair. No. He *had* to have her. He loved her far too much to let her go. If her parents would not countenance the union, then he'd sweep her off to Gretna Green and—The fantasy abruptly faded. Charlotte was too delicate, too pure to be married over an anvil in the still of night. He had to convince her parents to countenance the match. It was the only way. Rupert dropped his head into his hands and stared down at the dismal list.

If he sold the carriages and four of the horses, he could possibly pay off his debts and still have a little to live on. He straightened slowly, smoothing the paper as he considered what else he should do. They would have to practice economy, of course. But it could be done. Restless, he returned the pen to the holder, picked up the paper, and stood. Perhaps Anna could help him. She knew about practicing economy and what it would take to run a household.

He had just reached the door of the library when Anthony entered. Rupert forced himself to meet Anthony's quizzical gaze. "There you are," Rupert said, wishing he didn't feel so guilty.

Anthony's dark gaze rested on the paper in Rupert's hand before he said, "I'm surprised to find you here and not in the nursery or riding with Miss Thraxton."

"I'm on my way to see Anna now."

Anthony's jaw tensed at the way Rupert so casually used Anna's name. "You sound as if you have become very familiar with my governess." He didn't mean to put emphasis on the word "my," but somehow it came out that way.

It had been hell, but for the past two weeks Rupert had been with Anna for every one of her daily rides. It was all Anthony could do to speak in a civil tone.

Rupert didn't appear to notice. He just stared down at the paper in his hand, his brow creased. After a moment, he lifted his gaze to Anthony. "I've been taking stock of my life. Anthony, due to certain circumstances, I feel it is time I settled down."

An ominous weight shifted to Anthony's stomach. He reached out and took the paper from Rupert and silently read through it. "This is all you own?"

"It's not much but—"

"What are you planning?"

Rupert turned away, as if afraid to face him. His voice, when it came, was strained and taut. "Anthony, I'm in love."

"With?" Anthony asked silkily, his jaw aching with the effort to keep from ramming his fist in Rupert's face.

Rupert winced. "You know. How did you find out?"

Anthony didn't trust himself to speak, so he remained silent.

"Anthony, she's an angel. I can't live without her."

She was not an angel. She was an infuriating, independent woman and it would take an equally strong-willed man to be her partner. Anthony thought about saying as much to Rupert, but the bitterness in his heart would not allow it. He looked down at the list in his hand and noticed that he'd crumpled it into a tight ball. As if the words came from someone else, he heard himself ask, "Does she feel the same for you?"

"I think so. I hope. Oh, I don't know! We . . . we have not spoken because of her obligations."

Anthony frowned. "Obligations?"

"To you."

Good God, she felt she had to finish her duty to the children before she took up her own life? She saw Anthony as an obligation and nothing more. It was the most lowering moment of Anthony's life. "What can I do to help you?"

Rupert hesitated. "You can release her, Anthony. Let her go."

"She's free to go whenever she wants," Anthony snapped, "and she knows it."

A crease rested between Rupert's brows. "We didn't mean to . . . I never thought it would happen like this."

"No. No, of course not."

Rupert swallowed. "I hope you will forgive us."

Anthony turned and walked to the window. "There's nothing to forgive," he said tightly. How could Anna be in love with Rupert? Even though Rupert had admitted as much, Anthony refused to believe it. He fisted his hands and shoved them into his pockets, staring with unseeing eyes at the garden below.

After a moment, he heard Rupert sigh, and then leave. The door closed behind him.

The pressure in Anthony's chest increased and he rubbed at his shoulder to ease the ache. Damn Anna Thraxton. She'd invaded his household, set everything on end, forced Rupert to fall in love with her, and now she was planning on blithely dancing away.

And Anthony would just have to let her go, his hands tied by his determination to do the right thing. He thought of Rupert's list and managed a bitter smile. The boy was deeply in love, you could see it in his eyes, in the way his eyes brightened the second he mentioned Anna.

Anthony unlatched the window and threw it open, then stood leaning out, breathing deeply from the garden below. He'd stood in this same window not a month before and watched Anna perform her magic on Desford. Though far from perfect, the boy's behavior was improving daily. All of the children had blossomed under her touch and so, in all honesty, had Anthony.

And now he was going to lose her. He closed his eyes and rested his forehead against the window. If Rupert was right and Anna returned his regard . . . He pushed away from the window and turned to his desk. He would show Anna how false her feelings for Rupert were. It was impossible that she could react to Anthony's touch and be in love with another man—he refused to believe it.

Perhaps he needed to remind Anna of the fire between them. The idea took hold and grew. He would *show* Anna how he felt, show her in a way that would leave no room for anything else.

A thumping sound from the hallway preceded Sir Phineas into the room. "Greyley! How are you today? I left my book on the table and I've come to get it—" The older man stopped when he saw Anthony's expression. "Good God, no one has died, have they?"

"No. I was just thinking about—" *What? Seducing your granddaughter?* Anthony managed a thin smile. "It's nothing."

"It has to be something," Sir Phineas said, closing the door and then limping into the room. He found his book on a small table by a chair that sat beside the fireplace, then he lowered himself into the chair and looked at Anthony with an expectant gaze. "What has you looking like a thundercloud? Not Anna, is it? She has that effect on some people."

Anthony looked into Sir Phineas's bright blue eyes and wondered how much he could tell the old man.

As if he read his thoughts, Sir Phineas smiled. "Come, boy. You've no one else you can trust. None of your brothers is here."

That was true. Besides, what did Anthony have to lose? "I'm at a loss and it's not a feeling I relish."

"None of us do. Tell me about the matter and maybe I can think of something."

"I don't know if you are aware or not, but I'm engaged to Miss Charlotte Melton."

"So I've heard." The old man pursed his lips thoughtfully. "Don't think I've seen the announcement in the papers."

"We haven't posted the banns yet. She is in mourning for several more months."

"I see."

"At the time I offered for her, she seemed perfect. She's young and unspoiled by London life. A very gently bred young lady."

"Sounds like a paragon. But you don't look elated."

Anthony smiled without humor. "I'm not. Since I made the offer I've changed my mind. I do not wish to marry her."

"May I ask what has changed your mind?"

Anthony met the old man's inquisitive look with a steady gaze.

After a moment, Sir Phineas raised his brows. "Ah! I see. Cry off from your engagement then."

"I cannot," Anthony said shortly, jamming his hands back into his pockets. "As much as I wish it, I cannot do anything so dishonorable."

"The St. John pride makes itself felt." Sir Phineas sighed. "This is a quandary."

Silence rested between them. Sir Phineas seemed lost in thought, staring down at his feet. After a moment he looked up. "It's unfortunate that society has decreed that men cannot cry off from an engagement, but women can. Bloody unfair, if you ask me, but there's precious little we can do about it."

"I cannot be dishonest."

"Then disenchant her by being too honest. Women always get in a taking over the most ridiculous things. I daresay you'll think of something, Greyley. For what it's worth, you have my blessings."

"Sir Phineas, do you know what this would mean?"

A smile touched the old man's face. "I hope it means that someone we both care about will be made very happy. Someone who deserves the very best."

Anthony's throat tightened painfully. "There is the possibility that she loves another." The words burned his tongue.

Sir Phineas thought the turmoil on Greyley's face showed a good deal of promise. His one worry had been that the earl would not truly care for Anna, but apparently that fear was unfounded. "What makes you think Anna loves anyone? Damned secretive, that girl. Not one to wear her heart on her sleeve."

"My cousin Rupert seems to think she—" The earl stopped, white lines appearing at either side of his mouth.

"Ah, the young Mr. Elliot. He seems an impetuous sort. And not always correct in his assumptions."

A light gleamed in Greyley's gaze. "Perhaps you are right. It's just that Anna seems to seek him out, while she avoids me."

"Daresay she's afraid she'll reveal too much." Sir Phineas picked up his book and stood. "She's a proud woman, my Anna. But trust me, my boy, there's always hope. And when that fails, there's guile and wile."

"There are times when I see a bit of your granddaughter in you."

"I daresay there's more than a little." Sir Phineas flashed a brief smile. "But before you approach Anna, I believe you have something else to see to."

Anthony nodded briefly. "I'll take care of it this very afternoon. Whatever occurs, I cannot follow that path."

"Excellent," Phineas said, hobbling to the door, the thick carpet muffling the thump of his cane. "If you need any help, you know where to find me."

Sir Phineas gave the earl a reassuring wink and then left, content that things were progressing very satisfactorily indeed. Whistling merrily, Phineas made his way back to the nursery.

Lady Putney waited until the thumping of his cane faded into the silence before she stepped from behind the suit of armor by the library door. Though it had been closed, she'd been able to hear enough of the conversation to know what Greyley was about.

Anger dripped through her. Were none of her sons worth the effort she'd expended in their behalf? Fools, every one! She'd been counting on Rupert to woo that red-haired harridan away from Greyley, and what had he done but force the issue. The earl was more infatuated than ever, even to the point of trying to trick Charlotte into crying off.

Lady Putney's mouth thinned. She would have something to say to that. Within a remarkably short time, she was in a carriage and on her way to Melton House.

Charlotte pressed her hands to her heated cheeks, trying to comprehend what she'd been told. "It cannot be true."

Lady Putney's overpainted face softened with seeming sympathy. "It's true, my dear. I shouldn't have told you, but I thought you had the right to know."

Charlotte swallowed, aware of a sinking feeling in the region of her stomach. Her parents had lost their entire fortune, every last pence? It seemed impossible. But here was Lady Putney, who was not only one of Mama's dearest friends, but also her beloved Rupert's mother, telling her the facts as she knew them.

At the thought of Rupert, Charlotte clenched her hands before her. "It's hard to believe. My father was just talking of purchasing some additional lands."

"He probably will, once he has the money Greyley has promised."

Charlotte's gaze flew to Lady Putney's. "What money?"

Lady Putney shook her head sadly. "They didn't tell you about that, either? I vow, but I could pinch your mother for her stubbornness. She didn't want to worry you, which I'm sure is to her credit, but still . . ." She sighed.

Charlotte placed a trembling hand to her forehead. Her mind whirled with the information Lady Putney had given her—her mother had overspent on the household expenses, their man of business had made some imprudent improvements on the estate, her father had made some poor investments . . . Charlotte suddenly remembered that her father had seemed in an ill mood lately, which she had attributed to all the talk of the wedding, for Mama seldom spoke of anything else. Now his moodiness took on a far more horrible meaning.

Lady Putney looked about the sitting room with a sad gaze. "It will be difficult seeing someone else in this dear house. I shall always think of you when I come."

Tears welled in Charlotte's eyes. "The house—" She could not say it.

Lady Putney seemed to suddenly realize the depth of Charlotte's distress, for she took Charlotte's hands in her own. "Oh, my dear! Forget I said anything about it. I'm sure something will occur to right your family fortune. Perhaps even—wait. What am I thinking of? Your marriage to Greyley will fix everything!"

Charlotte's hands curled into fists, her nails biting into the tender flesh of her palms. For the last two days she'd been trying to find a way to tell Mama that she had no wish to marry Greyley. For the first time in her life she was in love, and she wanted Rupert or no one.

Now it seemed that even that choice was stripped from her. She gazed at the small red pillow that adorned the settee. She and Mama had embroidered it only last week. "My marriage to Greyley will save the house?"

Lady Putney gave her hands one last pat. "It will save everything. Once you are a countess, your family will be beyond the touch of any moneylenders, no matter how powerful they are."

Dear God, but this was horrible. Her family was in dire straits, so serious they dared not tell her, and all the while, they were counting on her to save them. It was horrible. Yet the thought of not being with Rupert was agony.

The door opened and Mama rustled in, greeting Lady Putney and admonishing Charlotte to serve the tea. As she did so, Charlotte watched her mother with a careful eye. She finally decided that Lady Putney was right. Mama didn't look well at all, and twice she made a reference to the cost of Charlotte's wedding gown, a fact that made Lady Putney look at her with a significant air.

If only Rupert had a fortune! She knew he'd save her and her family. But he was not a wealthy man. He'd already told her of his lack of expectations, his hopes of living in the cottage in Derbyshire. For the last week Charlotte had dreamed of living in that quaint cottage. She'd help with the household expenses, too, and perhaps raise a sweet little goat for milk and cheese. Rupert would have been so pleased with her and they would have been blissfully happy.

Charlotte closed her eyes, a faint trembling in her legs that made her glad she was sitting. The truth of her situation was obvious. As much as she loved Rupert, she would have to marry Greyley. The thought left her gray and cold, like ashes in the bottom of the fireplace.

Mama and Lady Putney talked for the better part of a half hour while Charlotte helplessly mulled her way through her new circumstances. She was so preoccupied that she barely noticed when the butler announced a visitor, and it was a shock to see Lord Greyley escorted into the room.

In the past, she'd always seen him with a tentative air, part of her not really believing that they would actually be wed one day. And if they were, the day was so far removed that Charlotte was able to allay her fears and anxieties. But today, looking at his broad shoulders and noticing the way he dominated the room without even trying, made her feel small and insignificant. Her heart fluttered when the earl bowed over her hand and pressed his lips to her limp fingers.

It seemed as though Greyley was looking at her more intently than usual. Charlotte managed a perfunctory smile and murmured something incoherent. That seemed to be all he expected, for he turned his attention to her mother and Lady Putney.

Charlotte stared miserably down at her hands, which were clenched in her lap. What could she do? She couldn't imagine life without Rupert, but there was no help for it. She would marry Greyley and be a proper wife, yet every night she would dream of Rupert and his cottage in Derbyshire.

Feeling like the most miserable person alive, Charlotte tried to think of the bright side of her situation. She would be a married lady and a countess, which would give her social standing in London. Perhaps she could become a leader of fashion, and host a number of elegant parties. Charlotte imagined herself as a dashing young matron of society in a futile effort to cheer herself up.

"Charlotte," Mama's voice broke in on Charlotte's musings, a note of reproof lingering in the air, "the earl has asked you no less than two times what you think of the weather."

"Oh!" Charlotte said, forcing herself to take note of her surroundings. She glanced at the earl and found him disturbingly close, his dark eyes almost hawklike. "I-it has been unusually warm," Charlotte stammered miserably. "I've heard that it is even warmer in London." Rupert had told her that, Charlotte remembered with a pang.

"You need not worry about London. I daresay we'll never go there."

Charlotte paused. "Never?"

"Oh, once every five or six years, perhaps. But only when the season is over. I find it too crowded otherwise."

Lady Melton gave an uncertain laugh. "Lord Greyley, surely you'll go more often than that. After all, you have an impressive town residence and—"

"I'm selling it."

Charlotte blinked. She loved the Greyley London house. Located in Mayfair, it was the most stylish establishment on the street. "You . . . you cannot sell it!"

"Cannot?" He crossed his arms over his chest and leaning back in his chair, looking astonishingly self-satisfied. "I can do anything I want."

Anger rallied Charlotte's spirits somewhat. Oh, how she wished she were more like Anna. Anna would have made sure her feelings were known. Charlotte glanced at the earl from beneath her lashes, noticing the way he watched her, his lids lowered, a faint smile on his face. He was insufferable, Charlotte decided. And she was to marry him. The thought made her furious.

For one instant, Anthony thought he'd managed to raise Miss Melton's ire enough to get her to engage in a good, healthy argument. But as he watched, the flash of irritation melted away, to be replaced by her usual anxious look.

Charlotte had never been very comfortable in his presence, Anthony reflected with irritation, wondering how he'd ever come to the conclusion that he would be happy with such a lackluster bride.

Suddenly anxious to see this charade at an end, Anthony said loudly, "I'm also thinking of moving from Greyley House."

Lady Melton's mouth dropped open while Charlotte gasped. "You cannot mean that!" she said. "I would miss Mama and—"

"You'll be my wife, Charlotte. You won't need your mother any longer." There, he thought with satisfaction. That should settle things. Lady Putney was frowning and even Lady Melton, that implacable statue of calm, was beginning to look disturbed.

"Lord Greyley," she said now, "you cannot mean to whisk Charlotte away."

"Once she's married, she'll have far too much to do seeing to my needs."

"Your . . . needs?" Charlotte said in a voice that was barely above a whisper.

"Mine and the children's, of course."

Lady Melton managed a smile. "I thought the children would be going to live with Lady Putney." She looked at Lady Putney as if seeking assurance.

It was not far in coming. "I'd love to have the children live with me once Greyley's married! Charlotte could never handle all five of them."

"She'll have plenty of help from the servants," Anthony said. "And once we have a few children of our own, five or six perhaps, then she'll—"

"Five or six . . ." Charlotte stood, one hand pressed to her stomach. "My lord, may I speak with you in private?"

Lady Melton looked astounded. "Charlotte, that is highly improp—"

"Mama," Charlotte said, an unexpectedly firm light in her eyes. "I will speak with Lord Greyley on the terrace. We will remain in sight at all times, but I *must* have private speech with him."

Anthony raised his brows. He'd never heard Charlotte speak with such resolution. Perhaps it was a good sign. He wasted no more time. "We will stay within sight of this window."

Lady Putney immediately chimed in, "An excellent idea, Greyley." She turned to Lady Melton and said in a smooth voice, "The impetuousness of youth! I daresay Lord Melton was just as impatient a suitor, wasn't he?"

Lady Melton nodded, though she looked far from assured. "I suppose."

Anthony went to the door that led to the garden and opened it. Charlotte passed by in a nervous rustle of lace.

The last thing Anthony heard as he shut the door was Lady Putney's pleased titter. "Such love birds," she said.

Anthony stifled a spark of annoyance and walked quickly to the nearest bench, careful to remain in sight of the terrace door. He had no wish to be forced to wed Charlotte because of a breach of etiquette.

As soon as they reached the bench, he motioned for Charlotte to sit. Instead of taking his place beside her, he remained standing. "What did you wish to say?"

Charlotte twisted her hands together. "My lord, I . . ." She swallowed as if unable to go on.

"Yes," Anthony said, a bit more kindly now. This was certainly awkward, and he felt a momentary pang to cause the child such discomfort. But it really was for the best. "Charlotte, if there is something you wish to tell me that is difficult, perhaps I can guess—"

"No," Charlotte said quickly. "I have something very important to say and I will say it now." She took a deep breath, lifted her eyes to his. "My lord, I am very glad we are to wed."

Anthony almost recoiled a step. "You won't mind living away from your parents?"

"I-I shall miss Mama. But it is my duty as your wife to live where you will."

"And the children? You would take care of them all? If we have six of our own, it will make eleven in all."

Charlotte bent her head. "Yes," she whispered.

Damn it! This wasn't what he wanted. Anthony took an impatient turn on the terrace, coming to a halt directly in front of her. "I will expect my wife to be obedient, too."

He tried to imagine saying such a thing to Anna and couldn't even begin to picture it. She'd have burned his ears with her opinion on that topic.

Charlotte didn't seem to like it, either. She suddenly stood, arms crossed in front of her, an expression of irritation on her heart-shaped face. "Wollstonecraft was right when she said that society considers women as nothing more than chattels of society. I, for one, do not wish to be a chattel. We will marry, my lord, and I will try to be a good wife, but don't expect me to—"

"Wollstonecraft?" He couldn't imagine Lady Melton condoning such a work in her daughter's hands.

"Miss Thraxton lent me her works." Charlotte shot him a dark glance from beneath her lashes and tossed her head. "I found her to be very enlightening. Anna has been bringing me books and essays and—"

"That little—" Anna's morning rides suddenly took on a

new meaning. "So the busy Miss Thraxton has been visiting you often, has she?"

"Yes, she has. And I enjoy talking to her very much."

"I wager you do."

"She's been most generous. I wanted to be ready for our marriage. If it weren't for her I don't know if I'd have had the strength to—" Charlotte stopped and looked away.

A slow anger simmered through Anthony's veins, then exploded to a roaring boil. If Anna hadn't stuffed Charlotte's head full of nonsense, Anthony was sure he would now be a free man. But thanks to Anna and her tendencies to attend to everyone's business but her own—He made an abrupt bow to Charlotte. "I'm sorry to leave you, but there's something I must do." Without waiting for an answer, he turned on his heel and strode out of the garden, calling for his mount as he went.

Chapter 25

Never underestimate the importance of what a woman says in bed. It's one of the few places they will tell you exactly what they are thinking.

Lord Nicholas Montrose, the Earl of Bridgeton,
to his brother-in-law, Chase St. John, while riding
the park at Hibberton Hall

"**I** have a splinter," Selena said, holding her finger in front of Anna's face, so close that Anna couldn't see anything but a blurry blob.

Anna held the child's hand away and then grimaced. "You're going to have to wash those grimy fingers if you want me to see anything."

Selena stuck her finger in her mouth, pulled it out, and wiped it on her dress. "There. All clean now."

"That wasn't what I had in mind," Anna said dryly. She pulled a handkerchief out of her pocket and wiped Selena's hands. "Now let me see."

She turned the child's finger this way and that. Finally, frowning, she shook her head. "I don't see a splinter."

"That's because Desford has already gotted it out for me. I just wanted you to see where it was."

"Oh," Anna said, smiling in spite of herself. "I daresay you were very brave."

"Yes, I was. I only screamed a little."

The little girl beamed so proudly that Anna chuckled and swooped her into her lap. Selena obediently snuggled against her, the faint scent of lemon lifting from the child's hair.

She rested her cheek against Selena's curls and watched the other children playing Catch the Cat. It was late afternoon and the sun shone across the lawn, casting long shadows. It was cooler now and all the children wore coats. Elizabeth's and Marian's long white dresses fluttered against the deep green grass as they ran. Richard was chasing Desford, both of them laughing loudly. Anna sighed. Her time at Greyley House was at an end.

The children were doing well, even Desford had settled in somewhat, though she still detected an occasional flash of rebellion in his eyes. Lily had worked out well and the children loved her. Usually by the time Anna reached this stage with her charges, she had already found her next employment. But for some reason she hadn't written a single letter of inquiry. Tomorrow, perhaps, after the children presented the play, she'd start making preparations to move on.

She caught the sound of Elizabeth's laughter and a feeling of sadness weighted her. In the short time she'd been at Greyley House, she'd grown to love these children—more than she should. She wasn't sure if it was because she'd been more open to them, knowing they were under Anthony's care, or if they were just dearer. Whatever it was, it made her throat tighten painfully to think of leaving.

"You're holding me too tight," Selena said, shifting in Anna's arms.

Anna loosened her hold. "Sorry, sweetheart. I was just thinking."

" 'Bout what?"

Anna rubbed her chin against the child's curls and didn't answer. As much as she would miss the children, she would miss Anthony more. But as much as it hurt to leave, it would kill her to stay.

"Uh oh," Selena said suddenly. "Lord Greyley is coming and he appears angry. Do you think he's remembering all his lost shoes?"

Anna followed the child's gaze across the lawn. Anthony strode toward her with long, purposeful steps. The dark expression on his face made her heart sink. *Oh dear, what has happened now?*

He stopped before her, his gaze hot. "I want a word with you."

She waited.

His gaze flickered to Selena and then back to Anna. "Not in front of the children."

Anna stiffened at the preemptory voice. "Lord Greyley, as you can see, I'm busy. Selena has a splinter in her hand."

Always willing to garner attention, Selena held out her finger toward Greyley.

A scowl crossed the earl's face. "Does it hurt?"

"Not anymore," Selena answered.

"I'll give you a shilling to go and play."

Selena pursed her lips. "Two shillings."

"Done."

Selena hopped out of Anna's lap. "I think I'll go play Catch the Cat," she announced, then held out her hand.

Face grim, Anthony dug into a pocket and produced two shillings.

The little girl examined the coins carefully before placing them in her pocket. Then she turned to Anna. "If you need me, yell loud. I'll find a big stick."

"Thank you," Anna said, touched by this show of loyalty.

Selena sent a dark look at the earl, then marched off.

"Greyley, there was no need for you to be so rude. The children are—"

His hand clamped about her wrist and he hauled her to her feet. Anna was instantly aware of the heat of his grasp. "Release me at once."

"You can either come with me now, or I'll pick you up and toss you over my shoulder. You and I have something to discuss."

Anna yanked her arm free. A welter of emotions stirred inside her, upsetting her peace and sending hot sparks through her. "I will not be threatened in such a manner. If you wish to speak to me, you will ask me nicely or—"

One moment she was standing in front of him, her feet on solid ground, and then she was upside down as Greyley marched across the lawn, Anna hanging over his shoulder like a sack of potatoes.

She beat on his back with her fists and tried to kick, but all that won her was his hand placed more firmly on her bottom, and his low growl of displeasure.

"Damn you, Greyley! Release me now!"

"No." He continued to march on, unaffected by the stares of the children.

"Lily!" Anna called.

"Yes, miss?" came the tentative answer.

"Take the children back to the nursery and see that they get their dinner."

"Yes, miss!"

Anna tried to shake the hair from her eyes. Marian and Elizabeth had their hands clasped before them, a beatific expression on their faces as if they were witnessing the dramatic close of a romantic play. Selena was sucking on her finger and shaking her head, as if chastising them for their improper behavior. Desford and Richard wore huge grins.

"This is absurd, Greyley," Anna hissed. "Everyone can see."

"I don't care about everyone," he returned, striding across the terrace as if she weren't hanging over his shoulder. "We're going to talk and there's not a damned thing you can do about it."

"If you'll put me down, I'll gladly meet you in the library!"

He opened the door and entered the house. "And be interrupted by your grandfather? Or Rupert? Or Lady Putney? Or one of those blasted children? Every time I try to have a word with you, someone interrupts us. I'm not having any more of it."

He was mounting the stairs again and she closed her eyes and prayed that he did not drop her. "Greyley, please let me down."

"No," he said, reaching the top of the stairs and striding down a long hallway. "Not yet." He reached a doorway and kicked it open, then carried Anna across a dark room. Suddenly, she was flying through the air. She landed on her back with a startled "oof" on something soft. Greyley left her to lock the door. Then he began opening curtains.

Anna lifted herself on her elbows and shoved her hair from her face. She lay in the middle of a large, red curtained bed, so big that it could have easily slept six people. "Good heavens, this is your bedchamber!"

"So it is." He came to stand by the bed, staring down at her with such an intent expression that hot color touched her cheeks.

She collected her wits and scooted off the bed, trying to right her clothing with trembling hands. "Are you mad?"

A strange light glinted in his eyes. "Oh, I'm mad. I'm beyond mad. And it's all your fault."

Anna couldn't draw a breath. She stood facing him, intensely aware of the bed behind her. "Anthony, this is foolish. I'm leaving."

"No," he said, moving forward so that his knees held hers against the edge of the bed. "You aren't going anywhere. We, my troublesome little governess, are going to settle this thing between us once and for all."

Anna shoved him as hard as she could. Caught off guard, he staggered back a step. It was all Anna needed. She ran, making it halfway to the door before she was unceremoniously picked up, carried back to the bed, and tossed onto the counterpane again. This time Anthony joined her on the bed, his body covering hers.

She tried to push him away, but he captured her hands and held them over her head, his broad chest blocking the light from the windows. He leaned across her, his face inches from hers. "Stop it, Thraxton."

"I'm not discussing anything in your bedchamber."

"Fine. Then we'll do something other than talk." His gaze traveled down her face, lingering on her mouth, her chin, then below. "But you and I are staying here until we reach an agreement."

"An agreement about what?" she asked through clenched teeth. His body heated her through her gown.

"We cannot ignore what is between us, Anna."

Anna jutted her chin. "I am not attracted to you, Greyley."

A warm smile settled on his lips. "Aren't you?" He leaned forward to whisper in her ear, his heated breath sending hot chills across her skin. "Not even a little?"

She closed her eyes, but that made her immediately aware of how his chest rubbed against hers, of his hands about her wrists and the power of his body as it brushed her. She was burning with need, with the desire to touch him and be touched.

The silence about them grew and thickened. Anna moved restlessly, her hips pushing against his.

His breathing grew more strained. "God, Anna. Do you know what you do to me?"

"No," Anna gasped, trying hard to still the thundering of her heart, the restless heat that was growing inside her. "We'll talk," she blurted out, suddenly desperate to put some space between them.

Anthony placed a single, warm kiss on her cheek. "I just came from seeing Charlotte. She has been reading some interesting books of late."

Charlotte. Anna tried to ignore the fact that Anthony was now placing feather light kisses on her neck. "Mary Wollstonecraft wrote some marvelous—"

"I know what she wrote." He lifted his head to look at her. "Why, Anna? Why did you visit Charlotte?"

"Because she was obviously ill-suited to be your bride. Someone had to watch out for her interests."

A frown settled between his brows. "And you were going to help her?"

"Something like that," Anna said uneasily. "I just wanted her to be able to stand up for herself. I thought it would make her better suited to be your countess."

"What you made her is obstinate." He cursed softly, his eyes glinting. "Do you have any idea what you did, you and your interfering?"

She hadn't interfered. She'd helped. And once Greyley wed Charlotte, he would be glad she had—though the thought brought Anna no pleasure, only pain.

She couldn't think about that unless she wanted to burst

into tears in front of Anthony. And that, she vowed, would never happen.

She risked a glance at him through her lashes. He was regarding her with a peculiar mixture of frustration and something else . . . something like . . . desire. For an instant Anna imagined what it would be like to have Anthony make love to her, to be with her and no one else. The thought warmed her, swelling her breasts and peaking her nipples, making her skin quiver in anticipation.

The time had long come for her to leave. Lily was more than capable of taking care of the children, and Anthony would be marrying Charlotte soon. Nothing held Anna at Greyley.

The thought was strangely freeing, and to still the emptiness of her heart, she lifted her mouth to his. He froze for a moment, startled. But she didn't let that deter her. She increased her efforts, slipping the tip of her tongue over his lower lip.

He moaned and opened his mouth, the kiss searing. Heat flared and Anna wanted more. She wanted Anthony with her, beside her, inside her. She wanted to leave Greyley House with something that was just hers . . . a memory of a moment when she was more than just the governess.

Anthony groaned against her mouth, his hands tangling in her hair. Anna lifted her hips and rubbed them against his, instinct pressing her further and further. Anthony broke the kiss and lifted himself on one elbow. He untied her gown and tugged it down until only her thin chemise separated them. Then he was undoing his own cravat.

Within moments, his coat, cravat and shirt lay on the floor. Anna splayed her fingers over his skin, savoring the feel of him, of his warm skin, of his muscled body. Every inch of her trembled with excitement as he undid the lacing on her chemise and bared her breasts.

His gaze flickered to hers. "I've dreamed of this."

"So have I."

He kissed her, his mouth devouring hers, his hands on her arms, her breasts, teasing her nipples to readiness. Anna ached against him, wanting more. Needing more. Anthony lifted just enough to pull her dress and chemise free and then she was naked beneath him.

Anna wrapped her arms about him and let the feeling wash over her. She was intensely aware of everything—of his warm scent, of the feel of his hard muscled arms about her, of the rough feel of his breeches against her bare legs . . . every inch of her skin tingled with awareness. Her stomach tightened as heat built inside her and she linked a leg over his and pulled him to her. "Anthony, give me . . ."

It was both a plea and a cry. A shaky laugh escaped him and he raised on one elbow to look down at her. "I shall give, my love, until you can take no more." Within seconds, his breeches were gone and he lay atop her. "Anna, I want to be gentle, but you have to—"

She placed her fingers to his lips. "No talking." She moved her hips against his, feeling the strength of his arousal. "I want this," she whispered, opening her legs to him and running her hands over his arms, his shoulders, to his back and lower.

Anthony buried his face in her neck and groaned. She had no idea what she was doing to him, and he was helpless to resist her. Teeth gritted, he rose over her and positioned himself between her thighs. She waited, her hands curled about his arms, her head tilted back, the lovely line of her throat exposed. God, but she was beautiful. He'd imagined her there, her glorious red hair spread over his pillows, her naked skin gleaming in the late afternoon sun, but the reality was so much sweeter, so much more that it overwhelmed his senses.

But he could not take her without readying her, making sure she received the full enjoyment of the moment. He placed his hand on the plane of her stomach, kissing her neck as he touched her softly, gently, stroking her nether curls with a feather-soft touch. She gasped when his fingers brushed the inside of her thigh and then found the delicate folds. Moist heat dampened his fingers and he gritted his teeth with the urge to bury himself inside her.

She was so beautiful. He stroked her gently, then more firmly, watching as she tossed her head and arched toward him, her breasts rising toward him. Anthony bent and tasted her, taking a nipple in his mouth. He laved it mercilessly, moving his fingers faster, deeper. Within seconds she stiffened, lifting her hips from the bed as the passion took her.

Anthony didn't wait for her to regain her breath. He lifted himself over her, and then slowly, ever so slowly he held himself against her, each movement taking him further into the heat. Beneath him, Anna moaned softly, wrapping a leg about him as she held him to her. She held nothing back, offering all, and Anthony marveled at her openness.

Suddenly he was moving, rising and falling into the sweetness of her. After a first astonished gasp, Anna quivered, then rose to meet him, enveloping him in a heat that shook him to the core. As he'd expected, she was not a pliant partner, but wild, untamed, nipping at his shoulder, her hands never still as she touched and stroked, her long legs locked about him, as if she would hold him there forever.

Anthony cupped his hands about her bottom and held her tight, burying himself in her heat. She moaned and he felt her tremble deep inside as she gave herself to the pleasure. It was an agony and an ecstasy, holding still as she writhed around him, her heat igniting his own.

He was delighted to see that Anna wasn't about to let this

moment slip by without living every second of it. She wrapped herself around him, holding tightly, trying to soak in every nuance of the passion that washed through him. When he finally stilled, they lay locked in each other's arms as their breathing returned to normal.

It was heavenly, lying in the warm bed with his arms about her, her warm, naked skin against his. She buried her face in his neck and held tightly. Outside, the sun finally gave way to night, twilight sinking into blackness.

Anthony sighed heavily. "I don't want to move." He rubbed his cheek against her hair and kissed her forehead, then rolled over to his side, pulling her with him, tucking her neatly against him.

After a while, she stirred. "That was . . . nice."

"Just nice?" he asked, a little affronted.

Her eyes shimmered silver. "*Very* nice. So nice I'd like to do it again."

He laughed softly and captured a thick curl in his hand and wound it around his finger. "You are a brazen vixen, Anna Thraxton." He rubbed against her in a suggestive manner. "Fortunately, I love brazen vixens."

She gave him a lazy, sated smile. Something flickered through her eyes, something sad and tender.

Anthony bent to kiss her mouth, trying to capture the sadness and remove it. "What is it?"

Her expression immediately shuttered. "I was just thinking of tomorrow."

"What happens tomorrow?"

She turned her head away, saying nothing.

Unease settled in Anthony's chest. He turned her face to his. "What happens tomorrow?"

A faint smile touched her mouth. "The children are performing their play."

Anthony had a feeling that wasn't the answer she had intended to give. But before he could say more, Anna sighed and pushed herself up on her elbows, her hair falling over her shoulders and pooling on the bed at her elbow. "I need to dress. One of the servants could come at any time, and it would be awkward."

"We haven't talked yet."

A faint smile touched her lips. "I think we've said quite a lot."

"Yes, but we haven't solved anything. Anna, I care for you."

She smiled, her heart in her eyes, a gleam of hope in the silver depths that made him ache. "Yes?"

His jaw tightened. If he could not convince Charlotte to release him, there would be no "and." "Anna, give me some more time—"

She placed her fingers over his lips. "This is a perfect moment, Anthony Elliot," she whispered. "Don't spoil it with words." She bent and pressed her lips to his, softly, gently, her hands traveling lightly over his back, sending trills of pleasure through him.

Anthony captured her hands. "Wait here." Then he rose and went to the dresser and searched for a moment. Finally finding what he was looking for amid the fobs and cravat pins, he returned to the bed and lay beside her.

A crease rested between her brows. "What is it?"

Anthony captured her hand. He kissed her ring finger and slid the talisman ring over it.

Anna held her hand to the light. "What's this?"

"A family treasure. Legend has it that whoever has the ring in his possession will meet the love of his life."

She made a movement as if to take it off. "Then it's not for me—"

"Anna, the ring has nothing to do with marriage. It's for finding the love of my life, and that is you." He bent and kissed her finger once more, this time teasing the palm of her hand as well. "Keep it. For me."

Anna closed her hand over the ring. She had his love. It was something—but it wasn't enough. "I cannot accept this."

"You already have."

She pulled away. "No." Had she any pride left, she would rise from this bed and walk away. But somehow her pride had disappeared, and with it all hope that she and Anthony could ever be happy. She couldn't ask him to walk away from his honor—it would change him. And she loved him just the way he was.

"We are hopeless," she said, managing a smile through her tears. "You can't walk away from your commitments, and I cannot allow myself to be beguiled into an untenable situation."

He enveloped her in a powerful hug, resting his head against hers, his breathing warm on her ear. "Please, Anna. I will take care of you. You and your grandfather will never want for anything."

Each word he said drove a wedge between them. Anna felt as if they were staring at each other over the brink of a chasm, a chasm so deep and so wide that it could never be bridged. Her heart ached as if someone had squeezed it in a vise. "No."

He brushed his lips over Anna's, nipping at the delicate corners of her mouth. "Don't think. Just stay with me. We'll take this one day at a time. Something will happen. It has to."

Anna closed her eyes. It was so tempting. The ring on her finger seemed to burn. It was a pity the legend was wrong. What she felt for Anthony couldn't be love. Love didn't feel so despairing. So hopeless.

Her fingers closed about the ring and she turned into his embrace, pressing her naked body to his. Without words, she showed him what she felt and he responded instinctively, worshipping her in a way that left her crying his name.

Later, much later, she lay curled in his arms. Anthony's steady breathing stirred her hair, sending a shiver of repletion through her. She savored the feel of him, his scent, his warm arms about her. Outside, the moon shone, sending long tendrils of light across the bed, warming their naked limbs to silver.

She wasn't sure how long she lay there, but eventually, as the night deepened, she slipped from his warm embrace and stood in the silver moonlight. Slowly, she dressed. Before she went to the door, she pulled the narrow circlet from her finger and laid it on the dresser. Careful not to make any noise, she turned and left.

Dawn brought a bright swish of pink and purple to the morning sky. Anna stood on the front step of Greyley House, her traveling pelisse neatly buttoned about her neck, a pair of clean gloves in one hand, her best walking shoes laced up her feet.

She'd left a letter for Grandpapa telling him to come and meet her in London as soon as possible. She was sure that Greyley would provide a carriage. The thought of Anthony tightened in her throat and she blinked back tears.

It had been difficult to leave the children. She'd gone to the nursery and awakened them. They'd seemed to know what was coming, for Elizabeth burst into tears before Anna could say a word. She'd hugged them all, even Desford, who had returned her embrace with a surprisingly fierce hug.

"Would you like the carriage ordered, my lady?" Jenkins

asked quietly. He seemed especially somber this morning, a fact Anna appreciated.

"Yes, I—"

A phaeton whirled into the drive and approached the front steps. As it drew closer, Anna could see Rupert in the seat, the reins in his hands.

He pulled up to the steps and dismounted. Anna caught a glimpse of his face and noted how white his mouth appeared. "Jenkins," she murmured to the butler, "Thank you for everything."

Jenkins bowed and Anna gathered her skirts and descended the stairs to Rupert's side. "What's happened?"

His gaze was wild, his hair mussed as if he'd grasped it at some point. "It's finished, Anna. I went to see Charlotte this morning and—" His voice broke and he clamped his mouth together, white lines appearing at either side.

"Rupert, I'm sorry," Anna said softly. "But . . . perhaps it is for the best."

His eyes blazed and he snapped, "How can you say that?"

"You are overset, but there is no need to flare up at me. I haven't done anything."

Rupert slumped. "I know. Anna, I'm sorry. It's just that . . . I love her. And she told me she didn't want to ever see me again. It was as if . . . she didn't care."

Anna nodded, unable to say anything more, her own tenuous control threatening to break.

With an obvious effort, Rupert gathered himself. He caught sight of her luggage for the first time. "Are you leaving, too?"

"I must."

Something in her voice must have given her away, for he nodded. "I understand." He turned with an impatient movement. "Here. I have no wish to stay, either. I might as well drive you to London; it'll be a hell of a lot faster than Grey-ley's outdated conveyance."

Anna considered the high perch phaeton with a wistful look. He was right—the phaeton would make the trip in half the time of the lumbering carriage. Besides, she didn't look forward to hours of a solitary ride, with no one to distract her from her thoughts. Sighing a little, she picked up her port-manteau and handed it to Rupert. "I would be honored to ride with you to London."

A faint smile touched his mouth. "Who knows? Maybe I will stay in town for a while. I sure as hell don't want to ever come back here."

Anna glanced around at the bleak house that rose beside them, at the expanse of green lawn, at the carefully trimmed trees. As forbidding as it was, it felt like home, and her chest ached to leave it. She cast a last glance up at the dark windows and climbed into the phaeton beside Rupert.

From an upstairs window, Lady Putney watched as her son drove off with the governess. Any other mother would have experienced heart palpitations at the thought of so un-worthy a match, but Lady Putney was no ordinary mother. The sight of Anna sitting in a curricle beside her son, her bags strapped to the back, made her smile.

Lady Putney dropped the curtain back in place and climbed into her bed. She would sleep another two or three hours and then she'd rise and attend the children's play. Smiling to herself, she drifted off to sleep.

Meanwhile, down the hall, someone else stood at their window and watched the phaeton bowl out of sight. Eyes narrowed, Sir Phineas puffed thoughtfully on his cigar, blow-ing the smoke out the opened window. He wasn't about to give up his dreams of scampering grandchildren.

There had to be a way . . . He puffed harder on the cigarillo. After several moments, a slow grin touched his face, and it was with a noticeably light step that he went to dress. He needed to talk to the children. They would know what to do—he'd bet his last groat on it.

Chapter 26

*From what our sister has told me, the only things An-
thony and Miss Thraxton have in common are stubbornness, an intractable sense of what is right, and an
astounding desire to conform everyone to their way of
thinking. They are perfect for one another.*

Chase St. John to his brother, Brand St. John,
upon meeting each other on the road to London

Several hours later Sir Phineas opened the door to the library. "Are you coming to see the children's play? They
are ready to begin."

Anthony was standing by the window, his face drawn and
set. Sir Phineas noted the signs of strain with approval. It
wouldn't be fair for Anna to suffer alone. "Everyone is already assembled in the dining room."

The earl's frown deepened. "Everyone?"

"Lady Putney, Sir and Lady Melton, and Miss Charlotte
Melton."

"Who invited the Meltons?"

"I believe the children did. They wanted a proper audience."

"That's odd." The earl's brow lowered. "Where is Rupert?"

Sir Phineas shrugged. "I haven't seen him since early this
morning."

"Lovely," Anthony muttered. God, what a coil. He'd

woken to an empty bed, still haunted with the feel of Anna. He'd almost risen and gone to her room, but the sounds of the household stirring to life had halted him.

What was it about her? Every time he closed his eyes, he saw her, tasted her, felt her heat surround him. He moved restlessly, turning back to the gray morning. Anna might think they had no future, but he knew otherwise. All he had to do was convince her of that.

But for now, he had to deal with Charlotte. Perhaps he could use the play to his benefit—another opportunity to show her how unsuited they were.

Sighing, he followed Sir Phineas to the dining room. The children had hung a painted canvas behind the wide opening that led to the foyer, making a natural stage area. Chairs had been placed near the curtain in two narrow lines. Sir and Lady Melton sat in the front row of chairs, Charlotte beside them.

Seeing Anthony, the Meltons rose and made their greetings. Anthony shook hands with Sir Melton, said a few brief words to Lady Melton, and bowed over Charlotte's hand.

"Perhaps you'd care to sit here?" Sir Phineas indicated an empty chair on the front row by Charlotte.

Banishing the urge to tell Sir Phineas to mind his own business, Anthony took the seat and fixed his gaze on the drawn curtain, imagining Anna just behind it.

A rustle moved the curtain and then Elizabeth stepped forward. Dressed in a blue satin gown, a conical hat on her head, a long veil draped over one shoulder, she curtsied. "Good evening, gentle ladies and gentle men." She launched into a short monologue describing the aspects of the play about to be presented.

Apparently the rendition was a telling of the family history of sorts. As Elizabeth droned on, Anthony's attention wandered and he stole a glance at Charlotte. She sat staring straight ahead, her eyes focused in the distance, her mind obviously elsewhere. Anthony tried to think of some obnoxious vice he could adopt that would so disgust her that she would recoil in horror. Perhaps if he mentioned that he snored . . .

The play went on and on, seeming interminably long, though in reality only twenty minutes passed. A whole parade of illustrious Elliot ancestors marched across the makeshift stage. Gradually drawn in, Anthony was impressed with the amount of knowledge the children conveyed about each of the time periods. Truly, Anna had wrought miracles.

Once in a while, one of the children forgot the lines. Immediately a soft voice whispered a prompt from behind the curtain. It had to be Anna. Anthony found himself staring at that place in the curtain, imagining himself with her, hidden from sight, his mouth on hers. He stirred restlessly, leaning back in his chair and shoving his hands into his pockets. Immediately, his fingers closed over the small circle of the talisman ring that Anna had left in his room.

The feel of the warm band of silver eased his frustration. He was far from through with Anna Thraxton. He was a St. John, damn it, and when a St. John wanted something, he made it his, one way or another.

The play continued. To everyone's amusement, there were plenty of gaffes—Marian came out wearing her costume inside out and Desford stumbled against a table that collapsed beneath him. Once, while in the middle of a mock sword fight, Richard's sword got tangled in the scenery and he yanked the curtain down on his head.

Sir and Lady Melton seemed to enjoy the show immensely, clapping and laughing aloud, as did Sir Phineas.

Everyone but Anthony and Charlotte, who sat side by side as if turned to stone.

Anthony stole a glance down at her and noted that she seemed as pale and wan as he felt.

Suddenly Lady Melton stiffened, her gaze on the stage.

The children had moved to current times, and were standing in the midst of a fairly accurate rendition of the nursery. And there, wearing a red wig, was Elizabeth, her chest filled with rags to give her an inkling of Anna's curvaceous figure. If the wig and enhanced bosom hadn't told Anthony who Elizabeth was supposed to be, the book of Greek poetry clutched to her breast would have.

"Miss Thraxton," Desford called, coming onstage wearing one of Anthony's best coats, the arms rolled up. "I've come to sweep you away!"

"Oh, Lord Greyley," the fake "Anna" simpered. "This is highly improper."

Anthony sat stunned as Desford walked up to "Miss Thraxton" and planted a loud kiss on her cheek. But worse was her reaction—she turned and kissed him back, blushing adorably.

"What the hell?" Sir Melton said loudly, sending a glare at Anthony. Lady Melton, meanwhile, sat as if mesmerized, her mouth opening and closing, though no sound came out.

"Children!" Lady Putney stood and scurried to the stage, but Sir Phineas blocked the way with his cane.

He took her arm and said quietly, "I fear it's too late, my dear Lady Putney. The truth is out." She struggled as if to free herself, but Sir Phineas led her to a chair and pushed her into it.

Despite the rustle in the audience, the actors plunged on. "Anthony" began chasing "Anna" about a table until Richard walked in.

Desford skid to a halt and glowered at the new arrival. "It's Rupert! Why have you come?"

Elizabeth clasped her hands together and said in her best stage voice, "He has come to steal me away, for I love no one but him."

Charlotte bound to her feet. "*What?*"

Anthony covered his eyes. He didn't know whether to laugh or shout or just leave, but he had the feeling that the entire world was careening madly out of control.

Lady Melton lurched out of her chair and went to enfold Charlotte in a protective embrace. "My dear, dear child!" Over Charlotte's curls, Lady Melton glared at Anthony. "We won't stand for this, Greyley."

Anthony sighed and hauled himself to his feet. "I'm sorry about the play. I didn't know—"

"I'm sure you didn't," Lady Putney said. "If anyone is to blame for this, it is that woman, Anna Thraxton. She's the one who—"

"No!" Charlotte broke free from her mother's embrace, her deep blue eyes brimming with anger. "I will not believe it of Anna."

Everyone was in a turmoil. Everyone except one person. Anthony caught Sir Phineas's calm gaze where he sat watching the whole as if the play had moved from the stage to the audience.

The old weasel, Anthony thought with grim amusement. He'd known all along.

Lady Putney sighed. "My dearest Charlotte, I warned you about the children, did I not? They are completely unmanageable, which you will discover when you wed Greyley. Fortunately I am more than willing to take them to live with me at—"

"No," came a voice from the stage. Desford stepped forward, his hands fisted at his sides. "We don't wish to live with you."

Lady Putney's face grew red, though she tried to smile. "Now Desford, I'm sure that Miss Melton doesn't want to hear—"

"I don't like Miss Melton, either," the boy continued in a dogged voice. "It's because of her that Miss Thraxton left."

Anthony's attention riveted on the small boy. "Left?"

"Of course you ask about *her*," Lady Melton huffed.

"Mother," Charlotte said, "be quiet."

"Where," Anthony asked ominously, "is Miss Thraxton?"

Desford glared. "She left. Because of you."

Elizabeth nodded. "She didn't want to stay and watch you marry Miss Melton."

"How do you know that?" Anthony asked. Desford's gaze flickered to Sir Phineas.

The old man cleared his throat. "I, ah, may have told them that during one of my many conversations. I can't remember."

"Doesn't matter," Selena piped up, taking her finger out of her mouth. "She's coming back. I know she will."

"She'd better," Anthony muttered, his heart a stone in the center of his chest. He glanced at Lily, who'd come out from behind the curtains. "Take the children back to the nursery."

It took Lily twice as long as it would have taken Anna, but she managed to herd the children out without too much incident.

As soon as they were gone, Anthony said, "I'm going after her."

"Good for you," Sir Phineas said with an air of great satisfaction. "If you leave now, you will catch them before they reach London."

Anthony frowned. "Them?"

"Yes, 'them.'" Lady Putney gave a shrill laugh. "Miss Thraxton eloped with Rupert this morning."

"You're lying," Charlotte snapped.

"I saw them," Lady Putney said, "They were riding together in my son's phaeton. That hussy even had her portmanteau strapped behind."

Charlotte stamped her foot. "That bounder! That cheat! Just this morning he told me that he loved *me!*" She paused, her face quivering. "And I sent him away."

"I should hope you did," her father huffed. "Rupert Elliot has no prospects."

"I know. He has been painfully honest. Or he was," Charlotte said, a tear running down her cheek. She looked sadly at her father. "I knew you had made some bad investments and you needed money. My marriage to Greyley was the only way to save us all."

Lady Melton's brow creased. "Bad investments? Where did you hear that?"

Charlotte stared at Lady Putney.

"Did you say such a thing?" Sir Melton demanded.

Lady Putney gave an ingratiating smile. "I-I merely repeated what I had heard from the town gossips—"

"You said Mama had told you everything!"

"No! You just misunderstood me, my dear."

Charlotte's gaze narrowed. "I didn't misunderstand anything. You lied, didn't you?"

"Charlotte!" her mother said in a reproving tone. "I'm sure there is an explanation. Calling someone a liar is not very ladylike."

"Sometimes I don't want to be a lady," Charlotte said. As if in illustration, she twisted her handkerchief until it ripped in two. "If I ever see Rupert Elliot again, I'm going to strangle him!"

"An understandable thought," Sir Phineas said gently. "I daresay he deserves it. However, before you can strangle him, you must find him." He met Anthony's gaze. "You will need to hurry."

"I'll go at once," Anthony said. He bowed to Lord and Lady Melton. "If you will excuse me, I have an urgent errand to run."

Lady Melton murmured her outrage while Sir Melton ground his teeth. Charlotte, meanwhile, grabbed Anthony's sleeve. "I am *not* leaving you to deal with Rupert. If anyone has the right to ring a peal over his head, it is I." Charlotte's willful face hardened into a fierce expression. "And I will, too."

Anthony was too impatient to argue. "I'll order the carriage for you, but I'm riding ahead." Without waiting to see her answer, he turned on his heel and left.

Anna knew that she'd made a mistake riding with Rupert before they reached Bedfordton, only two miles from Greyley. Too distraught to pay attention as he should, Rupert feathered a corner too tightly and locked the wheel of the phaeton on a signpost. It had taken thirty minutes and the help of a passing wagon full of farm laborers on their way to Bristol to get the phaeton back on the road.

Rupert, determined to make up lost time, set the horses to such a fast pace that Anna felt it necessary to mention the importance of safety. This did not sit well with Rupert, who prided himself on his handling of the ribbons, and after a brief exchange, he and Anna were soon embroiled in a full-fledged argument.

Their attention was so focused on berating each other and relieving their pent-up emotions that they didn't notice the huge bank of clouds gathering along the horizon until a rumble of thunder interrupted their sniping comments. Soon afterward the rain began to fall, huge fat drops that stung their faces and made it almost impossible to see. Within moments Anna and Rupert were soaked to the skin.

Though the rain didn't linger, it left the two in the worst of spirits. Rupert seemed determined to drown his feelings by imbibing freely from a pocket flask he produced the second they reached the main road. As he drank, his speed increased. Anna, having learned how sensitive Rupert was to comments on safety, could only hang on and pray that they did not hit a hole in the road.

But something worse than a hole in the road lay in wait. As they rounded a bend at breakneck speed, an old dray lay overturned in the center of the muddy road, a farmer and his wife standing to one side, a thickly muscled labor horse still harnessed to the mess.

Rupert saw the dray the second he rounded the corner, and he desperately tried to guide his grays to one side. But the old farm horse took fright the second the phaeton came bowling past.

The huge horse neighed loudly, then took off in an awkward gallop, the overturned cart dragging behind, the distraught farmer chasing it. Rupert struggled to hold his own team under control.

Just as it seemed he'd succeeded, the farm horse turned sharply and the back of the dray cracked into the phaeton, splintering the rear wheel and sending the delicate carriage tumbling.

Anna remembered nothing but a huge blur and a sharp pain, and then she was lying in a ditch, her skirts over her face, Rupert's colorful curses filling her ears. She closed her eyes, and blessed blackness swept her away.

Sometime later, the black receded and she struggled back to consciousness. Anna opened her eyes and found herself in the common room of an inn, Rupert hovering near, a bandage on his head spotted with blood. A relieved expression crossed his face. "Thank God! I was worried you would never wake up. Greyley would never forgive me."

"Damn Greyley," Anna muttered. How like Rupert to be worried about her only for the sake of saving his own skin, though she doubted Anthony would care. He was far too busy with his precious Charlotte to give any thought to her. To Anna's horror, tears rose to her eyes and she had to fight a depressing need to gulp back a sob.

"Perhaps I should get the landlady," Rupert said, backing away when he saw the tears, a wild expression in his eyes. "I daresay your head hurts and Mrs. Tuffins will know what to do."

"I don't want Mrs. Tuffins," Anna said, gathering herself. She pressed a hand to her head and found that she possessed a bandage that matched Rupert's in size. After touching it gingerly, she unwound it, wondering at the state of her hair. "I just want to get back to London."

"We'll get there," he said grimly. "One way or another."

It was that "another" that bothered her. She ran a tentative hand over her forehead, glad to find nothing more alarming than a knot the size of a walnut over one eye.

Heavens, but she must look a fright. Sighing at the thought, she pushed herself upright. Black spots swam before her eyes, but she grit her teeth and waited for them to subside.

"Maybe you need a glass of water? Or some ale. There's some excellent brandy here, too. I think it must be smuggled because even Greyley doesn't have stock like this—"

"Rupert," Anna said through her teeth, "if you must prattle, could you please not mention Greyley?"

"Lud, you're touchy, aren't you? There's no need to get in a snit," Rupert said in a sulky tone.

Anna swallowed a retort. They were both in ill humor and right now all she wanted was a little quiet so that she could collect herself. But even as she sat on the old worn settee, her head against the high back, her eyes closed against the annoying throbbing behind her forehead, she was on the verge of a torrent of tears. It was as if all her emotions had gathered behind her eyes and were determined to leak out.

She heard Rupert take a chair nearby. He sighed loudly, but Anna ignored him. After several more sighs, he said, "I've messed up everything."

A tear slipped from beneath Anna's lashes and fell down her cheek. She wiped it away, fairly certain Rupert hadn't seen, for he said in a dismal voice, "I should have listened to you and been more careful."

"How . . ." She swallowed the lump in her throat. "How will we get to London now?"

"I've asked to hire a curricle. It's old and it will be uncomfortable, but the phaeton is a complete loss. One rear wheel was crumpled and the shaft was broken in two. It will take weeks to fix it."

Anne pressed her lips together to keep them from quivering. Good God, but this was untenable, she *never* cried. Yet another tear joined the first, closely joined by something that sounded suspiciously like a sob. Anna gulped, miserable and embarrassed, but unable to stop.

"Anna, don't." Rupert moved to the edge of the settee and pulled her head to his shoulder, all brotherly solicitude. "Damn my pride. I should never have driven so wildly."

Rupert's shoulder wasn't as broad as Greyley's. Nor was he able to make her feel completely and totally surrounded, yet it was comforting to have a shoulder to cry on and Anna made the best of it, sobbing loudly against his coat and letting the tears fall. They finally subsided and Anna was left with nothing more than a hiccupping gulp. Still, she pressed her face against Rupert's shoulder while he rested his head against hers, taking comfort in the embrace as much as she.

Thus it was that Anthony, following the mangled trail of the runaways, found Rupert and Anna sitting in a little ivy-covered inn, enfolded in what appeared to be a lovers' embrace.

Anthony froze on the spot, his wet greatcoat dripping a steady stream of water onto the worn carpet, his heart thudding painfully. He'd arrived at the scene of the accident just as they were hauling the ruined phaeton away, and the sight had chilled him to the bone, especially when no one seemed to know the condition of the occupants, except that someone seemed to think the young lady had been injured, for she'd been carried from the scene.

For the next twenty minutes as he galloped wildly for the nearest inn, Anthony had been haunted with visions of Anna pale and injured, calling his name, or worse, cursing him with her last breath. Which was why seeing her locked in Rupert's embrace was something more than a rude shock.

"What the hell is this?" Anthony roared.

Rupert stumbled to his feet, his face pale. "Anthony! I didn't think you'd—I mean, I never thought you—"

"Obviously," Anthony growled, all pretense at civility burned away in one hot second. "She's mine, damn you!"

"Yours?" Anna stood, forcing her weak knees to stiffen. "Since when?"

"Stay out of this," Anthony ordered, his attention on his

opponent. He yanked off his greatcoat and threw it in the corner, then undid his coat.

Rupert's eyes gleamed and he yanked his cravat free and pulled off his coat.

"What are you doing?" Anna pressed a hand to her stomach. It felt queasy and she guessed it had less to do with the bump on her head than it had to do with the two lumps who were getting ready to fight before her. "I can't believe this. Anthony, please—"

"Rupert, you are a dead man." Anthony unbuttoned his waistcoat and yanked it off, his gaze locked on the younger man. "I hope you're prepared for this, for I owe you a good trouncing."

Rupert's waistcoat was already gone and he stood, fists poised, excitement and anger equally melded in his expression. "Are you through yammering yet, Greyley? Or are you going to fight?"

Anna sank back onto the settee and closed her eyes. It was worse than trying to reason with the children, and she was just too tired to deal with it. Besides, what would be the use? The worst thing that could happen would be that one of them would end up with a black eye, and somehow, in the overall events of the day, that didn't seem all that horrible.

So Anna quietly sat while the two men circled each other warily. Anthony landed the first blow, and it almost lifted Rupert from his feet. He staggered back, recovering at just the right moment, then returned with amazing fury to land a punch to Anthony's chin.

Anthony shook it off, but his gaze narrowed and he was more careful after that. If it hadn't been for Rupert's evident anger, they would have been sorely mismatched. As it was, the younger, slighter man was giving as good as he got.

Anthony feinted to the right, then came around with a smashing left hook that sent Rupert head over heels into the table. Chairs tumbled over and Anna noticed Rupert was slow to rise.

She took the opportunity to intervene. "That's *quite* enough."

Anthony's gaze met Anna's. A frown passed over his face. "Anna! What happened to your forehead—"

Rupert landed a punch on Anthony's left jaw and Anthony, his attention riveted on Anna, stumbled backward, hit a low stool, and fell to the floor, hitting his head on the hard plank floor.

"Ow!" Rupert hopped up and down, holding his fist in his other hand. "My thumb!"

"Serves you right, you stubborn whelp," Anthony muttered, climbing back to his feet, his gaze still fixed on Anna. Ignoring Rupert, he made his way to her side.

He placed a finger under her chin and lifted her face to his, drawing in a sharp breath when he saw her forehead. "Is that from the ride here?"

"Yes, we had a little accident."

The door flew open and a small figure dressed in pale blue stood in the bright light.

"Charlotte!" Rupert cried, tucking his bruised hand into his pocket as if to hide it.

Charlotte caught sight of Rupert's face and gasped. Besides a lump on his head, Rupert's left eye was rapidly swelling shut and a bloody cut graced his chin.

Stiff with outrage, Charlotte turned blazing eyes on Anthony. "What have you done to him?"

Anna opened her mouth to explain, but Anthony's hand closed painfully over her elbow. She noticed that his gaze was on Charlotte, his expression intent. A slow, lazy smile flitted across his face, and he shrugged. "Rupert insulted my honor. We were just settling the issue when you arrived."

Charlotte went to Rupert, who immediately placed an arm about her shoulders. He held her to him, a beatific expression on his face.

Charlotte nestled there for only an instant before she leveled a look of blazing contempt on Anthony. "You are a beast! I never want to see you again!"

Once again, Anna opened her mouth to speak, but Anthony was quicker. He slipped an arm about her waist and pulled her against him. Still a little wobbly, she allowed him to hold her there.

Anthony glinted a smile at Charlotte. "I take it our betrothal is at an end?"

"I will never marry you. *Never!*"

Rupert turned his beloved in his arms and looked into her face. "Charlotte! Your father—"

"I don't care about my father. Rupert, I love you. And if you'll have me . . ." A lone tear streaked down Charlotte's face. "Oh, please say you meant it when you said you'd wait for me, that you loved me."

"Oh, Charlotte, I do love you! So much! We'll go to your father and we'll talk to him. I'm not a rich man, but I can take care of you. I'll have to sell off my stable, but I can do it. I have it all figured out and—"

Charlotte kissed him, pulling his mouth to hers and leaning against him as if her entire heart was held in his arms.

Anna blinked. "Well," she said after a moment, in which she and Anthony silently watched the younger couple. "That was certainly surprising."

"No, it wasn't," Anthony said, sending Anna a stern glare. "And it would have happened much sooner had you not been so intent on interfering."

"Interfering? I was trying to help."

"Did it ever occur to you, my delightful troublemaker, that I did not want my betrothal saved? That I wished for the timid Miss Charlotte to break it off?"

That was certainly welcome news, but Anna managed a sniff. "I thought you said she was the perfect wife for you."

"It has been many weeks since I realized Charlotte was far from being the perfect wife for me," he returned gruffly. He put his arms about Anna's waist and looked down into her eyes. "You are the perfect wife for me, every troublesome, irritating inch. If you will have me."

Happiness swept through Anna, so powerful that it almost made her rise on her toes and place a kiss on Greyley's handsome mouth. "It will cause a scandal; I'm just a governess."

"I don't care."

"People will talk."

"They always do."

"They will say you are an Elliot after all."

He brushed his fingers over her chin, her cheek, as if trying to memorize her features. "I don't give a damn what they say. I love you and only you."

Warm in the circle of his arms, Anna toyed with his shirt buttons. "Really?"

"Really." He grinned. "Besides, Charlotte wasn't tall enough for me. I can't even hug her without straining my neck."

"Hm. I can see where that might have been a problem."

Anthony nodded. "And her hair was far too blond. I prefer red hair myself."

"You do?"

Anthony's eyes glinted with something that made Anna's heart pound.

She pursed her lips. "How do you feel about . . . proud noses?"

He smiled, lifting a finger to touch the tip of hers. "They add character. Small, pert noses are a decided irritant."

Anna sighed her satisfaction and permitted Anthony to draw her head to his shoulder. For a moment they stood thus, heart to heart, their bodies absorbing the warmth of each other.

Anthony didn't think he'd ever felt so completely whole. So alive. Or so in love. Life with Anna would be busy and troublesome and never quiet, and he was certain they'd argue at least ten times a week. But afterward . . . He smiled, thinking of all the ways they would make up for their disagreements.

She stirred against him. "There are a few things we need to discuss."

"Oh?" He asked, placing a gentle kiss beside the bruise that marred her forehead, the memory of his fears when he'd seen the broken phaeton beside the road returning.

"Anthony, I want to keep the children."

She did, did she? "Even Desford?"

"Especially Desford." She hesitated. "And I would like for you to build that house you promised me . . . only for Desford. He needs a house of his own."

Rupert looked up from where he had been talking quietly to Charlotte. "Desford can afford his own house."

Anthony frowned. "How?"

"Apparently my brother made some better investments than we'd realized. Desford owns a ruby mine."

"*That's* why your mother wanted the children," Anthony said.

Rupert nodded.

"That's the end of Lady Putney staying at Greyley House."

He eyed Rupert for a moment. "I don't suppose you'd consider taking her off my hands."

"No," Rupert said. "Never." He reached over and gathered his coat, pulling it carefully over his bruised hands, Charlotte helping him. "If you don't mind, Greyley, Charlotte and I will be off. I need to speak with her parents before my mother causes any more problems."

Anthony grinned. "Very well, whelp. And while you're out, see to it that you put something on that eye of yours. You look like hell."

Rupert chuckled. "So do you. Take care, Greyley." With Charlotte tucked beneath his arm, Rupert left.

Anna watched them go with a sigh. "I do hope Lord Melton won't cause too much of a problem. Rupert is a dear boy, but life hasn't left him with much."

"If it will make you happy, I will see to it that Rupert is comfortably fixed."

"Do you have enough money to do that?"

"Oh, I think I can find it somewhere." He lifted an arrogant brow. "I'm a wealthy man, Anna."

"How useful!" Anna pursed her lips. "Perhaps we can assist Lady Putney, too. As much as I dislike her, I hate to see someone displaced. I wonder if we can't just let her stay at Greyley until—"

Anthony kissed her. Kissed her so hard and so thoroughly that it was several moments before she could think, much less speak, and when she could speak, she only managed a rather weak "Oh my!"

"Get used to it," he said roughly. "That's the way I'm going to keep you from focusing your meddling on anyone other than me or the children."

Warmth spread through Anna and she grinned happily up

at him. "Then I had better get busy. There are a lot of things I want to change."

"About me?"

"No. About your bedchamber. That bed is far too large for just one person." She traced her finger across his bottom lip. "And I was thinking . . ."

"I love the way you think," he said gruffly. "But not as much as I love you." Within minutes Anna was wrapped in a cloak and on her way home to Greyley, certain, for the first time in her life, that she was exactly where she wanted to be.

Epilogue

I love a good wedding. Especially when it isn't mine.

Brand St. John to Lady Julia McLean, Viscountess Hunterston,
at the wedding of the Earl of Greyley to Miss Anna Thraxton

Sir Phineas took a deep puff of his cigarillo. The rich
smoke filled his lungs and sent a peaceful surge all the
way to his toes. Stretching mightily, he leaned back in
the leather chair and placed his feet on the desk, admiring the
shine of his new shoes.

It was peaceful here, despite the hum of the wedding
guests who were even now leaving Greyley House, having
enjoyed Lord Greyley's lavish hospitality. Carriages rimmed
the long drive as, one after another, the late stayers made
their way back to their own homes.

With a happy sigh, Sir Phineas refilled his glass from a
decanter of nearby port, silently commending Anthony's private stock. That was yet another thing he liked about his new
grandson-in-law—the man had impeccable taste. "Of course
he does," Phineas murmured, toasting the air. "He married a
Thraxton, didn't he?"

And did it in style, too. Phineas took an appreciative sip of port. The wedding had been held in a small chapel not ten minutes from the house, only immediate friends and family in attendance. But the reception had been far more elaborate. Anthony had thrown wide the doors to Greyley, and the huge house had been filled with the cream of the *ton*.

He'd been unstinting in the lavish affair, the house festooned with garlands of flowers and yards of pale blue and cream silk. Anna had protested over the amount of money spent, but Anthony had held firm. The reception had been one of the social events of the year.

Sir Phineas understood the earl's desire for the huge event—he'd faced down the gossipmongers who would whisper "governess" every chance they got, with gilt-edged invitations, cases of the best champagne, and an array of delicate ice sculptures that caused a constant murmur of appreciation. Oh yes, Sir Phineas liked his new grandson-in-law quite well.

Now all was right with the world; the Thraxtons were once again established in the eyes of society and Sir Phineas was exactly where he'd wanted to be—in Greyley's luxuriously appointed library. Yawning in contentment, he rose to flip his extinguished cigarillo out the window, then returned to his comfortable chair. He propped his feet on the desk, leaned back, and closed his eyes. Time lolled to a stop . . .

"*Sleeping?*" piped a young voice so close to his ear that he bolted straight upright and almost fell out of the chair.

Selena stood at his elbow. She grinned at him, her white gown sporting a green stain, twigs sticking out of her mussed curls.

His heart slowed to normal and he grinned in return. "Running from Lily, are you?"

She nodded, then leaned closer to whisper. "She tolded me it was bath day. I don't like bath day."

"Hm. I suppose you want to hide in here, with me."

Selena climbed into his lap and snuggled against him. "Thank you."

"You are incorrigible," he said, mussing her curls. "Where are the others?"

A sly smile tickled the little girl's face. "It's a secret."

Chuckling, Sir Phineas hugged her to him and lit another cigarillo. He'd just settled back in his chair when the door flew open and Brand St. John stormed into the room. "Where is he?" the young man demanded, his mouth white, something clutched in his hand.

"Where is who?" Sir Phineas asked.

"My brother, that mangy, ill-begotten lump of—" Brand caught Selena's wide gaze and reddened. "Anthony. I want to speak to Anthony."

"He's gone. Left for the honeymoon not ten minutes ago." Sir Phineas made a perfect smoke ring while Selena giggled.

Brand's face showed disbelief. "I thought they weren't leaving until tomorrow!"

"Oh, I sent them off. After all, I'm here to see to things."

"Yes, but—" Brand stared with a bemused expression at a small glittering circlet that lay in his palm. "What the hell am I supposed to do with *this*?"

Sir Phineas pulled Selena more comfortably into his lap so that he could lean forward to peer at the ring. "Ah, I've heard about that thing. Anna told me about it."

"Did she mention that Anthony ordered Jenkins to hide it in my piece of cake?" Brand asked sourly. "I nearly broke a tooth."

"I thought I broked a tooth once," Selena piped up. "Only it was a rock in my peas."

"It's not quite the same thing," Brand grumbled. "What do I do now? Everyone has already left. I'll have this blasted thing until Michaelmas."

"If you are fast enough, you might be able to find your brother Chase. I saw him not twenty minutes ago talking to a handsome young widow as she sat in her carriage in the drive. I daresay he's there still."

Brightening, Brand spun on his heel and left. Sir Phineas laughed softly. He wasn't sure he believed that nonsense about the talisman ring any more than the St. Johns themselves. Still . . . Anthony *had* had it in his possession when he'd won Anna, so perhaps there was a little something to it after all. Sir Phineas blew another smoke ring and watched it drift to the ceiling. Perhaps the dashing Brand St. John was on his way to an adventure of his own.

Sir Phineas decided that he was going to enjoy being a part of the St. John family. It was a perfect place for him, especially since he so loved happy endings. Chuckling softly, Sir Phineas rubbed his chin against Selena's soft curls, lolled back in the chair once more, and propped his feet back on the wide desk.

mccomesy

olv   cross   AJ
comp   Bennett
         W glover   MR
kim   MB.
glover   Bucknin   Marke

                          8-31-04
McCleod, Nem   paula
                          stich
                          Ben